THE WHITECHAPEL WIDOW

EMILY ORGAN

Storm

Ebook ISBN: 978-1-80508-878-3
Paperback ISBN: 978-1-80508-880-6

Cover design: Ghost
Cover images: Shutterstock, Adobe Stock

Published by Storm Publishing.
For further information, visit:
www.stormpublishing.co

ALSO BY EMILY ORGAN

The Baker Street Murders

Death in Kensington

Churchill & Pemberley Series

Tragedy at Piddleton Hotel

Murder in Cold Mud

Puzzle in Poppleford Wood

Trouble in the Churchyard

Wheels of Peril

The Poisoned Peer

Fiasco at the Jam Factory

Disaster at the Christmas Dinner

Christmas Calamity at the Vicarage (novella)

Writing as Martha Bond

Lottie Sprigg Travels Mystery Series

Murder in Venice

Murder in Paris

Murder in Cairo

Murder in Monaco

Murder in Vienna

Lottie Sprigg Country House Mystery Series

Murder in the Library

Murder in the Grotto

Murder in the Maze

Murder in the Bay

PROLOGUE

Tragedy in the East End, said the newspaper headline. He ran his tongue over his lips as he indulged in the details of the latest murder.

More bloodshed. More terror. He chuckled as he folded up the newspaper and tossed it to one side. Then he smoothed out a clean sheet of writing paper.

He dipped his pen into the pot of ink and began to write. Red ink flowed from the gold nib as it scratched the paper and formed the first two words: *Dear Boss.*

He sat back and watched the ink dry, considering the words for his composition. Then, with a grin, he dipped his pen into the ink again and wrote the rest of his letter:

You probably thought I was done with ripping, but I'm ready to do my next one and it will be my best yet. Tell the police they can search for me all they want, but they'll never find me. My knife is ready and I've got a thirst for more blood.

Yours truly,
Jack the Ripper

ONE

Saturday 10th November 1888

William Langley tapped his foot then checked his pocket watch. 'I've got time to buy a newspaper.'

'Are you sure?' asked Emma.

'Absolutely.' He put on his hat, got up from his seat and pulled down the window of the train door so he could reach the handle on the outside.

Emma glanced out at the platform clock. 'But it's five minutes to ten.'

'More than enough time,' replied her husband brusquely, stepping out onto the platform. 'I can see the newsstand from here.' He slammed the door shut and strode off.

Emma got up and leaned out of the window, keen to see how far William would have to walk. The newsstand was about seventy yards down the platform; she could see the billboards propped up against its counter. Her husband walked briskly, his coat tails lifted by the chilly breeze which swirled around the station. A cloud of steam from the hissing engine enveloped him and he faded from view.

Emma pushed up the window and sat back in her seat. The platform clock showed it was now four minutes until the departure time of ten. Why hadn't William bought a newspaper sooner? She felt tense from the cold and the worry he wouldn't make it back to the train on time.

She told herself it was foolish to be anxious and rubbed her gloved hands together to warm up. At least she and William were travelling in comfort to Suffolk today. He'd booked a first-class compartment with plush upholstered seats. Her hat and travelling case rested on the shelf above her head. Fixed to the walls below both shelves were two framed rural scenes, two gas lamps and an oval mirror.

Passengers in winter coats hurried past the window and porters pushed hand trolleys stacked with cases. A young woman embraced an older couple as she bid them farewell and carriage doors slammed as people got on board the train. Clouds of grey smoke curled up into the iron arches of the station roof.

It was now three minutes to ten.

The journey to Suffolk would take about two hours. Emma and William were going to stay with William's aunt in Lavenham while they looked for a place to live. Emma felt excited about this change, even though she would miss London. She'd never lived anywhere else. William had told her the air in Suffolk would be good for her health. She was still troubled by a cough from an illness she had endured for much of October. She and William planned to live in a cottage with a garden. There would be no noise, smells or smoke from factories and they would be surrounded by a landscape so beautiful that it had inspired the painter Thomas Gainsborough. William had secured a position at a solicitor's firm and Emma was looking forward to involving herself in village life. Perhaps they would have children.

Two minutes to ten.

Surely William should be back by now?

Emma got up, pulled the window back down and leaned out. She could see the newsstand and people hurrying to get onto the train. But there was no sign of William. The guard looked up and down the platform, holding his whistle poised at his mouth.

Perhaps William had got into the wrong carriage. But that made little sense. Surely he would check he had the right carriage and compartment before boarding? She opened the door and stepped out onto the platform, hoping to catch sight of him.

'The train's about to depart, madam!' shouted the guard. 'Get inside and close the door, please!'

'I'm waiting for my husband!' she responded. But he'd already turned his back on her.

She climbed back on board. The clock said one minute to ten.

The guard shouted again and more doors slammed.

Emma leaned out of the window, frantically searching for William. She couldn't leave the train because there wasn't time to get the trunks out of the guard's van now.

Then she caught sight of a man running alongside the train at the far end of the platform. She smiled with relief.

William.

She waved to him.

But as he drew nearer, she realised he was taller than her husband. His limbs were long and lanky, and he didn't move like William. He stopped further down the train, opened a door and jumped on.

The guard blew his whistle and the engine's whistle responded.

Emma's heart leapt into her mouth. 'No! Wait!' she called out. But her voice was drowned out by the noise of the engine. Clouds of steam billowed into her face and the train pulled out of the station.

TWO

Emma sat back in her seat, her heart thudding heavily in her chest.

William would have heard the guard's whistle. He wouldn't have had enough time to get back to her and would have got into the nearest carriage. There was no corridor linking the compartments and carriages, so at the next stop, William would get off and find her.

Emma comforted herself with these thoughts as the train journeyed northeast. A grimy fog hung over the rooftops, spires and chimneys, and the enormous cylinders of Bethnal Green gasworks were spectral in the gloom.

The fog sat low over the flat expanse of Walthamstow Marshes and the grey, eerie light made Emma shudder. She pulled up the collar of her travelling coat and glanced around the empty compartment. For a moment, she felt as though she was the only passenger on the train. The fog would get thicker. What if the engine driver wasn't able to see the signals? Perhaps there would be an accident...

She tried to shrug off the sense of foreboding building in her stomach. Everything was going to get better. She and William were starting a new life together in Suffolk.

A coughing fit took hold of her and she took her handkerchief from her handbag to clasp over her mouth. The coughing didn't last as long as it had done in the past. Perhaps she was getting better. The clean countryside air would help her health return in no time at all.

Eventually the fog began to lift and colour returned to the view from the window. Green fields, autumnal trees and little white farmhouses. As villages and settlements rushed by, Emma caught glimpses of everyday life: carts waiting at the crossings, horses pulling ploughs in the fields and children waving at the train.

The train slowed as it neared a town with a large cemetery on its outskirts. Then came houses, factories, schools and a large church with a tall, pointed spire. The sign on the platform said Chelmsford, and a clock showed it was a quarter to eleven.

Emma pulled down the window once more, reached for the handle on the outside, and readied herself to open the door.

She stepped out onto the platform once the train had stopped and looked up and down. Passengers bustled in and out of the carriages and porters busied themselves with luggage. Surely William would find her? As the activity subsided and the platform emptied, a sickening dread lurched in her stomach.

He wasn't here.

Leaving the carriage door open, she ran to the guard. 'Excuse me,' she said anxiously. 'The train can't depart until I've found my husband.' He scowled, taken aback by her insistence. 'He went to buy a newspaper before the train left London,' she continued, 'and I don't know if he got back on the train.'

'I can't delay the express for your husband. It needs to depart in half a minute for Bury St Edmunds.'

Was William still at Liverpool Street station? Emma knew

she had to make a swift decision. 'I'll get off here and return to London,' she said. 'Please can you unload my luggage?'

The guard gestured to a uniformed boy close by. 'He'll help you. But you need to be quick.'

Emma ran back to her carriage compartment to fetch her hat and case. Then she dashed to the guard's van where the uniformed boy unloaded the two large leather trunks and put them on a trolley. The activity brought on her cough and she was grateful it was drowned out by the noise of the train.

The guard blew his whistle, the engine responded and the train pulled out of the station.

'Where are you going to, madam?' asked the boy.

'Back to London,' she said. 'My husband didn't get on the train in time.' She felt foolish. How could a simple train journey have ended up like this?

She followed the boy down the slope to a boarded walkway across the rail tracks. The boy checked both ways before pushing the trolley to the opposite platform. An icy wind whipped around them, tugging at Emma's coat and hat.

She consoled herself with thoughts of the cottage in Suffolk. Once she and William were settled there, they would laugh together about the time he missed the train at Liverpool Street station.

THREE

Miss Welton, secretary to the editor of the *Morning Express* newspaper, sat down at her desk to open the morning's post.

An envelope with an address scrawled in red ink caught her eye. It had an east London postmark. She deftly slit the envelope with her sharp letter opener and pulled out the folded piece of paper inside.

Dear Boss,

The last job was my best so far. I took my time over it and I heard how my handiwork drew a crowd, ha, ha. I have sharpened my knife for the next job and this time I will rip two of them. The police think they can catch me but they keep arresting the wrong ones, ha, ha. I shall keep on with my work because I'm too fond of blood to stop.

Yours truly,
Jack the Ripper

Miss Welton recoiled from the red ink, her hand trembling

as the letter fluttered onto her desk. She lurched to her feet, frantically wiping her fingers against the rough wool of her dress as bile rose in her throat. The morning sun streaming through her window seemed to dim, as if the evil contained in those blood-red words had cast a shadow over her orderly office.

Without a backward glance, she fled to fetch the editor.

FOUR

Emma arrived back at Liverpool Street station at a quarter past midday.

'Where are you going to, madam?' asked the porter who wheeled her luggage beside her.

'I'm meeting my husband at the newsstand there.' She pointed, wanting to sound purposeful.

'Have you seen my husband?' she asked the lean, mousey-whiskered man who was selling newspapers. 'He bought a newspaper from you shortly before ten o'clock this morning. He was supposed to get on the express train to Bury St Edmunds, but he didn't make it on time.'

'What does he look like, madam?'

'He's five foot eight, dark-haired, and has a dark moustache. He's wearing a top hat and a black overcoat, dark trousers and a dark waistcoat. Oh, and he has brown eyes.'

'And he bought a newspaper from me this morning?'

'Yes. Do you recall him? Perhaps you noticed him running for the express train and failing to get on it.'

'It's a sight I see often, madam. But I don't recall seeing anyone miss the train this morning. I'm sorry I can't be more helpful, madam. He may well have bought a newspaper from me this morning, but I sell papers to lots of people. I don't remember everyone, I'm afraid.'

'I realise that. Thank you for your help.'

'Are you all right, madam? I hope you don't mind me saying, but you look quite worried.'

She felt tears prickle her eyes. Why wasn't William waiting for her here at the station? Where had he gone?

Trains, voices and trolley wheels echoed in her head. Emma became dizzy as her senses overwhelmed her. She gripped onto the counter for support.

'Let me get you a seat.' The newspaper seller brought a wooden stool out from behind his counter and helped Emma sit down on it.

Her breath was quick and shallow. Her mind felt cloudy.

'How are you feeling, madam?' The newspaper seller's voice was kind. It was kinder than William had spoken to her in a long time.

'I'm all right, thank you.' She fumbled for her handkerchief and wiped the tear which trickled down her cheek. 'This is all so silly, I'm sorry. I can't find my husband and... well, I don't know what to do. May I sit here for a while?'

'You sit here for as long as you like, madam,' said the news-paper seller.

Emma took in some slow breaths and felt a little calmer. She recalled William's restlessness that morning, his impatience to get out of the door and his curtness with the hackney carriage driver. He'd seemed fidgety as they waited to board their train, as if something had been bothering him. They'd waited twenty minutes to board the train and yet he'd decided to buy a news-paper just five minutes before its departure time.

And now he was nowhere to be seen.

Was his disappearance deliberate?

She dismissed the thought from her mind. William would

turn up soon, she felt sure of it. He was probably checking the arrival times of the trains on the Bury St Edmunds line. He probably hadn't expected her to return to London so quickly. Any moment now, he would stride onto the platform and greet her with a smile and open arms.

The newspaper seller brought her tea and the platform clock ticked on to twenty minutes to one. Almost three hours since she'd last seen William. The reassuring thoughts drifted away and a cold fear took hold. What was she going to do?

Then a thought occurred to her. It seemed so obvious that she couldn't believe she hadn't considered it sooner.

William must have got on the next express train. He wasn't waiting for her at Liverpool Street station at all, he was currently on the train to Suffolk!

She smiled to herself and shook her head. If only she hadn't panicked at Chelmsford and come back again. Soon her husband would be at his aunt's house and expecting to see her there with their luggage.

She jumped to her feet and returned her cup to the newspaper seller. 'Thank you very much,' she said. 'I feel a lot better now.'

'My pleasure. I hope you find your husband. Do you need a hand with anything else?'

'No, I'm fine, thank you. I'm going to get on another train.'

FIVE

It was just after five when the train guard unloaded Emma's luggage at Lavenham station in Suffolk. The express train had taken her to Sudbury, then she'd taken a branch line to the village. It was dark and there were few people about.

'Is someone meeting you here, madam?' asked a porter.

'No. I need to get to the house of my husband's aunt.' She moved closer to a gas lamp so she could see in her handbag to retrieve her diary with the address written in it. 'Wisteria Cottage,' she added, after leafing through the pages.

'Where's that then?'

'I don't know.'

'You don't know?'

'I've never been here before. And I haven't met my husband's aunt before, either. Her name is Miss Hardy.'

'Thornhill might know her,' said the porter. 'I'll fetch him.'

He disappeared into the darkness, and Emma shivered alone on the chilly platform. She could see distant lights in windows. She pictured William sitting with his aunt in one of those rooms, wondering where she'd got to. She hoped the porter and Thornhill would hurry so she could find her husband and forget all about her difficult day.

She heard Thornhill's shuffling boots before she saw him. He was a large man in a thick, shabby overcoat and a flat cap. His bushy, grey beard covered his neck and much of his chest.

'Looking for Miss Hardy, madam? Wisteria Cottage?'

'That's right. My name is Mrs Langley.'

'I'm Thornhill.'

'Do you know Miss Hardy?'

'Never heard of her.'

'Oh.'

'I've lived here sixty-three years and never heard of a Hardy at Wisteria Cottage.'

A heaviness began to take hold in Emma's chest. 'Perhaps I wrote the name down incorrectly.' She looked at her diary again, her fingers fumbling with the little pages.

'You've got the right village, have you?'

'Yes, I'm sure of it. I've written Lavenham here.'

'Aye, you're in Lavenham.'

'I don't understand...'

'I'll tell you what we'll do, Mrs Langley,' said Thornhill. 'My pony and trap are just outside the station here. I'll take you to the Angel Hotel. They've got a warm fire and hearty food in there. You can ask the folks about Miss Hardy at Wisteria Cottage and, if it comes to nothing, they've got comfortable rooms so you can stay the night. You must've had a tiring journey and you don't want to be out in the cold and dark for much longer.'

'Thank you, Mr Thornhill,' Emma responded, trying to quell the anxiety in her chest.

A fire blazed in the grate in the bar of the Angel Hotel.

Emma took off her hat and gloves and ignored the curious glances from people at the neighbouring tables. They were clearly wondering who the smartly dressed stranger was.

A young freckle-faced woman brought a plate of bread and boiled beef and a mug of beer to her table. Emma didn't feel hungry, but it would have been rude to refuse the food. She broke off a piece of fresh bread and it was deliciously soft with a crisp crust. As she ate, Thornhill joined her at the table.

'I can't find anyone who knows a Miss Hardy,' he said. 'Or Wisteria Cottage. Perhaps you wrote it down wrong, Mrs Langley?'

'Perhaps I did.' Emma took a sip of the refreshing beer and gave it some thought. Could she really have written both the aunt's name and the cottage name incorrectly? 'I know I'm not mistaken about Lavenham,' she said. 'My husband and I have talked about the village a great deal. I've heard it's very old.' She had seen little of it in the dark.

'It's old, all right,' said Thornhill. 'But it doesn't appear to be home to the lady you're looking for.'

'I don't understand. My husband must be here somewhere.' She told him how she'd lost William at Liverpool Street station.

Thornhill beckoned to the young woman who had served Emma's meal. She came over to the table, wiping her hands on her apron.

'Have you been working here all day, Milly?' he asked.

She nodded.

'I don't suppose you've had a traveller from London in here today, have you? Wears a top hat and a black overcoat. Dark moustache, apparently. Five foot eight.'

Milly shook her head. 'Don't remember seeing him. We've not had many travellers in today.'

'Would you mind asking around?' Thornhill asked. 'And ask your ma and pa as well.'

Milly nodded and went off to the bar.

'It's a strange one, Mrs Langley,' said Thornhill, shaking his head. 'You've lost your husband and you're looking for a lady who no one's heard of. There's something funny going on if you ask me.'

SIX

After a restless night at the Angel Hotel in Lavenham, Emma returned to London the following day. She no longer had a home so she decided to call on her former landlords Mr and Mrs Solomon. They lived next to the house Emma had once shared with William. It was in Northampton Square, a pleasant location in Clerkenwell where smart townhouses overlooked a garden in the centre of the square.

'Mrs Langley? Is everything all right?' Mrs Solomon asked with a start. Her kindly, lined face was framed with steel-grey curls.

'Not really.' Emma felt her voice crack as she replied.

'You'd better come in. Ronald, come and get the trunks,' she yelled over her shoulder before gently pulling Emma inside.

A short while later, Emma sat in the parlour of the Solomons' home with a glass of brandy in her hand. It was a comfortable room with paintings of rural scenes on the wall and a shaggy cat asleep on the hearthrug. Mr and Mrs Solomon listened intently as Emma told them about her search for her husband. She'd given them a fond farewell the previous morning, and now she felt embarrassed about having to return.

'I hoped William had come back to the house,' she said. 'Although I don't see why he would have because you're getting it ready for the new tenants.'

'We've not seen him, have we, Ronald?' said Mrs Solomon.

Mr Solomon shook his head, running his hands over his bald head.

'What a troubling situation,' continued Mrs Solomon. 'I'm sure Mr Langley would never run off deliberately.'

Her husband gave a sigh, as if he wasn't so sure. 'Have you reported this to the police?' he asked Emma.

'No. It doesn't seem serious enough for that.' Or was it? It was now half past six on a Sunday evening and she hadn't seen William since ten o'clock the previous morning. Perhaps she had to consider reporting his disappearance.

'I think you should tell the police,' said Mr Solomon.

'I agree,' said Mrs Solomon. 'But before you do that, Mrs Langley, I insist on you having some supper. We've got a nice cut of beef left over and some potatoes, too. After that, there's prune pudding with sugar and cream. We can't have you going hungry.'

After supper, Emma and Mrs Solomon walked to the police station on King's Cross Road. Mrs Solomon carried a lantern as they made their way through the maze of streets. Fog curled around railings and streetlamps, and hazy silhouettes of people and carriages passed them in the gloom. Light glowed from a lamp hanging over the entrance to a public house. A sign in the window advertised mild ale at a penny for half a pint and muffled laughter sounded from within.

'Let's hope we don't bump into Jack the Ripper,' said Mrs Solomon with a nervous laugh.

'Oh, don't say that!' The thought brought on Emma's cough.

'He won't come over to Clerkenwell. Whitechapel and

Spitalfields are his hunting grounds. Places where poor, unfortunate women wander the streets in search of money. You don't get so much of that around here. And besides, the pair of us would soon see him off, wouldn't we?'

'I'm not so sure. He carries a very sharp knife,' Emma replied, glancing around nervously.

'He wouldn't come near us if he saw us now. It's the unfortunates he's after. The ones who can't defend themselves.'

Emma tried to feel reassured by Mrs Solomon's words, but the back of her neck prickled. She quickened her step, keen to get out of the damp and the dark.

A loud, drunk man was being pinned to the floor by two constables when Emma and Mrs Solomon arrived at the police station.

'Mind your language in front of the ladies!' warned one of the constables as he grappled with the drunk's legs. A tirade of obscenities followed, and the desk sergeant hurriedly showed them to a small room away from the noise. They were joined a few minutes later by a constable with a large nose and a receding chin. He introduced himself as Constable Morris and they sat at a table together.

He took out his notebook. 'How can I help?'

'My husband is missing,' said Emma. As she said the words, they didn't seem real to her.

'And your name is?'

'Mrs Langley. Emma Langley. My husband is William Langley.'

'And when did you last see your husband?' asked the constable.

'Yesterday,' said Emma.

'Only yesterday?' He frowned. 'So there's a good chance he'll probably turn up again somewhere in a day or two.'

'You can't be sure of that, Constable,' said Mrs Solomon. 'Please listen to what Mrs Langley has to say.'

'Has he done this sort of thing before?'

'No,' said Emma.

'So he's never gone away before?'

'No. Well... he has. He goes away for work.'

'How long for?'

'Usually a few days. But he hasn't gone away for work this time.'

'How do you know that?'

'Because of how he disappeared.'

'And how did he disappear, Mrs Langley?'

Emma explained the events of the previous day while the constable made notes. By the time she'd finished, Emma's throat felt tight and tears stung her eyes.

'I realise this isn't pleasant to consider, Mrs Langley...' The constable paused, his face colouring as he scratched his chin. 'But is it possible your husband has been deliberately deceitful?'

Reluctantly, she had to acknowledge it could be true. William could have deliberately left the train without planning to return. He could have invented the aunt and the address in Lavenham. But why?

'How was your husband's mood before he supposedly disappeared?' asked Constable Morris.

Emma didn't want anyone to think badly of her husband, but she realised she had to be truthful. 'Irritable,' she said quietly and then added, 'a little restless.' She recalled his fractious temper the previous morning. She'd assumed he'd been anxious about the move to Suffolk.

'Is your husband prone to irritability and restlessness?' asked the constable, fixing her with his gaze.

'Sometimes.'

'Did he seem preoccupied?'

'Yes, I suppose he did.' Emma wiped her brow. 'Why are you asking me these questions?'

'I've learned a bit about human nature over the years. If your husband was planning something, then it's likely he wouldn't have been his usual self—'

'Planning something? What do you mean?'

'I could be mistaken, but...' He scratched his chin again and cleared his throat. 'If he'd been planning to leave you on the train, then it's no surprise his mood was irritable and restless yesterday. He knew what he was going to do.'

Emma's jaw clenched. 'You think he deliberately didn't get back onto the train? He planned to leave me on it so I would travel to Suffolk without him?' Her heart pounded at the thought.

'That's my impression, Mrs Langley. And if there's truth in it, then I'll say it's a most deplorable and cold-hearted act which a charming young lady such as yourself doesn't deserve. Unfortunately, some men behave like scoundrels.'

'My husband isn't a scoundrel!'

'Perhaps he isn't, Mrs Langley. Perhaps there's another explanation for this. But let's look at the facts. He got off the train just before it departed and made little effort to get back onto it on time. When you returned to Liverpool Street station, he wasn't there waiting for you. When you got to Suffolk, not only was there no sight of him, but you discovered he'd given you a false name and a false address.'

Emma stared at a scratch on the table. A faint ringing sounded in her ears. Then her vision grew cloudy.

'Mrs Langley?' The constable's voice sounded far away. '*Mrs Langley?*'

When Emma came round, she was sitting on the floor, propped

up against the wall. Mrs Solomon wafted some smelling salts beneath her nose. 'Oh, my poor dear,' she muttered.

Emma turned away from the salts, her head stinging from their potency. William had chosen to leave her. But why? And where was he now?

Mrs Solomon helped her back onto her chair.

'How are you feeling, Mrs Langley?' asked the constable.

'Tired.'

'You've had a difficult weekend,' he said. 'I recommend a few days of rest.'

'Where?' said Emma bitterly. 'I don't have a home anymore.'

'You can stay with us,' said Mrs Solomon gently. 'Ronald won't mind.'

'So that's settled then,' said the constable abruptly.

'But what about my husband?' said Emma. 'Will you search for him?'

'Your husband appears to have taken himself off by his own accord. And while it's a very unfortunate incident, it's not a matter for the police to investigate, I'm afraid.'

'Then how will I find him?'

He shrugged. 'You can ask his family and friends if they've seen him. I'm sure someone will have. The very most I can do is circulate his description to the other divisions in the Metropolitan Police. Perhaps someone has reported something about him. But it's unlikely.'

SEVEN

Emma couldn't get to sleep that night; her cough seemed more incessant again. She lay propped up on pillows, exhausted. A thin line of light crossed the ceiling, cast through the gap in the curtains from the streetlamp outside.

Occasionally, a carriage passed through the square. Emma felt comforted by the rattle of its wheels and the sound of horses' hooves, the knowledge that someone else was awake.

She felt grateful Mr and Mrs Solomon had put her up for the night. But where was she going to live? The house she had shared with William was about to be let to new tenants so she couldn't return there. Before her marriage, Emma had lived with her cousin, Agnes, and her husband in Euston, but they had since moved out of London. Apart from Agnes, Emma had no other family. Her brother, Alfred, had been murdered four years previously. Before his death, he'd sunk into opium addiction and he'd lost his life in a squalid opium den in Limehouse. Emma's parents had never come to terms with his death and both had died just a few years afterwards.

And now William had gone too.

She had to find him. She wanted to ask him why he had left

her. If he had wanted to leave, then why hadn't he told her? Why had he chosen to abandon her without an explanation? It was a cowardly act.

She hadn't expected William to be a coward.

Eventually, she sunk into a deep, dreamless sleep and was woken by voices downstairs.

William. He'd returned.

Her head spun with drowsiness as she climbed out of her warm bed and felt around for her shawl to put over her night-clothes. She opened her door and there was just enough light from the lamp in the downstairs hallway for her to see her way.

She descended the stairs to find four people in the hallway. Mr and Mrs Solomon stood with Constable Morris and a red-haired man with a bushy moustache and a pipe in his mouth. He wore an overcoat and held a bowler hat in his hand. They all turned to face her, their expressions sombre.

'Perhaps you'd like to get dressed, Mrs Langley, and speak with these gentlemen in the parlour?' said Mrs Solomon.

'What's happened?'

'We'll explain everything,' said the red-haired man.

Emma dressed hurriedly, her mind racing. Why were the police here when she'd been told William's disappearance wasn't a matter for them to investigate?

Perhaps there'd been an accident.

She dashed back downstairs to the parlour, light-headed and her mouth dry. Mrs Solomon guided her to an armchair. 'Please tell me what this is about,' Emma said, perching on the front of the seat cushion.

The red-haired gentleman took his pipe from his mouth. 'I'm Detective Inspector Bradshaw,' he said. 'I'm a detective inspector at H Division and I work at Commercial Street station.'

Emma knew the police station. It was in London's East End

and the detectives there were busy investigating the Whitechapel murders.

'I apologise for the lateness of the hour,' he continued. 'But it's quite necessary, I'm afraid.'

Her chilly hands trembled in her lap as she waited for his explanation. Her eyes fixed on his face with its freckled complexion and red moustache.

The Solomons' shaggy cat strolled across the room, oblivious to the tension.

'We're visiting you tonight with news about a gentleman we believe to be your husband,' said the inspector. 'He was attacked in Whitechapel on Saturday night and found in the early hours of yesterday morning, at a quarter to one. Unfortunately, he died from his injuries.'

'No, no, it can't be William,' Emma said, getting to her feet. She began to pace the room, her hand at her throat. 'He's never been to Whitechapel. He has no reason to go there.' Her mouth felt dry.

The inspector's expression remained impassive. 'He had no identifying papers on him.'

'It's not William.' She refused to believe it.

'When Constable Morris here put out word yesterday evening about a gentleman missing from Liverpool Street station, I realised his description matched the description of our deceased chap.'

The inspector's calm demeanour angered her. Had he any idea how upsetting his words were? 'I think you're mistaken,' she said. 'This man you've found must be someone who looks like my husband.' Attacked in Whitechapel? It seemed impossible. She felt sure William had never been there.

'It would be helpful if you could come along with us now and take a look at him.'

'Now?' She felt a cold knot in her stomach.

'Yes. He's in the mortuary at the London Hospital.'

If it was William, then it explained his disappearance. But Emma couldn't accept the thought he might be dead. She didn't want to lose all hope of seeing him again.

'You can bring someone with you to the mortuary if that would help, Mrs Langley.'

'I can come with you,' said Mrs Solomon in a kindly voice.

Emma's breath felt shaky as she replied, 'Thank you.'

EIGHT

A four-wheeled hackney carriage was waiting for them outside in the square. Emma sat next to Mrs Solomon, and the police officers took the seat opposite them. The carriage moved off and Emma shivered despite her warm coat. Passing streetlamps illuminated her companions' faces and Detective Inspector Bradshaw's pipe filled the carriage with swirls of smoke. Mrs Solomon lowered a window.

'What happened to the gentleman who died in Whitechapel?' Emma asked nervously. She didn't want to consider that he could be William. 'How was he attacked?'

'He was stabbed,' said the inspector.

'Jack the Ripper!' cried Mrs Solomon. 'He's attacking gentlemen now!'

'No. I'm certain this has nothing to do with the recent Whitechapel murders. This attack was of a different nature,' the inspector replied quickly.

'So what happened?' Emma probed.

'At a quarter to one yesterday morning, about twenty-four hours ago, the injured gentleman hailed a hansom cab on Whitechapel Road, close to Green Dragon Yard. He asked to be taken to a lodging house in Canrobert Street in Bethnal Green.'

Emma couldn't imagine William staying in an East End lodging house. She felt even more convinced the police were mistaken about his identity.

'Why did he ask to be taken to a lodging house?' asked Mrs Solomon. 'Why didn't he ask for a doctor if he was injured?'

'That's a good question,' said the inspector. 'He gave no indication to the cab driver he was injured. He clearly didn't wish to reveal he'd been attacked. Perhaps he'd been involved in trouble of some sort. A fight, perhaps. Even an attempted robbery. Maybe he was worried he would be arrested.'

'It can't be William,' said Emma. 'He would never have been involved in a fight or a robbery.'

'All I can do is speculate at this stage, Mrs Langley. Anyway, the cab driver took the gentleman to his destination in Canrobert Street. When they arrived at the lodging house, the driver opened the hatch in the roof and asked the passenger for the fare. When there was no response, the driver got down from his seat and had a look inside the carriage. In the light of the cab's lamps, he could see the gentleman slumped to one side, as if asleep. All attempts to wake him failed. And then he noticed blood. He called out for help and the landlady from the lodging house came out to assist. She told the driver to take the gentleman to the London Hospital, so that's what he did. A doctor at the hospital confirmed he was deceased.'

'How horrible!' said Mrs Solomon, shaking her head.

'A postmortem on the gentleman confirmed he died from a single stab wound to his abdomen,' said the inspector. 'It was a deep wound which the doctor estimates would have caused his death within half an hour. We think, therefore, that he was attacked at about quarter past midnight at the very earliest. It's possible he had no idea how serious the wound was. He had no papers on him, so we've been unable to confirm his identity.

However, when I learned from Constable Morris here that Mr Langley was last seen at Liverpool Street station less than a mile from Green Dragon Yard—'

'It can't be him,' interrupted Emma. She turned to the window and wiped away the condensation with her gloved hand. She could see little outside.

She wasn't supposed to be here. She was supposed to be in Suffolk with her husband. How had their plan gone so wrong? Had he really invented his aunt as part of an elaborate ruse to leave her?

They arrived at the London Hospital and climbed out of the carriage into a cold, foggy yard. Faint lights glimmered from windows high in the tall hospital buildings. The inspector led them to a door which he rapped on officiously.

Emma felt dizzy and her chest was tight. She didn't want to go into the mortuary, but she had to. She had to find out if the dead man was her husband.

A sombre, bald mortician admitted them into a wood-panelled room. The smell of disinfectant mingled with an unpleasant dank odour. Emma wrinkled her nose as it hit the back of her throat.

'This is Mrs Langley,' said the inspector. 'She's here to view the body of the gentleman stabbed in Whitechapel early yesterday.'

The mortician nodded, picked up a lantern and led them to another door.

'I'll wait here,' said Mrs Solomon, her voice quivering. 'If that's all right?'

'Yes, of course,' said Emma. Her landlady looked pale.

She followed the mortician and police officers into a long brick room with a row of coffins resting on trestle tables.

The odour was much stronger here, and Emma felt her stomach turn.

The mortician stopped by the fourth coffin and handed his lantern to the inspector. Then he gripped both sides of the coffin lid and lifted it.

The body was wrapped in a sheet. The mortician rested the lid against the neighbouring table and lowered the sheet from the face. The inspector removed the pipe from his mouth and held the lantern close so Emma could see the man's features.

He didn't look like William – at least, not as she remembered him. His jaw sagged and his mouth hung open. His skin was pale and waxy.

She recoiled, her hand flying to her mouth. The face was slack, unfamiliar, yet undeniably William's. Her chest constricted as she forced herself to look at him properly. This couldn't be real.

'Is this your husband, Mrs Langley?' asked the inspector.

She nodded, unable to speak. The room seemed to tilt and spin around her.

It was him. The police hadn't been mistaken.

A storm of emotions crashed over her: grief, horror, confusion, anger. Why had he been in Whitechapel? What had happened to transform her vital, handsome husband into this lifeless shell?

She wanted to reach out and touch his face, to somehow make sense of it. But she couldn't bring herself to do it. The William she had known was gone, leaving behind only questions and a growing sense of betrayal.

The mortician's voice seemed to come from far away. 'You may spend more time with him if you wish.'

'No.' The word came out as a whisper. 'I can't...' She turned and fled, brushing past Mrs Solomon. The door banged behind her as she stumbled into the yard, gulping in great gasps of the cold night air. She bent over, hands on her knees, fighting back waves of nausea.

NINE

Emma sat with Detective Inspector Bradshaw and Mrs Solomon in a glum room at Commercial Street police station. It had grey wainscoting and a small fireplace. Police notices were pinned to a board above the fireplace and a clock on the mantelpiece showed the time was almost two. Constable Morris had returned to King's Cross station, his help no longer needed.

'Have you any idea what your husband could have been doing in Whitechapel, Mrs Langley?' the inspector asked her.

'No. I've never known him to come here,' Emma replied, her mind and body numbed. She rubbed her forefinger on the table just to check she could feel its texture.

'Did he have any family or acquaintances here?'

'No.' Emma was consumed by an odd floating sensation, as if none of this was real. She was a widow now. It seemed impossible to grasp.

'How long were you married for?' asked the inspector.

He was already using the past tense. William was dead but she couldn't yet comprehend it.

'Four months.'

'And when did you first meet?'

'April.'

'So you knew your husband for seven months in total?'

'I suppose it must have been.' It didn't seem long at all.

The inspector puffed on his pipe and examined a piece of paper in front of him. 'These are Constable Morris's notes from the conversation you had with him yesterday evening. It says here your husband was a solicitor.'

'That's right. For Cardwell and Theobald. A firm in Holborn.'

'But he'd given his notice because you had both decided to move to Suffolk.'

'Yes.'

He examined the notes again, absently stroking his red moustache. Mrs Solomon stifled a yawn. Emma sat rigid in her chair, her mind oddly blank as she watched him read. The numbness worried her – shouldn't she feel something? Anger, grief, fear? Instead, there was only this strange, hollow emptiness where emotion should be.

'Your husband got off the train at Liverpool Street station and never returned,' said the inspector. 'Constable Morris seems to think he did this deliberately.'

'Yes.'

He looked her in the eye. 'Do you think he did it deliberately?'

Emma sighed. 'I'm beginning to think now he must have done. There were obviously things he was keeping from me.'

'Such as what?'

'The fact he came to Whitechapel.' She rubbed her brow. 'He never once mentioned this place to me.'

'You think he may have visited Whitechapel in the past?' The inspector gave her a demanding stare.

Emma felt weary of his questions. 'I don't know,' she said. 'But something brought him here, and I'd like to know what.'

'This is a personal question, Mrs Langley, but it's important

I ask it.' The inspector sat back in his chair. 'Was your marriage happy?'

She knew she was supposed to reply that it was. But it took her a moment to find her answer. 'Yes,' she said. She couldn't possibly admit anything to the contrary. Especially in front of Mrs Solomon.

'You're quite sure about that?' he asked.

'Yes. I was unwell a few weeks ago, and that put a strain on things. But everything was going to be better once we moved to Suffolk.' She cleared her throat and smoothed her skirt.

'And what makes you say everything was going to be better?'

'William and I were in agreement about it.'

'But the Suffolk plan wasn't real, was it? According to Constable Morris's notes, the aunt wasn't real. And neither was her address.'

'But... but we had a letter from her.' William had shown her the letter a few weeks previously. She felt a bitter taste in her mouth as she realised now he'd either forged it or lied about its contents.

'Did you see the letter?' asked the inspector.

'I saw it in William's hand.'

'Did you read it?'

'No. He told me what it said.'

'It would be useful to find that letter. Where would it be?'

'It must be in my husband's trunk.' His trunk sat unopened in a spare room at Mr and Mrs Solomon's house.

'We'll need to look through that trunk,' said the inspector, pointing his pipe at her. 'I'll send some men over later today if that's all right. So you're adamant your marriage was happy, Mrs Langley, even though it appears your husband deliberately left?'

Emma realised she would appear naïve if she continued to

insist there had never been problems. 'Perhaps it wasn't completely happy.'

'Were there disagreements?'

'Sometimes. But all married couples have disagreements, don't they?'

He nodded. 'Did he ever mention he wanted to put an end to the marriage?'

Her head ached as she searched for the right response. 'No.'

'Did you ever express a wish to end the marriage?'

'No. I didn't want to. I just assumed everything would get better.'

'Better than what?'

His questions were coming too fast. Her breathing felt quick and shallow. 'Better than how things had been.' Her answer sounded foolish.

'Was your husband a drinker?'

She hesitated. 'Not really.'

'Was he prone to losing his temper?'

She winced as she thought of the times she'd cowered from him. There was no use in lying. 'Yes.' Then she caught Mrs Solomon's eye and felt the need to justify William's behaviour. 'But only if someone caused it.'

'A man is responsible for his own temper, Mrs Langley. Was your husband cruel to you?'

'No. He wasn't a cruel man.'

'He appears to have deliberately deserted you. Is that not cruel?'

'Perhaps he didn't. Perhaps he got off the train and something distracted him or he saw someone he knew and ended up leaving the station with them and...' Emma trailed off as she tried to think of other possibilities.

The inspector's expression hardened. 'Where were you between the hours of midnight and one o'clock yesterday?'

A horrifying thought entered Emma's head. 'You don't think I attacked my husband, do you?'

'I have to consider all possibilities,' the inspector said, spreading his palms on the table.

'Mrs Langley would never have murdered her husband, Inspector!' Mrs Solomon said, outraged.

'If her alibi holds up, then she won't be a suspect,' he replied.

'I was in Lavenham in Suffolk,' said Emma.

'Where did you stay in Lavenham?'

'At the Angel Hotel. Just ask in there and they'll remember me. You can ask in the post office too because I made inquiries there. And speak to Mr Thornhill. He took me to and from the station in his pony and trap.'

'What was your impression of Mr Langley, Mrs Solomon?'

'My impression?'

'Yes. What sort of man was he?'

She gave Emma a sideways glance as tiny beads of sweat began to form on her brow. 'He was, erm...'

Emma wondered why she was hesitating. Was it possible she'd disliked him?

'He was what?' asked the inspector.

'He was a professional gentleman and had a respectable manner about him.'

'But what about his character?'

'I really couldn't say.'

'But you knew him?'

'Yes.'

'So why can't you say?'

'It's not fair to Mrs Langley.'

'Please don't worry on my account, Mrs Solomon,' said Emma. She could feel anger stirring again. 'William's dead now, so you may as well come out with it.'

Mrs Solomon sighed.

'What was your impression of him?' the inspector asked again.

She paused, her shoulders sagging as she looked pitifully at Emma. 'He wasn't the sort of gentleman I trusted,' she said. 'In fact, I only accepted Mr and Mrs Langley as tenants as his wife was so likeable. But as for Mr Langley... I'm afraid I didn't like him very much at all.'

TEN

He knelt down, rolled back the rug and took the penknife from his waistcoat pocket. He slipped the penknife beneath the corner of the floorboard and lifted it. In the space beneath were stored his writing implements.

He took out the pen, writing paper and a pot of red ink. Then he replaced the floorboard, rolled back the rug and took his special stationery over to the writing desk.

After smoothing out a clean sheet of paper, he unscrewed the lid from the pot of ink, picked up his pen and dipped it in.

Red ink. The colour of blood.

He pushed the tip of his tongue against his upper lip as he began to write.

Dear Boss,

I won't keep you waiting for much longer, and you know how I like to spring a surprise, ha, ha. I've bought a new knife and it's even sharper than the last one. I can't wait to use it for my next job. I told you I would rip two of them next time, but I think I will do three. I won't stop there, I will keep the police busy for a long time yet.

Yours truly,
Jack the Ripper

ELEVEN

Emma had first encountered William in Hyde Park. She'd been walking around the Serpentine lake with her cousin, Agnes, on a warm Sunday afternoon in April.

Agnes had been complaining about changes to the services at church while Emma had been struck by the handsome features of a gentleman walking towards them. He had sharp cheekbones, a well-defined jaw, a brown moustache and large dark eyes. His clothes were smart, and he was watching her with a smile playing on his lips.

Emma blushed. She expected him to pass by and was flattered when he stopped.

'I'm so sorry to interrupt your conversation.' His voice was soft and well-spoken. 'I wonder if you could tell me where you bought your bonnet? I would like to buy a similar one for my sister for her birthday.'

He was interested in her bonnet and not her. Emma tried to hide her disappointment. 'I bought it from a shop on Edgware Road about two years ago.'

'Which one?'

'Houghton's. I shouldn't think they still stock the same bonnet, but they may have something similar.'

He grinned. 'That's very helpful. I'm William Langley, by the way.' He removed his hat. 'It's a pleasure to meet you.'

'And you too, Mr Langley. I'm Miss Holland, Emma Holland. And this is my cousin, Mrs Agnes Jones.'

William gave Agnes a nod, then his eyes swiftly returned to Emma. 'Do you walk here often?'

'Yes, quite often. When the weather's nice. And it looks to be improving now, doesn't it?'

'It does indeed. It's a glorious day today. It's going to be good all week. I'd say we quite deserve it after all that rain, don't you?'

'Yes, I'd say.' Emma realised she was smiling broadly at him. She pursed her lips and tried to appear a little more demure.

'Well, I won't detain you any longer, Miss Holland, Mrs Jones. However, I hope to see you here again.'

'Indeed.' Emma couldn't help grinning again. 'Goodbye Mr Langley.'

He went on his way.

'He seemed like a charming gentleman,' said Emma.

'A little too charming if you ask me,' replied Agnes.

William had worn a crimson silk necktie that day, fastened with a pearl pin. Emma now held the necktie in her hand, looping it absent-mindedly around her fingers as she recalled the first time she'd met her husband.

Her thoughts were interrupted by Mrs Solomon hauling a painting with a heavy frame into the sitting room. 'You left this in the house, Mrs Langley,' she said. 'I'm guessing you decided it was too big to take with you to Suffolk.'

'Oh, yes. I'd forgotten about it. It belonged to William.'

It was a large, dark picture painted in loose, soft brush-strokes. It depicted a woman standing alone, her navy-blue dress blending into shadow. She held a hat in her hand and had a sombre, enigmatic gaze. Emma had never liked it very much; she thought it too dingy.

'Would you like Ronald to hang it in the room you're staying in?'

'Thank you. But I don't suppose I'll stay with you for long. I don't want to—'

'Oh, don't worry about that at the moment. I'll ask Ronald. It will be nice for you to have something familiar on the wall.'

A knock sounded at the door.

'Looks like the police are here,' said Mrs Solomon grimly, peering out of the window.

'They want to go through William's trunk,' said Emma.

A short while later, Emma watched as two constables emptied the trunk in an upstairs room. Her husband's belongings were tossed out onto the floorboards with little care.

The trunk contained mainly clothes: jackets, shirts and trousers which William had worn for work. There were hats and shoes too, and a few books including William's favourite: the *Strange Case of Dr Jekyll and Mr Hyde*.

'Where did your husband keep his personal papers, Mrs Langley?'

'In his writing desk. But he emptied it and I assumed he'd packed everything in the trunk.'

'Could the papers be in your trunk, madam?' The constable gestured at her trunk which was in the corner of the room.

'No, none of his papers are in there.'

'Would you mind if we check?'

'You don't believe me?' She felt her cheeks grow hot.

'It's not a case of not believing you, madam. We need to be thorough in our investigation,' the constable replied gruffly.

'I'll empty it out for you.' Emma strode over to her trunk and began pulling out all her belongings. Everything she owned was here. She'd sold her parents' home and the furniture in Hillingdon after her marriage. She'd kept a few small precious items such as her father's pocket watch and her mother's jewellery. Everything else had gone. She'd made good money from the sale of the house and it had been invested in a savings account with the money from her inheritance too.

'There,' said Emma, once she'd emptied the trunk. 'That pile of papers is mine. You can look through it if you like, but my husband's papers aren't there.' She'd placed the pile next to her folded undergarments, and both constables fixed their eyes elsewhere, too embarrassed to look in more detail.

'We'll take your word for it, madam,' one of them said.

'Are you sure the papers are not in my husband's trunk?'

'Quite sure, madam.'

William's diary and correspondence appeared to be missing. And as Emma looked through his belongings on the floor, she realised other items were missing too. His brush and comb, his shaving mirror and his favourite cufflinks. Items which he presumably hadn't wished to be parted with. And where was the small overnight case he took with him when he went away? The one with his initials on it, WJL.

Her head began to spin, and she sank into the chair by the window.

'Are you all right, madam?' asked one of the constables.

'No. I'm not. My husband's diary and papers are missing. He must have taken them. But where are they now?' His papers included personal information such as the details of their bank account. 'What if the papers fall into the wrong hands?' she asked.

The constables didn't have an answer.

Detective Inspector Bradshaw entered the room.

'Have you found any witnesses?' she asked him. 'Someone must have seen my husband in Whitechapel.'

'We're making inquiries, Mrs Langley. In the meantime, I have some further questions for you.'

She got to her feet. 'How will that catch William's murderer?'

'Would you mind joining me in the parlour downstairs? This won't take long.'

'There's nothing more I can tell you.'

'Do you keep a diary, Mrs Langley?'

'Yes.'

'Then please bring it with you.'

Mrs Solomon brought in tea for Emma and Detective Inspector Bradshaw as they sat in the parlour. 'Would you like me to sit with you?' she whispered in Emma's ear as she placed the tea down.

'Thank you, Mrs Solomon. I'll be all right for now, and you've already been helpful enough. The inspector says it won't take long.' Emma tried to reassure her.

'That's right, it won't,' he replied as he leafed through his notebook looking for something. The Solomons' cat rubbed its head against the inspector's shins and he tried to move his legs away. Emma thought it amusing when cats paid the most attention to people who liked them the least.

The inspector cleared his throat and asked Emma about several specific dates while she consulted them in her diary.

'He was away,' said Emma for each of them.

'I'm trying to establish what your husband was up to before his death, Mrs Langley. Obviously, you were unaware he was in Whitechapel, so your husband may not have always been truthful about where he was going and what he was doing.'

'I see.'

'What about Monday the sixth and Tuesday the seventh of August?'

Her head ached. 'How many more dates are you going to ask me about?'

'These are the final two.'

'No, he wasn't working away then.'

'So he was home, but it's possible he went out for the evening?'

'No, we went out for a meal together on the evening of the seventh to celebrate our one-month wedding anniversary.'

'I see. And where did you go?'

'To the Holborn Restaurant.'

'Very nice. I like the table d'hôte menu there.'

'Yes, that's what we had.'

'It's good value for three shillings and sixpence. What about the previous evening?'

'We were both at home.'

'Is it possible your husband went out without you noticing? Perhaps late at night while you were asleep?'

The question alarmed her and she couldn't understand why the inspector was suggesting it. 'He wouldn't have done it,' she said.

He folded his notebook closed. 'Thank you for your time again, Mrs Langley.'

It felt puzzling and the inspector wasn't giving her a proper explanation. 'I don't understand why you're asking me about these dates. How does it help you find who murdered my husband?'

'We're trying to establish if your husband was caught up in something.'

'Like what?' She stared at him, challenging him to elaborate.

The inspector scratched his temple. 'If he was involved in something of a criminal nature, then it's possible someone murdered him in revenge.'

'Criminal?' She felt sure the inspector was mistaken. 'What do you suspect him of?'

'We don't suspect him of anything at the moment, Mrs Langley. Please don't be alarmed by it. These are early inquiries.'

Emma sighed.

'Please be assured we're doing what we can, Mrs Langley.'

'I've heard that before. And nothing was done.'

The inspector frowned. 'When?'

She took a moment to steady her nerves and clear her throat.

'When my brother was murdered.'

'Your brother?'

'Yes. His name was Alfred Holland,' she said. 'He was murdered four years ago. He was shot in an opium den in Limehouse.'

'Good grief, I recall that now. He was your brother? They caught the culprit, as I recall. Excellent work from Scotland Yard.'

'No, it wasn't the Yard which solved it.'

'It wasn't?'

'No. I'm afraid to say the police were no use at all. The case was solved by someone else. A news reporter called Penny Green.'

TWELVE

The inquest into William's death was held at the Working Lads Institute on Whitechapel Road. It was a narrow, red-brick building topped by a pointed gable. Attractive stonework edged its tall windows.

Emma arrived with Mrs Solomon in a hansom cab and stepped out into the grey, drizzly weather. The imposing facade of the London Hospital stretched along the opposite side of the street.

The inquest was held in the library where portraits of the royal family hung on the walls. The careworn faces and shabby clothes of the jury contrasted with the stiff collars and smart black jackets of the professional gentlemen. Emma and Mrs Solomon found a space at a table close to Detective Inspector Bradshaw who acknowledged them with a nod.

The coroner was an authoritative, square-faced man with a bushy moustache. He summoned Detective Inspector Bradshaw first. The inspector explained how William had hailed the hansom cab on Whitechapel Road and had died on the journey to the lodging house in Bethnal Green.

A doctor then described the wound which William had suffered and explained death occurred as a result of blood loss.

Emma fidgeted with her hands as he spoke. She didn't enjoy listening to the detail of her husband's fatal injury. It was hard to believe something so awful had happened to him.

Her turn came to give evidence. She got to her feet and related the story of being abandoned on the train and searching for her husband. As she listened to the monotony of her voice, she realised there was no emotion in it at all. Her eyes were dry. She'd cried no tears for William yet. What did the jury think of her? Surely they expected her to weep?

After she'd spoken, she sank into her seat and the coroner called another witness.

'Albert Bexley, your honour.'

'And your occupation?'

'I'm the landlord of the Ten Bells public house on Commercial Street.'

Emma watched him with interest, wondering what he was doing here. He was a broad-shouldered, stocky man with a heavy jaw. His jacket sleeves were tight around his upper arms and the buttons strained at his stomach.

'Can you tell the inquest when you saw Mr Langley on the weekend of his death?'

'He came into my pub about a quarter past eleven on Saturday morning.'

Emma felt her jaw drop. William had left her on the train and gone to a public house?

'Was he a regular visitor to the Ten Bells?'

'Quite regular, yes.'

Emma's husband had never mentioned the place to her. She caught Mrs Solomon's eye and her landlady gave her a look of pity.

'And how was he when he arrived at your public house?'

'He was a bit out of breath and looked bothered about something.'

'Did he say what was bothering him?'

'No. And I didn't ask.'

'Why not?'

'It was none of my business. He asked for a pint of his usual and—'

'What was his usual?'

'Whitbread's London Stout, your honour. He had a pint of that and then two or three more. Possibly four.'

'Did he talk to anyone else in the bar?'

'Exchanged a few pleasantries with a few people, but I didn't notice him in conversation with anyone. He went off after that.'

'What time did he leave?'

'Must have been about one.' He smoothed the front of his jacket, as if attempting to relieve the strain on the buttons.

'And did you see him again after that?'

'Yeah, he came back later.'

'At what time?'

'About four o'clock.'

'And how long did he stay for?'

He ran a hand over his hair. 'It's difficult to say because the bar got busy.'

'But he was there until the evening?'

'Yeah. At least nine o'clock. Possibly later.'

While Emma had been travelling to Suffolk and searching for him, he'd spent his time drinking in a bar. She shook her head. It didn't sound like the man she had known.

The next witness was a lady with a lined face and sunken cheeks covered with red rouge. She wore a tall hat decorated with colourful ribbons and a threadbare woollen shawl. The fabric of her dress had faded to a dirty grey and colourful buttons had been sewn onto the bodice to brighten it up. How did this woman know William?

'Your name please,' asked the coroner.

'Louise Granger.' Her voice was raspy. 'But everyone knows me as Lady Lou.' She grinned to reveal a few yellow teeth, then winked at one of the jurors.

'And where do you live, Mrs Granger?'

'That depends. Sometimes it's Thrawl Street, sometimes it's Flower and Dean Street.'

'You live in lodging houses?'

'That's right, your honour. Wherever I can find a bed.'

'And you saw Mr Langley on the weekend of his death?'

'Yes, your honour.'

'How can you be sure it was him?' asked the coroner.

'The description of him was the same. Everyone was talking about the gentleman who died and I realised I spoke to him that night. He was lost and it was dark. That's one of the problems we've got here. There ain't enough streetlamps. Everyone's been saying that for years, but when are they going to listen to us? They're just happy for people to keep getting murdered. As long as it doesn't happen up in the West End, they don't care.'

'And do you have a profession?'

'Yes I do. I'm a fruit seller.'

Some of the jury members sniggered. The coroner gave them a sharp look.

'What time did you see Mr Langley?'

'It was shortly after half past midnight because I'd just heard the bells of St Jude's. I think it was St Jude's anyway. I know for sure it wasn't St Mary's because they're still building it after the fire.'

'And where did you see him?'

'In Green Dragon Yard. I was walking up from Whitechapel Road.'

'Have you any idea what Mr Langley was doing there?'

'He was lost.'

'Did he say where he had been?'

'No. And I didn't ask him because it wasn't my business.'

'Green Dragon Yard is a dark, narrow thoroughfare which runs between Old Montague Street and Whitechapel Road. It's not the sort of place a gentleman such as Mr Langley would normally be seen. Were you surprised to see him there, Mrs Granger?'

'You can call me Lady Lou like everyone else does, your honour. I wasn't surprised to see him in Green Dragon Yard because I'm used to seeing all sorts about the place. And there are more of them these days. They come here looking to see the places where the murders have happened.'

'In the middle of the night?' the coroner asked.

'Who knows what they're thinking? It ain't my place to say.'

'In the light of the recent atrocities in the area, were you not worried about walking alone in a dark alleyway?'

'Yeah, it worries me, your honour. But I've got no choice. If I've not got enough money for a bed, then I have to go out and find it. The doss houses don't let you in if you've not got the money.' The woman cast her eyes downwards and shook her head sadly.

Emma felt a pang of sympathy for Mrs Granger. It was wrong that people in such desperate poverty were forced out onto dangerous streets at night.

'Let's return to Mr Langley,' said the coroner. 'You came across him in Green Dragon Yard just after half past twelve and you say he was lost.'

'Yeah.'

'You spoke with him?'

'Yeah. He asked me how to get to Whitechapel Road and I told him he had to carry on the way he was going. I saw him just before the street narrows by the lamp and I don't think he wanted to carry on down that way because it's as dark as a tomb down that bit.'

'So you saw his face quite clearly?'

'Yeah. Handsome chap, he was. Polite and spoke like a proper gentleman.'

'Was he in distress at all?'

'No. But I think he'd had a bit to drink.'

'What makes you say that?'

'By the way he walked. And everyone out in Whitechapel at that hour has usually had a bit to drink.' She gave a cackle.

'Yourself included, Mrs Granger?'

'I enjoy a tipple. I ain't ashamed to admit it.' She winked at the juror again.

'Did Mr Langley seem injured to you when you encountered him?'

'No. He hid it very well.'

'You didn't see any blood?'

'No. He had a thick coat on. If I'd known he was hurt, I would've told him to get to the hospital. But maybe he thought it was nothing serious. I don't know how. If someone stabbed me like that, I'd know about it.'

'Did you exchange any more words with Mr Langley that night?'

'No, he went on his way and so did I. Didn't see him again. Then I heard about the man who hailed the cab near Green Dragon Yard and that he'd died. I knew then he must've been the gentleman I spoke to.'

'Did you see anyone else in Green Dragon Yard that night?'

'I think someone passed me at the bottom end of the street, but it was so dark I couldn't see who it was.'

THIRTEEN

The next witness shuffled to the stand: Tommy Fletcher, a lean man with sharp features and darting eyes that made him look more rat than human.

'You saw William Langley shortly before his death?' the coroner asked him.

'Yeah. On the evening of Saturday the tenth of November, your honour. I saw him in the Ten Bells.'

'Did you know him well?'

'Not that well. I knew his face, though.'

'Did you speak to him that evening?'

'Yeah. Well, he spoke to me first. I was playing cards with two friends and he asked if he could join us. So we played cards, then we decided we wanted to be a bit more serious about it.'

'A bit more serious? What do you mean by that?'

'Well...' He ran the back of his hand across his nose. 'I don't like to say, sir, it might get me into trouble.'

'We're only interested in the facts surrounding Mr Langley's death,' said the coroner. 'You won't get into trouble for anything.'

'All right then.' He shifted his gaze around, looking at

everyone but the coroner. 'Well, we wanted to play for money, you see. So that's why we went to mine.'

'Your home?'

'Yeah.'

'And where do you live?'

'On Finch Street, your honour.'

'How many went to your home to play cards, Mr Fletcher?'

'Four of us.'

'And how long did you play cards for?'

'Until about midnight.'

'And how did Mr Langley get on? Did he win money? Lose it?'

He wiped his nose again. 'He lost a bit.'

'And how did he feel about that?'

'He wasn't too happy about it. He was quite drunk too.'

'Did he argue with any of you?'

'Yeah, I had to ask him to leave because he accused us of cheating. Then I made a joke.'

'What sort of joke?'

'I told him he'd better get out and do some murdering because he looked like Jack the Ripper.'

His comment was met with gasps.

'And why did you say that?'

'Because he looked like how they describe the Ripper on the handbills they're always giving out. It was just a joke.'

'Did he find your joke amusing?'

'No. He probably would've found it funny if he hadn't just lost his money.'

'What mood was he in when he left your home?'

'A bit angry.'

'Was he aggressive?'

'A little bit. But I wasn't too worried because there were three of us and one of him.'

Emma now had a good idea of how William had spent his

last day. But why had he chosen the East End instead of a nicer, safer part of London? And playing a drunken, late-night game of cards with men he barely knew was out of character. She couldn't understand it.

The cab driver who'd been hailed by William on Whitechapel Road spoke next. His name was Samuel Carter and his soft-spoken voice belied his appearance. He was a tough-looking, rough-skinned man with greying hair and pale eyes. He described how he'd taken William to the lodging house in Bethnal Green and then discovered he had died during the journey.

'I just wish there was something more I could've done,' he said. 'If he'd told me he'd been attacked, I would've taken him straight to the hospital. I don't understand it.' He wiped his eyes.

Emma felt sorry for him. He must have had a terrible shock.

As the inquest concluded for the day, the coroner stated there were three hours of William's time unaccounted for on the tenth of November. 'Detective Inspector Bradshaw,' he said. 'May I request you and your men make every effort to discover what Mr Langley was doing between the hour of one o'clock, when he left the Ten Bells public house, and the hour of four o'clock, which is when he returned.'

'Yes, your honour.'

The inquest was adjourned to allow the police time to make further inquiries.

Emma stepped out onto Whitechapel Road with Mrs Solomon.

'You poor thing,' said her landlady. 'That must have been very difficult for you to listen to. I can't believe your husband left you on that train and went off to drink and play cards! Why on earth did he do such a thing? Perhaps he was unwell.'

'Unwell?'

'Yes. Maybe he had a nasty fall and hit his head. The injury must have caused him to act strangely. Something wasn't right with his mind, was it? Perhaps it explains why I didn't like him very much. I'm sorry if it pains you to hear me say it, Mrs Langley, but I like to speak the truth. And his behaviour shortly before his death was appalling. What was he thinking?'

'I wish I knew.' Low, grey clouds rolled overhead and a cold wind whipped spots of rain onto Emma's face. It felt refreshing after the warmth of the crowded library. She glanced up and down the street. She took a deep gulp of fresh air to steady her nerves.

'I would like to have a look around... I want to find Green Dragon Yard.'

'Very well. I'll accompany you. You don't want to be walking around here on your own.'

FOURTEEN

Whitechapel Road was a wide, lively thoroughfare. Newspaper reports of the recent murders had described the area with sensationalist horror, but Emma didn't feel any sense of menace on the busy high street. She and Mrs Solomon headed west, passing the railway station and then a grocer's shop with fruit and vegetables heaped in crates outside. A newspaper seller with a bundle of papers under his arm shouted out the day's news. Next to him, a young shoeblack rested on his box as he waited for the next customer.

They passed a general store advertising Sunlight soap, Champions mustard and selected eggs, fine and fresh. A baker's boy wheeled his handcart past them and the smell of fresh bread made Emma's stomach grumble.

Music drifted from somewhere and they came across a young man playing the harp. Emma stopped to listen. It was a popular tune she'd learned on the piano as a child. She could even recall the finger for each note and then there had been a tricky bit which had taken ages to master without her fingers tripping over on the notes.

When the musician finished, she put some coins in his hat.

Then a tiny, pale-faced girl offered her matches from a little tray. Emma bought a box, even though she didn't need any.

'Are they Bryant & May matches?' asked Mrs Solomon once the match seller had moved on.

Emma examined the box. 'I'm afraid so.'

'Let's hope they treat their workers fairer these days after the matchgirls' strikes.'

They passed a boot seller, a public house and a hat polisher before coming across a little archway within the buildings. A crooked sign above it read *Green Dragon Yard.*

Emma stopped. 'This is the place where William hailed Samuel Carter in his hansom cab.' She glanced up and down the road which was busy with carts, carriages and horse-drawn trams. 'I want to follow the route he took that night.'

She stepped into the dingy, narrow passageway.

'Really, Mrs Langley?'

'You don't have to accompany me, Mrs Solomon.'

'I insist on accompanying you. It's not safe.' Her brow furrowed, and Emma knew she felt nervous about straying from the main road.

'It's not dark yet,' she said. 'I'm sure we'll be fine.'

'I hope so.' Mrs Solomon gripped her handbag with both hands and followed.

The passageway was covered for a few yards before opening out into a narrow lane lined either side with small, mean-looking houses. Many of the window panes were broken or missing. Shutters hung from broken hinges and paint peeled on rickety doors. Some of the doors stood open and sallow-faced women wearing grimy aprons watched them pass. Emma and Mrs Solomon made their way along the uneven cobbles, around filthy, foul-smelling puddles. Children with bare feet and grubby faces happily tossed an empty can to each other, seemingly oblivious to the poverty of their surroundings.

Pieces of broken furniture and other rubbish had been

discarded in the street and an old man sat on a milk churn, smoking a clay pipe. 'Are you ladies from the church?' he asked them hopefully.

'No, we're not,' said Emma. She could understand why he'd asked the question. Middle-class ladies in this area were often missionaries. 'My husband was attacked in this street on Saturday night,' Emma said. 'Did you hear or see anything?'

'He was your husband? I'm sorry to hear it. I didn't see anything, I was asleep when it happened.' He shook his head. 'I don't know what's come of this place. I came here from Ireland as a young man. Years ago you didn't have to worry about murders or anything like that. The streets were as safe at night as they were in the day. And now you've got a lunatic murdering women and the police can't do anything about it. They've got no hope of catching him, if you ask me. It's all gone to ruin and I don't know how it's going to end up.' He took his pipe from his mouth and pointed it at them. 'But however it ends up, I'm glad I'll be in my grave before then.'

Emma nodded her thanks even though he'd been little help, and they went on their way. They passed dark archways and miserable courtyards and Emma realised how extensive the maze of streets was. She couldn't imagine how anyone could navigate this place properly at night. It was little wonder William had got lost.

'There's a lamp,' said Mrs Solomon, pointing to a lantern attached to a wall on a crooked bracket. 'It's one of the first I've seen here. It makes you realise how dark it must be at night.'

'I wonder if this is close to the place where Lady Lou says she encountered William,' said Emma.

'It could be.'

Mrs Solomon turned to look at the way they had just come. 'Someone must have stabbed him back there where it was completely dark,' she said.

'I don't see why a stranger would have attacked him for no reason.'

'It can happen, though.'

Emma sighed. 'I suppose so. In which case, we have little hope of finding who did it.'

They eventually reached the end of Green Dragon Yard and found themselves on a street lined with shabby stores and workshops. Opposite, two women chatted outside a garment shop where rows of old clothes hung from hooks and lay in heaps on tables. Some shop signs were written in Hebrew script; many Jewish people had recently arrived here having fled persecution in Russia. A man strolled past, balancing a tray of beigels on his head and ringing a bell to draw attention to his wares.

Emma felt a little better now they had left the misery of Green Dragon Yard. 'William must have walked along this street,' she said. 'But from where?'

'I think the man he played cards with said Finch Street,' said Mrs Solomon. 'We could ask where it is.' Emma sensed from the tone of her voice that she was reluctant to do so.

'Perhaps we've done enough looking around for today,' said Emma.

'Yes, I think so. I can understand why you want to find out where your husband went that day, but we're unlikely to find any clues. You have to leave that to the police, Mrs Langley.'

'They didn't do much for my brother, Alfred,' Emma replied bitterly.

'But it might be different this time,' Mrs Solomon said softly.

Emma thought back to the last conversation she'd had with Detective Inspector Bradshaw. He'd mentioned William might have been caught up in something of a criminal nature. He might have been murdered in revenge. And then he'd asked her about all those dates...

William had played cards with a man. What had his name been? He had made a strange joke. *I told him he'd better get out and do some murdering because he looked like Jack the Ripper.*

Tommy Fletcher.

She stumbled and fell against Mrs Solomon.

'Goodness!' She grabbed her arm to steady her. 'Are you all right, Mrs Langley?'

FIFTEEN

Emma tried to gather herself. She didn't want to share the disturbing thought that had entered her head. Could William really have been Jack the Ripper? It seemed impossible.

But maybe it wasn't.

William's work had often taken him to other cities. He'd travelled to Birmingham, Bristol, Leeds and Manchester. He'd told Emma he'd been visiting clients of the law firm he worked for, Cardwell and Theobald. But had he told her the truth?

Emma had had no reason to doubt him at the time. But now she had learned from the inquest that he'd regularly visited the Ten Bells public house. She couldn't understand why he'd gone to that place when there were countless public houses nearer to his home and work. Why had he never mentioned it to her?

It was clear he'd had something to hide, and Emma was fearing the worst.

William had been in Birmingham the previous week and had returned home at lunchtime on Friday the ninth. Early that morning, Jack the Ripper had murdered Mary Kelly in her room in Miller's Court on Dorset Street. Emma wasn't exactly sure where Dorset Street was, but she knew it wasn't far from the Ten Bells public house.

She pictured how William had been when he'd returned home that day. He'd told her he'd had a busy week and felt tired. He hadn't been very talkative and had busied himself with packing for their journey to Suffolk the following day.

Had he been to Birmingham? Or had he been in Whitechapel?

Emma shuddered. It seemed ludicrous that she was considering the possibility William had been capable of murder. And the attack on Mary Kelly had been exceptionally violent. The details in the newspaper had been gruesome. People said Jack the Ripper was a madman who had escaped from an asylum because only a lunatic could commit such dreadful crimes.

But Jack the Ripper had to hide somewhere. Was he capable of behaving like a gentleman so no one would suspect him?

William had never been violent. He'd said some cruel things to her, but he had said sweet things, too. He'd had a quick temper, but he had also been quick to apologise.

Yet he had hidden things from her. And she suspected he'd hidden far more from her than a few visits to a public house.

She considered now the lies he must have told her. She'd believed every word. She'd trusted him. How could she have been so foolish?

'I'm going to ask someone for help,' Emma told Mr and Mrs Solomon at breakfast the following morning.

'Who?' asked Mrs Solomon as she buttered a slice of toast.

'The lady who found my brother's murderer. She's a news reporter.'

'A lady news reporter?' said Mr Solomon, looking up from his newspaper. 'How unusual.'

'She writes for the *Morning Express*,' said Emma.

'I prefer *The Times*,' said Mr Solomon.

'She found your brother's murderer, Mrs Langley?'

'Yes. She's solved quite a few cases. Her name is Penny Green.'

'And you think she'll be willing to help?'

'I hope so.'

But Emma wasn't as confident as she sounded. She'd last seen Penny Green four years ago, and the circumstances had been rather dramatic.

SIXTEEN

Fleet Street bustled with people: messenger boys, clerks, reporters and printers in ink-stained aprons. Everyone was hurrying to meet a deadline. The names of well-known newspapers were emblazoned in large letters on the front of the buildings. Telegraph wires were strung between the rooftops and the road was busy with traffic. Fleet Street felt important. From this place, news was distributed across the country, empire and beyond. Emma felt a buzz of excitement. She could understand why Penny worked here.

She reached the *Morning Express* offices, pushed the door and stepped inside. She was greeted by the thunderous roar of printing presses in the basement. A man in an apron dashed down the staircase without giving her a second glance. A sign on the wall for the editor's office pointed up the stairs so Emma followed it.

On the corridor upstairs, she heard the tapping of typewriters. Framed editions of the *Morning Express* hung on the walls, including a commemorative edition celebrating the Queen's golden jubilee the previous year. The floorboards creaked beneath her feet as she decided which door to knock on. She chose one marked *Miss Welton, Secretary to the Editor*.

She knocked and stepped inside when she heard the voice from within.

'Can I help you?' A prim, grey-haired lady sat at a desk and barely looked up. She was clearly busy.

'I'm sorry to trouble you. My name is Mrs Langley and I'm looking for Miss Penny Green.'

The name caught Miss Welton's attention. She peered over the pince-nez on the end of her nose and looked Emma up and down. 'Miss Green? She hasn't worked here for some years.'

'Oh.' Emma felt her heart sink with disappointment. She hadn't considered that Miss Green might have left the newspaper.

'Are you a friend?' asked Miss Welton.

'An acquaintance. Miss Green helped solve my brother's murder.'

The secretary raised an eyebrow. 'Did she indeed? She was always quite good at that sort of thing. Who was your brother?'

'Alfred Holland. He died four years ago in Limehouse.'

'Yes, I recall that now. It must have been quite dreadful for you and your family.'

'It was. I don't know what I would have done without Miss Green's help at the time. Can you tell me where she is now?'

'I don't know, I'm afraid. I could ask the editor, but he's extremely busy.' Miss Welton got to her feet. 'If he knows the answer to your question, then I don't suppose it will take up too much of his time.' She smoothed her dark dress and left the room.

She returned moments later with a tall, jovial man with small eyes and a thin moustache. He greeted Emma with a smile. 'I hear you're looking for Penny Green?'

'Yes. She helped solve the murder of my brother.'

'I'm very sorry to hear about your brother, Mrs Langley. I'm

Mr Edgar Fish, and I'm the editor of the *Morning Express*. I had the pleasure of working with Miss Green for ten years. I'm afraid she left this newspaper three years ago.'

'Do you know where I can find her now?'

'Well, for one thing, her name's changed,' said Mr Fish. 'She's now Mrs Blakely.'

Emma recalled the name. 'Did she marry the Scotland Yard inspector?'

'Yes she did. Detective Inspector James Blakely. They married three years ago and that's when Mrs Blakely left the newspaper. Although I recall she wrote a few occasional articles after that. They lived in St John's Wood, but I can't tell you if they're still there now.'

'I don't suppose you know where in St John's Wood?'

'I don't know, I'm afraid. The Blakelys never invited Mrs Fish and I for dinner. Rather remiss of them wouldn't you say?' he quipped, a hint of bitterness in his voice. 'Mind you, Mrs Blakely is being kept busy these days now she's a mother.'

'She's a mother?' Emma couldn't help but feel surprised to learn this. 'I never imagined she would have children.'

'Neither did she!' He laughed.

'I was hoping she might be able to help me with something,' said Emma. 'But it sounds like she's too busy.'

'Can anyone else help?'

'I don't know. It's regarding the murder of my husband, William Langley. He was attacked in Whitechapel on Saturday night.'

Mr Fish's jaw dropped. 'He was your husband! Goodness, how awful. Please accept my most sincere condolences, Mrs Langley. We've reported on the incident so I'm quite familiar with the facts. If Mrs Blakely was still a news reporter, then she would have been reporting on the case, I'm sure of it. How unfortunate for you that both your brother and husband have lost their lives in such barbaric circumstances. I'm not sure Mrs

Blakely will be able to help you this time, but her schoolboy inspector husband might.'

'Schoolboy?'

He narrowed his eyes as he smiled. 'I used to call him that, it was a little joke of mine back then. Thinking about it now, I realise how much I miss Penny. I should call her Mrs Blakely, really. I was very fond of her. We rarely agreed on anything, but it meant our days were never boring.' He chuckled. 'If you do find her, please tell her Edgar Fish sends his regards.'

SEVENTEEN

Disappointed, Emma lingered on Fleet Street for a few moments as she decided what to do next. Surely Penny Blakely was too busy with her family to help her? Her former colleagues hadn't seen her for a few years. It was likely she had no interest in working on murder cases anymore.

She had trusted Penny once before. Emma's instincts told her she had to speak to her.

She walked along the street and found the nearest post office. There, she looked in the directory for the Blakelys in St John's Wood. She found an address for Mr J Blakely at twenty-five, Henstridge Place.

She walked to Farringdon Street railway station to catch the Metropolitan Underground Railway to St John's Wood Road.

As Emma approached number twenty-five, she felt a growing sense of apprehension. She had last seen Penny and James when her brother's murderer had been caught. Emma had been extremely agitated at the time. She had also been in possession of a gun... She shook her head, trying to dispel the unpleasant memory. She could only hope Mrs Blakely had forgotten the details of that incident.

She could hear a baby crying on the other side of the door. She took in a breath and decided to keep her visit as short as possible. If the timing of her visit was inconvenient, then she felt sure Mrs Blakely would tell her.

The door opened and Penny Blakely stood there, resting an unhappy infant on her hip. Her fair hair was pinned up, and tendrils were falling loose about her face. She wore an apron over a plain day dress and round, gold-rimmed spectacles. Her brown, intelligent eyes had dark circles beneath them. The baby stopped crying and stared wide-eyed at Emma, its face red and wet. Penny's skirts moved and a young boy came into view. He clung onto the skirts and peered cautiously at her.

'Miss Holland?' said Penny with surprise.

'I've become Mrs Langley since we last met. And I don't wish to trouble you at a time like this. You're clearly very busy.' Emma suddenly felt embarrassed at turning up unannounced.

'There's nothing I would like more than another adult to speak to. The baby's tired and she'll settle down to sleep shortly. Please come in and tell me how you've been.'

Emma followed Penny into the bright sitting room. It had large windows and comfortable chairs. A tabby cat eyed her from the windowsill. Wooden building blocks were scattered across a colourful oriental rug.

'Why don't you build your tower again, Thomas?' said Penny.

'Don't want to,' he said shyly, still clinging to her skirts. She gestured for Emma to sit in an easy chair while she lowered herself onto the sofa with the children.

'I called at the *Morning Express* offices and they told me you were no longer a news reporter,' said Emma.

'Yes, I left a few years ago. I miss the work but I have other priorities now. How have you been?'

'All right.' She felt a lump in her throat. 'Sort of all right, anyway. I got married earlier this year.'

Penny was about to reply when the baby grabbed her spectacles. 'Let's be careful with these,' she said, trying to uncurl the chubby little fist. The baby laughed, pulled the spectacles from her face and flapped them up and down.

'Florence thinks this is a wonderful game,' said Penny, trying to steady the baby's arm. 'She's already broken two pairs.' A second later, the spectacles were flung onto the floor.

Thomas laughed.

Penny bent forward to retrieve her spectacles. 'Luckily, these aren't broken.' With a grimace, she folded them and put them in a pocket in her apron. 'Now I shall just have to be content with being unable to see anything properly.'

Emma hadn't seen Penny without her spectacles before. Despite her evident tiredness, she had attractive features, and Emma guessed she was nearing the age of forty. 'How old are the children?' she asked.

'Thomas is two years and six months, and Florence is six months old.'

'And how does motherhood compare to being a news reporter?'

'Reporting on the news was much easier!' Penny laughed. 'There were moments which were difficult, of course, but I felt I was in control most of the time. I find it quite remarkable that I never feel much in control as a mother. I have countless daily demands to meet and...' Penny trailed off. 'Goodness, I haven't offered you a cup of tea!'

'Please don't worry about making tea,' said Emma. 'I won't stay long.'

'But I want a cup of tea.'

'Then I shall make it.' Emma got to her feet. She'd assumed

Penny and James had a lady to help, but there was no evidence of one.

Once Emma had made the tea, Penny encouraged the children to sit on the rug with the building blocks. Baby Florence was propped up with cushions so she could see her older brother playing and he appeared to enjoy the audience.

'Thank you again for your help with my brother's case, Mrs Blakely.'

'Please call me Penny.'

'All right, then you must call me Emma.'

Penny smiled. 'I think your brother's killer would have been found eventually. Maybe I helped it happen a little quicker.'

'I think you're being modest. You helped me during a very difficult time.'

'And how have you been since then?'

Emma felt tears prickle her eyes. 'I've recently been widowed.'

'I'm so sorry to hear it. I noticed you're wearing a mourning dress, but I didn't wish to remark on it until you mentioned it.'

'My husband died on Saturday,' said Emma. 'He was murdered in Whitechapel.'

Penny gasped. 'Just a moment... Your surname is Langley. I didn't make the association when you first told me your name. I read all about it in the papers. Your husband was William Langley?'

Emma nodded.

'Oh my goodness, what an awful time you must be having.'

'It isn't easy. There's quite a long story behind it, you won't want to hear it all.'

'But I do,' said Penny. 'As long as you're happy to tell me. And hopefully the children will allow us to talk.'

Penny listened and Thomas entertained his little sister while Emma related the events of the previous weekend.

'So I'm not sure what to do next,' said Emma, after she had

finished her explanation. 'And there's something which troubles me more than anything.'

'And what's that?'

Emma took a deep breath before she spoke. 'I'm worried my husband may have been Jack the Ripper.'

EIGHTEEN

Penny let out a gasp. 'What makes you think that?'

'The police have been asking me about him,' said Emma. 'I think they suspect him.'

'Goodness.' Penny ran a hand over her brow. Florence began to cry.

'Oh dear,' said Penny, picking her up. 'She's tired. Both the children usually sleep around now. If you could bear with me, Emma, I'll take them upstairs to their cots. If they both sleep, we may even get an hour to talk about this. Do you have enough time?'

'Of course.'

'It might take me a while to settle them. Please help yourself to something to read from the bookshelf.'

Emma glanced at the books on the shelves but didn't read the titles on their spines. She thought instead of the burden she was placing on Penny. Had sharing her fear with her been a mistake? Now Penny would feel obliged to help her.

Florence's cries carried downstairs, reminding Emma that Penny had other responsibilities. She couldn't expect her to give up any of her valuable time.

But Penny had said she was happy to talk some more today, so maybe that would help a bit. Hopefully Emma could feel reassured that William had nothing to do with the Whitechapel murders.

Emma found a book of poems by the Brontë sisters and returned to the easy chair. The tabby cat jumped down from the windowsill and strolled over to greet her with its tail held high. Then it sprang up onto her lap and purred loudly as it made itself comfortable.

Penny returned fifteen minutes later. She brought with her a pile of papers. 'It looks like Tiger approves of you,' she said with a smile. 'She's very good at finding a comfortable lap. Let's sit at the dining table and I'll show you my notes.'

'Notes?' Emma eased the sleeping cat from her lap and placed her gently on the easy chair. Tiger blinked a few times, then curled up again into her sleeping position.

'My notes on Jack the Ripper,' said Penny. 'I may not be a news reporter anymore, but I've been following every twist and turn of the recent events.'

Emma smiled. She'd had no idea Penny had been collecting information about the murders, but it made sense to her that she had. If she'd still been a news reporter then she would probably have been writing about them.

She followed Penny into the dining room where Penny pulled her spectacles out of her apron pocket, spread out the papers and they sat down. They included newspaper cuttings, hand-drawn maps and pages of neat handwriting.

'How have you found the time to do all this?' asked Emma in amazement.

'I do it in the evenings. James thinks I'm foolish because it's all for nothing. But it could count for something, couldn't it? You never know.'

Emma nodded. 'And what does your husband make of the recent murders?'

'He's frustrated that little progress is being made. He's not been working on the case, but some of his colleagues are and they've been finding it quite a challenge. Now tell me why you think your husband could have been Jack the Ripper.'

'The police seem to suspect it. Detective Inspector Bradshaw at H Division asked me for William's whereabouts on several dates. When I checked my diary for those dates, I realised William had been away during many of them.'

'Away where?'

'Birmingham, Bristol, Leeds and Manchester. That's what he told me. He said he had to go away for work. I believed him at the time.'

'Presumably you had no reason not to.'

'No. I trusted him. But I think now he lied to me because he'd been spending his time in Whitechapel.'

'But that doesn't make him Jack the Ripper.'

'Perhaps not. But there was something someone said at the inquest. A man joked that William had looked like Jack the Ripper.'

'And what did he look like?'

'He was five foot eight, dark-haired and had a dark moustache.'

Penny sorted through the papers on the table. 'I've written the descriptions of him somewhere. Here we are.' She picked up a sheet of paper. 'The descriptions vary,' she said. 'That's not surprising because eyewitness accounts are unreliable. And some people like to think they've seen him but are actually mistaken. I've summarised the descriptions as well as I can.' Penny looked down at her notes. 'He's believed to be between the ages of twenty-six and thirty-eight years old.'

'William was thirty-two,' said Emma.

'And his height is around five foot six or five foot seven. William was five foot eight, you say?'

'Yes.'

'So a little bit taller.'

'But not too dissimilar.'

'No. Most of the descriptions state he has dark hair and dark eyes.'

'Like my husband.'

'And a dark moustache. Although I think I recall a description stating he had a fair moustache. Lots of gentlemen have moustaches. And I should think there are many gentlemen in London who would match this entire description. Let's consider the clothing. He apparently wears a long dark overcoat and some claim it has a fur collar and cuffs.'

'William didn't own a fur-trimmed coat. Although he had a couple of long, dark overcoats.'

'And a dark felt hat.'

'Yes, William had one like that. Although it's probably a common hat.'

'Very commonplace, I should say. Then there's a waistcoat, sometimes light in colour, and dark trousers. Button boots and gaiters. All those items of clothing are owned by many gentlemen.'

'William fits the description,' said Emma. 'But so will many other people.'

'Yes, they will. I think the descriptions of Jack the Ripper are interesting because they describe a very ordinary-looking man. He has no distinguishing features which set him apart from other people. And that explains why he escapes detection, doesn't it? If he looks like every other gentleman, then he doesn't look suspicious, does he? His ordinariness is his shield.'

Emma shuddered. 'We could pass him in the street without knowing.'

'Yes, we could. Let's look at the dates of the attacks. You say the police have already asked you about these?'

'Yes. And William appears to have been away for a number of them.'

Penny searched through the papers on the table until she found what she was looking for. 'The first victim was Martha Tabram,' she said. 'She was thirty-nine and murdered in the early hours of the seventh of August. James tells me his colleagues aren't convinced she was a victim of Jack the Ripper because the nature of the attack differed from the others. However, a knife was used as the weapon and the assault was still exceptionally violent. Poor woman.' She gave a shudder.

'The inspector asked me about William's whereabouts that night,' said Emma. 'And as I told him, he wasn't away then. But when you described how ordinary the murderer appears to be... he can only be someone who's able to fool everyone around him.'

'He certainly has some cunning about him. The next murder, possibly the first murder committed by Jack the Ripper, was early on Friday, the thirty-first of August.'

'While William was away,' said Emma. 'Or so he claimed. He returned late that evening.'

'The victim was Mary Ann Nichols,' said Penny. 'People knew her as Polly. She was forty-three years old and had been living in a lodging house in Flower and Dean Street. Do you know Flower and Dean Street?'

'No.'

'It's possibly one of the worst streets in London. The lodging houses there are overcrowded and overrun with vermin. I really don't know how the landlords get away with running establishments which are so diabolical. Polly's body was found at twenty to four on the thirty-first of August in Buck's Row. It's a little street behind the railway station on Whitechapel Road.' Penny sighed and looked up from her notes. 'Her injuries were detailed in the newspaper reports. I'm sure you've heard how viciously these poor women were attacked.'

'Yes,' said Emma. 'It's horrific.'

'The next victim was Annie Chapman. She was forty-seven

and lived in lodging houses in Whitechapel and Spitalfields. She was last seen talking with a man at half past five in the morning on the eighth of September. Her body was found shortly before six in the yard of number twenty-nine, Hanbury Street.'

'William wasn't away then,' said Emma. 'But the inspector asked me if he could have gone out at night without my knowledge.'

'And could he have done?'

'I suppose he could have if I'd been too deeply asleep to hear anything. But if he'd gone out and done something terrible like that overnight, then surely I would have known? How would he have been able to act normally the following day?'

'Most people wouldn't be able to,' said Penny. 'But I think that's what makes Jack the Ripper difficult to catch. He acts normally most of the time.' She searched through her papers again. 'This doesn't make cheery reading, does it? But it needs to be solved. This man can't continue what he's doing.' She picked up a piece of paper. 'This is what I was looking for. It describes the night of the double murder.'

Emma felt a chill on the back of her neck. The night of the double murder had not just shocked the community in East London, but the entire country. The details had been widely reported in the newspapers and she'd read them as avidly as everyone else.

'It was the night of Saturday, the twenty-ninth of September,' said Penny.

'When William was away in Birmingham,' said Emma. 'At least, that's what he told me.'

'The first victim was forty-four-year-old Elizabeth Stride, and she lived in a lodging house on Flower and Dean Street. The same street as Polly Nichols. At one o'clock on the morning of the thirtieth, a man drove his horse and cart into Dutfield's Yard on Berner Street. The horse shied at something, and that's when the man discovered Elizabeth's body. The police believe he may have disturbed the attacker, because Elizabeth had died just moments earlier. Jack the Ripper didn't have time to inflict the awful injuries on her. He must have left the yard when he heard the horse and cart approach.'

'And to think he was that close to being seen!' said Emma.

'It's frustrating that he got away, isn't it? The fact he couldn't complete the attack meant he attacked again that same night. Catherine Eddowes's body was found just forty-five minutes later in Mitre Square in the City of London. She was forty-six years old. She had recently left the Bishopsgate police station after being shut in a cell there to sober up. She left the police station at one that morning.'

Emma shook her head. 'If only she had remained there for the night. I realise a police cell is a miserable place to sleep, but at least she would have been safe.'

Penny nodded. 'These women were extremely vulnerable. This man preys on the weak.' She balled her fist and banged it on the table. 'It makes me so angry!'

She returned to her notes. 'October passed without an attack and we all hoped we'd seen the end of them. But then came the murder of Mary Kelly last week. She suffered the most brutal attack of all because she was murdered in her home. The killer had the benefit of privacy and time.'

Emma felt nauseous.

Penny gathered the papers together. 'I sincerely hope your late husband isn't Jack the Ripper, Emma. From what you've told me, he clearly lied to you and misled you. But the man who's committing these awful crimes in Whitechapel is a monster.'

'I don't believe I married a monster,' said Emma. 'But what was William doing in Whitechapel? I need to find out. And maybe he was murdered because someone thought he was Jack the Ripper.'

'A case of mistaken identity?' said Penny. 'It's possible.'

'He told me he went away for work,' said Emma. 'So his employer, the law firm Cardwell and Theobald, will be able to confirm when he was away. I could visit them and ask.'

'That sounds like an excellent idea,' said Penny. 'It's something the police should do, and I'm sure they'll get round to it. But they're also extremely busy.'

Emma sighed. 'But even if I can prove William wasn't Jack the Ripper, I don't know how anyone can find the person who killed him. There seem to be no clues at all.'

'Finding the truth is like untangling a knot,' Penny said, leaning forward. 'Sometimes it feels impossible, but you have to keep pulling at the threads. Ask the right questions. Look where others haven't thought to look. Watch for the patterns that don't quite fit.'

NINETEEN

'Emma Holland?' said James at dinner that evening, his face had turned pale. 'The woman who tried to shoot me?'

'She didn't actually mean to—'

'She was here in our house?'

'Yes,' said Penny. 'We had a long conversation.'

He laid down his knife and fork.

'It was four years ago, James.'

'That doesn't change what happened. Imagine if she'd been successful! We would never have married. Thomas and Florence wouldn't even exist!'

'But they do exist, so there's no use in thinking like that. And besides, Emma didn't mean to point the gun at you. She wasn't thinking straight. She was consumed by some sort of mania caused by the murder of her brother.'

'So you're defending her.'

'I'm just trying to explain why she acted as she did. It was a moment of madness. She hasn't forgotten about it and she apologised for it again today.'

'She apologised to you. But not me.'

'Because you were at work, James. Oh, do please be reasonable, Emma has just been widowed.'

'I'm sorry to hear it.' He picked up his cutlery again. 'It was a surprise to hear she'd called on you. What was her reason?'

'Her husband, William Langley, was murdered in Whitechapel on Saturday night.'

'He was her husband? Good grief.'

'She wants some help. She wants to find her husband's murderer.'

'Presumably H Division are working on it.'

'They are, but they're short of men, aren't they? And they're so busy with the Whitechapel murders that I'm not sure they have the time.'

'Even so, that's for them to manage. I'm sure they'll do all they can.' He sawed his knife through the tough piece of beef on his plate. The meal she had prepared was poor, but he was being polite about it.

'And Emma is also worried her husband may have been Jack the Ripper,' said Penny.

James groaned. 'Not another one! We have about two dozen people each week telling the police their husband or son or brother or cousin or whoever is Jack the Ripper. It's no wonder H Division and the Yard are struggling to make any progress.'

'But it seems H Division themselves suspect William Langley. An inspector asked Emma about the dates of the murders and apparently his whereabouts for those dates couldn't be accounted for. Emma has reason to be concerned. I suspect her husband was having an affair, and that's why he left her. I didn't want to ask Emma directly about an affair because I didn't want to upset her even more.'

'Or maybe there wasn't another woman and perhaps he was Jack the Ripper,' said James. 'But if he was, then surely Emma would have suspected something before now.'

'Not necessarily. The murderer is able to wander the streets and approach these women without raising suspicion. Why? Because he looks and acts ordinary. William Langley also appears to have been fairly ordinary but if his wife never suspected him of anything, then why would anyone else?'

'It's a fair point,' said James. He sat back in his chair, having consumed the tough piece of beef.

'I'm sorry dinner wasn't very good,' she said.

'It filled a hole,' he said, wiping his mouth on his serviette. 'Didn't we have the same yesterday evening?'

'Yes.' Penny didn't enjoy cooking, and she wasn't particularly good at it. The housekeeper, Mrs Oliver, had left a year ago, and they had struggled to find a suitable replacement. Penny reasoned she had time to look after the children, do the housework and cook herself.

James was quiet as he cleared their plates from the table.

'What is it?' she asked him.

'What is what?'

'You seem preoccupied about something.'

'Not preoccupied,' he said. 'Just a little concerned.'

'About what?'

'About you.'

'Why?'

'I'm worried the visit from Emma Langley is going to mean you get involved in something. You have the children and the house to look after now, and you barely—'

'I barely what?'

'I didn't mean to say that. I just... well... you've already spent an awful lot of time studying the Whitechapel murders and I've no idea why.'

'It interests me. It keeps my mind active.'

'Very well. But please don't allow Emma Langley to drag you into anything. The police will work on her husband's case and there's no need for you to get involved. You can't, not now you're a mother. The children are very young and they have to come first.'

Penny sighed and gave a nod. 'They will always come first, James.'

TWENTY

Penny looked through her folder of notes and newspaper cuttings while Thomas and Florence slept the following afternoon. Could it really be possible William Langley had been Jack the Ripper?

He had clearly been a duplicitous man, but that didn't mean he was a murderer. His absences from home were suspicious, but perhaps they could be explained by his former employer. Emma had said she would visit the law firm and find out more. Penny wondered how she'd got on.

It was unfortunate William Langley had borne a resemblance to the descriptions of Jack the Ripper. But what of his character? Penny leafed through the pages in front of her to find the notes she had made on this. Newspaper reports had speculated on the type of man who was capable of committing such atrocities and Penny felt it would be useful if she could show these notes to Emma. With a bit of luck, Emma would realise the reports didn't describe her husband at all.

Penny found her page of notes and read through it. The man responsible for the Whitechapel murders had earned his nickname after a letter claiming to be from him was signed,

"Jack the Ripper". The letter had been sent to the Central News Agency at the end of September and had bragged about his evil deeds. The letter was believed to be a hoax, but the name of the signatory had stuck.

Some thought Jack the Ripper was a lunatic who had escaped from an asylum. Others wondered if his actions were caused by a drink delirium or an epileptic seizure. It was speculated that he acted unconsciously while in the fit of a nerve storm and had no recollection of his actions at all.

There was little doubt he deliberately targeted unfortunate women. Some reports suggested he was seeking revenge for being wronged by a prostitute, others believed he was driven by religious zeal to clean the streets of vice. Penny suspected he targeted unfortunate women because they were vulnerable.

And then there was the knife. Some said Jack the Ripper was so skilled with his weapon that he could be a butcher or a surgeon. Others said there was no skill to his violence at all.

Many of the reports were sensationalist. As well as being described as a lunatic, Jack the Ripper was called a madman, a man-monster and a ghoulish assassin with a lust for blood. It was enough to strike fear into the heart of everyone living in Whitechapel. Penny lamented the fact some members of her profession enjoyed frightening their readers with melodramatic prose.

'You look rather busy, Penny,' said James.

She startled. She'd been so consumed by her notes that she hadn't noticed her husband enter the dining room.

'What are you doing at home?' she asked.

'That's a warm welcome.' He smiled and bent down to kiss her. 'I thought I'd call in because I've just been to St John's Wood police station. D Division have arrested a notorious swindler.'

'That's excellent news! Who is he?'

'His name is Barnaby Ratcliffe, and he's been running a

fraudulent insurance company. For the past few years, people across London have reported being swindled by this company. The Yard got involved and coordinated efforts to find the man behind it.'

'How was he swindling people?'

'He was going from door to door selling life insurance policies, just like any other insurance salesman. But his policies aren't worth the paper they're written on. I've heard of some very sad cases indeed. People have been paying Ratcliffe's men each month only to discover the life insurance policies are non-existent when their family member dies.'

'So the life insurance policies pay nothing?'

'Nothing whatsoever. Ratcliffe keeps the money for himself. He's made thousands of pounds from the fraud.'

'What a horrible man!'

'He employed two accomplices to collect money on his behalf and D Division arrested all three of them in St John's Wood this morning.'

'That's excellent news! You must be very happy about it all.'

'I am. There's little doubt Barnaby Ratcliffe is going to prison for an extremely long time. He and his men are being taken down to the Yard in a Black Maria so I need to join them down there shortly. I thought I'd pop in to see you.' He paused to look at her before he said softly. 'You're not trying to solve the Jack the Ripper case, are you?'

'No.' Penny chewed the end of her pencil. She wished it was possible to solve the case, but she didn't have access to all the information the police had. 'I'm hoping I can rule out William Langley,' she said.

'And can you?'

'Not yet. I need to speak to Emma Langley again.'

'Really?'

She didn't like his questioning tone. It suggested he didn't understand the difficulties Emma was enduring. 'Yes. I think she needs some help.'

He gave a laugh. 'May I remind you, Penny, that Emma Langley once tried to shoot me?'

'We've discussed that already. She temporarily lost her mind,' Penny said frustratedly.

'Maybe she temporarily lost her mind a second time and murdered her husband?'

'No! That's quite impossible.'

'I don't think it is,' said James. 'From what you've told me, William Langley was a scoundrel. Emma took her revenge by following him to Whitechapel and attacking him. The trouble with this crime is that it happened in the middle of the night, and there are no witnesses. But from what I've learned of the case so far, Emma and her husband did not have a happy marriage. He abandoned her, and she must have been extremely angry and upset about it.

'Imagine she then discovered him in the street in Whitechapel. He was probably the worse for a drink because we know he went to the Ten Bells and played cards. Perhaps Emma tried to reason with him. Perhaps she didn't intend to murder him at all. But she was upset, possibly intent on revenge, and maybe he said something which enraged her.'

'But she would have had to have had a knife on her, wouldn't she?' said Penny. 'The person who murdered William Langley had armed themselves with a weapon.'

'Many people in Whitechapel are arming themselves at night, Penny. I think it's entirely sensible that Emma Langley could have gone to Whitechapel that night looking for her husband, with a knife because she was worried about being attacked by Jack the Ripper.'

'No, I don't agree at all. Emma didn't even know her husband was in Whitechapel.'

'That's what she says. But we only have her word for it that he left her on the train.'

'No. There were witnesses.'

'Who?' asked James.

'The police would find some if they asked around. And besides, she certainly has alibis who saw her in Suffolk on the night of her husband's death.'

'That's what she's told you.'

'And I'm sure it's true! It's something which is easily proved so I don't see why she would lie about it.'

'Very well. But you realise it's important not to believe everything she says?'

'Yes, I know the importance of that,' said Penny. 'And I also consider myself to be a good judge of character. I don't think Emma is lying to me.'

'If you say so.'

Penny sighed. 'A few years ago, I would have been able to help Emma properly. I was a news reporter on the *Morning Express* and I would have written articles about William Langley's murder and travelled all over town asking lots of questions. I can't do that anymore.'

'No. Life has changed, hasn't it? It's not the sort of thing a wife and a mother does,' James said gently.

'No, it's not.'

'Although you're trying to, aren't you?' he said, casting his eyes over the table. 'This is why you get all these papers out whenever you have a spare moment.'

'I like to keep my mind busy. But I'm probably wasting my time with it all.'

A cry came from upstairs. Florence was awake again. Penny began tidying up her papers. She felt exhausted. Florence didn't sleep well at night and both children kept her busy during the day. It wasn't easy looking after them and cooking and cleaning.

There seemed to be little time for anything anymore. Not

even cooking a decent meal. She made little effort with her appearance. She had lost interest in styling her hair or wearing nice clothes. Instead, she pinned back her hair and wore practical clothes that she could put an apron over.

She was lucky James didn't complain. Many other husbands would be less tolerant.

'Why don't we look for a new housekeeper?' said James as he helped her gather up the papers.

'Because no one is as good as Mrs Oliver was. And the last housekeeper was dreadful. She did everything wrong, and I had to spend my day pointing it out to her. I reasoned it was less work in the end to do everything myself.'

'We can find someone else who's good.'

'I'm sure we will, eventually. But only after we've employed more hopeless ones. I don't think I can cope with the hard work involved with that.'

'I can ask a colleague of mine,' said James. 'Detective Browning. His sister is apparently looking for a new position. You can't possibly take on more without a housekeeper. In fact, I forbid it.'

'You forbid it?' She stopped and stared at him. She had never imagined James trying to stop her from doing something.

He appeared to reconsider. 'Perhaps *forbid* is too strong a word... I advise against it. But do you understand what I'm trying to say, Penny? Before you can help Emma, you need someone to help you.'

TWENTY-ONE

A tea-coloured fog hung over Bedford Row. Emma's coat and hat were damp from the twenty-five-minute walk she'd made from Clerkenwell.

As she looked for William's former law firm, a hansom cab emerged from the fog. Emma gave it a passing glance, then was struck by something familiar about the driver.

She stopped and stared. The driver slowed the horse to a stop, too. 'Sorry, I'm not for hire,' he said, perched high on his seat. 'I'm already booked.'

'Mr Carter?' He was the rough-skinned, pale-eyed cabman who William had hailed on the night of his death. He wore a shabby bowler hat and had a rug over his knees. 'I recognise you from the inquest into my husband's death,' she added.

'Oh, Mrs Langley. I recognise you as well, now you mention it. I'm so sorry about what happened to your husband, I wish I could've done more to help him.'

'You did all you could. If you'd known he was injured, you would have taken him to the hospital. I don't understand why he didn't ask for help.'

'Me neither. He must've thought he was going to be all

right.' He shook his head. 'I hope the police find out what happened that night. He didn't deserve it. And you most certainly don't deserve it, Mrs Langley.'

'Thank you. I'll let you go on your way.'

He tipped his hat, and the horse trotted on.

The law firm was in a smart, four-storey, terraced building. The clerk behind the desk in the marble entrance hall told Emma she would find Cardwell and Theobald on the third floor.

Once she'd climbed the stairs, Emma reached a corridor. The door nearest to her stood ajar and she could hear voices and smell tobacco smoke. Peering in, she saw half a dozen men sitting at desks divided by wooden partitions. Emma stepped inside and approached the junior clerk who sat nearest to the door. He had thick, unruly hair which he'd tried to oil into place.

'I would like to speak to Mr Cardwell or Mr Theobald, please,' she said.

'May I ask what it's regarding?'

'I would like to speak to one or both of them about my husband, William Langley. The late William Langley, I should say. I'm his widow.'

A brief expression flickered on the young man's face. She couldn't tell what it signalled. Caution maybe. Or even contempt. 'I shall make some inquiries for you.' He got up from his seat, walked past his colleagues and headed for a door at the back of the room.

The clerk hadn't offered Emma his condolences. Had it been deliberate or just the gaucheness of youth? While she waited, she recalled her visit to Penny Blakely the previous day. She'd found her welcoming and helpful. She also appeared to understand Emma's predicament. It was a shame Penny was no longer a news reporter and was unable to help her as she had in the past, but Emma hoped she would become someone she could call on for advice.

The door at the back of the room opened and a broad man in a dark suit and a burgundy striped waistcoat stepped out. He had thinning, grey hair, a bulbous nose and heavy jowls. His face was glum as he approached Emma, but he forced a smile when he caught her eye. 'Mrs Langley? I'm Mr Theobald. How do you do?' He held out his hand, and she shook it. His handshake was firm but clammy. 'I was very sorry to hear of the death of your husband. On behalf of everyone here at the firm, I extend my deepest sympathies to you.'

'Thank you.'

'We can talk in the boardroom,' he said. She followed him out of the room and along the corridor to a room with a long, well-polished table. Portraits of important-looking gentlemen hung on the wall and the view from the large sash windows was obscured by fog.

Mr Theobald pulled out one of the chairs for Emma to sit in, then placed himself in the large chair at the head of the table.

'I've read about the circumstances of your husband's death,' he said. 'I can imagine it must have caused you great distress.'

'It has,' said Emma. 'I don't understand how it all came about. I can only hope the police will find the answers.'

'I'm sure they will. How can I help?'

'I'd like to learn more about where William travelled to while he was working for you. He went away quite a lot and I know he visited Birmingham and Manchester and a few other places. I'm wondering if there's a record of where he went and when. I wrote down some of the dates in my diary, but if I could obtain some details from you, then I could give it to the police.'

'The police?'

'Yes. They've asked me for details of his whereabouts over the past few months and I can only rely on my memory or what I've written in my diary. If your firm could provide a record of the places he visited, then I'm sure that will answer their questions. Perhaps William kept a diary here?'

Mr Theobald scratched his head and Emma didn't like the way his brows knotted together, as if he felt confused about what she was saying.

A pause followed. Then he cleared his throat. 'If I understand you correctly, Mrs Langley,' he said, 'you've stated your husband used to go away for work on a regular basis.'

Emma nodded.

'I'm afraid I'm unable to provide a record of him having done so because he stopped working here some time ago.'

'I'm aware his employment with you ended this month,' said Emma. 'We had planned to move to Suffolk.'

'I see. Well, I can confirm your husband left his employment here in July.'

TWENTY-TWO

'July?' The news felt like a punch to Emma's stomach.

'Yes,' said Mr Theobald. 'Your husband left this firm about three and a half months ago.'

'Three and a half months?' she repeated in shock.

'I apologise, Mrs Langley, if you were not aware.'

'I wasn't aware. No.' She stared at the table; its polished sheen reflected the dim, foggy light from the window. The room felt cold all of a sudden. She recalled William cheerfully setting off for work and giving her a kiss as he departed. She remembered how he'd been reluctant to discuss his day at work or his trips away because he'd said he found his work dull. 'I've been working all day,' he would say. 'The very last thing I want to do when I get home is discuss it.'

And now she understood why. He hadn't even been there.

'Is it possible he took up a position elsewhere?' she asked, hopefully.

'He may have done, but I couldn't tell you, I'm afraid.'

Emma felt her face flush. The situation was embarrassing. What did Mr Theobald think of her? It was obvious William had lied to her and now Mr Theobald knew she'd believed every word.

'I'm sorry I had to inform you of this,' he said. 'I thought your husband would have—'

'Told me?' She met his gaze. Anger balled in her stomach. 'Yes, I thought he would have too. But I'm discovering he's not the man I thought he was.'

Mr Theobald gave a slight nod and didn't seem to know what to say.

'Why did he leave his job?'

He scratched his head again. 'There was a difference in opinion between your husband and some of his colleagues.'

'There was an argument?'

'A series of disagreements. I wish to state your husband was an intelligent gentleman who conducted himself well with his colleagues and our clients. He didn't leave on bad terms.'

'You asked him to leave?'

'I had a conversation with him in which I suggested it was for the best.'

Emma could feel frustration bubbling within her. 'I hope you don't mind if I speak directly, Mr Theobald,' she said. 'But I find your language tactful and rather lacking in detail. Please don't feel you must speak about my husband in flattering terms because he's dead. I would like to know exactly why he left this law firm.'

He raised an eyebrow and gave a little exhale. 'Very well. I shall tell you everything, Mrs Langley. Your husband worked here for a year and a half. He arrived with a reference from another law firm which I later found out he had falsified.'

'Oh.'

'That said, Mr Langley acquitted himself well to begin with. Many of our clients liked him, in fact, I can say he charmed them. I wasn't concerned about him until I heard reports he was occasionally absent with little explanation.

There were also reports of rudeness when a colleague disagreed with him. He could be imperious and thought his opinion counted more than the opinions of others. This law firm has an excellent reputation, and I got the impression he wished to be considered the finest solicitor employed here. It was an arrogant assumption, considering his relative youth and inexperience. Any right-minded gentleman would naturally defer to the older, more senior gentlemen in his company. But I'm afraid he was insubordinate, and I can imagine he was a difficult pupil at school. To coin a well-known phrase, Mr Langley was too big for his boots.'

'So you dismissed him?'

'Only after several conversations about the matter. And unfortunately he lost his temper with me.'

Emma sensed Mr Theobald wasn't the sort of man someone should lose their temper with.

'And that was that, I'm afraid. I had to ask him to leave. I can only imagine he was too embarrassed about the whole affair to admit it to you.'

'Yes, I think he must have been.' Had there been any sign William had been dismissed from his job? She thought back to July when they had been newly married. William had seemed his normal self. How could he have found it so easy to pretend everything was fine? And how had he managed without a salary for over three months? Had he earned money elsewhere?

'I can see this comes as quite a shock for you, Mrs Langley.'

'Yes. It does.'

'If there's anything I can help with, do please ask. It's a regret of mine that everything I've just told you will be making you feel even worse. That's why I kept my conversation tactful and lacking in detail to begin with.'

'It's not your fault,' said Emma. 'It sounds like my husband wasn't a particularly good employee.' She wanted to add he hadn't been a particularly good husband, either.

'Do you have a solicitor looking after your affairs?'

'No. I suppose I need one, don't I? I don't think William left a will, and I can't find any of his personal papers.'

'Oh dear. Well, please let me offer you the services of one of my solicitors, free of charge.'

'That's very kind of you.'

'If you can't find your husband's will or any other personal papers, then you will need a solicitor to help you, Mrs Langley. There will be financial matters to sort too. Have you told the bank your husband has died?'

'No. Not yet.'

'Do you have a death certificate?'

'Yes. The coroner gave it to me.'

'You'll need to take it to the bank to inform them. The solicitor will be able to help you with everything else.'

'All right. Thank you.'

'It's the least I can do to help the widow of a former employee.'

'Thank you again, and I appreciate you taking the time to speak with me today.'

Emma got up from her seat and Mr Theobald did the same.

'Just one more question,' she said. '*Did* my husband ever need to travel away for his work?'

'No he didn't, Mrs Langley. All the clients he dealt with were here in London.'

'I see.'

It was another blow. More lies.

Emma blinked away tears as she descended the staircase. How could her husband have behaved so despicably? Had he really cared nothing for her feelings at all?

TWENTY-THREE

Mr Theobald waited for Mrs Langley to leave before he went into Mr Cardwell's office.

'How did it go, Edward?' asked Robert Cardwell, peering at him intensely over the rim of his glasses and placing the papers he'd been reading on the desk in front of him.

'Well enough. I feel rather sorry for the poor woman. I don't think she had a clue what Langley was like. It's come as quite a shock to her.' He sank into the leather-buttoned chair by Cardwell's fireplace. 'Can you believe the scoundrel told her he was still working here?'

Cardwell gave a bemused snort. 'That doesn't surprise me. Presumably he was too proud to tell her we'd let him go. It's not the sort of thing a man likes to admit to his wife.' He sat back in his chair and steepled his fingers. 'What does she know?'

'Not much, I don't think. If Langley didn't tell her he'd left the firm, then I can only guess he didn't tell her much about what happened before then.'

'You can only guess? So you don't know for sure.'

'I think if she knew something, then she would have brought it up. She grew rather annoyed with my tactfully worded responses and asked me some direct questions. But none of her questions suggested Langley had told her exactly what happened here.'

'Good. It sounds like he kept it to himself.'

'I think so. And it's probably just as well; his widow is no fool. She's a demure young lady, but I think she has a keen mind, too. Hopefully she won't call on us again. But if she does, then we need to handle her carefully. She's not the sort to accept generalisation and obfuscation.'

'Interesting. It sounds like we shouldn't underestimate her. When did she and Langley marry?'

'Early July, I think it was. We sent Andrews and O'Brien to the wedding.'

'Yes, I recall that now. And Langley left us when?'

'The twenty-seventh of July.'

'So he worked here for three further weeks after they married and he mentioned no word to her about leaving his employment here. I'm confident he kept her in the dark.'

'We could have a problem with the police, though.'

'Why?' Cardwell unsteepled his fingers.

'Mrs Langley told me they've been asking her questions about her husband's whereabouts. Apparently, he explained his absences to her by telling her he went away for work.'

'I see.'

'And that was the reason she called here. She wished to confirm his whereabouts with us.'

Cardwell rubbed his brow and gave an ominous laugh. 'Oh dear. I can't imagine the look on her face when you told her he'd never travelled away for his work.'

'As I've said, I feel rather sorry for her.'

'Women should know better than getting mixed up with a chap like Langley.'

'Yes, they should. But he fooled us too, didn't he?'

'Fooled you, Theobald.'

'He fooled both of us. That reference was exceptionally well forged.'

'It didn't take us long to work him out, though.'

'So what about the police?' asked Theobald.

'If they come here and ask us questions, then we don't know anything, do we? Langley's supposed absences occurred after he left our employment.'

'Very well.' Theobald got up from the chair. 'Hopefully, the widow will be content with what I've told her and will stay away.'

'I'm sure she'll calm down. It only happened on Saturday, she'll still be in a state of shock the poor thing. Are we sending anyone to the funeral?'

'I'll go.'

'But that will give her the opportunity to ask you more questions.'

'Not at the funeral, she won't. I won't hang about there for long, and she'll be distracted by the other mourners.'

'Right you are, Edward.'

'And I offered her the services of a solicitor free of charge.'

Cardwell smiled. 'And she accepted?'

'Yes, she did. I'll ask O'Brien to do it. It will mean he can keep an eye on things.'

'An excellent idea, Edward. Well done.'

TWENTY-FOUR

William's bank account was held at Wyndham and Co on Lombard Street in the City of London. It was a narrow street with tall, formal buildings. Smartly dressed gentlemen hurried by and a shoeblack appeared to be doing a brisk trade outside Barclays Bank.

The banking hall of Wyndham and Co had a vaulted ceiling, tall marble columns and a tiled floor. Clerks sat behind high mahogany desks lit with ornate lamps.

After explaining to a clerk the reason for her visit, Emma was shown into a comfortable, wood-panelled office where a bank manager greeted her with a sympathetic face. 'Please accept my condolences, Mrs Langley.'

She thanked him, but she was growing tired of everyone's sympathy and sombre mood. She had become someone who people felt sorry for. A widow in mourning.

'A solicitor will be managing my late husband's affairs,' she said to the manager. His name was Mr Blythe, and he was a grey-faced man with steel-rimmed spectacles. 'However, I'm currently unsure of my financial position. My husband looked after the accounts. He had two, I believe. A current account and a savings account.'

Mr Blythe gave a solicitous nod. 'Probate has not been granted to you yet, I take it?'

'No, not yet.'

'Hopefully things will progress quickly, and you'll be granted probate soon. It depends on how your husband left his affairs.'

Emma had assumed his affairs were in order, but now she'd learned he probably hadn't had a salary for over three months. What money had they been living on?

'For peace of mind, can you please tell me how much is in each account?' she said. 'I don't have any income, but I do have a lot saved. It was my inheritance, and we were going to use the money to buy a home in Suffolk.'

'Of course. Do you have your account number?'

'I'm afraid I don't. My husband's personal papers appear to be missing.'

He frowned. 'How odd.'

'I'm sure I'll find them soon enough.'

'Indeed. Well, I can certainly look at the accounts for you, Mrs Langley. Please bear with me while I fetch them.'

A lady in a starched white apron and stiff cotton hat served Emma tea as she waited for Mr Blythe to find the accounts.

It had been five days since William's death and she hadn't yet cried for him. Surely a wife should cry for her dead husband?

She had loved him once. But his desertion of her had swiftly turned her bitter. And his lies had left her wondering who he really was. She thought back to their wedding day. It had poured with rain, an omen of what was to come. William had been overjoyed that day, the happiest she'd ever seen him. She had been happy too, genuinely believing she was marrying a man who loved her. But now she was beginning to believe she had married an actor. She hadn't known the real William Langley at all.

Mr Blythe took his time. His brow was furrowed when he returned to the room with two folders under his arm.

'I've found the accounts,' he said. He sat down at the desk, avoiding her gaze.

'And?'

He opened one of the files. 'The current account has a balance of five shillings.'

'Oh.' Nausea swirled in her stomach. It would barely cover two weeks' rent. 'And the savings account?' she managed to ask.

He opened the other file. 'There aren't any savings.'

She began to feel faint.

'No savings? What do you mean?'

'The account is empty.'

Her inheritance.

Emma fell back in her chair, trying to catch her breath.

Mr Blythe grimaced, unsure what to do. 'Can I get you anything, Mrs Langley?'

'No, thank you.'

She got up from her chair and paced the room. 'When was the last withdrawal?'

He consulted the file. 'The fifth of November.'

'And how much was it?'

'Forty-seven pounds.'

She stopped. 'Forty-seven?' William's salary had been just over seventy pounds a year. 'And the rest of it?'

'The rest of it?'

'I inherited five thousand pounds from my parents. Is it not in the account?'

'Not now, no.'

'So it's all been withdrawn over the past four months?'

'Yes.'

Her ears began to ring, then she felt her knees give way beneath her.

TWENTY-FIVE

After Emma and William's first meeting in Hyde Park, she'd returned there exactly a week later. Agnes had been too busy to accompany her, so Emma went on her own. She completed a lap of the Serpentine lake without seeing William. Disappointed, she was about to walk back to Euston when she noticed him approach. Her heart flipped, and she felt a pleasant tickling sensation in her stomach.

William removed his hat as he approached. 'Miss Langley!' He grinned and looked even more handsome than she remembered. 'How lovely it is to see you here again. And you're wearing a different bonnet this time.'

'Yes.' She blushed. 'How well observed of you.'

'It's the sort of detail I like to notice. Is your cousin not accompanying you today?'

'No, Agnes has another engagement.'

'Oh.' He glanced around, scratching his chin. 'Well... I hope you don't think it improper of me to suggest it, but do you mind if I accompany you on your walk this afternoon? I promise you I'll be entirely respectable about it.'

'I suppose some company would be nice.' She tried not to appear too enthusiastic, fearing it was unladylike.

'Excellent.' He replaced his hat. 'Clockwise or anti-clockwise?'

'I beg your pardon?'

'Around the lake. You're walking clockwise and I'm walking anti-clockwise. Which direction do you prefer?'

'Oh, I really don't mind!' she laughed.

'Then let's go clockwise as that's the one you'd already chosen.'

William was enjoyable company. As they walked, he told her he was a solicitor at a law firm in Holborn. She told him she lived with Agnes and her husband and worked as a piano teacher.

'I've always wanted to play the piano,' he said. 'Perhaps you can teach me?'

'If you're a willing student, then it wouldn't be too difficult.'

'Oh yes, I'm a willing student, all right.'

'But I usually teach children. I'm not used to teaching adults.'

'If you speak to my friends, they'll tell you I'm little more than an oversized child.' He laughed. 'I'll be quite easy to teach. Although I can't promise I'll be any good at the piano, I was quite hopeless at the violin at school.'

At the end of their walk, they agreed to meet at the same time and at the same place a week later.

Their walks around the Serpentine became regular, and sometimes Agnes would accompany them. Emma didn't like Agnes being there because the conversation was more staid in her presence. But she agreed to it because it was more respectable to have a chaperone.

After each meeting, Agnes would say something critical about William. Emma assumed she was jealous because

William was more interesting and attractive than Agnes's husband.

'I think he's trying too hard to impress you,' said Agnes after a walk one weekend.

'He doesn't need to try,' said Emma. 'We already have a great deal in common.'

William proposed marriage on his birthday at the end of May. It had been six weeks since their first meeting and Emma was in love. William was amusing, clever, generous and kind. He bought her jewellery, flowers, chocolates and pretty ornaments. After the loss of her brother and parents, Emma had finally met someone who helped her feel happy again.

Agnes didn't approve of the engagement. And she didn't attend their wedding in July. At the time, Emma had been heartbroken by her cousin's absence, convinced Agnes was simply jealous of her happiness. Now she wondered if Agnes had seen something in William that she had been too blind – too desperately in love – to notice.

It had been a small wedding. William's parents had also died, and he admitted to Emma that he'd invented his sister so he'd had an excuse to talk to her about her bonnet on their first meeting.

'We don't need a lot of guests at our wedding,' he said. 'The only person I want there is you, Emma.'

The sky on the day of William's funeral was leaden grey, just as it had been on their wedding day. The service was held in the chapel at Abney Park Cemetery in Stoke Newington. The tall, pointed spire of the cemetery chapel rose out of the morning mist.

Emma walked towards the spire, her footsteps crunching on the gravel path. The air felt chill and damp on her face. Ornate tombs, obelisks, and statuettes receded into the surrounding mist. Here and there stood the faint silhouette of a tree.

Everything was silent.

She had chosen not to accompany the hearse. She felt no need to play the part of a loyal wife. William had chosen to leave her. He'd lied to her and deceived her. He had taken all her money. On the morning of his funeral, she felt anger instead of grief.

What did her future hold? Not so long ago, she had hoped for children. She had pictured raising them in a pretty cottage in Suffolk. She would have bought them a piano and shared her love of music with them.

All her dreams had evaporated now. She'd made the mistake of relying on another person to help them come true. Someone she had foolishly assumed would always be by her side. She would never trust another person the same way again.

Movement up ahead caught her eye. A tall, elegant lady in a long black dress, cloak and hat.

Emma quickened her step to get a better look. But either the mist shifted, or the figure turned off the path. She couldn't work out which.

The woman vanished.

Mr and Mrs Solomon joined her for the service in the chapel. Only a dozen people attended. Mr Theobald occupied a pew on his own and she acknowledged him with a nod.

The lack of mourners was telling. William had clearly made few friends during his brief life. Emma noticed a couple in their sixties who sat close together, their faces drawn and sombre. The gentleman's face was familiar in some way, as if Emma had met him before.

It was cold in the chapel and her stomach felt tight and

knotted. She followed the service with little attention to the words spoken or the hymns sung. Resentment prevented her from immersing herself in the proceedings.

Once the service had concluded, she rose to follow William's coffin out of the church. From the corner of her eye, she noticed someone leave by the chapel door, as if they were in a hurry. Who had it been? She looked around at the glum faces, unable to spot who was missing.

As she left the chapel, she felt a strange sense of detachment. Her anger had gone, and she felt no emotion at all. It was an odd, dreamlike sensation which she wanted to wake up from.

'Mrs Langley?' The couple she'd noticed earlier were now speaking to her. She turned to meet their lined, harrowed faces. 'We're Mr and Mrs Langley,' said the lady. 'William's parents.'

Emma stared at them, wondering for a moment if she had misheard. William had told her his parents had died.

'William's mother and father?' she said.

'Yes,' said Mrs Langley. Her eyes narrowed, as if she was puzzled by Emma's response.

Emma glanced down at the ground, trying to gather her thoughts. She recalled William's sombre tone as he had told her both his parents were dead. It appeared to have been another lie.

'We're so very sorry for your loss,' said William's father.

Emma met his gaze, unsure how to reply. She couldn't tell them William had told her they were dead. It would be hurtful for them to hear such a thing on the day of their son's funeral.

She forced a smile. 'It's nice to meet you at last,' she said. 'It's a shame we didn't meet while William was alive.'

'Yes, it is,' said his father. 'A great shame. I don't know if he discussed us with you, but we became estranged from him about eight years ago.'

Emma wanted to ask what had caused the estrangement,

but she knew this wasn't the time to do so. 'I'm sorry you had a difficult relationship with your son.'

Why had William lied to her about his parents' death? Perhaps he hadn't wished to explain the estrangement. Or maybe he'd lied about them to build rapport with her in the early days of their courtship. His tactic had worked. Emma had believed he'd understood what it was like to have no close family. She had thought she'd met a like-minded soul.

'We're sorry we didn't meet you sooner,' said his mother. 'We heard William had married, and I'm pleased to see he married such a pleasant young lady. I can only hope you managed to instil some sense into him during your short marriage.'

'No, I don't think I ever achieved that,' said Emma. She felt a bitter taste in her mouth. 'I must be frank with you, Mr and Mrs Langley, I am discovering a few unpleasant things about your son which I didn't know before his death.' Their expressions grew even more harrowed. 'But today is not the time to discuss that,' she added. 'Today, we must remember William for what he was. A husband and a son.'

Her eyes remained dry at the graveside committal. William's mother kept wiping her face with a black handkerchief, and Emma imagined she was filled with regret for missing out on a relationship with her son. The day was probably much harder for William's parents than it was for Emma.

Once the coffin had been lowered, the mourners began to leave.

Mr Theobald shook Emma's hand. 'Mr O'Brien will contact you regarding Mr Langley's affairs,' he said. She thanked him and glanced over his shoulder as he bid her farewell.

Among the headstones stood the figure of a woman. Tall

and elegant. The same figure Emma had seen on the path before the funeral.

It seemed the woman was here for William. Who was she? Emma took some steps towards her. But the lady turned and moved away from her. Within seconds, she had disappeared again into the mist.

TWENTY-SIX

'Your children are adorable, Mrs Blakely.' Baby Florence grinned as Mrs Tuttle bounced her in her lap. Thomas laughed as he drove a wooden toy train to and fro over her feet.

'You're very good with them,' said Penny.

'I've had my own, that's why. It comes naturally, doesn't it?'

'Does it?' Penny wasn't sure she agreed. 'Perhaps it becomes more natural with time.'

Mrs Tuttle was the sister of James's colleague, Detective Browning. She was about fifty-five with greying, mousy brown hair. She had a cheerful, round face and a double chin.

'So what would you like me to do around the house, Mrs Blakely? Cooking? Cleaning? That sort of thing?'

'Yes. Exactly that sort of thing.'

'That's no trouble at all. You don't have a very big house so it won't take a lot of work. I'll have time to look after these two as well if you'd like to take yourself off shopping one morning, Mrs Blakely.'

Penny didn't enjoy shopping. But the thought of occasionally being able to leave the house on her own was very appealing. 'That sounds good, Mrs Tuttle,' she said. 'Would eight shillings a week suit you?'

'That would suit me very well, Mrs Blakely. How about I start tomorrow for a week's trial? Then we can see how we go after that.'

'Perfect.'

'I'm pleased you like Mrs Tuttle,' said James at dinner that evening.

'I hope she's a good cook,' said Penny.

'I'm sure she will be.' James stuck his fork into an overboiled potato and it broke into floury clumps.

'Then hopefully you'll have something nice to eat tomorrow evening.'

'Yes, hopefully. I've missed good... Oh no, sorry. I didn't mean to say that.'

Penny pretended she hadn't heard. 'She said she can look after Thomas and Florence occasionally too, but I'm not sure they'll like that.'

'That's because they're only used to you looking after them. It won't do them any harm to spend time with someone else. They'll probably get a bit upset to begin with, but they'll soon get used to her.'

'I'm not sure how I feel about it, though.'

'Surely it's a good thing, Penny. You'll have more time.'

'But she might do things differently to how I want her to.'

'And what's wrong with that?'

'I like things done in a certain way.'

'I understand that. But Mrs Tuttle is very experienced and she'll probably have some helpful suggestions. If you only want things done your way, then you end up doing everything yourself.'

'She might have too many suggestions and try to change

everything. Or she might be horrified by the way I do things here and tell her family about it. Including your colleague Detective Browning.'

'She won't do anything like that.'

'How do you know?'

'Because you told me she was a very nice lady. And Browning's a decent chap too. I think you're worrying too much about it, Penny. And besides, she suggested a week's trial, didn't she? Try it for a week and see how it goes.'

'All right then.' Penny stuck her fork into her own floury potato and tried to overcome her guilt about leaving the children with someone else. Wouldn't they worry she was deserting them? And would Mrs Tuttle know what to do if one of them fell unwell or had an accident?

Awful thoughts about what could go wrong swirled in Penny's mind. She could only feel happy if she was with the children all the time. No harm could come to them then.

But was she truly happy being with them all the time? As much as she loved motherhood, she also craved adult company and conversation. She wanted to go out and travel by train, omnibus and tram without having a perambulator and a young child to worry about. The thought of doing as she pleased was liberating. As was the thought of investigating a case again. The murder of William Langley was perplexing. She wanted to get out with Emma Langley and work with her to discover the truth behind his death. Mrs Tuttle's help would allow her to do that. All she had to do was put her trust in a lady she had only just met.

It seemed a difficult thing to do.

TWENTY-SEVEN

William had first mentioned Suffolk when Emma had fallen unwell in the middle of October. A cough became a fever and Emma had lain in bed for a week. William's work had kept him busy, but he had bought her flowers, a new hat and a necklace. They were gifts Emma couldn't make use of until she recovered, but Mrs Solomon had visited regularly and helped nurse her back to health.

'It's the London air,' William had said to Emma when she was recovering. 'It's no good for your lungs. You need to be in the countryside. I've had a wonderful idea while you've been lying on your sickbed. Let's move to Suffolk.'

'Suffolk?' She had never heard him mention the place before.

'I have an aunt there.'

'Do you?'

'I've never been close to her, but I took the liberty of writing to her a few days ago and she's already replied.' He grinned and pulled a letter out of his pocket. 'She says we can stay with her. She lives in a charming village with a pretty, ancient church and lots of friendly shops.'

'It sounds lovely.' Emma liked the idea of visiting the place, but she still felt too weary to walk around her own home.

'And the countryside is so beautiful that famous artists paint it,' said William, his eyes twinkling. 'We can stay with my aunt while we look for a cottage to rent. Can you imagine what lovely cottages they have there? Beautiful old cottages with oak beams and thatched roofs. And delightful little gardens with roses growing over the front door.'

'The roses won't be blooming now,' said Emma, keen to dampen her husband's enthusiasm for the time being. She felt too tired to consider the idea.

'No, not now. But they will in the springtime. Can you imagine how lovely that would be?'

'Why are you suddenly thinking about Suffolk?' asked Emma. 'I thought we were planning to buy a property in London.'

'Yes, but I've been thinking about it ever since you've been laid up in bed with this awful illness. It's the smoky, filthy air here in London.' He gestured at the street beyond the window. 'It's bad for your health. What better place to go than Suffolk? We have somewhere to stay there and the air is clean and fresh. What do you say?' He fixed his keen gaze on her.

It sounded appealing. 'I suppose if we don't like it, we can come back to London, can't we?'

'Absolutely,' said William, patting her arm. 'How about we try it for six months? We can go for the winter and when spring arrives, we can decide whether we wish to stay there or return to London. My bet is that we'll want to stay and buy a house there. But let's try it, shall we? It's so bleak here in London. And seeing you so unwell breaks my heart. I want to see colour in your cheeks again.' He took her hand. 'I want you to be happy again, Emma.'

'But what about your job?' She felt concerned William hadn't given enough thought to the practicalities of the plan.

'I'll find work as a solicitor in Suffolk easily enough. I shall write off to some firms tomorrow.'

A few days later, William had told her he had been offered a job at a solicitor's firm in Lavenham. And from that moment onwards, they made plans for their move. Emma did her best to convince herself it was the right decision.

The day after William's funeral passed in a grey haze of grief. Emma moved through the house like a ghost, time stretching endlessly as she wondered if the crushing weight in her chest would ever lift. But that night, sleep came suddenly and deeply. She woke in the pale morning light with her mind crystalline and her purpose clear.

'I shall have to teach piano again,' she told Mrs Solomon on Sunday morning.

Her landlady took a pause from brushing the shaggy cat on her lap. 'A job? I'm sure there's no need for that, Mrs Langley. You're no longer buying a house in Suffolk and the life insurance money will come through soon.'

'I didn't take out a life insurance policy on William.'

'You didn't? Oh.'

'And the savings we had have all been spent.'

'By who?'

'William. He was dismissed from his job shortly after we married and he didn't tell me. I suspect we lived on my inheritance money while I thought it was being kept securely in a savings account.'

'What?'

'I thought we were living on his salary. I was foolish. I should have asked to see the bank accounts, but I trusted him with managing our money.'

'As any wife would have done. You weren't foolish, Emma.'

'And he didn't just live on the inheritance money, he spent it all.'

'All of it?'

'Every last penny.'

'What on?'

'I don't know.'

'What a devil! What a despicable...' Mrs Solomon trailed off and resumed brushing the cat, as if trying to calm herself. 'The more I learn about *that man*, the more I... How do you manage to stay so calm about it, Mrs Langley?'

'I don't know. I don't think I am calm. I feel like each new revelation knocks me over, and just as I pick myself up again, I get knocked over by another. I don't think I've even had the opportunity yet to even decide how to react. It just seems... endless. And exhausting.'

Mrs Solomon nodded. 'Yes, I can see that. I can't believe he took your money. He swindled you. And it pains me to say it, but I suspect that was his plan all along.'

'To take my money?'

'I'm afraid so. When did he learn about your inheritance?'

Emma thought back to their first days of courting. 'I suppose it was quite early on. I told him my parents had both died quite soon after we met. And I told him about Alfred's murder, so I suppose he deduced the family's money had come to me. And I also told him about my parents' house in Hillingdon and how I didn't want to live there because it brought back too many sad memories.'

'You sold the house, didn't you?'

'Yes, along with all the furniture, too. William encouraged me to do it and now I understand why.'

'All that while he was planning how to get his hands on your money, Mrs Langley. This sounds like a dreadful thing to say, but I'm afraid I shall say it. That man deserved to be murdered! I should think you're not the only person he swindled, there will be others too. And I suspect that's why he was murdered. Someone took the law into their own hands and put an end to him. That's really all there is to it.' She pulled a ball of cat hair out from the bristles of the brush.

Emma sighed. 'I think you could be right, Mrs Solomon.'

'I would like to find out who the murderer was. How are the police getting on with it?'

'I don't know.'

'What about the news reporter?'

'She's not a news reporter anymore. I think she would like to help, but she has two young children to care for.'

'That's a shame; from what you told me about her, she could have been useful. So how will you get back to teaching piano again?'

'I'll put an advertisement in the newspaper.'

'That sounds like an excellent idea. Please don't worry about paying us any rent for the time being.'

'No, I insist on it. I have a little money left from my house-keeping—'

'You're not to pay us anything for the time being. Not until you're able to earn a little bit.'

'Thank you, Mrs Solomon. I'm very grateful to you.'

'Don't mention it. But perhaps you can earn your keep by making us a cup of tea? I don't want to disturb Laurence while he's on my lap.'

TWENTY-EIGHT

Emma returned to Whitechapel. She wanted to find answers to her questions. What had happened to William's personal papers? And who was the mysterious woman who had attended his funeral?

She'd looked at a map of Spitalfields and Whitechapel in Clerkenwell Free Library and copied down some of the main roads and waypoints. Although she felt nervous about visiting the area, she resolved to keep to the main streets where she hoped she wouldn't meet with any trouble.

Emma began at the newsstand in Liverpool Street railway station where William had supposedly gone to buy a newspaper nine days previously. She doubted now he'd ever visited the newsstand, instead he would have made his way out of the station as quickly as possible.

She found the exit which led to Bishopsgate, a busy street running from north to south. What had William been thinking as he'd left the station that Saturday morning? Had he felt happy? Or regretful? It was impossible to know.

Cabs lined up outside the station, waiting for passengers. A steady rain fell, and Emma put up her umbrella. After waiting for a horse tram to pass, she crossed Bishopsgate and entered Brushfield Street. Ahead of her, at the end of the street, stood Christ Church Spitalfields with its columned facade and tall spire.

Spitalfields Market sprawled along the left side of Brushfield Street. Porters in heavy boots and flat caps busied around carts with crates of fruit and vegetables. Horses waited patiently, their ears flicking in the rain.

Emma walked briskly, heading for the church. When she reached the end of the street, she caught sight of the public house on the opposite corner: the Ten Bells.

It was a large establishment, occupying the corner of the street across the road from the church. The building was four storeys high and had a faded grandeur to it, with a pair of decorative columns flanking the shabby double doors at the entrance.

Emma crossed the road and approached the public house. Grubby curtains hung at the windows and a sign advertised spirits, draught beer and whiskey. She could hear laughter from within and didn't feel brave enough to step inside.

Why had William been a regular visitor to this place? Who had he met here?

The rain drummed on her umbrella and she pulled out the piece of paper which she had drawn her map on. She wanted to find Finch Street which had been the place where William had played cards with the men he'd met in the public house.

She worked out a route which would keep her on the main roads and headed along Fournier Street. It was lined with houses built by the Huguenot weavers exiled from France in the previous century. The homes had probably been attractive in their day but were now dilapidated. They were all inhabited, despite their condition. People sheltered in doorways from the rain and sat at broken windows. A lady hurried along the street with her shawl draped over her head.

Emma turned right into Brick Lane which was lined with tumbledown shops and businesses. A rag merchant's shop advertised for wastepaper, old deeds and parchment. The shop next to it sat empty, its shuttered windows plastered with faded, peeling bill posters advertising music hall shows and excursions by train.

Passers-by glanced at Emma, no doubt noticing her smart overcoat and hat. She was one of the few people carrying an umbrella. Some people around her seemed too poor or careworn to possess one.

Each public house she passed was busy. The establishments were well lit and provided a warm refuge from the rain and squalor.

Finch Street was accessed by a narrow alleyway off Brick Lane. Emma paused, cautious about walking through a place so dark and narrow.

Beyond the darkness of the alleyway, she could see daylight and a rain-soaked street. She mustered up courage and walked as quickly as she could through the alleyway. A pungent stench hit her nose and encouraged her to walk faster. Her boot skidded on something soft and slippery. She dared not stop to see what it was. Instead, she hurried on her way towards the daylight where the alleyway opened out into a miserable little street.

She walked through a puddle, attempting to wash her boots in it, then continued past the cramped little houses which lined the right-hand side of the street. On the left stood a high brick wall; the building beyond it looked like a school.

William had left his comfortable home and his marriage to come here. A wretched place where he had met his death. Why?

The rain continued to fall and a sense of futility set in as Emma reached the end of Finch Street. She was cold, wet and had found no answers. Perhaps she'd been foolish to think she would.

There was one more place she wished to visit before she returned home. She turned right onto Casson Street, then left onto Old Montague Street. Passing more scruffy shops, she reached Whitechapel Road and was delighted to see a hansom cab approaching. She put her hand out and hailed it.

TWENTY-NINE

The hansom cab hadn't travelled far before it had to stop at a large junction. Traffic stood still and people thronged the street. Emma realised they were all wearing black.

She lifted the hatch and asked the cabman what was happening.

'I forgot,' he said. 'I shouldn't have come this way.'

'Forgot what?'

'They're burying Mary Kelly today.'

Mary Kelly was the most recent victim in the series of Whitechapel murders. Ten days after her death, she was being laid to rest.

'Goodness,' said Emma. 'I hadn't realised.' Although she felt sure now that William hadn't been Jack the Ripper, a shadow of doubt still haunted her quieter moments, whispering of all the other secrets he had kept from her.

They waited on the road by the Blind Beggar public house. Police constables urged carts and carriages to move out of the way and tried to keep the crowds off the road. The rain fell and there was an eerie silence.

Emma's stomach tightened as she heard the approaching

sound of horses' hooves and carriage wheels. Two black horses came into view on the road joining from the left. They wore black coats and had tall plumes of black feathers attached to the top of their bridles. The carriage was open to the elements and carried a coffin with two wreaths on top of it and a cross of flowers.

People removed hats and shawls from their heads. Emma was moved by the number of people walking alongside the carriage, determined to accompany Mary Kelly on her final journey. Two black mourning coaches followed behind.

'God forgive her!' cried out a lady with tears streaming down her face. Similar cries followed and Emma struggled to contain her own tears for the poor soul as people wailed and wept. Some rushed forward to touch the coffin.

The funeral cortege turned left on Whitechapel Road and headed east. Emma wiped her eyes as she watched the procession move off ahead of her; the crowds filled the road behind it and followed.

It was a while before the traffic could move again. Emma tried to recover herself as the cab turned into the road the funeral procession had emerged from. As she dried her eyes, she realised she had cried more for a woman she had never known than she had for her own husband.

The hansom cab passed beneath the railway lines and turned into a maze of narrow roads with cramped terraced houses and tall, brick tenement buildings.

The driver opened the hatch in the roof. 'Where on Canrobert Street do you want?'

'The lodging house there.'

'Which one?'

'Is there more than one?'

'I don't know,' said the driver. 'Do you know the name or number?'

'No.'

'Well, it's not going to be easy to find. Do you know how long the street is? There's a stretch of it north of Bethnal Green Road, then it crosses Old Bethnal Green Road, then there's another hundred and fifty yards of it.'

'Would you mind helping me find the lodging house? And I'd like you to wait while I call there, please.'

'All right. As long as you've got the fare.'

'Yes, I have.' Emma had the rest of her housekeeping money in her purse. Most of it would have to be spent on the cab fare, but she didn't want to walk about the East End in the pouring rain.

Canrobert Street was lined with red-brick terraced houses. The cab driver slowed the horse so Emma could look out for a lodging house. Rainwater poured from broken guttering and an old woman eyed her suspiciously from a window.

'Oi!' called the cabman to a young man hurrying along the street. 'Where's the lodging house?'

'Which one?'

'The lady doesn't know which one. How many are on this street?'

The young man shrugged. 'Try up that way,' he said, pointing ahead of them.

Emma wished now she had written down the number of the lodging house. Then she saw a sign in a window advertising rooms for threepence a night. She lifted the hatch above her. 'Stop here, please.'

Emma climbed out of the cab and knocked at the door. The grubby pane of glass above the door had a faded sign in it saying, *Whitstable Guest House*.

A stocky lady with wiry grey hair and a pugnacious expression opened the door. 'After a room?' she asked.

'No,' said Emma. 'I'm making inquiries about my husband.'

'Why? What's he done?'

'He was murdered. Nine days ago. He died in a hansom cab—'

'He was your husband?' The landlady's eyes widened. Emma nodded, and the landlady shook her head in dismay. 'Terrible it was. He turned up in a cab just like you have just now. Only he was dead. The first thing I knew about it was when the cabman was hammering on my door loud enough to wake the dead. Only it didn't wake your husband, unfortunately. He asked me to help, but I took one look at the gentleman and knew there was nothing I could do. I told the cabman to take him down the hospital. So that's what he did.'

'Had my husband booked a room with you?'

'No. He must've asked to be brought here on the off chance I had a room spare. Which I did as it happened. Poor chap couldn't make use of it though, could he? The cabman was very shaken up by it all.'

'What time was this?'

'About half past one.' The landlady folded her arms and leaned against the door frame.

'Had my husband stayed with you before?'

'No.'

'Had you ever met him before?'

'No.' She gave a resolute shake of her head. 'Never seen him before in my life.'

'So how did he know about your lodging house?'

'I call it a guest house. Rooms are sixpence a night here. And you get a room for that, not just a bed like you get in those lodging houses over in Spitalfields. I can only guess someone recommended my place to him. That's how I find most of my customers. Word of mouth. I never advertise. Don't need to.'

'And you're quite sure my husband hadn't visited you before? He didn't call in and leave a bag or case of belongings with you?'

'No. Why would he do that?' The woman was starting to look miffed at Emma's questions.

'Some of his belongings are missing.'

'I'm sorry to hear it. But they ain't here, I'm afraid. And I can assure you the one and only time I saw your husband was when he was slumped over in that cab that night. I didn't get back to sleep after that. I hope you accept my sincerest condolences. I know what it's like to lose a husband. I've lost two of them.'

'I'm sorry to hear it.'

'Well, you've just got to get on with life, haven't you? There's no use in complaining about it. Anyway, I hope the police manage to catch the person who attacked your husband. Although if I were you, I wouldn't be holding my breath. If they can't catch Jack the Ripper, then there's not a lot of hope, is there?'

THIRTY

'This note is middle C,' Emma said to her new pupil, Beatrice Montgomery. Her family lived in a large, comfortable house in Park Crescent, Stoke Newington. They sat together at a well-polished baby grand piano next to French windows which over-looked an emerald-green lawn.

'Can you put your right finger on middle C?' Emma asked Beatrice. The young girl put her left finger on it. 'Your right finger,' said Emma. 'This one here.'

'When can I play a song?' asked Beatrice.

'When we've learned the notes.'

'How long will that take?'

'It will be quite quick if you pay attention. Now, see this note here? That's D.'

'Where's A?'

'We'll get to that.'

'Why aren't we doing A first? It's the first letter of the alphabet.'

'Yes it is, well done. We're beginning with C because it's in the middle.'

'Why isn't A in the middle?'

'That's a very good question. I don't know.'

Emma had forgotten how tiring it was to teach piano to young children. She left the house in Park Crescent half an hour later, feeling grateful for a few moments of peace. Fortunately, Beatrice's mother had paid her in advance for a month's worth of lessons. Emma had made three shillings today, and she hoped she would take on more pupils over the coming weeks.

Rays of pale sunshine peeked between the clouds. Emma walked past St Mary's Church and made her way along Church Street towards the high street. Her route would take her past Abney Park Cemetery, William's burial place.

Despite the resentment she felt towards him, it seemed wrong to pass his resting place without paying her respects. She turned in through the gates on the high street and made her way towards his grave. Stone tombs and headstones gleamed in the weak sunlight. It would be some time before Emma would be able to afford a headstone for William's grave. For the time being, a rectangle of freshly dug earth marked his place.

As Emma approached, she saw a woman ahead of her. Her head was bowed. Immediately she was reminded of the cloaked woman she'd seen in the mist at William's funeral. As she drew closer, she felt sure the woman was standing at the location of William's grave. She was dark-haired and wore a long black coat and a small, fashionable hat.

The woman noticed her. She turned and swiftly moved off in the opposite direction.

She was clearly avoiding her. Emma jogged after her. 'Excuse me!' she called out, when she was near enough to be heard.

The woman began to run.

'I need to talk to you!' Emma shouted after her. It wasn't easy running on the gravel path in heeled boots. The soles of her feet slipped and Emma knew she risked twisting an ankle.

The woman turned left, down a narrow path, then right. She was doing her best to lose Emma.

They passed an old woman with a horrified expression. Emma realised it was disrespectful to run in a cemetery, but she didn't want to lose sight of the mysterious woman a second time.

They zig-zagged through more narrow paths. Emma's legs ached and her corset restricted her breath. The woman ahead of her increased the distance between them. Emma was struggling to keep up as the woman fled through the gate and out of the cemetery.

'Wait!' Emma called again. She reached the gate, gasping for breath. After passing through it, she found herself on a street of terraced houses. The woman was about to disappear from view at the end of the street.

Emma followed, dodging around a milkman who pushed a handcart with a large urn of milk on it. Her legs ached. She realised now she had no hope of catching the woman. She reached a crossroads and saw she was on the high street again. Across the road from her sat Stoke Newington railway station.

Emma leaned against a lamp post to recover her breath.

The woman had clearly known William. And she wanted nothing to do with Emma. If only she could manage to speak to her.

She resignedly made her way towards the railway station to catch the next train back to Liverpool Street.

THIRTY-ONE

Liverpool Street station was cold and busy. The rattle of luggage trolleys, the hiss of steam, the hoot of whistles and the shouts of guards all echoed in the great arches above Emma's head. She felt tired and wanted to get home.

It was a thirty-minute walk to Northampton Square. Or she could travel by the underground railway to Farringdon Street and make the fifteen-minute walk from there.

She was debating which to do when she saw a familiar figure in the crowd ahead of her.

The woman from the cemetery.

She must have got on the same train from Stoke Newington.

Emma caught up with her then grabbed her left arm in a vice-like grip.

'Ouch!' The woman turned. Her face was pretty, with an upturned nose, dark eyes and prominent cheekbones. She wore rouge on her cheeks and her lips were coloured deep red. She was older than Emma, possibly thirty-five. And she stood about two inches taller. 'Get off me!'

'Why did you run away?'

'I don't want to talk to you.' She tried to shrug Emma off, but she held on.

'Why not?'

'Just let go of me!'

'Did you know my husband, William Langley? I saw you at his grave. I saw you at the funeral too. Please talk to me and I'll let go of your arm. I'm not angry with you, I'm just confused.'

The woman's face softened slightly and Emma released her grip. 'I don't know anything,' she said.

'William lied to me,' said Emma. 'And I want to know the truth.'

The woman shook her head. 'You won't want to hear it.'

'You're wrong. I do. I know what sort of man my husband was. Nothing you tell me will shock me, I feel sure of it.'

The woman gave a hollow laugh.

Emma gritted her teeth. 'Don't mock me.'

'I'm not. I'm just surprised you want to hear about everything.'

'Of course I do! I was his wife and I want to find out who murdered him. And if you won't speak to me about him then I can only guess you know something about his death.'

The woman's eyes widened. 'I don't know anything about it!'

'But tell me what you do know.'

'All right then.' The woman bit her lip and glanced around. 'Where shall we talk?'

'How about the dining room?'

A short while later, they sat at a small table in the corner of the railway station dining room. The tables were close together and most of them were occupied.

Thankfully, the room was warm. Emma took off her over-coat, scarf and gloves.

'I'm Lavinia Drummond,' said the woman. 'And I knew your husband as Billy.'

'Billy?'

'Everyone knew him as Billy.'

'Everyone?'

'His friends.'

'I don't know about these friends. Who are they?'

'I can explain. But it may take a while.'

A waitress came to their table, and they ordered tea. Lavinia took off her gloves and Emma noticed sparkling rings on her fingers. She also wore sparkling earrings and a necklace. The bodice of her gown was cut low and trimmed with lace, and she wore a fur stole around her neck.

She was polite and well-spoken, but she didn't seem entirely respectable.

'Why did you run away from me?' Emma asked her once the waitress had left.

'I don't like confrontations.' She fidgeted with her left earring.

'You thought I would confront you? Why?'

'Because of my friendship with your husband.'

'He never mentioned you.'

She smiled. 'No, I don't suppose he would have.'

'Were you more than friends?'

'Are you sure you wish to discover the answer to that, Mrs Langley?' Her brow furrowed.

'I think I already know the answer.'

A pause followed and Lavinia cleared her throat before she spoke. 'Very well. We began a love affair about two years ago.'

'Two years ago?'

'Yes.'

'So not recently?'

'Not recently. It was never a formal love affair because I'm not the sort of woman men wish to marry. My reputation is too ruined for that.' She sighed. 'So our relationship was intermittent. Billy wanted to look for a wife.'

'He never proposed marriage to you?'

'No. And I never expected him to.'

'How did you meet him?'

'We met in the Ten Bells in Spitalfields. I noticed him because he looked like a gentleman and he was handsome.' She paused and gave a brief smile. 'I don't think I should say anything more. He was your husband. You don't want to hear me talk about him in that way.'

'I'd rather you told me everything.'

'Well, you can probably understand why I was attracted to him. He was handsome and charming with it. We got on well and saw each other quite often. He took me to the theatres and restaurants in the West End. I enjoyed his company and I was flattered by his attention. But I knew he would never marry me, I had too much of a past for that. And besides, we didn't need to be married. He wasn't around all the time and I suspected there were other women. But I didn't mind that. The arrangement suited us both.'

'I think I saw you at his funeral.'

'Yes, I was there. I wanted to keep my distance. I didn't want to get in the way of anything.'

'Are you the reason he spent time in Whitechapel?'

'I don't think so. He knew a lot of people there.'

Emma sighed. William's attachment to the area had clearly begun long before she'd met him. It was a part of his life he'd kept secret from her. Why?

'William went away a lot,' said Emma. 'He told me he was travelling with his job. I realise now that's when he was with you.'

'He wasn't always with me,' Lavinia bristled. 'He spent time with other people, too.'

'Such as who?'

'Lots of people.' She glanced around. 'I don't want to say names, just in case.'

'Just in case what?' Emma was growing impatient.

Lavinia leaned in towards her and whispered, 'It's busy in here. You don't know who's listening.'

Emma took a sip of tea and tried to comprehend what Lavinia was telling her. Her husband, a solicitor, had secretly been spending his time in Whitechapel with a lady with a ruined reputation.

She told Lavinia that William had stolen her inheritance.

'It saddens me to hear he treated you so dreadfully,' she said.

'Perhaps I only have myself to blame.'

'No, don't say that!'

'Did you see him on the day he died?' asked Emma.

'Yes. But only briefly.'

'What happened?'

'He arrived at my house and asked if he could stay for a while. I refused.'

'Why?'

'Because I didn't like the look of him. He'd been drinking and I didn't like it when he was drunk. And he was agitated about something. He kept saying he'd done something terrible.'

'Did he explain any more than that?'

'No.'

'He could have been referring to the fact he'd abandoned me on the train that morning.'

'Oh dear.' Lavinia sighed. 'It probably was that. I didn't give it much thought at the time because he was drunk and he could be prone to exaggeration when he was in that state. I told him he could tell me about it later once he'd sobered up. He wanted to stay with me for a few days but I already had another friend staying with me so I told him there wasn't any space.'

'What time was this?'

'Lunchtime on the Saturday.'

'The coroner at William's inquest said three hours of his time that day are unaccounted for. We don't know where he was between one o'clock and four o'clock. Did he visit you during that time?'

'Yes, I think it must have been just after one.'

'And how long was he with you?'

'Not for long. I turned him away. So he asked for a case which he had left at my house a few days before.'

'He left a case with you?'

'Yes.'

'A small overnight case with his initials on?'

'Yes. That was the one.'

'And what was in it?' asked Emma.

'I don't know.'

'Personal papers and a few belongings of his are missing. They must have been in that case.'

'Perhaps they were. I paid little attention to it. He called in on the previous Tuesday or Wednesday and asked me to look after it for him. I put it in a cupboard and it stayed there until he asked for it again on the Saturday.'

'So he left you that day with the case.'

'Yes.'

'Do you know where it is now?'

'No, I don't. That was the last time I saw him.' She paused and bit her lip.

Emma waited for her to resume.

'That's what I feel awfully guilty about.' Lavinia's voice cracked as she spoke. 'If I'd let him in, then he would still be alive. That's why I visited his grave today. I wanted to be alone with him for a moment so I could say sorry.'

'It's not your fault.'

'I feel partly responsible.'

'Why? Do you know who attacked him?'

'No. I have no idea who did that. No one does.'

'You need to tell the police what you know.'

'I don't get along with the police that well. And I'm not sure it would help.'

'Yes it would! It would help them find out what he did during those missing three hours. And why didn't you speak at the inquest?'

'I wasn't summoned.'

'You could have volunteered what you knew.'

She gave a slight smile. 'People like me tend to avoid officials, Mrs Langley. It's usually more trouble than it's worth.'

'But in this case it would really help. Please won't you tell the police that you saw him that day?'

'All right then. If you think it might help, then I'll do it. I can see it's important to you.'

'Thank you. And what about his other friends?'

'What of them?'

'I need to know who they are.'

'Not here. Call on me tomorrow. Would eleven o'clock suit you?'

Emma nodded.

'I live on Fleur de Lis Street,' said Lavinia. 'It's not as nice as the name suggests. Number seven.'

'Thank you. I'll see you then.'

They left the dining room and went their separate ways. As Emma buttoned up her coat, she caught sight of a man watching her. He had a brown moustache and wore a bowler hat and a long dark coat.

As she returned his gaze, he turned and walked away towards the Bishopsgate exit. There was something unpleasant about him but she couldn't understand what. A cold shiver ran down her spine.

THIRTY-TWO

Lavinia Drummond sat at her dressing table. The face staring back at her from the looking glass was tired and lined. The candle cast a flickering light on her features and created unflattering shadows beneath her brow and nose.

She mourned the loss of her beauty. It had left her like a withered rose or a twilight sky. The smooth, firm skin and full lips had gone.

All she could do these days was paint her face. Red lips, pencilled eyebrows, dark powder around her eyes and rouge on her cheeks. Wearing makeup, she could still appear beautiful to some gentlemen, but her painted face was just a mask.

She picked up a linen cloth and began rubbing at the rouge on her cheeks. Tomorrow she had agreed to speak to Emma Langley. But was it a good idea?

She liked Emma. And she felt sorry for her. But she worried now that her pity for her had encouraged her to say too much. It wasn't safe to talk about Billy Langley. Everyone knew that.

Lavinia rubbed the cloth over her eyes and up into her brows, removing the pencil lines she'd carefully drawn that morning. Then she dipped her fingertips into a pot of cold cream and applied the soothing balm to her face.

When she'd asked Emma to call on her, she had planned to tell her everything. But now her mind was changing. Emma would tell the police and everyone would know Lavinia had talked. Although she wanted to help Emma, she also had to consider her own safety.

She stared at herself in the looking glass, the cold cream giving her face a ghostly pallor. The church clock struck midnight. Lavinia picked up another cloth and began to wipe off the cream.

The candle flame dipped, as if disturbed by a sudden draught. Lavinia paused, the skin on the back of her neck prickling. She glanced around her bedroom. It was large, with a high ceiling, and sparsely furnished. The candlelight didn't reach the furthest corners.

Her door was shut and locked. She could hear horse's hooves and carriage wheels on the cobbles outside. That was normal for this time of night. Fleur de Lis Street was never quiet.

Reassured that everything was all right, Lavinia finished wiping her face and unpinned her hair. The thick, dark locks tumbled past her shoulders and she picked up the mother-of-pearl hairbrush from her dressing table. It had been a present from Billy.

As she brushed her hair, she smiled at the memory of him presenting it to her in a gift box tied up with a large red bow. Her heart ached with the sense of loss. It was difficult to believe she'd never see him again.

She'd warned him he was putting himself in danger, but he hadn't listened. And he'd got her involved, too. She should have refused. She'd been so foolish!

A thud sounded downstairs. She stopped, her breath caught in her throat.

Then another thud.

Lavinia put her hairbrush down. Had she left a window open? Perhaps a breeze had caught a door.

Pulling her shawl around her shoulders, she picked up the candle holder and stepped over to her door. The floorboards creaked beneath her bare feet.

She turned the key in the lock and quietly opened the door. All was still and quiet on the landing. The candle flame bent and flickered as she held it out in front of her.

Another noise came from downstairs. This time a creak rather than a thud. Was someone down there? Her heart raced as she tiptoed back to her bedroom and pulled the revolver out from beneath her mattress.

Then she headed back to the stairs and began to descend. The steps were cold, and a draught swirled up the staircase, extinguishing the candlelight.

Lavinia stopped and waited for her eyes to adjust to the gloom. Her heartbeat pounded in her ears.

A noise came from the sitting room. It sounded like the opening of a drawer.

'Who's there?' she called out. Her voice quavered with fear. 'What do you want?'

There was no reply.

Lavinia felt her way down the remaining stairs, desperate to get to the front door and raise the alarm out on the street.

As she reached the bottom step, she held her breath. Everything was silent now. Was it possible she'd imagined the noises? It was late, and she was tired.

She turned towards the door just as a powerful hand clamped over her mouth, fingers digging into her cheeks. Terror shot through her as she was yanked backwards, her scream muffled against the palm pressed tight against her face. Her fingers found the revolver's trigger and squeezed.

Nothing happened. The mechanism was jammed.

THIRTY-THREE

A grimy yellow fog sat over the rooftops as Emma left Northampton Square that morning. By the time she reached Fleur de Lis Street, it had sunk lower and thicker. The street was at the northern end of Spitalfields, close to Commercial Street police station and Bishopsgate Goods Yard.

It was easy to see why William had been attracted to Lavinia Drummond. She was tall, elegant and pretty. Would he have married her if she hadn't lost her reputation? Emma wondered if he'd loved her. Perhaps he had. And perhaps that was why he'd called on her after abandoning Emma on the train.

It seemed he'd felt troubled by what he'd done. He had visited the Ten Bells to drown his sorrows, and then he'd told Lavinia he had done something terrible.

Emma had never seen William drunk during their brief marriage. Although he'd enjoyed the occasional whiskey when they were together, it seemed he had only drunk to excess during his visits to Whitechapel.

And he had called himself Billy.

Her husband had been leading two separate lives and she had been completely oblivious to it. She told herself it wasn't her fault and yet she still felt gullible and foolish. Had he realised that when he'd met her that first time in Hyde Park? Had it been obvious to him that she'd been a naïve yet wealthy young woman? Men like William were good at spotting their prey. Her jaw clenched with anger and she turned her thoughts to finding Lavinia's home.

She walked along the street looking for number seven. A sad-eyed man wearing an advertisement board for a music hall handed her a leaflet. She gave it a cursory glance. Top billing was the Barbier Twins with their Marvellous Juggling and Balancing Entertainment. She pushed it into her coat pocket and continued on her way. Ahead of her, a group of people grew more distinct in the fog. They gathered outside a scruffy townhouse with paint peeling from its railings and sash windows.

A police constable blocked the doorway, his face grim. The crowd pressed closer, their hushed voices carrying on the chill morning air. Emma's heart quickened as she caught fragments of their whispered conversation.

'Another killing...'

'... found her this morning...'

'... so much blood...'

She touched the arm of a woman hunched beneath a patched shawl. 'What's happened?'

The woman turned, her face pale. 'Murder. Poor soul never stood a chance.'

'It's him again,' someone hissed. 'The Ripper's back.'

Ice flooded Emma's veins.

Through the crowd, she could just make out the number on the door – was that a seven? Her gaze fixed on the dark doorway as dread pooled in her stomach. 'Who lives here?'

'Miss Drummond,' the woman in the shawl whispered.

'Lavinia.' The name fell from Emma's lips like a stone.

'That's the one.' The woman crossed herself. 'God rest her soul.'

THIRTY-FOUR

Emma's mind span as she waited with the crowd for news. She struggled to believe it. She hoped Lavinia would step out of the house at any moment and reassure her she was safe.

But the more time dragged on, the more Emma feared for her. The fog grew thicker and small flakes of soot floated in the murk.

Then Detective Inspector Bradshaw stepped out of the building, distinctive with his bushy red moustache and his pipe in his mouth.

Emma called out to him, pushing her way through the crowd.

'Mrs Langley?' He raised an eyebrow. 'What are you doing here?'

'I arranged to meet Lavinia Drummond here this morning. It's not her, is it?' Emma asked, her heart pounding.

He gave a sniff. 'Let's talk in the police station.' He nodded towards the end of the street.

She knew then Lavinia was the victim. She felt her body tremble as she followed the inspector through the crowd. It didn't seem real. Bradshaw addressed the onlookers in a loud voice. 'I'd like to make it clear this was not an attack by Jack the Ripper! There's nothing to see here! Go back to your homes and get out of this dreadful weather.'

'I don't have a home,' said a lady with a gaunt face.

'A public house then, madam. Go and keep yourself warm somewhere.'

At Commercial Street police station, they sat in the same room Emma had been questioned in ten days previously. The grey wainscoting made the light dingy, but a lively fire burned in the small fireplace.

Detective Inspector Bradshaw exhaled a cloud of pipe smoke. 'Your connection to Miss Drummond is interesting, Mrs Langley,' he said. 'And an unlikely one. How did you know her?'

'I'd like to know what happened to her,' said Emma. 'Please can you tell me before I answer your questions?'

'Very well. A friend of Miss Drummond found her at the foot of the stairs this morning. She was attacked with a bladed instrument and appears to have died from a single wound to the abdomen. A revolver was found next to her but the chamber was jammed. We don't know yet if it belonged to her or her assailant. The doctor estimates she died last night between the hours of midnight and two o'clock.'

Emma shuddered. 'How awful.'

'Yes, it is. How did you know her?'

'I only met her for the first time yesterday. She knew my husband well.'

'Is that so?' He raised an eyebrow and made some notes.

'She began a love affair with him two years ago,' Emma said quietly, feeling her cheeks growing hot.

'And when did you discover this?'

'Just yesterday. I told her to speak to the police about it and she agreed that she would. But obviously she didn't get round to it. It could be the reason she was attacked. Maybe she knew something about William's murder. Maybe someone didn't want her to talk.'

'We shall look into it.' He put his pipe in his mouth.

Emma felt a snap of irritation. 'If you'd carried out your inquiries properly, then you would have found out about her relationship with my husband. She saw him on the day he died and would have been an extremely helpful witness at the inquest. But she didn't attend because she wasn't summoned.'

'She could have volunteered her information. She lived about fifty yards from this police station.'

'Yes, she should have, but she didn't want to. You should do more to make reluctant witnesses speak. You can't rely on people coming forward.'

'I understand your frustration, Mrs Langley. Please be assured we're doing what we can. Now, what did she tell you about your husband?'

Emma sighed. 'I shouldn't have to do your job for you. You should have spoken to her.'

'But we didn't and sadly she's now dead. The very best we can do is hear her account from you, Mrs Langley.'

Emma told him everything she could remember from her conversation the previous day. 'And when we left the dining room at Liverpool Street station, I saw a man watching us.'

'What did he look like?'

She gave him the description.

'How old would you say he was?'

'Between thirty and forty-five.'

'Can you be more precise?'

Emma gave it some thought. 'I'm afraid not.'

'Anything distinctive about him?'

'No. He just looked ordinary. But perhaps he was watching Lavinia and following her. Perhaps he killed her.'

A knock at the door interrupted them. A sombre-faced gentleman with mutton chop whiskers and keen eyes stepped in.

'I apologise for the interruption, Bradshaw, but I've just heard about this business on Fleur de Lis Street. What do you think we're dealing with?'

Bradshaw straightened his posture. 'Not the Whitechapel murderer, sir. This one's different.'

'I see. You're quite sure of that?'

'Yes. A different mode of attack without any of the, er...' Bradshaw gave Emma a sidelong glance, as if wary of using unpleasant words.

'Mutilations?' said the whiskered man.

'Yes, sir. Just a single stab wound.'

'He could have intended to do something more,' suggested the whiskered man, placing his hands on his hips. 'Maybe something disturbed him, as it did in Dutfield's Yard.'

'I'm not sure that it did, sir. She wasn't found until this morning,' said Bradshaw.

'Very well.' He turned to Emma. 'I should have introduced myself sooner, madam. I'm Inspector Abberline.'

'I'm pleased to meet you, Inspector. I'm Mrs Langley.'

'William Langley's widow?'

Emma nodded.

'I'd like to extend my commiserations to you, Mrs Langley. Hopefully my colleague here will give you all the assistance you require. I won't disturb you any longer.' He turned back to Bradshaw. 'Come and find me when you're finished.'

'Of course, sir.'

'Inspector Abberline is a busy man,' said Bradshaw once the inspector had left. 'He worked here for fourteen years before being moved to A Division then Scotland Yard. Unfortunately for him, he knows this area so well that he's been brought back here to investigate the recent atrocities.' He gave a bemused shake of his head. 'But with Abberline in charge, I feel sure we'll catch the culprit soon. Now, where were we?' He checked his notes. 'Ah yes. Did Miss Drummond mention a disagreement with anyone? Did she seem worried about her safety?'

'No. Her murder has to be connected to my husband's murder though, doesn't it? They were both attacked late at night and both died from a single stab wound.'

'I wouldn't like to make that assumption just yet, Mrs Langley.'

'Why not?'

'Because it's too early to tell.'

'But I think they must be connected!'

'Your opinion has been noted, but you must allow me and my men to carry out our investigation.' He folded his notebook closed. 'Thank you for your time today, Mrs Langley. This has been most useful.'

THIRTY-FIVE

Emma felt light-headed as she left Commercial Street police station. She leaned against the stone wall of the building to recover.

She had little faith in Detective Inspector Bradshaw. After investigating William's murder for ten days, he'd been unaware of his relationship with Lavinia Drummond.

'Do you mind me asking if you're all right?' A lady in a smart coat and hat had emerged from the grimy fog, a look of concern etched across her face.

'Thank you, I'm just gathering my thoughts,' said Emma trying to still her shaky voice.

'You look quite upset.'

'I am, actually. Someone I have just met has died and I'm struggling to understand it.'

'Miss Drummond?'

'Yes. Did you know her?'

'No, but I've heard all about it this morning. It's dreadful. Come with me to Quaker Street. It's close by. I'll get you a cup of hot, sweet tea. I work for a charity which helps the poor here.'

'I'm not poor,' said Emma.

The lady smiled. She was fair with wide blue eyes and an attractive, heart-shaped face. 'No, but you're in shock, and you need something to help you feel better. I'm Miss Mary Fairchild, by the way.'

'I'm Mrs Emma Langley. It's nice to meet you.'

Emma crossed Commercial Street with her and they entered a street which ran alongside the railway lines. The rumble of passing trains was muffled by the fog.

'Isn't the weather awful?' said Mary. 'We need a good wind to pick up and blow all the fog away.'

A malty odour from a brewery grew stronger as they walked. Eventually, they reached a stall which had been set up in front of a little red-brick building with a sign on it saying, *Sunday School*.

The stall had two large urns on it and neatly stacked bowls and cups. A smartly dressed lady stood behind it.

'This is Mrs Langley,' said Mary. 'She's had a terrible shock, so I offered her a cup of tea.'

'Oh dear,' said her companion with a pitying smile that made Emma flinch. 'Here you are.' She handed Emma a cup of tea and she thanked her. 'Would you like a cup of tea too, Mary?'

'No thank you. Please save it for the people who need it.'

Emma sipped her tea which was cooling rapidly in the cold air.

'We serve tea and soup here,' said Mary proudly. 'On a day like today, people need some warmth inside them. Many of them work outside, that's if they can find work. And others struggle to heat their homes. They don't have proper clothing to keep them warm, either. We're not making a big difference to their lives, but it's something.'

'Yes it is,' said Emma. She glanced around, wondering where the people in need were. Perhaps they avoided this stall because they didn't like the pitying looks from the ladies running it.

'Did you know Miss Drummond well?' asked Mary Fairchild.

'No. I'd only just become acquainted with her. She knew my late husband.'

'Your late husband? I'm so sorry.'

'He was murdered in Whitechapel twelve days ago.'

The ladies gasped. 'Oh my goodness,' said Mary. 'You're his widow?'

Emma nodded.

'I heard about the murder. It was dreadful. I don't understand why someone would have attacked him like that. And it's even more shocking that the police haven't found out who did it. Mind you, they seem incapable of finding the monsters who roam these streets at night. Fortunately, I don't live here. I'm only here during the daytime. When dusk falls, I make sure I leave. I feel so sorry for what happened to your husband.'

'And now Miss Drummond is dead too,' said Emma. 'I think the same person murdered her.'

'You think so?'

'Yes. Although the inspector I spoke to earlier doesn't share my view.'

Mary shook her head. 'It pains me to say it, but I don't think the police have been doing enough. If only they would offer a reward for information leading to arrests! If they did so, then I'm quite sure they would catch the people who do these things. People around here need money. If they know something about the Whitechapel murderer, then I'm sure a reward would encourage them to speak up.'

'The vigilance committee is offering a reward,' said her companion.

'Yes, that's true, Doris. But if the Metropolitan Police offered one, then it could be a large reward.'

'I think the decision rests with the Home Office,' said Doris.

'Does it? Well, they can afford an enormous reward, I feel sure of it. Anyway, those are my thoughts on the matter. But none of this helps find the person who murdered your husband, Mrs Langley. And poor Miss Drummond who lost her life last night. The streets around here need better lighting. That would deter bloodthirsty criminals.'

'Better lighting wouldn't have helped Miss Drummond,' said Doris. 'She was murdered in her own home.'

'The dark streets allowed the murderer to arrive and leave unseen,' said Mary.

'So does the fog. Better lighting is no use in the fog. The light just gets swallowed up by it.'

'If you say so, Doris.' Mary pursed her lips, as if she was growing tired of Doris disagreeing with everything she said. 'Anyway, we can only do what we can, can't we?'

Emma nodded and drained her cup.

'Thank you for the tea,' she said. 'How long have you been doing this for?'

'Two years,' said Mary. 'I like to do what I can around here.'

'You do lots to help the people here,' said Doris. She turned to Emma. 'Miss Fairchild helped the East End matchgirls in the summer.'

'You were involved with that?' said Emma. 'I read all about it in the papers.'

'Oh, I just did what I could,' replied Mary.

Over a thousand women and girls employed at the Bryant & May match factory had refused to work that summer. They had protested about poor working conditions, low pay and a debilitating medical condition called phossy jaw. It wasn't the first time they'd gone on strike, but this time their cause had been supported by the social reformer Annie Besant. The workers had appealed to her for help and her involvement had secured better terms for them. The success of the strike had led to the formation of the Union of Women Matchmakers. It was the first time working women had managed to enforce change in their working conditions.

'You worked with Annie Besant?' asked Emma.

'Only because my aunt knows her,' said Mary. 'All you can do is hope you can make a difference. Sometimes you can and sometimes you can't. Oh look, here comes someone!' A slow-moving figure shuffled towards them in the fog. 'Hello!' she called out to them. 'Would you like some soup?'

THIRTY-SIX

Penny stepped out of Ludgate Hill railway station and into the tea-coloured fog. It was fortunate she knew this area well, otherwise it would have been impossible to find Fleet Street.

She crossed New Bridge Street and entered Bride Lane which took her past St Bride's Church.

Mrs Tuttle was minding Thomas and Florence, and she had ordered Penny to go out for a shopping trip. She'd told her she looked tired and needed to do something enjoyable by herself.

Thomas and Florence would wake up from their afternoon sleep soon. How were they going to react when Mrs Tuttle greeted them instead of their mother? Penny envisaged inconsolable tears and upset. It seemed unnecessarily cruel just so she could have a short while to herself.

She faltered in her step for a moment, wondering if she should go back home. But if she returned early, Mrs Tuttle would think she didn't trust her to look after the children. With a sigh, she continued on her way and resolved to make her trip quick.

It had been three years since she'd last visited Fleet Street. Most of it was hidden in the fog today, but Penny could see it had changed little. If anything, it was busier. The people hurrying along the pavement did their best not to bump into each other in the poor visibility.

The familiar offices of the *Morning Express* newspaper were soon upon her and she stopped. The thought of entering the building made her nervous. Would she know anyone working here now?

The editor, Mr Sherman, had left the newspaper three years previously. He'd been replaced by the proprietor's nephew, Crispin Childers. Penny assumed Miss Welton had left with Mr Sherman, and her colleagues, Edgar Fish and Frederick Potter, had told her they would be leaving too.

Ever since Emma Langley had mentioned she'd visited the offices looking for her, Penny had felt an urge to return. She missed working as a reporter.

Penny stepped in through the door and was greeted by the roar of printing presses and the smell of ink and paper.

She smiled as she climbed the staircase, recalling the many times she had dashed up these steps with an article in her hand for the deadline.

Little had changed in the corridor upstairs. The floorboards still creaked and a few new framed editions had been hung on the wall.

A woman stepped out of the secretary's office. She was immediately familiar with her long black dress and the pince-nez on the end of her nose.

'Miss Welton? You're still here?'

Miss Welton startled, then gave her an uncharacteristic smile. 'Mrs Blakely! Is it really you?'

'Yes.' Penny felt tears in her eyes; she never thought she would feel emotional about encountering the dour Miss Welton again. 'How have you been?'

'Very well, thank you. The daily grind goes on as usual. How's your family?'

Penny began telling her about the children when a gentleman stepped out of the editor's office. He was a tall, broad man with small eyes and a mousey-brown moustache. He was a little stockier than Penny remembered.

'Edgar!' she said.

'Mrs Blakely!' He held out his hand and gave her a firm handshake. 'How wonderful it is to see you again! Have you missed us?'

'Yes.' She felt tears again. 'A lot. And you're all still here!'

'Yes, why wouldn't we be?'

'You said you were going to leave when Crispin Childers took charge.'

'I did leave. For two weeks. But no one else would have me, so I had to come crawling back again. But as luck would have it, Childers didn't turn out to be much good at all. We knew that would be the case, didn't we? He only lasted a few months, then I took over the helm.'

'You're the editor?' Penny laughed.

'Yes.' He bristled. 'What's so funny?'

'I never thought you would become the editor, Edgar. I'm sorry, I didn't mean to laugh. I'm sure you're doing excellent work here.' She hadn't read the *Morning Express* for some time because doing so reminded her of the career she'd had to stop.

'He is,' said Miss Welton, patting Edgar on the shoulder. 'He's been the editor for nearly three years now and he does an outstanding job.'

'And the best thing about it is Potter is very jealous,' added Edgar.

'Frederick is still here?'

'Yes. He's still the parliamentary reporter. I'm never sure how much work he actually does, but he's part of the furniture. Come into my office and have a cup of tea!'

Penny followed him.

'It's Sherman's old office. You remember it, don't you?'

'Of course I remember it,' said Penny. 'Although I was only ever summoned to this room when I was in trouble.'

'I've tidied it up a bit. At least I did when I first moved in. But it turns out I'm just as untidy as Sherman was. There's something about this job which makes everything untidy. It's because I'm so busy the entire time. It's a lot of work getting a newspaper out every day.'

'Yes, I remember that being the case.' Penny moved a pile of papers from a chair and sat down. Edgar took his seat behind the editor's desk.

'So how's the schoolboy inspector?' he asked.

It was an old jibe which had always annoyed Penny. 'He's very well, thank you. But you can't still call him that.'

'My apologies. Old habits die hard but I shall put a stop to it. And the children? How many do you have now?'

'Two. And they're both delightful.'

'Lovely. Mrs Fish is expecting our third child soon. Wonderful things, aren't they children? So much fun. I don't know what we'd do without a nanny, though. Where are your children today?'

'They're being looked after by our new housekeeper.'

'Not a nanny? We've got a housekeeper, a maid, a cook and a nanny now. I advise getting as many people in as possible.'

'Perhaps we will.'

'Good.' Edgar's face grew serious for a moment. 'I feel the need to get something straight before we proceed any further. You've not come here today to ask for a job, have you? Much as I admire your work, Mrs Blakely, you know I can't employ a reporter who's also a wife and a mother.'

'No, I realise that, Edgar. This is purely a friendly visit for old times' sake.'

'Oh good.' He relaxed again. 'If you were still working for this newspaper, you would be the chief reporter on this Jack the Ripper chap.'

'I've been following it closely. It's dreadful, isn't it?'

'The police are getting nowhere with it. I think you could have had it solved if you were still a reporter, Mrs Blakely.'

'Oh, I doubt it. He appears to be a master at evading detection.'

'What does your husband make of it?'

'He knows it's a troublesome case. And it's gained such notoriety now that there's a lot of misleading information about.'

'Absolutely. All these nuisance hoax letters don't help. We had one sent here.'

'Did you?'

'I'll find it for you.' Edgar leafed through the piles of paper on his desk. 'Here you are.' He passed it across the desk to Penny and she read it. It was written in red ink.

Dear Boss,

The last job was my best so far. I took my time over it and I heard how my handiwork drew a crowd, ha, ha. I have sharpened my knife for the next job and this time I will rip two of them. The police think they can catch me but they keep arresting the wrong ones, ha, ha. I shall keep on with my work because I'm too fond of blood to stop.

Yours truly,
Jack the Ripper

'Ugh, how horrible,' she said, feeling the hairs on the back of her neck stand up.

'It gave Miss Welton quite a fright,' said Edgar. 'But I reassured her it was a hoax. I think every newspaper in Fleet Street has received at least one letter from him now. We print them because the readers enjoy them. Some say the letters are written by journalists. Isn't it ridiculous? And then there's been this latest murder in Whitechapel last night.'

'He's struck again?'

'The police say it wasn't Jack. The victim was a lady who was murdered in her home. A single knife wound, apparently. Like that chap who was murdered... Oh, I've just remembered something. His widow came in here looking for you. I think her name was Mrs Langley.'

'That's right. She found me.'

'She did? Excellent. Poor lady. Her brother was that chap shot in Limehouse and then her husband was murdered too. Awful. I suppose you had to tell her you couldn't do anything to help, that can't have been easy.'

'I'd like to help.'

'I can imagine...' He paused before continuing. 'But I'm afraid you can't.' He put his head to one side and gave a smile. 'Oh well, I'm sure you're far happier in your current position. Motherhood is surely the most fulfilling pastime for the fairer sex.'

Penny pursed her lips. She didn't like the assumption women enjoyed motherhood more than having a profession.

Miss Welton brought in the tea and they thanked her.

'Well it's nice having this chat with you, Mrs Blakely,' said Edgar. 'We didn't always see eye-to-eye, did we? But we got along rather well in the end. After you left to become a mother, I really didn't think our paths would cross again. But this is thoroughly pleasant.'

'It's nice to come back here. And I'm happy for you, Edgar. Mr Sherman was an excellent editor, but it was the right time for him to move on. And I'm not surprised to hear Crispin Childers failed in his task to edit the newspaper properly. You're doing really well.'

Penny couldn't help but feel envious. She would have liked

to have been the editor of a newspaper. She would have enjoyed the challenge of it.

'Thank you, Mrs Blakely,' said Edgar. 'If you find you have time on your hands and you would like to write the occasional article for the *Morning Express*, I'd be happy to publish your work again.'

'Would you really?' Penny asked, slightly taken aback by his offer.

'Of course.'

'But what about Mr Conway, the proprietor? He insisted on me leaving when I married.'

'He did, but you wrote for the paper on an ad hoc basis after that. I know you have little time on your hands, and I don't want to take you away from your family, but once you feel ready to write something, just let me know, won't you?'

'Thank you, Edgar.' Penny smiled. 'I will.'

THIRTY-SEVEN

Emma lay awake past midnight, cold and worried. She thought about Lavinia and how frightened she must have been in her final moments. Had the assailant been the person who'd been watching them as they left the dining room at Liverpool Street Station? Who was he?

The thin line of light from the streetlamp crossed the ceiling and cast itself on William's painting on the opposite wall. The glow illuminated the woman's face. She looked like Lavinia.

Emma glanced away, but her eyes were drawn back to the painting. Eventually, she got out of bed and went over to the window to pull the curtains across the little gap of light. But no matter how much she tried, the light still found its way through at the top where the curtains refused to properly meet.

Lavinia's face glowed in the gloom. Ghostlike and watchful.

Emma couldn't bear it. She pulled off her shawl, walked over to the painting and draped the shawl over it so she couldn't see the face. Then she climbed back into bed and turned away.

But she was even colder without her shawl. And Lavinia's eyes seemed to look through it.

The situation felt faintly ridiculous. Emma knew it was because she was tired and upset, but still she couldn't sleep.

She got out of bed again and removed the shawl from the painting. Then she gripped the frame and lifted it to free the picture wire from the hook on the wall. The frame was heavier than she'd expected. And the wire seemed stuck. Emma's arms ached as she tried to lift and pull the heavy frame away. Somehow, it remained attached to the wall.

Her arms shook with effort, and she knew they were about to give way altogether. Reluctantly, she let go of the painting.

It pitched heavily to one side, banged against the wall, then fell to the floor with a crash. Emma skipped out of the way so it avoided her feet. Her heart sank as she feared the painting was broken. And she'd probably woken Mr and Mrs Solomon.

She turned on the little lamp on her bedside table, then returned to the painting which now lay face down on the floor. One side of the back was detached from the frame and was slightly bowed. Emma knelt down and tried to push it flat. A label caught her eye:

G. Flynn, Picture Framer, Crispin Street, E1

The back of the frame wouldn't lie flat and Emma noticed there were no tacks holding it into position on the side which had become loose. They'd either fallen out during the fall, or they hadn't been there in the first place.

She lifted the picture upright, looking for tacks which could have fallen onto the floor. There were none.

She turned the picture over and, as she did so, a flash of white in the gap caught her eye. It looked like a piece of paper stuck between the canvas and the loosened back of the frame. Emma pulled the back open a little wider and pushed her fingers into the gap. She managed to grip the paper and pull it out. It was foolscap size and folded in half.

Emma rested the picture against the wall and unfolded the piece of paper.

It was covered in rows of numbers written in a neat, even hand.

A knock sounded at the door. 'Mrs Langley!' called out Mrs Solomon. 'Are you all right in there?'

'I'm fine!' Emma jumped up, folded the paper and got to her feet. She hurriedly put the piece of paper in the pocket of her nightgown as she made her way to the door. 'There's nothing to worry about, Mrs Solomon,' she said. 'I accidentally knocked the picture off the wall.'

THIRTY-EIGHT

'I wonder if Billy Langley's widow will stop by again today,' said Doris, as she helped Mary Fairchild fill the urn with vegetable soup. Steam and the smell of overboiled vegetables filled the chilly morning air.

'I shouldn't think she will,' said Mary.

'I didn't even know he was married!' said Doris. 'Of course, I didn't mention that to her when I saw her. Did you know he was married, Mary?'

'Only when I read about his death in the newspaper.'

'But you didn't know before then?'

'No.'

'Perhaps I'm speaking out of turn...' began Doris, as she fixed the lid on the soup urn. 'But he didn't act like a married gentleman, did he? He was actually... Well, I don't quite know how to put this. I can't really think of a better description... Oh, I shall say it, anyway. He was actually quite flirtatious at times.'

'That's inappropriate, Doris. Gentlemen are not flirtatious. And besides, he's dead now. You mustn't speak of him like that.'

'Well, I didn't know how else to say it.'

'There was no need to say it at all!' snapped Mary. 'I'll see if that kettle's boiled yet.' She dashed into the Sunday school, blinking away the tears in her eyes.

THIRTY-NINE

Emma called at Penny's home, keen to show her the paper she'd found hidden in the picture frame.

A round-faced, middle-aged lady knelt with Thomas on the hearthrug in Penny's sitting room. They were playing with a jack-in-the-box together.

'This is Mrs Tuttle,' said Penny, cradling baby Florence. 'She's helping me with the house and children.'

'Hello!' Mrs Tuttle winced as she got up. 'Ouch, my knees. I should never have got down into that position. It's a pleasure to meet you...'

'Emma.'

'Hello Emma.' She turned to Penny. 'I'll make some tea, shall I?'

'That would be lovely. Thank you, Mrs Tuttle.'

They sat down and Thomas picked up the jack-in-the-box and took it over to the tabby cat on the windowsill.

'Please don't tease Tiger with that again, Thomas,' said Penny. 'She doesn't like it.'

'She does!'

'No, she doesn't. Move it away from her, please.'

'She likes it!'

'Thomas, can you do what I asked you, please?'

'Tiger likes it!'

'If you're going to continue arguing with me, Thomas, then I'm going to have to take the jack-in-the-box off you and you won't be able to play with it anymore. I don't think you'd like that, would you?'

He pushed out his lower lip and Florence grabbed Penny's spectacles. 'Oh no,' said Penny. 'I keep forgetting to take these off. Can you let go please, Florence?'

The baby laughed. A clown jumped out of the jack-in-the-box and Tiger leapt off the windowsill and ran off.

'Thomas! What did I tell you?' Florence threw Penny's spectacles onto the floor. 'Oh, good grief.'

Emma picked up the spectacles.

'Thank you,' said Penny. 'And would you mind holding Florence for a moment while I confiscate the jack-in-the-box?'

'Of course.' Emma swapped the spectacles for the baby and stood motionless with the infant in her arms. She couldn't remember the last time she'd held a baby and she felt nervous about doing something which might upset her. Florence stared at her with her large blue eyes and pushed her little fist into her mouth. Emma smiled at her and the baby smiled back. The moment felt warm and comforting.

Penny put the jack-in-the-box high up on the bookcase. 'You can have it back when you play nicely,' she told Thomas.

'Not fair!'

Penny sighed and collected Florence from Emma. 'I'm sorry about all that. How are you?'

'I'm fine,' said Emma. 'Although I have a lot to tell you.'

FORTY

Mrs Tuttle offered to look after the children while Penny and Emma talked in the dining room. Even though Emma had said she was fine, Penny thought she looked tired and pale.

She poured the tea and listened as Emma told her she'd discovered William had called himself Billy. He'd left his job without telling her, he'd taken all her money and she'd found a woman who'd had a love affair with him.

Then the woman had been murdered. The murder which Edgar had mentioned to Penny the previous day. A lady called Lavinia Drummond. Penny had read about it in the newspaper.

'Detective Inspector Bradshaw doesn't think the attack on her was connected to William's murder,' said Emma. 'But I think it could be the same person.'

'Police officers like to be cautious with these cases,' said Penny. 'They like to consider all the possibilities. But I agree with you, Emma. I think the same person could have attacked both your husband and Miss Drummond.'

'I saw a man watching us as we left the dining room in the railway station. I gave the inspector a description of him.'

'Someone was watching you?'

'It felt like it. I suppose I could be mistaken but I didn't have a good feeling about him. I'm worried that Lavinia might have been murdered because of me.'

'Why?'

'She knew about William's life in Whitechapel and perhaps someone didn't want her to talk to me. Maybe they wanted to silence her?'

It was a valid concern. But Penny didn't think it was fair Emma should feel responsible. 'The only person to blame for Lavinia's death is the murderer,' she said.

'What if the murderer comes for me next?' Emma asked anxiously.

'I can understand why you're worrying about that. In fact, it's a familiar feeling. When you start looking into a murder case, there's usually someone who doesn't want you to. But you're doing the right thing. You did well to befriend Lavinia and learn a little more about her and your husband. Plenty of women would not have wanted to do that,' Penny said, trying to reassure her.

'I suppose I quite liked her. She was very different from me, but she seemed thoughtful and intelligent. I even envied her a little. She knew William for longer than I did. And he was fond of her because of who she was, not because she inherited a substantial sum of money.'

Emma's red-rimmed eyes began to fill with tears as she spoke. Penny rested a hand on her arm. 'I'm sorry he treated you like that.'

'I was foolish!' Emma sobbed.

'People who behave like your husband did are manipulative. They know exactly what to say and do to make you fall in love with them.'

Emma nodded. 'He managed that, all right.'

'But you're discovering the truth about him now. And I wouldn't be envious of Miss Drummond. Maybe your husband was fond of her, but it may not have been entirely reciprocated. She turned him away when he was drunk, didn't she? And she clearly had a past which made it difficult for her to marry. Many people would have looked down on her. She probably wished to be honourable and respectable, but knew it wasn't a possibility. That must have been difficult for her, even if she was as pretty and likeable as you describe her.'

'I feel desperately sad that she's dead,' Emma choked. 'I barely knew her, but she didn't deserve to die in that manner. And I think she could have helped the investigation into William's murder.'

'Which could be why someone killed her,' said Penny.

'Then late last night I found this.' Emma took a piece of paper out of her bag, unfolded it and placed it on the table.

Penny peered closely at it. 'Numbers,' she said. 'What do they mean?'

'I don't know. I found this hidden in a painting which had belonged to William. I accidentally knocked it off the wall and noticed the back wasn't properly attached to the frame.'

'So someone hid the piece of paper in there?'

'Yes.'

'Is this your husband's handwriting?'

'It doesn't look like it to me. Unless he disguised it. But it's possible he didn't know it was there.'

'Where did he get the picture from?'

'I've no idea. There's a label on the back of the picture with the address of the picture framer on it. I wrote it down.' Emma pulled another piece of paper out of her bag and read from it, '"G. Flynn, Picture Framer, Crispin Street, E1."'

'A postcode in the East End,' said Penny, the cog in her mind beginning to turn. 'It could be Whitechapel or Spitalfields.'

Emma sighed. 'Everything seems to lead back to that same part of London.'

'Perhaps it's a code,' said Penny. 'And maybe it belongs to the picture framer, G. Flynn. It's interesting he's in the East End. I think we need to pay him a visit. Shall we go on Monday afternoon?'

'That sounds like a good idea, but I'm not expecting you to spend time on this with me, Penny. You have your children to look after.'

'Yes I do. But I can spare some time.'

'Really?'

'Yes. Not much, but I want to help. I miss doing this sort of work.'

Emma gave her a relieved smile. 'Thank you, Penny. I appreciate it. So much has happened since William died that it's been difficult to think straight.'

'Well I'm more than happy to help. That's what friends are for.'

'Friends?'

Penny had said the word without thinking. 'Yes. You already feel like a friend to me, Emma.'

Emma smiled and she hurriedly wiped a tear from her cheek. 'Thank you, Penny.'

Penny felt a lump in her throat as she tried not to shed a tear herself. She had to help this woman. She picked up the teapot. 'More tea?'

'That would be lovely.'

FORTY-ONE

'You plan to visit a shop in Whitechapel?' said James at dinner that evening. 'I don't think it's a good idea at the moment. With all these unsolved murders, it's not a safe place for a mother of two children.'

'I'll have Emma with me,' said Penny. But she knew this wouldn't be enough to persuade James.

'Frankly, it's dangerous for her to be involved too. Both her husband and a woman she arranged to meet are dead. If I was Emma, I'd be staying well away from the East End. I don't think she realises the enormity of what she could be getting herself into. I realise you've done this sort of thing before, but times were different then, Penny. You only had yourself to think about.'

James was right. Penny took a mouthful of onion soup which was delicious. Mrs Tuttle was an excellent cook.

'Emma wants to find out what happened to her husband,' she said.

'Why? He was a scoundrel.'

'Yes, he was. But I don't think it's wrong of her to want

answers. And now Miss Drummond has been murdered too, she has even more questions.'

'I'm sure she does. But it's down to H Division to investigate.'

'They're not doing enough. And that's not surprising because they haven't even got enough men to catch Jack the Ripper.'

'I'm sure that's not true.'

'It's what everyone says.'

James laid down his soup spoon and looked her directly in the eyes. 'No one outside the police force knows how difficult this case is, Penny. It's very easy for people to criticise when they don't know the full facts. H Division would do more on Langley's case if they didn't have this awful Whitechapel murderer to catch, but that doesn't mean you and Emma need to work on it. You're no longer a news reporter. And to be honest with you, Penny, you put yourself in danger quite a few times in the past. You made some foolish mistakes, and you were lucky you emerged from it all unscathed. But now you're a mother, you simply can't take risks like that anymore. I don't want our children having their mother threatened or injured. Or even worse.'

Penny's jaw felt tight. Had James forgotten who she was before she became a mother? He seemed too ready to dismiss her desire to work on the case. She conceded, however, that she'd been foolhardy in the past. 'I suppose I agree with you in part,' she said. 'But does that mean I must sacrifice everything because I'm a mother? You know how much I enjoyed working on those cases. It was extremely rewarding to solve them. Sometimes the work was difficult and harrowing, but it was thrilling too. You know what I'm talking about, James. It's why you're a detective inspector for Scotland Yard.'

'Yes, I do know what you're talking about. But it's different for me. I don't have the same domestic responsibilities as you. I earn the salary to support this family. If something were to happen to me in the course of my work, it wouldn't be as awful for the children as if something happened to you.'

Penny got up from her seat. 'Perhaps you can help with this, James? You could come with us to Whitechapel and wait nearby when we visit the picture framer.'

'When am I supposed to do that? I'm busy working on the case against the swindler Barnaby Ratcliffe.'

'It would only take an hour of your time on Monday afternoon.'

James shook his head, then picked up a piece of bread and wiped it around his empty soup bowl. 'Penny, you're relentless once you get an idea about something.'

'Of course I am. How else do you think I managed to be the only lady reporter on Fleet Street for ten years?'

James smiled at her.

'I know I can't do the job I used to,' she continued, pacing the room. 'Not at the moment, anyway. But I would like to do something, so perhaps there's a compromise somewhere. You know me well, James. Please understand, I just want to help Emma Langley. She really doesn't have anyone else.'

'Fine. I understand.'

'Thank you.' She stepped over to him and rested a hand on his shoulder.

He sighed. 'But if you put yourself in danger—'

'I won't! I promise.'

FORTY-TWO

Emma waited to meet Penny at the Bishopsgate entrance to Liverpool Street station the following Monday.

Mr O'Brien, the solicitor from Cardwell and Theobald, had visited her that morning to begin work on settling William's affairs. Emma thought there was little use in applying for probate if there was no money left.

People climbed into the successive line of cabs which waited on the road outside the railway station. It was a grey day with an icy breeze.

Emma didn't feel part of the activity around her. She felt like an observer looking in on a world which was getting on with its everyday business. Perhaps it was the effect of grief. Or perhaps it was the sense she couldn't move on with her life until she knew what had happened to William and Lavinia.

She smiled when she saw Penny approaching. She wore a blue overcoat over a fitted jacket and a long woollen skirt. Her blue velvet bonnet was tied beneath her chin with a large bow.

Then Emma saw someone accompanied her. Penny's husband James. He looked solemn in a bowler hat and dark overcoat. Emma hadn't seen him since the incident with the gun. She felt her stomach tighten with shame.

'Emma! You remember James, don't you?' said Penny.

'Yes, I do. And I'd like to apologise for the incident when—'

James held up a gloved palm. 'There's no need to apologise, Mrs Langley. It's all forgotten about now.'

'But I—'

'You have other things to worry about,' he said. 'I was very saddened to hear what happened to your husband and his... friend, Miss Drummond. I hope the culprit can be caught before he causes any more trouble.'

'Thank you. I hope so too.'

'We can't be too long,' Penny said to Emma. 'James needs to get back to the Yard and I need to get back to the children.'

'And I have to teach a piano lesson at half past three,' said Emma.

'So we're all busy!' Penny smiled. 'Let's go. Crispin Street is just behind Spitalfields Market.'

Emma felt safe walking through the area with a Scotland Yard detective inspector in tow. The people who watched from doorways or stared at her smart clothes didn't seem so menacing now.

It had been kind of James to say the incident with the gun had been forgotten about. But did he really mean it? It was difficult to imagine he didn't still bear her some resentment.

Spitalfields Market occupied the right-hand side of Crispin Street. On the left was a grocer's shop, a public house and a carpenter's workshop. The picture framing shop had an elegant frontage of carved wood. It had two bay windows above wooden panels with a polished geometrical design. The door was flanked by two carved wood columns which were joined by a decorative arch at the top. *G. Flynn, Picture Framer* was written in neat gold lettering on the shop's sign. Paintings with intricate frames hung in the windows and ornate mirrors reflected the faces of Emma, Penny and James.

'G. Flynn is clearly a proud man,' said James. 'His shop looks a little out of place here, doesn't it? I think it would fit in much better in the West End.'

'He clearly has enough customers,' said Penny.

'Who? I can't imagine many people here being able to afford picture frames.'

'There must be some. Now, where are you going to keep watch?'

'That's a good question.' James glanced around. 'I could walk up and down the street, I suppose. Or maybe I'll lean against that lamp post over there. Whatever I do, someone's going to suspect me of being a police inspector. In places like this, people can sniff us out from fifty yards away.'

'Very well,' said Penny. 'We'll see you shortly.'

James walked off and Penny pushed open the shop door. It set off a small tinkling bell.

FORTY-THREE

Inside, the shop was dingy and smelled of wax, oils and tobacco smoke. Pictures and frames hung on the walls and were propped up against the counter. A clock ticked steadily from somewhere. Emma wasn't sure why, but she felt an unpleasant tingle on the back of her neck.

'Hello,' said a low, slow voice. A man emerged from the shadows, rubbing his palms together. He was slender and pale, and his oiled dark hair was combed back from his face. His dark moustache had neatly curled ends, and he wore a dark red velvet waistcoat and a silk cravat. His eyes were almost black and his brow low and prominent. 'How may I help?' An obsequious smile played on his lips.

'Mr Flynn?' said Emma.

'That's me.'

'I'm Mrs Langley. The widow of William Langley who was murdered in Whitechapel a couple of weeks ago. Did you know him?'

He rubbed his palms slowly, and his smile faded. 'I met him once or twice. It's a pleasure to meet you, Mrs Langley, and I was very sorry to hear about his untimely demise.'

'This is Mrs Blakely,' said Emma. 'She's a former reporter for the *Morning Express* newspaper.'

'A lady reporter? How interesting. And why are you no longer a reporter, Mrs Blakely?'

'I've retired from it now. But I'm helping Mrs Langley find out what happened to her husband.'

'I see.'

'My husband owned a painting which you framed,' said Emma. 'And I found a piece of paper inside the frame with lots of numbers on. Would you know anything about it?'

He stroked his chin. 'How odd. Perhaps you would like to join me for tea and we can have a little chat?'

Emma didn't want to. There was something reptilian about Mr Flynn. She and Penny exchanged a glance, and she realised they would have to have tea with the man if they wanted to know more.

He led them up a narrow staircase and to a small, tidy living room with tall windows overlooking Spitalfields Market. The furniture was carved dark wood and furnished with red brocade.

Emma and Penny perched uneasily on a sofa while Mr Flynn settled into an armchair and crossed one leg over the other. He wore shiny, pointed leather boots with buttons up the side. He rang a bell and an old lady in an apron appeared in the doorway.

'Tea please, Mother,' he said.

She nodded and left again. Emma managed to hide her astonishment that Mr Flynn treated his mother like a maid.

'A piece of paper with numbers on,' he said to Emma. 'Do you have it with you?'

She nodded, pulled the piece of paper out of her bag and passed it to him. He examined it closely, tapping his chin with his forefinger.

'What is it?' he asked eventually.

'We were hoping you might be able to tell us.'

'No.' He passed it back to Emma. 'I have no idea at all.'

His mother brought in a tray with a teapot, milk jug and three cups on it. She placed it down on a little mahogany table.

Emma and Penny thanked her, but Mr Flynn remained silent as she left the room.

'Have you ever seen any pages of numbers like this before?' Penny asked him.

'No. Never. It was hidden in a painting, you say?'

'Yes,' said Emma. 'You framed the painting according to the label on the back of it.'

'I probably did. And you think I put the page of numbers in the frame too?'

'We don't know how it got there,' said Emma. 'I can't ask my husband about it so I thought we would inquire with you. Do you remember framing the picture for my husband?'

'No, I can't say that I do.'

'But you met him once or twice.'

'Yes, I did. He came in here to look around. Pleasant chap.'

'Do you know what he was doing in Whitechapel at the time of his death?' asked Penny.

'I don't know. Seeing friends maybe?' Mr Flynn leaned forward in his chair and poured out the tea.

Emma took a sip of tea. It had an unpleasant musty flavour. She swallowed the mouthful and concealed her grimace.

'When did you last see him before his death?' Penny asked.

'A few weeks before. I passed him in the street and we greeted each other. I have a theory about his murder, though.'

'What do you think happened?' asked Emma.

'I think it was a case of mistaken identity. I think someone saw him on that dark night and thought he was someone else. I think they mistook him for Jack the Ripper. It was only the day after Mary Kelly's murder, wasn't it? They must have thought he was Jack and exacted their revenge on him.'

'Did you know Lavinia Drummond?' asked Penny.

'Yes, I knew the unfortunate creature. I suppose it was always going to end that way.'

'Why do you say that?'

'The murderer would have been one of her clients. You know she worked as a prostitute, don't you?'

Emma felt a flush of embarrassment creep up her neck. She tried to compose herself and gave a slight nod, not wishing to show she'd been unaware of it. Although Lavinia had told her she was a lady of low reputation, Mr Flynn's revelation was still a shock to her.

'A very dangerous profession,' he continued. 'There are some unpleasant characters about and poor Miss Drummond appears to have encountered one of them. It's only a matter of time in that line of work.'

'You can't blame her for her death,' said Emma.

He held up his hands in mock defence. 'I'm not blaming her. The man who did it is to blame. But if you choose that profession, there's an inherent risk, I'm afraid.'

Emma wanted to argue that many women were forced to do such work out of desperation, but she sensed Mr Flynn wasn't the sort of man to reason with.

'Talking of unfortunate women,' he said. 'Lady Lou probably knows more than she's letting on. She was the last person to see Mr Langley before he encountered his murderer. That's what she says, anyway.'

'You think she could be lying?' asked Penny.

He shrugged. 'I don't know. But there are many people who don't want to tell the truth because it might be inconvenient for them. So instead, they make up stories to protect themselves. Make of that what you will.' He jumped to his feet. 'I must get on, ladies.'

'Of course.'

Emma and Penny left their half-drunk tea and followed him

downstairs to the shop. Emma felt relieved to be leaving the place.

'This here is my livelihood,' he said. 'I've been doing it for nearly twenty years. My father had this shop before me.' He stopped and picked up an oil painting of a milkmaid. 'I don't just make new frames; I restore old ones too. Take this picture, for example. It's by an amateur painter and isn't worth anything. The frame, however, is quite exquisite. It can be restored to look as good as new.' He turned the picture around. 'Look at these tacks which have been hammered into the back to attach the canvas to the frame. It can take a long time to prise them all out. If I want to get to work on a frame quickly, I need to get the canvas off. So I get a nice large sharp knife and I rip through the canvas.' He made a slashing motion with his hand.

Emma gasped and stepped back.

'The knife has to be very sharp to do the job quickly,' added Mr Flynn. He grinned, displaying his little teeth again. 'And with my sharp knife, I can rip that canvas off within seconds.'

FORTY-FOUR

'How was Mr Flynn?' James asked once Penny and Emma had joined him at his lamp post.

'Horrible,' said Emma.

Penny thought she looked even paler than usual. She linked her arm through hers. 'Come on,' she said. 'Let's find somewhere for a nice cup of tea instead of that strange-tasting brew which Mr Flynn's mother made.'

'His mother was there?' said James.

'Yes. Although she appears to be his servant.'

'Really?'

They walked briskly down Crispin Street.

'Mr Flynn claims he knows nothing about the code,' said Penny.

'Do you think he was telling the truth?' asked James.

'I'm not sure. I think I shall take it to Mr Hobhouse.'

'Of course!' James smiled. 'He's an expert code breaker.'

'Who's he?' asked Emma.

'An old friend of my father's,' said James. 'And he's very old. Actually... I've not heard about him for a while. I hope he's not—'

'Oh, I'm sure he's still alive, James,' interrupted Penny. 'We must be hopeful.'

They turned right, and headed for Bishopsgate.

'So why was Mr Flynn horrible?' asked James. 'What did he do?'

'He was perfectly polite,' said Emma. 'But he gave me the creeps. And his shop gave me the creeps. Everything was so dark and dingy and his voice was just... chilling.'

'And when he mentioned his sharp knife, I'd really had enough,' said Penny. 'He was either trying to scare us or it was his idea of a joke.'

'That sounds rather untoward,' said James.

'And he was unsympathetic towards Lavinia Drummond,' said Emma. 'He said it was probably only a matter of time before one of her clients murdered her.'

'That's a nasty thing to say,' said James, looking incensed.

'He should be investigated,' Penny chipped in.

'For what? The police can't get involved just because he gave you the creeps and said nasty things.'

'Well I wish they could,' said Penny. 'There's something not quite right about him. Couldn't he at least be asked if he has an alibi for the times when William and Lavinia were murdered? Surely that can rule him in or out.'

'I agree,' said Emma. 'And he mentioned Lady Lou too, didn't he? She was a witness at William's inquest. I recall her name was Louise Granger. She told the inquest she lived in lodging houses. If we ask around, I'm sure we'll find someone who knows where she is.'

'Shall we do that tomorrow afternoon?'

'Yes, good idea.'

'Tomorrow?' said James. 'Does that mean I need to accompany you here again?'

'I'm sure there's no need,' said Emma. 'I've encountered Lady Lou and I think we'll be safe with her.'

James gave Penny a sceptical glance.

FORTY-FIVE

Gideon Flynn watched the two women from his living room window. They joined a man who was leaning against a lamp post. Had he been waiting for them? He wore a bowler hat and an overcoat. He looked like a detective.

The three of them walked down the street and disappeared from view. The women were probably reporting the conversation to the police officer. Gideon felt sure he had let nothing slip. Or had he?

He turned away from the window and recalled the conversation in his mind as he knelt down and rolled back the rug. He smiled as he remembered the startled expressions on the women's faces as he told them about his sharp knife. He'd had to do something to ensure they never came back to his shop again.

Gideon took the penknife from his pocket and lifted the corner of the floorboard with it. He was in the mood for writing letters.

After lifting out his writing paper, pen and pot of red ink, he replaced the floorboard and rolled the rug back into place. He carried everything over to his writing desk and laid it out.

'Gideon?' came a voice from beyond the door.

'Not now, Mother. I'm busy.'

He sat at his desk and unscrewed the lid from the pot of ink. There weren't many places in London where you could buy red ink. The only supplier he had found was a stationer's in a little street off Charing Cross Road.

He picked up his pen, thought for a moment then put it down again.

His thoughts were distracting him. Was the man really a police officer? And were the women really working for him?

If so, he could be in trouble.

FORTY-SIX

Penny travelled by omnibus to Westminster the following morning, hoping Mr Hobhouse still lived on Little Smith Street. Four years ago he'd helped her and James decipher a code linked to the murder of a hotelier, Nathaniel Gallo.

A light drizzle fell as she climbed off the omnibus in Parliament Square. The Big Ben clock tower loomed over her, piercing the low cloud with its tall spire. Penny's route took her around Westminster Abbey and its walled yards and gardens.

Little Smith Street was a short narrow road lined with tall, gabled buildings. She passed an ecclesiastical bookshop with crooked bow windows and gargoyles carved into its stonework. A few doors along stood the narrow house she recalled from before. The name *Hobhouse* was etched on a tarnished bronze plaque and worn stone steps led to an ancient oak door.

Penny sounded the heavy bronze knocker and waited. An elderly housekeeper eventually answered and led her up a narrow staircase to a room filled with bookshelves and a fug of tobacco smoke.

Mr Hobhouse worked at a desk by the window. He had thin

wisps of white hair and wore a pair of spectacles. A second pair rested on his large forehead.

'Mrs Blakely!' He got up from his seat, wincing at some indeterminate pain. 'I haven't seen you since your wedding. How are you?'

'I'm very well, thank you. And you?'

'Oh, I can't complain. How's young James?'

Penny smiled at the description. 'He's very well too. His work and fatherhood are keeping him busy.'

'I can't quite believe he's a father now. He doesn't seem much older than a lad himself. I remember his little round face and mischievous grin as if it were yesterday. Where's the time gone, eh?'

'That's a good question.'

'Now the last time you visited me, you brought with you a nice little example of the Vigenère cypher. Have you got something else for me today?'

'Yes, I have.' Penny pulled the piece of paper out of her bag and handed it to him. He swapped his spectacles and peered at it.

'Very interesting. Where did you find this?'

'A friend found it hidden in a picture frame.'

'Intriguing.'

'It's unusual because it's written in numbers. In fact it may not even be a code.'

'It looks like a code. The use of numbers suggests it could be the Beale cipher.'

'What's that?'

Mr Hobhouse swapped his spectacles around again. 'It's a code which was invented by a mysterious gentleman called Thomas J Beale. In 1822, he left a locked box in a safe at the Washington Hotel in Lynchburg, Virginia. He later sent a letter to the hotel saying the box could be opened if he didn't return for it within ten years. Beale said the box contained coded papers which would be unreadable without a key. You remember me telling you before that a key is a piece of text needed to decipher a code, don't you?'

'Yes, I remember that.'

'Good. Well Beale told the owner the key text would be sent to him. Ten years came and went and neither Beale nor the key text turned up. Beale was never seen again.'

'How mysterious!'

'The hotel owner finally opened the box in 1845. Inside were three pages of code and a letter from Beale. The letter described how Beale and some friends had mined gold and silver at a place a few hundred miles north of Santa Fe and buried the treasure somewhere in Lynchburg. Attempts were made to decipher the code and a friend of the hotel owner managed to decipher the page which describes how Beale buried gold, silver and jewels worth thousands of dollars in iron pots. The friend realised the Declaration of Independence had been used as the key text for the page. But the keys for the other pages haven't yet been determined.'

'So they remain undeciphered?'

'Yes. The ciphers were published in a pamphlet three years ago and many people are working on them. Myself included.'

'I'm sure you'll solve it, Mr Hobhouse,' said Penny.

'Maybe. But even if I do, I'm a long way from Lynchburg, Virginia.'

'So if the code we've found is the Beale cipher then it's possible we may never solve it if we don't know what the key text is.'

'Exactly,' said Mr Hobhouse. 'But I'll give it a go. Call on me again the day after tomorrow. I should have some answers for you by then.'

FORTY-SEVEN

Emma and Penny met at Liverpool Street station that afternoon and made their way to Thrawl Street. The drizzle had stopped but the sky was a leaden grey.

'What did Lady Lou tell the inquest?' Penny asked Emma.

'She said she was walking up Green Dragon Yard from Whitechapel Road. I visited the street to see what it's like. It's a narrow alleyway and not very pleasant. Lady Lou says she met William just after half past midnight and he told her he was lost. He asked her the way to Whitechapel Road, and she told him to continue in the direction he was going. They met near a streetlamp, but the section of alleyway he then walked down was unlit and very dark. She said he seemed reluctant to carry on that way.'

'But it seems he did.'

'Yes, he must have done, because the cab driver found him on Whitechapel Road.'

'Did she say anything else about him?'

'Only that he seemed to be under the influence of drink. She also said she thought she passed someone in the unlit part of the alleyway, but she couldn't be sure.'

'And it's important to remember this is Lady Lou's account,' said Penny. 'There was no one else there, so we only have her word.'

'I don't see why she would lie.'

'Mr Flynn thought it was possible, didn't he? I know he's an odious man, but that doesn't mean we should disregard everything he says. Lady Lou could be lying if she's the person who murdered your husband.'

Emma thought of the jovial lady at the inquest. 'It's difficult to imagine her attacking William,' she said. 'But she could have done. And perhaps she did it because she wanted to steal the case William was carrying. She wouldn't have necessarily known what was in it, perhaps she was hoping it contained something valuable.'

'It's important that case is found,' said Penny. 'If Lady Lou took it then it could have been hidden in one of the lodging houses around here.'

They reached Thrawl Street. It was lined with tall, grim-looking tenement buildings. Boards and rags covered broken window panes and notices advertised beds for fourpence a night. People chatted in doorways while dirty-faced children played on the cobbles.

'We shall have to speak to these people,' said Penny, quietly. 'Although I can tell by their expressions they don't trust us. They probably think we're Christian missionaries.'

They approached two women and a man by a doorway. Their faces were lined and gaunt, and Emma suspected they were younger than they looked.

'Do you know where we can find Lady Lou?' Penny asked.

'Not seen her,' said one of the women.

'But you know who she is?'

'I know her face. Never spoken to her.'

'Do you know which lodging house she's staying at?'

'No.'

'Never mind, thank you.'

They walked on and found a woman in an old grey shawl sitting on a vegetable crate. Penny asked her if she knew Lady Lou.

'I'll tell you if you give me fourpence for my bed tonight,' she replied sharply.

'All right.' Penny opened her bag, took some coins from her purse and handed them over.

The woman examined the coins before replying. 'Yeah, I know her.'

'Do you know where she is?'

'No. Not seen her for a few days,' she said as she curled her fingers tightly around the coins.

'I'm not sure I got my fourpence worth there,' said Penny with a smile.

Flower and Dean Street ran parallel to Thrawl Street and was just as miserable. Two men argued over a handcart, their words slurred with drink.

A woman with a broom had swept up some rubbish and was looking through it. A young baby was swaddled to her chest by a grubby shawl.

Penny offered her fourpence before she had even asked for it.

'We're looking for Lady Lou,' Emma said to her. 'Do you know where we can find her?'

'Why are you asking?' said the woman, leaning on her broom.

'We've heard she might know something about the murder of William Langley,' said Emma. 'He was my husband.'

'The man who was murdered? Your husband? I'm sorry to hear it. I heard Lady Lou saw him that night, but I think she's gone away.'

'Gone away?' said Penny. 'Where?'

'She said Jack the Ripper tried to murder her.'

'Goodness,' said Penny. 'She was attacked?'

The woman smiled, revealing she only had a few teeth. 'Not exactly, Lou likes to make a fuss. But she said she was approached by him. You know what he does, don't you? He talks to women before going off with them somewhere. And before they know it, he gets his knife out.'

Emma shuddered.

'Lou said she met him on Hanbury Street, near where Annie Chapman was murdered. He grabbed her arm and tried to pull her into a courtyard. She showed him her knife, and he ran away. She'd taken to carrying a knife after the first few murders.'

'How frightening!' said Penny. 'When was this?'

'About five days ago. I think it properly scared her because she left the area. She said she was going to stay with a friend who lives near the Adelphi.'

'The Adelphi by the Strand?' asked Penny.

'Yeah. So I don't know if that's where she went, but that's where she said she was going.'

'Thank you,' said Emma. 'You've been very helpful.'

The woman returned to her rubbish and Emma and Penny walked in the direction of Liverpool Street station.

'The Adelphi,' said Emma. 'That's the place with the underground arches, isn't it?'

'Yes,' said Penny. 'Where thieves, pickpockets and prostitutes ply their trade. Lady Lou must have been very frightened if she's chosen that place over Whitechapel.'

'So we have to go to the Adelphi to find her?'

'Yes. I think that will have to be tomorrow's excursion.'

They crossed Commercial Street and Emma glanced over her shoulder.

On the corner of Flower and Dean Street and Commercial

Street stood a woman watching her. She looked familiar and Emma realised it was Mary Fairchild from the charity which gave out tea and soup to the poor.

Emma raised her hand to acknowledge her, but Miss Fairchild turned away.

FORTY-EIGHT

Gideon Flynn drained his cup of tea and folded up the *Morning Express* newspaper. The editor of the newspaper should have received his letter today. The newspaper had printed the previous letter he'd sent, hopefully his latest effort would be published too.

His mother shuffled in to tidy away the tea tray.

'Have you set up the tape machine, Mother?'

'Not yet, Gideon.' Her voice was frail and her bony fingers fumbled with the tea cups.

'Please get on with it. We need the odds.'

The tinkle of the bell sounded from the door in the shop.

'Oh no. We have a customer. Let me see to that.'

As he descended the stairs, he hoped the two ladies hadn't returned with their police detective friend. He was relieved to discover his visitor was someone he knew.

'Hello Mr Gallagher. How are you?'

'Well enough.' He was a short, stocky man with a crooked nose. He was the owner of a boxing club and a general store.

'You've come to collect your monthly cheque?' said Gideon. He nodded.

Gideon went behind the counter and took out a key from his pocket which was attached to his waistcoat on a gold chain. He stooped and unlocked a safe where he kept customers' cheques.

He pulled out the envelope with Gallagher's name on it, closed the safe again, and locked it.

Mr Gallagher gave a grunt when he handed the envelope to him. 'It'd better be a good return this month,' he said in a threatening tone.

'Investments aren't always predictable, Mr Gallagher.'

He gave Gideon a sharp look. 'That doesn't bode well.'

Gideon watched him rip open the envelope with his thick fingers. There was a pause while he looked at the sum on the cheque. 'Four pounds. Is that all?'

'The investment hasn't performed enormously well over the past month, Mr Gallagher. I did explain this—'

'Yeah, you did explain it, I remember it well. But this is the third month in a row where I've received a cheque like this. It's not what I was expecting.'

Gideon remained calm and recited his well-rehearsed commentary on the unpredictable nature of the horse racing industry.

Mr Gallagher listened with a sneer on his face. 'So in summary, then, it's everyone else's fault, but not yours. Am I right?'

'I need not remind you, I'm sure, that your investment has received some excellent returns in the past and I'm entirely confident you will receive cheques like that again, Mr Gallagher. There are lean times and lucrative times—'

'I don't need a lecture from you,' said Mr Gallagher. 'Do you think I'm stupid? I want to see your numbers.'

Gideon smiled. 'I don't make my numbers available, I'm afraid. I keep them secret because I can't have anybody copying my strategy.'

'I don't think anyone's tempted to copy your strategy given the disaster it's been for the past few months,' said Mr Gallagher. 'I demand to see your numbers now!'

'That simply isn't possible, Mr Gallagher.'

His face reddened. 'In which case, I want my money back.'

'Mr Gallagher. It's invested. And besides, the contract you signed committed your funds for three years.' Gideon took a step closer to him to make his point clear. 'Only a year has passed since you signed.'

'To hell with the contract!' spat Mr Gallagher. 'I consider you to be in breach of it! The returns you're giving me are not what you promised. And you can lecture me about the state of the horse racing industry, but I think you're trying to get away with giving me as little as possible.'

'That's simply not the case, Mr Gallagher. How about we sit down with a glass of port and—'

'I'm not interested in sitting down and listening to your platitudes, Flynn. I want to see your numbers. And if you're not going to show me your numbers—'

Gideon raised a finger at him. 'If I were you, I'd be careful about what you say next, Mr Gallagher.'

'Why's that?' He jutted his chin.

'Do you know who the last person to challenge me was?'

'No. I'm not interested.'

Gideon clenched his fist. 'Oh, but I think you should be.'

'Why?'

'If I tell you his name, then you'll know why.'

Mr Gallagher stepped closer. 'What's his name?'

Gideon lowered his voice and fixed Gallagher with a sharp stare. 'What *was* his name, you mean? His name was Billy Langley.'

FORTY-NINE

'How was Lady Lou or whatever she calls herself?' asked James when he got home from work that evening.

'We didn't see her,' said Penny as she wiped Florence's face and hands with a damp cloth. 'She's left Whitechapel because apparently Jack the Ripper tried to attack her.'

'Goodness, really? Did she report it?'

'I don't know. Emma and I are going to look for her at the Adelphi tomorrow.'

'The Adelphi? That crime-ridden slum between the Strand and the river?'

'Yes. Apparently, that's where she is now. I shouldn't think it's any worse than Spitalfields and Whitechapel. Florence, please don't chew the cloth, I've just cleaned you with it.' She tried to extract the cloth from the baby's balled up fist. 'Isn't it astonishing how strong babies can be?'

'Yes, it is. I can't say I'm happy about you going to the Adelphi, Penny. And tomorrow will be the third day in a row with you working on this case. I'm worried that Emma Langley is expecting too much from you. As it is, you've already had an unpleasant encounter with that Flynn character.'

'He's no worse than other miscreants I've met over the years. Emma was far more bothered by him than I was and that's because she's younger and probably hasn't met many unpleasant men like him.'

'Apart from her husband.'

'Oh yes. Apart from him.' Florence finally let go of the cloth and Penny put it in her apron pocket.

'Well, perhaps once you've met Lady Lou, you can have a bit of a rest,' said James.

Penny laughed. 'A rest? Why do I need a rest?'

'Because you're busy and I don't think you should get too tired.'

'I don't feel tired at the moment. I'm fine.'

'All right then. Well, let's see how we get on. At least the children seem happy with Mrs Tuttle minding them.'

'Yes, it's working out quite well. It means I have a few hours each afternoon to work on something. And it also means the house is tidy and you have a lovely meal cooked for you each evening, James.'

'I suppose I can't complain about that. It's been a tiring day.' He sat down in an armchair. 'We've made progress with the swindler Barnaby Ratcliffe. It appears he's spun a web of villainy across London.'

'How?'

'By encouraging others to join him. And the reason crooks such as Ratcliffe operate for so long without detection is because they get help. People and businesses protect them. Often quite reputable people too.'

'So you have more arrests to make?'

'Possibly. The first thing I need to do is speak to a law firm which has apparently been advising Ratcliffe.'

'Really? Did the law firm know he was a criminal?'

'That's what I need to find out. The firm's in Bedford Row, Holborn. Cardwell and—'

'Theobald?'

'Yes. Do you know it?'

'No. But I do know William Langley used to work for the firm.'

FIFTY

Villiers Street was a narrow thoroughfare which sloped down towards the river. On one side stood Charing Cross railway station, and a row of lively shops and restaurants stood on the other.

Emma preferred the salubrious streets of the West End to the misery of Whitechapel, but even in this part of London squalor wasn't far away. She knew the Adelphi had a notorious reputation.

'James told me something interesting yesterday evening,' said Penny. 'He's investigating a criminal who carried out a life insurance swindle. Apparently, he sought advice from Cardwell and Theobald. Isn't that the law firm your husband worked for?'

'Yes,' said Emma. 'What an interesting coincidence.' She recalled her conversation with Mr Theobald. Did he seem the sort of man to mix with criminals? He'd seemed respectable, but she couldn't be sure. 'Will they be in trouble over it?' she asked.

'I don't know,' said Penny. 'I suppose it depends on how much they were aware of the criminal's activities. James is speaking to them today so I'll let you know what he finds out.'

'Yes, please do. I hope they've not been involved in anything criminal because they've provided me with a solicitor to sort William's affairs. All free of charge.'

Penny slowed her step. 'Have they? That's unusual.'

'Mr Theobald said he wanted to help the widow of a former employee.'

'What was the reason for William leaving the firm?'

'Apparently William was insubordinate, and Mr Theobald described him as being too big for his boots. And William lost his temper with him.'

'So William left the company on bad terms,' said Penny. 'Why would Mr Theobald offer to help his widow after that?'

'I can only imagine he feels sorry for me.'

'Or perhaps there's more to it than that,' mused Penny. 'Perhaps he gains something from it.'

'Such as what?'

'I don't know. Let's wait and see how James gets on and we can think about it further.'

Penny's inquiring mind impressed Emma. She hadn't thought of questioning Mr Theobald's apparent generosity. Had she been naïve once again?

They turned off the street and onto a path which ran alongside Victoria Embankment Gardens. The trees had almost lost their leaves and their branches stood stark against the cold grey sky.

'I've heard the Adelphi was very grand in its day,' said Penny. 'It was a parade of large townhouses which were built on the riverside. The houses were built on top of a colonnade of arches to raise them above the level of the river. In those days, the riverside was where we're walking now.'

'Really?'

'Yes. These gardens on our right were built about twenty years ago when the Victoria Embankment was constructed. The Thames was narrowed and now the riverside is about one hundred and fifty yards from us. When the embankment was constructed, it was built in front of the Adelphi's colonnade. That's why the arches and the space behind them are now underground.'

'You're very knowledgeable about this area, Penny.'

Penny laughed. 'It's only because I've written many articles about London over the years. I'm in danger of sounding too knowledgeable like my dear old friend Mr Edwards. I wonder what he's doing now?'

They walked through an alleyway before reaching a narrow road flanked by tall, grand buildings. They approached a dark archway.

'Here we are,' said Penny. 'I think this place is primarily used for storage vaults, but it's also a good hideaway for people who don't want to be found or seen. Hopefully it won't take long to find Lady Lou.'

Emma's heart thudded heavily as they stepped through the archway.

'Why didn't we think to bring a lantern?' whispered Penny, her voice echoing in the darkness.

An acrid odour filled Emma's nose. 'Do people actually live down here?'

'I think so. And despite this smell, I think I'd prefer it here to the streets of Whitechapel at night.'

In the gloom, Emma could see barrels and crates stacked behind barred gates. Lanterns flickered ahead of them.

'By rights, anybody can walk through here,' whispered Penny. 'But I think the informal residents do a good job of making it feel unwelcoming.'

'I suppose they're naturally suspicious,' said Emma.

She startled as she caught sight of an old, twisted face in the dim light of a lamp. It grinned and she realised she was looking at an elderly man.

'Who's come to pay Uncle Eddie a visit then?' he croaked.

Then a cackle echoed around the vaults and made Emma's heart beat faster.

'We're looking for Lady Lou,' said Penny in a confident voice. 'Have you seen her?'

'She's around somewhere.'

They walked on. Emma faltered as a lantern moved swiftly towards them, then she saw it was being carried by a boy no older than twelve. He gave them a sidelong glance as he passed.

'Who goes there?' said a hoarse lady's voice. 'Someone without a lantern by the looks of things.'

'We're looking for Lady Lou,' said Penny into the darkness.

'Keep going.'

'Thank you.'

They continued towards another light and Emma heard the strains of someone singing a popular music hall song in a raspy voice.

'Someone sounds happy,' said Penny.

As they walked towards the light, Emma could see a woman sitting on a barrel. She wore a tall hat decorated with colourful ribbons. She stopped singing as they stepped into the light from her lantern.

'Oh hello!' She smiled to reveal her few teeth.

'Lady Lou?' said Emma.

'That's me. Who's asking?'

FIFTY-ONE

'I'm Emma Langley, the widow of William Langley. I recognise you from the inquest.'

'Oh yeah. I remember,' said Lady Lou.

'This is my friend Mrs Penny Blakely. We're trying to find out more about my husband's murder and I'm hoping you can help.'

'Well I never,' said Lady Lou. 'Don't tell me you've come all the way down here to find me.'

'We have,' said Emma. 'We looked for you in Whitechapel and heard you'd left.'

'Yeah, well, that's because Jack the Ripper nearly got me, didn't he? And he'd have killed me if I hadn't had my knife with me. I showed it to him and I told him, "Don't you think about ripping me to pieces, I'll do it to you first." You should have seen him run!' She laughed. 'He got the shock of his life. No woman had never said that to him before!' She laughed again.

'But you left Whitechapel, even though he ran away?' said Penny.

'Oh yeah, I didn't want that happening to me again. I knew that if I acted brave, then I could scare him. But inside, my heart was all of a flutter.' She flapped her hand at her chest to demonstrate. 'And I'll tell you something else,' she said. 'I knew it was him from the moment I saw him. It was his eyes. There was evil in them. I knew then he was a man who did bad things.'

'It sounds like you did very well to escape,' said Penny.

'I won't get myself murdered, that's for sure. He made a mistake choosing me. I wish he'd stayed longer so I could have used my knife on him.'

'You would have killed him?'

Lady Lou nodded. 'Nothing worse than what he did to those poor women. But I don't want to face him again. That was enough for me. That's why I came here. I miss my friends in Whitechapel, but I ain't going back until they've caught him.' She pulled her shawl closer over her shoulders.

'When did you see William Langley on the night of his death?' asked Penny.

'About half past eleven. I was on... Where was it again? Oh yeah. Green Dragon Yard.' Emma recalled Lady Lou telling the inquest she'd seen William at half past twelve. 'He was lost, poor soul. So he asked me how to get to Whitechapel Road. He wanted to hail a cab.'

'Did you see anyone else around?' asked Emma.

'Not at that time, no. He was on his own.'

'Did he have a case with him?'

'Now you mention it I think he was carrying something, yeah.'

'That case has been missing since his murder,' said Emma.

'He must've dropped it when he was attacked,' said Lady Lou. 'Then someone must've found it and nicked it. That's what happens round there. People will nick anything. Especially a gentleman's case. That's all I can tell you. Let's hope they get his murderer.'

'And Lavinia Drummond,' said Emma. 'Did you know her?'

Lady Lou rolled her eyes. 'She had high opinions of herself.'

Emma wondered if she'd been envious of Lavinia's youth and beauty. 'Have you any idea who could have attacked her?'

'Well lots of people would've wanted to because she looked down on the rest of us. Thought she was a lady. She could pass for a lady, that's for sure. She looked like one. But she was no better than the rest of us. So who did that one? I don't know.' She shrugged.

'The same person who murdered my husband?' said Emma.

'I wouldn't like to say. There's been so many murders now, who knows?' She yawned and Emma suspected she wasn't going to tell them much more.

'Thank you for talking to us, Lady Lou,' said Penny. She gave her some coins.

'It was a pleasure, and that's very kind of you. Now the pair of you get out of here before you get mistaken for a pair of gentlewomen street walkers.' She gave a loud laugh then vanished into the shadows.

FIFTY-TWO

'What was all that about then, Lou?' said Eddie once the two ladies had gone. He limped towards her.

'Listening in, were you?'

'I heard some of it. Who were they?'

'The widow of that Langley chap who got murdered. And some friend of hers. Wanted to know everything that happened when I saw him. I'm tired of talking about it, to be honest. It's all people want to talk to me about. I didn't mind at first, but I'm bored with it now.'

'They'll tire of it soon enough.'

'I hope so. What else do they want me to say? I didn't see who did it and that's that.'

Lady Lou went over the conversation in her mind. Had she remembered all the facts right? She didn't see Billy until Green Dragon Yard. She saw him at half past eleven. Or was it half past twelve? She couldn't remember which time she'd told the two ladies.

She had never met him before. That was the important thing to tell people. As long as she kept that part of her story straight, she was fine.

She gave a sniff. Poor Billy Langley. And he'd been such a handsome young chap, too.

She had never betrayed anyone before.

'Fancy a drink, Lou?'

'Yeah. Go on. You paying, Eddie?'

'No, you can. Didn't those gentlewomen give you some money?'

She chuckled. 'You don't miss anything, do you, Eddie?'

FIFTY-THREE

'Do you think Lady Lou told us the truth?' Emma asked Penny once they were out in the grey daylight again.

'I don't know. She admits she carries a knife which makes me wonder if she murdered William.'

Emma felt her stomach turn. 'I don't want to suspect her. I quite like her. But I suppose it's possible, isn't it?'

'I'm afraid so,' said Penny. 'Although I don't know what her motive would have been. Perhaps we could have questioned her more about William, but her answers may not have been reliable. Do you really think she met Jack the Ripper?'

'The story seemed exaggerated to me,' said Emma, 'but it's difficult to be certain. I think she's probably very good at lying.'

'Yes, I think she is,' said Penny. 'It's hard to know what to believe.'

'I hope she wasn't lying,' said Emma. 'And that her encounter with William was just as she described it. That would mean William wasn't Jack the Ripper.'

'For that reason, I hope so too,' said Penny. 'Was her story about encountering William consistent with what she said at the inquest?'

'Yes. Although she told us she saw him at half past eleven and told the inquest it was half past twelve. The later time makes more sense because the cab driver picked him up at a quarter to one.'

'So Lady Lou made a mistake. An innocent one, maybe? Or a sign she's forgetting the story she's made up? I think she needs to be interviewed by the police again. I don't think she's a reliable witness, I'll speak to James about her.'

They turned into Villiers Street and walked uphill towards the Strand. 'Have you got time to meet tomorrow?' Penny asked Emma. 'I need to call on Mr Hobhouse and find out how he's got on with deciphering the code.'

'I'd love to find out if he's deciphered it. I finish teaching at three.'

'Brilliant.' Penny smiled. 'I'm happy you called on me for help. It's giving me an opportunity to feel like myself again.'

'How do you mean?'

'Working on puzzles like this. I feel like it's the sort of thing I'm meant to do. I feel guilty saying it because I love my children very dearly, and I love being a mother too. But I'm enjoying helping you. Oh dear, this doesn't sound good. I'm not considering at all the awful circumstances you've found yourself in. I'm sorry.'

'There's no need to apologise,' said Emma. 'I'm happy I called on you too, Penny. I worried I was making an unreasonable request of you, though. I realised how busy you were.'

'Yes, but I was forced to find someone to help me. And I've been very lucky with Mrs Tuttle, the children have really taken to her. She's good with them, and I know they love her company. So now I feel I'm achieving some balance with my life. I can enjoy being a mother, but I can also enjoy working on a case again.'

'That's good to hear,' said Emma. They walked on. The grey sky was darkening and lights glimmered in the shops. She felt a twinge of sadness. 'I don't suppose I shall ever know how busy motherhood can keep you.'

'What makes you say that?'

'I haven't got a chance of becoming a mother anytime soon, have I? When I married William, I assumed it would happen. But now he's gone, I've realised I've lost more than just a husband. I've lost the chance to be a mother.'

Penny took her arm. 'No. That chance isn't gone. You're young. You're not even thirty yet. There's plenty of time for you to meet a new husband and have a family with him. Just a few years ago, I swore I would never get married or have children and now look at me.' She laughed. 'Life works out for you one way or another and it's rarely how you plan it to be.'

Emma smiled at her but it was hard to shrug off the overwhelming feeling of sadness. 'I can't imagine how I'd meet a new husband. I certainly don't feel I can trust someone again.'

'And that's completely understandable. You'll need some time to recover from this. Life will have something in store for you, even if you don't become a mother. Maybe you have other callings instead. The children you teach now will carry memories of you into their futures. Some of them will stop playing music but others will become accomplished at it. A few may become professional. And they will always remember Mrs Langley, their first piano teacher.'

Emma blushed at the thought. 'You don't need to flatter me like this, Penny!'

'But it's true, isn't it? None of us truly knows the impact we have on other people's lives. Life is full of surprises. I never imagined we would meet again after we solved your brother's murder, and yet here we are. Tragedies have a strange way of bringing people together, don't you think?'

Emma nodded. 'Yes, they do, Penny.'

FIFTY-FOUR

'How are you getting on with the widow, O'Brien?' asked Edward Theobald.

'She told me Langley took all her money and it's true. He spent just about every penny he had, sir.'

'You've looked through all his bank accounts now?'

'Yes.'

'So there's no chance of us getting anything back. That's a shame.'

'With all due respect, sir, that would be difficult.'

'Officially, yes. But unofficially, it would have been quite straightforward with you working on the probate. You would have found a way to recoup our money, I'm sure.'

'I'll keep working on it, sir. Perhaps there was an account his widow was unaware of.'

'I hope there is. Keep going, O'Brien.'

A knock at the office door interrupted them.

'What is it?' said Edward.

His secretary stepped into the room. 'There's an inspector from Scotland Yard here to see you, sir.'

He felt an uncomfortable twinge in his stomach. 'An inspector from the Yard? What can he possibly want?'

'He didn't say, sir. He says his name is Inspector Blakely.'

O'Brien's brow furrowed.

'I'll see him off,' Edward said to O'Brien. He got to his feet. 'Thank you for the update.'

'Shall I show the inspector in, sir?' asked the secretary.

'Yes, go on then.'

O'Brien left the room, and the inspector stepped in with his bowler hat in one hand and a large brown envelope in the other. He wore an overcoat and had a square boyish face and blue eyes. 'Mr Theobald,' he said. He tucked the envelope beneath his arm and held out his hand. His handshake was firm. 'I'm Inspector Blakely of Scotland Yard.'

'So I've heard.' Edward pointed at the chair opposite him and sat down. 'This can't take long. I have an appointment in ten minutes.' This wasn't true, but he planned to give the inspector as little time as possible. Reassuringly, he looked too young to have had much experience.

The inspector placed the envelope on the table next to his chair. What was in it? Edward tried not to stare at it too much. 'I'm here to inform you that Mr Barnaby Ratcliffe has been arrested,' said the inspector.

Arrested? Edward's heart skipped. How had he not known about this? He pulled a disinterested expression and wiped his clammy palms on his trousers. 'I'm not familiar with the name.'

'He's a confidence trickster,' said the inspector. 'He's been carrying out a life insurance policy scam. He and two accomplices go from door-to-door selling policies which never pay out.'

'Scandalous.'

'We estimate there could be hundreds of victims across London. They faithfully paid their premiums each month to men they thought were from the insurance company, but when the time came to claim their money, they realised they had signed contracts which weren't worth the paper they were written on. After some painstaking work by the Yard and the rest of the Metropolitan Police, D Division arrested Ratcliffe and his accomplices in northwest London twelve days ago. They've been charged with a variety of fraudulent activities.'

'That's excellent news, Inspector. Good work by Scotland Yard. Thank you for sharing your success with me.' He made a show of looking at his pocket watch.

'And you're quite sure you're not familiar with the name Barnaby Ratcliffe, Mr Theobald?'

'I don't recall the name.'

'Well, that's interesting. Because we've spent a great deal of time going through Mr Ratcliffe's papers. In order to facilitate his deception, he created a business which appeared legitimate. He did this by enlisting the assistance of professional firms. From what I can see from Ratcliffe's papers, Cardwell and Theobald have done quite a bit of work for him. Can you confirm that?'

Edward felt the inspector's eyes on him, gauging his reaction. Why had he not chosen Cardwell for this interrogation? He calmed his breathing, desperate to appear as nonchalant as possible.

'I can't confirm anything, Inspector, because I really know nothing about it. I need to speak to my colleagues and find out if they remember this chap. What's his name? Radcliffe?'

'Ratcliffe. I'm perplexed to hear you know nothing and can't recall, because the correspondence we've found suggests you and Ratcliffe have met in person several times.'

What a fool Ratcliffe had been. Why hadn't he destroyed his papers? Mr Theobald drummed his fingers on the arms of his chair as he thought. Continuing his denial would probably look foolish now. It was probably better to admit some involvement with Ratcliffe to keep the inspector happy and hopefully send him on his way.

'I'm sure you can understand that I'm bound by client confidentiality, Inspector,' he said. 'But as your allegations of Barnaby Ratcliffe's supposed wrongdoing are of a reasonably serious nature, then I shall tell you what I know.'

'I would be grateful if you could.'

'I once met with Mr Ratcliffe in the distant past when he sought my advice on a legal matter relating to his company. Now I must stress that I did not at any time have any reason to doubt his business was completely legitimate.'

'It's interesting you should say that, Mr Theobald,' said the inspector. 'Because I have some papers which demonstrate you were aware his business was not completely legitimate.' He picked up his brown envelope, pulled out a file and leafed through it.

Edward felt his jaw clench. He stared at the papers in the file, desperately trying to read them even though they were upside down. What exactly did the inspector know?

'Here it is,' said Inspector Blakely, pulling out a sheet of paper. 'Correspondence advising Mr Ratcliffe what to do when a complaint about his practices was made by a rival insurance firm.'

'May I see it?'

'Of course.' The inspector handed the letter to him.

Edward remembered it well. Why had Ratcliffe kept it? What a halfwit that man was.

He decided a dismissive laugh was the best response as he handed the letter back to the inspector. 'The complaint came from a rival firm, Inspector. You expect that sort of behaviour from a competitor, don't you? When we wrote that letter, we had no idea Mr Ratcliffe's business was acting illegally in any way. As I recall, we merely offered advice on how to respond to the complaint, just as we do to any business which faces unfounded accusations. There's no evidence at all which shows this firm had any knowledge that Mr Ratcliffe's firm was acting illegally. If indeed, it was acting illegally. Have you considered the life policies didn't pay out for other reasons? Some people lie when they take out policies and if that's discovered when they make a claim, then the money isn't paid to them. I'm sure you're aware of how it all works.'

The inspector tucked the letter back into his file. 'Tell me about William Langley.'

Edward startled, surprised by the sudden change in topic. 'What?'

'He worked for your firm, is that right?'

'Yes. But what does that have to do with anything?'

'You're aware he was murdered in Whitechapel earlier this month?'

'Yes. Very sad indeed.'

'When did he leave this firm?'

'At the end of July.'

'And why did he leave?'

'He was dismissed.'

'Why?'

'Because his work here simply wasn't up to scratch, Inspector, that's why.'

'That's the reason you gave him?'

'Something along those lines, yes.'

'You can't remember the exact reason you gave?'

'Well, it was probably the usual tactful wording which one gives to employees who aren't much cop. I forget now. It was months ago. He was no good at it, so we let him go.'

The inspector said nothing, waiting for Edward to continue speaking. The silence grew until it became unbearable. 'What else do you want me to say, Inspector? That's that. Now, if you don't mind, I need to get to my next appointment.'

'Of course.' Inspector Blakely picked up his envelope and

got to his feet. 'Thank you very much for your time today, Mr Theobald.'

Edward remained calm while the inspector left the room. Then he thumped his fist on his desk. 'Damn it!' he shouted. 'Damn it! Damn it!'

He marched across his office, opened his door and strode off to find someone to shout at.

FIFTY-FIVE

'The police need to interview Lady Lou again,' said Penny to James at dinner that evening. They dined on beef brisket from the butcher's shop with mustard sauce and vegetables. 'Emma and I think there's a possibility she murdered William Langley.'

'And what makes you say that?'

'She was one of the last people to see him alive, and there's no one else to support her story. And she carries a knife.'

James raised an eyebrow. 'Does she?'

'She says she carries a knife to protect herself from Jack the Ripper. In fact, she told us a tall tale about how she frightened off Jack the Ripper with her knife.'

James raised both eyebrows. 'A tall tale? You don't think there's any truth in it?'

'I don't know for sure. It's difficult to know whether she's talking sense or not. And for that reason, I think the police need to speak to her again. Not as a witness, but as a suspect.'

'Why would she have murdered William Langley?'

'We think she might have wanted to steal the case he was carrying at the time.'

'How do you know he had a case with him?'

'Lavinia Drummond said he collected it from her home that day and Lady Lou confirmed to us he was carrying the case when she saw him.'

'But why would she admit to that if she stole the case? Surely if she didn't want any suspicion to rest on her, she would have denied seeing him with it?'

'Possibly. But maybe she's not that clever. Or maybe she is clever. I really don't know, James. But I do know her statement at the inquest can't be relied on. She told us she saw William at half past eleven but she told the inquest it was half past twelve. The police need to know that. Can you speak to H Division about it?'

James sliced a carrot in two and pierced both halves with his fork. 'It's not that simple, Penny.'

'Why not?'

'H Division aren't going to take kindly to me ordering them who to interview.'

'But they have to listen to you. You're from the Yard.' She pleaded.

'If only they would! Relations between H Division and the Yard aren't at their best at the moment.' He rested his fork on his plate and ran a hand over his brow. 'There's a lot of disagreement over how the Ripper case is being handled. The very last thing that's needed is me telling Bradshaw how to do his job.'

She leaned forward. 'But he's not doing his job!'

'That's your opinion, Penny.'

'Don't you agree with me?'

'It seems he could do more, but it's not my place to tell him that.' He picked up his fork again.

'So what can we do?'

'He may listen to Emma.'

Penny frowned. 'So Emma needs to ask him to interview Lady Lou?'

'It's worth a try.'

'And if he doesn't listen to her?'

'There's not much more we can do.'

She flung down her knife and fork. 'Oh, this is so frustrating!'

'I thought you weren't going to get too involved with this case, Penny.'

'When did I say that?'

'We had that long conversation, didn't we? The one about the children coming first and the fact you can't do the job you used to... and the rest of it.'

'I'm not doing as much as I used to. But I can't help getting angry about incompetence!'

'Who's incompetent?'

'The police.'

'It's unfortunate timing that William Langley happened to get himself murdered at the same time H Division are trying to solve all the other Whitechapel murders. Perhaps he could have planned it for another time? Last year would have been better, before all these atrocities happened.'

'This isn't a laughing matter, James. And don't forget it's not just Langley, Lavinia Drummond was murdered too. And you should have heard how dismissive Lady Lou was about her. I thought she was extremely cold-hearted about her.'

'In the way only a murderer could be?'

'Exactly!'

'Ask Emma to speak to Bradshaw at H Division. He might surprise us and actually listen to her.'

'I suppose that's all we can do.' Penny picked up her knife and fork again.

'I spoke to Mr Theobald today,' said James.

'Oh yes, how was he?'

'He lied for most of our conversation. He's a terrible liar. He can't be a very good lawyer.'

'So was he involved with the swindling?'

'Undoubtedly. We'll have to prove it, but I don't think it's going to be too difficult. I asked him about William Langley too.'

'And what did he say?'

'He couldn't give me a firm reason why Langley was dismissed. He muttered something about him being no good at his job, but I found his response rather vague.'

'As if he didn't want to tell you the exact reason for his dismissal?'

'Yes. And I find that odd.'

'Cardwell and Theobald are giving Emma the services of one of their solicitors free of charge.'

'Really?'

'She thinks they're just being kind, but I told her they must have a reason for doing it.'

'To keep an eye on her?'

'It must be that.'

'Why?'

'I don't know. But it seems like an attempt to keep control of the situation.' Penny had a thought. 'How many people at Cardwell and Theobald knew they were working with a criminal?'

'I don't know. We've only found evidence on Theobald so far. But hopefully we can implicate Cardwell soon and there could be others, too. Ratcliffe kept a lot of paperwork, which is very fortunate, but it means there's a lot to go through.'

'Do you think William Langley knew about Ratcliffe?'

James pursed his lips. 'Now that's a very interesting thought indeed, Penny.'

FIFTY-SIX

Emma met Penny in Parliament Square the following afternoon. A cold wind whisked around the square and tugged at their coats.

'James interviewed Mr Theobald yesterday,' said Penny. 'He's sure he lied for most of the conversation. James suspects Theobald knew Barnaby Ratcliffe was a criminal.'

'So Cardwell and Theobald could have been involved with something criminal?'

'It's possible. I certainly wouldn't trust anything they say or do. James and I suspect the solicitor they've loaned you could be keeping an eye on you.'

Emma felt a chill in her stomach. 'What a horrible thought!'

'I'm sorry, Emma. I realise it's not what you want to hear. But all you need to do is tell the solicitor you don't need his help anymore.'

'What explanation shall I give?'

'You don't have to give one. But you could say you have an uncle who's a solicitor and he's offered to do the work instead. Something like that, maybe. We could be mistaken and it might be nothing to worry about. But I think it's best to keep your distance from Cardwell and Theobald just to be sure.'

They left Parliament Square and headed towards Little Smith Street. 'I also spoke to James about Lady Lou and he's reluctant to ask H Division to interview her. He says he can't tell them how to do their job. He thinks it would be best if you spoke to Detective Inspector Bradshaw.'

'I can try, but I don't think he'll listen to me. That's why we're doing this in the first place, isn't it? The police seem unable or reluctant to follow all the leads.'

'You've brought a friend with you, Mrs Blakely,' said Mr Hobhouse, giving Emma a warm smile. She was amused to see him wearing two pairs of spectacles at the same time.

'This is Emma Langley,' said Penny. 'She found the code hidden in the painting. Have you managed to decipher it?'

'Oh yes, it was quite straightforward.' Emma felt a skip of excitement in her chest as Mr Hobhouse walked over to his desk and pulled some papers out of a drawer. 'It's the Beale cipher,' he said. 'As I thought it would be.'

'But didn't you need a key text?' asked Penny.

'Yes. I tried the one which Beale had used, the Declaration of Independence. And it worked! Clearly the author of this code didn't wish to bother coming up with his own key text.'

'I'm afraid I don't understand,' said Emma.

'It's quite simple,' said Mr Hobhouse. He cleared a space on his cluttered desk, laid out the papers and swapped his spectacles. 'Come and have a look at this while I explain.'

Emma and Penny joined him at his desk by the window.

'Here's a copy of the Declaration of Independence,' he said, pointing at a bundle of paper. 'It's a little over 1,300 words long. For ease of use, I've marked every tenth word, can you see? Ten, twenty, thirty and so on. The Beale cipher looks at the first letter of each word. Let's say, for example, I would like to write the letter 'n' in Beale cipher. Now you can see here that the tenth word in the Declaration of Independence is 'necessary'. "When, in the course of human events, it becomes necessary." So for the letter 'n', I write the number ten. If I wished to write the word 'never', then I would need to write down five numbers. Each number would correspond to a word in the key text. So, after ten I would put thirty-seven for 'e' then... Oh, just a moment...' He peered at the paper, turned it over, then turned it again. 'Ah, got it. It looks like eight hundred and seven for 'v' and so on. Simple, isn't it?'

'If you say so,' said Penny. 'But it must take ages to write and decipher.'

'Yes, it can take a while,' he replied. 'But that's encryption for you. You don't want to make it easy for anyone, do you?'

'So the person who wrote the coded message I found also used the Declaration of Independence as a reference point,' said Emma.

'Yes. And we're lucky they did,' said Mr Hobhouse. 'If they'd used another text, then we could still be trying to puzzle it out. There is no equivalent to the Declaration of Independence here in Britain, so I suppose the author used what had been used before. But they could have used anything. A book of the Bible perhaps, a work by Dickens or even a recipe for bread pudding.'

'We're lucky they didn't choose to be that imaginative,' said Penny.

'Quite so,' said Mr Hobhouse. 'And here's your decoded message, ladies.' He handed them another sheet of paper.

'It looks like a list of names,' said Emma.

'And addresses,' said Penny. 'With amounts of money next to them. What does this mean?'

Mr Hobhouse shrugged. 'That's what I can't help you with, I'm afraid.'

'Thank you, Mr Hobhouse,' said Penny. 'We don't know what this list means, but we'll find out. You've done all the hard work for us. How much do we owe you?'

He waved a dismissive hand. 'Nothing. You're young James's wife. I don't expect payment from family and friends.'

FIFTY-SEVEN

Emma and Penny examined the list of names and addresses as they sat in the comfortable coffee room of the Chester Hotel in Westminster.

'They're all in the East End,' said Penny. 'I find it difficult to believe they're not somehow connected to Mr Flynn's picture framing shop.'

'Do you think they're customers?' asked Emma.

'Why would he write the names of his customers in code? And let's not forget he denied knowing anything about the code. If these people are customers, then surely there's nothing to hide?'

'I suppose we shall have to visit them and ask them,' said Emma. 'But there are about thirty names here.'

'It's going to take a long time to speak to all of them, isn't it? We could call on a few and ask them why they think they could be on the list. Perhaps they're all members of a gang or a secret society.'

'And the amounts of money?' said Emma.

'Money earned, paid or owed. Wages, perhaps? It's difficult to say. As you've suggested, Emma, we need to speak to them.' Penny glanced at a clock on the wall. 'Hopefully Mrs Tuttle won't mind looking after the children for a little while longer. And before we leave here, I'm going to write out a copy of this list. Experience has told me you should always have more than one copy of everything.'

Emma and Penny travelled by omnibus from Westminster to the Bank of England. There, they caught a second omnibus to Whitechapel.

'Let's begin with an address we know,' said Penny.

Emma looked down the list until she saw a familiar street name. 'Old Montague Street,' she said. 'I know where that is.'

'J Dyer is the name of the person there,' said Penny. 'And ten shillings is written next to their name. Hopefully, they'll be happy to talk to us.'

The address on Old Montague Street was a butcher's shop. A row of carcasses hung on hooks outside. Inside, the metallic smell of raw meat made Emma's stomach turn a little. A dark-eyed young man behind the counter greeted them. He held a large knife and wore a white apron over a shirt with collar and tie.

'Mr Dyer?' Penny asked him.

He nodded.

'J Dyer?'

'No, that's my father. John.'

'Is he here?'

'No.'

A woman appeared in the doorway behind the counter, her arms folded. She was dark-eyed like the young man, but a generation older. Emma guessed she was his mother.

'Why are you asking about my husband?' she asked warily. Her manner was confrontational.

'We found his name on a list,' said Penny.

'What list?'

'It's just a list of names and addresses. And amounts of money. For J Dyer it says ten shillings.'

Mrs Dyer stepped out from behind the counter. 'Let me look at that.' She snatched the paper from Penny as she held it out to her. 'I see Matthew Templeman is on here too.'

'Who's he?'

'He was a friend of John's.' She thrust the paper back at Penny.

'Do you know what this list means?' Emma asked her.

'Ten shillings is what John owed to begin with. I never knew he even borrowed any money. But the debt grew. Just like it always does with these people.'

'What people?'

'You really don't know? Moneylenders. That's who. They're the reason we lost our business. And now my son, Andrew, and I run this shop for a friend while John is detained at Her Majesty's pleasure in Wandsworth gaol.'

'He's in prison?' said Penny. 'That must be extremely difficult for you.'

'It is. John stole money to repay the debt. He was ashamed of what he did. But he did it because they threatened him.'

'Who?'

'The moneylenders,' said Mrs Dyer.

'Do you know who your husband borrowed the money from?'

'No. He wouldn't say. He was too frightened of them. So he was sentenced to two years in prison.'

'When was he imprisoned?' Penny asked.

'Four months ago,' said Mrs Dyer. 'Where did you get that list from?'

'I found it hidden in a painting,' said Emma.

Mrs Dyer let out a humourless laugh. 'Well, that's some find, isn't it?'

'What do you know about Matthew Templeman?' Penny asked.

'He was a friend of John's.'

'Was?'

'He died earlier this year.'

'When?'

Mrs Dyer sighed as she thought. 'Not long after John went to prison.'

'Was Mr Templeman's death sudden?'

'I'd say so. He fell off the Imperial Warehouses in Leman Street.'

'Fell?'

She nodded. 'It was ruled an accident.'

'Thank you for your time speaking to us, Mrs Dyer,' said Penny. 'You've been very helpful.'

'The least you could do is buy something in return,' she said. 'How about some mutton chops at ten pence a pound? If you want them trimmed, we'll do them for a shilling a pound. Or there's rump steak for a shilling a pound, brisket for five pence and ribs for eight pence. Tongue is eight pence for both fresh and salted. What takes your fancy?'

FIFTY-EIGHT

It was getting dark as Emma and Penny left the butcher's shop, each of them carrying cuts of meat for supper. The shops and businesses on Old Montague Street were well-lit, but many of the narrow side streets had already been plunged into darkness.

'The list must be the names of people who owe money, don't you think?' said Emma.

'It could be. Mrs Dyer said her husband owed ten shillings, and that was the amount written next to his name,' said Penny.

'Mrs Dyer said her husband owed ten shillings to begin with. That suggests the amount increased.'

'And probably increased by a lot quite quickly,' said Penny. 'That's how these moneylenders make their profits, isn't it? They add unreasonable rates of interest and, before long, the person who borrowed the money has little chance of paying it back. It sounds like Mr Dyer stole to settle his debts.'

'Because he was threatened,' added Emma. She gave this some thought as they turned into Brick Lane. Had William written the list of debtors? Had he been the person who'd lent them the money?

'Oh dear,' she said, pausing by a garment shop.

'What is it?' asked Penny, resting her hand on her arm.

'My husband threatened Mr Dyer, didn't he? He forced him to turn to crime to repay him.'

'Can you imagine William doing that?' asked Penny.

'If you'd asked me that question a few weeks ago, then my answer would have been no. But now I really don't know at all.' A pause followed. 'The more I think about it, the more it makes sense,' continued Emma. 'He used my inheritance money to lend to people.'

'But most of them would have paid him back,' said Penny. 'So where's that money now?'

'That's a good question. It's certainly not in the bank accounts we had together. And I suppose the list puzzles me still. The code doesn't look like William's handwriting. And I never knew him to show any interest in code or ciphers.'

'So maybe he wasn't the moneylender,' said Penny. 'Perhaps he never knew the list was hidden in the painting.'

'I hope so,' said Emma. 'Despite everything, I don't like to think he was responsible for forcing people into debt and crime.'

'Maybe he wasn't,' said Penny. 'We can look up the cases of Dyer and Templeman in newspaper reports. I feel sure their predicaments would have been reported on. It will also give me an excuse to visit one of my favourite places.'

'Where's that?'

'The reading room at the British Museum.' Penny smiled. 'I haven't been there for a few years. Would you like to see it?'

'Yes I would.'

'Then let's go tomorrow.'

'I have a few lessons to teach tomorrow, but I should be able to find an hour.' A familiar figure ahead of them caught Emma's eye. 'Oh look! Isn't that Lady Lou?' A lantern on a public house illuminated her tall, elaborate hat and fussy clothing. She walked with a purposeful gait.

'Yes, I think it is,' said Penny. They watched as she crossed

Brick Lane and turned left into Flower and Dean Street. 'I wonder where she's going?'

'Let's follow her and find out,' said Emma.

They crossed the road and followed.

'I wish the police would speak to her again,' said Penny. 'It's frustrating. I can think of many cases which would have been solved more swiftly if they'd listened to someone.'

'You mean if they'd listened to you?'

Penny turned to her and smiled. 'I don't want to appear conceited but...yes.'

Three children ran past them, barefoot and laughing. Their tattered clothes looked too thin to keep out the cold and damp.

At the end of the street, Lady Lou paused. Emma felt fearful she might turn and see them. She grabbed Penny's arm, and they ducked into a doorway.

'Did she see us?' whispered Penny.

'I don't know,' said Emma, her heart thudding in her chest. Cautiously, she peered out from the doorway and there was no sign of Lady Lou.

'Quick!' she whispered. 'We don't want to lose her!'

They hurried to the end of the street and looked along Commercial Street. 'There,' said Penny, pointing to their right. Lady Lou was heading towards Christ Church. The silhouette of its spire was just visible against the darkening sky. Opposite the church, Lady Lou crossed the road and turned left into Brushfield Street.

Spitalfields Market was closed up for the day as Emma and Penny passed it. A musty odour of overripe fruit and vegetables lingered in the air.

'Crispin Street,' said Penny as they watched Lady Lou turn right. 'That's where Flynn the creepy picture framer is.'

They hurried on, keen to keep Lady Lou in their sight. Once they reached the corner, they slowed their step and watched as Lady Lou headed for the wood-carved shopfront. A little lantern flickered above the gold-lettered sign: *G. Flynn, Picture Framer*.

Lady Lou marched up to the door, pushed it open and disappeared from view.

'I wonder why she's calling on him,' said Penny. 'I can't imagine she has many pictures which need framing.'

They walked a little closer to the shop but remained on the opposite side of the street, within the shadow of Spitalfields Market.

The windows on the first storey were lit and the curtains drawn. 'That's the room we visited him in,' said Penny. 'I think I just saw movement there.'

Emma watched the windows closely and a shadow passed across the backlit curtain, as if someone had moved across the source of light.

'Yes, I think they're upstairs,' she said.

The pictures in the shop window were lit by Mr Flynn's lantern. One of them caught Emma's eye. 'I want to take a quick look at something,' she said. She crossed the cobbles and carefully approached the shop, keen not to be seen if Lady Lou or Mr Flynn suddenly appeared at the door.

The lady stared out from the picture, her dark dress blended with the background, and she held a hat in her hand. She had the same sombre, enigmatic gaze as the lady in William's painting. It wasn't the same picture, but it was remarkably similar. She tried to recall if the picture had been in the window when she and Penny had first visited Mr Flynn. She didn't remember seeing it.

A shout startled her. Lady Lou's voice came from the window above. The words were indistinct, but Emma could hear anger. She turned to where Penny stood in the shadows and gestured for her to join her. Penny scampered across the street and Emma pointed to the window above.

More shouting. This time, the voice was male.

Then a thud. As if a door had slammed.

'Let's go,' whispered Penny. 'We can't be seen here.'

They strode away, heading for the darkness across the street again. The sound of a sliding sash window quickened their step. Light spilled into the street from the opened curtain at the window. As they reached the corner of the street, Emma turned to see a man looking out.

Had he heard them? Or was he just getting some air?

'Come on,' whispered Penny. 'We need to leave.'

FIFTY-NINE

'This is a list of people who owe money,' said Penny as she showed James the deciphered code that evening.

'Owe money to whom?'

'We don't know. But my guess is William Langley. He kept the list hidden in the picture frame.'

'That makes sense.' James examined the list and Penny told him what she'd learned about Mr Dyer and Mr Templeman.

'Ideally we need to speak to the other people on the list, but it's going to be time consuming.' She watched his expression, hoping he might pick up on her hint that she needed help.

'Yes it is.' He sighed. 'I suppose this could be a criminal matter.'

'So the police might help?'

'Yes. I think it warrants some investigation. Let's not burden H Division with it until we can be sure about what this list actually shows. I'll ask my nephew Richard to look into it.'

James's nephew had recently begun working as a constable.

'But isn't he in K Division?'

'Yes. But it neighbours H Division, doesn't it? I'm sure he can make a few inquiries without upsetting anyone too much.'

'Thank you, James.' Penny kissed him on the cheek.

'Goodness. I should offer to help more often, shouldn't I?'

She decided to ask him for another favour while he was in a helpful mood. 'Are you still sure you can't ask Bradshaw to speak to Lady Lou? Emma and I saw her going into Flynn's shop today and we heard raised voices.'

'Lady Lou and Flynn arguing?'

'We can't be certain it was them, but I assume it was. The pair of them are suspicious.'

'Did you witness an argument between them?'

'No.'

'Did you hear the details of what it was?'

'No.' Her heart sank. She knew there wasn't enough evidence for the police to get involved.

'I can't go to Bradshaw with that, can I? It has to be actual evidence of wrongdoing. I agree they're suspicious, Penny. But we need to catch them at something before we can act. Has Emma spoken to Bradshaw yet?'

Penny blew out a sigh; the case felt frustrating. 'Emma doesn't think he'll listen to her. And I agree, he probably won't. Detective inspectors don't like ordinary people telling them what to do. And they are particularly averse to women doing it.'

James nodded. 'True. Let's all keep an eye on Flynn and Lady Lou. Once we can be certain they're up to no good, I'll have a word with Bradshaw.'

SIXTY

'It's been a long time since I last visited this place,' said Penny as she and Emma approached the steps of the British Museum. Its vast columned portico loomed over them.

'I used to come here as a child,' said Emma. 'The Egyptian rooms always fascinated me the most.' She smiled as she recalled how she and her brother had stared at the mummies and sarcophagi with ghoulish delight.

'I'm looking forward to bringing my children here once they're old enough to understand what they're looking at,' said Penny. 'But today we're here for the reading room. The newspaper archive in there will hopefully tell us more about what happened to Mr Dyer and Mr Templeman. James has asked his nephew Richard to call on the other debtors on the list. He's a constable for K Division and James feels sure he can make a few quiet inquiries for us.'

'That's excellent news!'

They walked through the entrance hall and out into a central courtyard, where a domed building stood in front of them.

'Here we are,' said Penny. 'I feel quite excited to have an

excuse to come here again! Fortunately, they allow me to renew my reading ticket each year.' She pushed open the oak door and they stepped inside.

Emma was struck by the beauty of the room. It was circular and dominated by an enormous dome over their heads. Daylight streamed through a circle of arched windows at the base of the dome and illuminated the decorative blue, white and gold plasterwork.

Three tiers of bookshelves covered the walls. The upper two tiers were accessed by galleries with ornate gold railings. Rows of desks radiated out from a dais in the centre of the room and people sat with their heads bowed, quietly studying.

'What a place!' Emma said in awe.

'And it hasn't changed at all,' whispered Penny with a grin. 'Let's go to the newspaper room.'

The newspapers were in a side room with large desks set at a sloped angle so a newspaper could be spread out on them and read with ease.

Emma followed Penny to a row of leather-bound volumes. 'Let's try old copies of the *Morning Express*,' she said. 'I've heard it's quite a reputable paper.' She gave Emma a knowing wink. 'Now when did Mrs Dyer say her husband was imprisoned?'

'Four months ago,' said Emma. 'So I assume it was July.'

Penny pulled out a volume which was marked *July to September 1888*. She carried it over to one of the desks and opened it.

'It's a shame we didn't ask for the exact date,' she said. 'But I sensed Mrs Dyer didn't like us asking her questions, so I didn't want to antagonise her.'

Penny slowly turned the pages of each newspaper as she and Emma searched for a mention of John Dyer's prison sentence.

'You look on the left-hand pages and I'll look on the right-hand ones,' said Penny. 'It may be well-hidden, perhaps little more than fifty words at the bottom of a column.'

It took a while to find, but Emma eventually spotted an article about a butcher jailed for theft.

'Here he is,' she said. '"At the Middlesex Sessions yesterday John Dyer, 47, a butcher, was brought up to receive sentence for breaking and entering the warehouse of Francis George Hardman at Clerkenwell and stealing items of jewellery worth one hundred pounds. Sir Andrew Masefield directed that the prisoner should serve two years' penal servitude. Counsel for the prisoner, Mr Thomas Haskins, said Dyer had previously borne a good character but had fallen into debt."'

'Well found!' said Penny. 'And what a sad story. He ended up stealing jewellery worth one hundred pounds for a ten-shilling debt. If only we could find out who he owed money to.'

They continued searching through the newspaper reports, and Penny found a report on the inquest into Matthew Templeman's death. 'It says here that Mr Templeman was a cooper, and he was fifty-eight years old,' said Penny. 'He spent the earlier part of the evening drinking in the Ten Bells public house. At nine o'clock that evening, shortly before sunset, Mr Templeman was seen in a distressed state on the roof of the Imperial Warehouses in Leman Street. He'd gained access to the building via an unlocked window. People grew concerned for his safety and urged him to come down, but he refused. A bystander, Thomas Haskins, entered the warehouse in an attempt to help Mr Templeman to safety. However, Mr Templeman tripped and fell to his death. The verdict was death by misadventure. Mr Templeman's wife gave evidence at the inquest stating that she didn't believe her husband would have deliberately jumped to his death. However, she stated he'd recently taken to drink because of mounting debts.'

'Thomas Haskins,' said Emma. 'A bystander when Mr

Templeman died and counsel for Mr Dyer. Is it a coincidence the two men have the same name?'

'Well noticed!' said Penny. 'It could be the same man.'

'How do we find out?'

'Let me think... Thomas Haskins, the lawyer for Mr Dyer, will be listed with the Law Society. We could find him and ask him if he's the same man who tried to help Mr Templeman. But even if he is... I'm not sure how it helps us. There's a danger we spend too much time on these small bits of detail.'

'Thomas Haskins the lawyer might be able to tell us who Mr Dyer owed money to,' said Emma.

'Yes, he might. That's a good point. We can visit the Law Society and look him up.'

Emma glanced at the clock on the wall; she only had twenty minutes to get to Hampstead. 'I'm afraid I have to get to a piano lesson.'

'That's all right. I'll visit the Law Society and let you know how I get on.'

SIXTY-ONE

Penny recalled the Law Society was on Chancery Lane, just a short distance from Fleet Street. As she walked the fifteen-minute route from the British Museum, she felt a skip of excitement. For years she had walked the streets of London, making inquiries and following leads. Today, she felt thrilled to be doing something similar again. Although the weather was grey and passers-by were glum-faced, Penny could feel herself smiling.

The Law Society was easy to find, housed in an imposing, classical building with towering Corinthian columns. Its edifice seemed too large for the narrow street of Chancery Lane.

Inside the marbled entrance hall she spoke to a clerk and then another before finally being referred to Mr Tipworth who would look at the register for her. He was a grey-haired man with a beak-like nose and mutton-chop whiskers. He led Penny to a musty room lined with leather volumes on bookshelves.

'What's the name of the gentleman you wish to look up?' he asked.

'Mr Thomas Haskins,' she said.

'And what date was he added to the register?'

'I don't know.'

'You don't know?' His eyes bulged, as if horrified by her response.

'No. Isn't it alphabetical?'

'Yes, it's alphabetical. But it's alphabetical by year. You really have no idea how long he's been practising?'

'No. Can't we just check each year?'

'Yes, we can. But have you seen how many years there are?' He gestured at the number of volumes with a sweep of his hand.

Penny peered closely at them. Each one was labelled with a gold-lettered year on its spine. 'I'd say anyone who was registered in 1810 is probably dead now,' she said.

'Well, yes. I think that's quite obvious.'

'So we don't have to look through all the volumes in this room, do we? I think 1875 onwards would suffice to begin with. I can help so there's two of us doing the work.' Penny followed this with a smile, keen to win him over.

'I'm the only person who's permitted to look in the register,' said Mr Tipworth sourly, pulling an elaborate silver pointer from the inside pocket of his jacket. 'Let's begin with 1880.'

Penny watched as he pulled out the volume and carried it to a little table by the window which was covered with a red velvet cloth. He laid down the book, opened it and turned to the letter H. Then he stooped over the pages and ran his pointer down the names. The end of the pointer had a little pointing silver hand on it.

'No Thomas Hardwick there,' he said.

'Haskins,' corrected Penny.

'It's Haskins now, is it?'

'It always was.'

'I thought you said Hardwick.'

'No.'

He sighed and ran the little silver hand down the names again. 'No Thomas Haskins for 1880. Let's try 1881.'

After fifteen minutes, the little silver hand found a Thomas Haskins who was registered in 1876.

'Could he be the chap you're looking for?' asked Mr Tipworth.

'I hope so. What details do you have for him?'

'His inn of court is Lincoln's Inn. His address is Fenners and Company, twenty-eight Bedford Row, Holborn.'

'Bedford Row?'

'Yes.'

'The same street as Cardwell and Theobald.'

'Is it? There are a few law firms in Bedford Row.'

'Do you have the details for Cardwell and Theobald?'

'What sort of details?'

'Their address.'

'Yes, they will be listed here. But we have to go into a different room for that.'

Mr Tipworth placed the volume back on the shelf and led Penny to another room which was almost identical to the previous one. The volumes on the shelves were labelled with letters of the alphabet.

'Cardball and Theo... what was it?' he asked.

'Cardwell and Theobald.'

'Oh. I thought you said something different the first time.' Penny waited as he carried out the familiar procedure of taking the book off the shelves, opening it at the little table by the window and running his pointer through the entries. 'Here they are,' he said. 'Cardwell and Theobald. They're at twenty-eight Bedford Row, Holborn.'

'The same address as Fenners and Company.'

Penny considered Thomas Haskins and how he appeared to have been involved with at least two of the debtors on the coded list of names. And now it seemed he had links with Cardwell and Theobald. What could it mean? She couldn't wait to share the information with Emma.

'Thank you, Mr Tipworth,' she said. 'You've been enormously helpful.'

'Have I?' His face cracked into a faint smile. 'I'm pleased to hear it.'

SIXTY-TWO

'How are you finding the piano teaching, Mrs Langley?' asked Mrs Solomon that weekend.

'I'm enjoying it. The children are delightful.'

'And their parents?'

'They vary.'

Mrs Solomon laughed and pulled her brush through Laurence's shaggy fur. 'Every self-respecting parent has ambitions for their children, I suppose. Too many ambitions in some cases.'

The doorbell rang and Laurence's narrowed eyes sprang wide open.

'Who can that be?' said Mrs Solomon.

'I'll go and see,' said Emma, getting to her feet. 'You don't want to disturb Laurence.'

'No, I don't. And Ronald won't have heard the bell. He's remarkably deaf these days.'

Emma went into the hallway and opened the door. 'Penny? Is everything all right?'

'Everything's fine.' She smiled, to Emma's relief. 'I'm sorry to disturb your weekend, I need to tell you about Thomas Haskins.'

'Come in.'

As Penny stepped into the hallway, spots of light rain sparkled on her clothes. She took off her spectacles and wiped them with her gloved fingers.

'Come and meet my landlady, Mrs Solomon,' said Emma.

They went into the sitting room.

'Oh, I'm sorry I can't be polite and stand up,' said Mrs Solomon. 'I don't want to disturb my cat.'

'It's quite all right,' said Penny. 'My name is Penny Blakely, by the way.'

'And I'm Mrs Solomon. I've heard all about you.'

'You have?'

'Yes, Mrs Langley told me how you used to be a news reporter and solved her brother's murder. Very impressive.'

'Thank you.'

'You might wish to speak in the parlour,' said Mrs Solomon. 'I'm sorry I can't move out of your way.'

'You have a delightful cat,' said Penny.

'Well, he's a bit of a nuisance really, but I love him all the same. I have to brush him every day otherwise his fur becomes all tangled up.'

'What's his name?'

'Laurence.'

'I have a cat too, she's called Tiger. When I lived in a garret room in Cripplegate, she used to wander about the rooftops.'

'Goodness me, that sounds quite dangerous!'

'Fortunately, she was fine, and she has a little garden now.'

'How lovely. Now go and have your chat together, I'm quite sure you didn't come here to talk about cats with me!'

.   .   .

'Thomas Haskins is a lawyer for a firm which occupies the same building as Cardwell and Theobald,' said Penny. 'The firm is called Fenners and Company. Did William ever mention them?'

'No he didn't. But they share offices with Cardwell and Theobald? That's more than just a coincidence, isn't it?'

'I think so,' said Penny.

'He's associated with at least two of the people on the list I found in William's picture,' said Emma. 'I'll pay him a visit on Monday. I think he must have known my husband.'

SIXTY-THREE

'Can you play the piano, Mrs Langley?' asked Emma's pupil, Beatrice Montgomery, the following Monday.

She smiled. 'Yes, I can play.'

'Can you play something now?'

'Oh no, this is your lesson now.'

'I want to hear you play something. Just quickly.'

Emma glanced at the polished keys of the baby grand piano in front of her. She hadn't played in a long time. 'It would have to be very quick,' she said. 'A minute and no longer.'

Beatrice grinned.

Emma decided on the first movement of Beethoven's *Moonlight Sonata*. It was relatively easy and it had been a favourite of hers as a child. She stretched her fingers out across the keys.

As soon as she began, the slow motion of the piece had a lulling effect. She felt the tension leave her shoulders, and she smiled as she realised her fingers recalled exactly what to do. She'd played this piece so often that her hands moved instinctively with the music. She closed her eyes, enjoying the sensation of the music coming from somewhere deep within her.

She could hear her father's soft voice again, guiding her through the piece and reminding her when to accentuate certain phrases and lighten her touch for others. 'Don't rush,' he'd always said. 'The skill is to slow down as much as you can.'

A minute passed and she paused.

'Don't stop!' whispered Beatrice. 'It's beautiful. I want to hear more.'

Emma continued and the steady rhythm of the music carried her through for the next few minutes. Eventually, her hands moved down to the bass notes to play the finishing chords.

A ripple of applause startled her. She turned to see Beatrice's mother, two maids and the housekeeper applauding her.

Her face immediately flushed hot. 'I'm sorry,' she said. 'Beatrice asked me to play something and I got a little carried away.'

'It was wonderful to listen to,' said Mrs Montgomery. 'You're very talented indeed, Mrs Langley.'

After the lesson, Emma travelled by omnibus to Holborn.

She stepped into the smart terraced building on Bedford Row.

'I would like to speak with Mr Haskins at Fenners and Company,' she said to the clerk behind the desk in the marble entrance hall.

'Mr Haskins no longer works for the company,' he replied briskly.

'Really? When did he leave?'

'Last month, I believe.'

'Where does he work now?'

'I don't know.' He glanced past her shoulder, as if keen to bring their exchange to a close.

'Oh.' She paused to gather her thoughts. 'What does Fenners and Company have to do with Cardwell and Theobald?'

'They're both law firms.' He rearranged some papers on his desk.

'I realise that. But they share this address. Are they actually the same company?'

The clerk's face stiffened. 'I'm afraid I'm unable to answer your questions, madam.'

Was it because he didn't know or didn't wish to say? Emma couldn't decide. 'Very well,' she said. 'Can I speak with Mr Theobald please?'

'You can inquire at his offices on the third floor.'

'Thank you.'

Emma climbed the staircase, wondering what had happened to Thomas Haskins. Had his departure had something to do with the list of debtors? Or had the reason been something more mundane?

'Mrs Langley.' Mr Theobald smiled when he greeted her, but his eyes remained cold. 'How are you getting on with Mr O'Brien?'

She didn't want to antagonise him at this moment by telling him she no longer wished to use his services. 'He's very helpful, thank you.'

'Any problems?'

'No. No problems with Mr O'Brien at all.'

'Good.' He paused and the brief silence made her feel unwelcome. 'So what can I help you with today?' He checked his pocket watch. 'I have about five minutes spare.'

'I came here to speak to Mr Haskins at Fenners and Company but I understand he no longer works for the firm.'

'Mr Haskins?' Mr Theobald's expression remained impassive. 'Yes, I believe he left the company.'

'Did you know him?'

'In passing. He worked in this building.'

'Is Fenners and Company part of Cardwell and Theobald?'

He checked his watch again then glanced around. 'I'm not sure why you're asking me these questions, Mrs Langley, but I'll do my best to help. Let's talk in the boardroom again.'

He strode on ahead of her and she sensed some irritability in his manner. It made her nervous.

Inside the boardroom, a maid was dusting the portraits of the distinguished gentlemen on the wall. She gave Mr Theobald a considerate bow and left the room. He pulled out a chair for Emma, then seated himself in the chair at the top of the well-polished table.

'Why do you wish to speak to Mr Haskins?' he asked.

'He's been mentioned in some news reports about people who've got into trouble because they owe money,' said Emma. Mr Theobald said nothing, so she continued. 'He appears to have been the counsel for a butcher called Mr Dyer who was convicted of burgling a warehouse. He stole to repay a debt. And then there was another poor gentleman, Mr Templeman. He also owed money but tragically fell from the Imperial Warehouses in Leman Street. A man called Thomas Haskins tried to save him but sadly failed. I'm wondering if it was the same Thomas Haskins in both cases.'

Another pause followed. 'Well, you would have to ask him that.'

'That's what I came here to do today, but I've learned he's left the company. Do you know where I can find him.'

'No, I'm afraid not.' He shifted in his chair and cleared his throat. 'How did you happen across these newspaper reports?'

'I found the names Mr Dyer and Mr Templeman on a list of people who owed money.'

He pushed his chair back and got to his feet. 'I apologise for cutting our meeting short, but I did say I only had five minutes available. As I understand it, Thomas Haskins left on bad terms.' He stepped over to the door, opened it and gestured for her to leave.

SIXTY-FOUR

'What is that widow up to, Edward?' said Cardwell.

Edward Theobald sat in the leather buttoned chair next to the fireplace in Cardwell's office. 'She's learned something, that's for sure. And she's working with a former news reporter called Mrs Blakely.'

Cardwell groaned. 'A news reporter? That's all we need.' He opened his snuff tin, placed a pinch of snuff at the base of his thumb and sniffed.

'A *lady* news reporter,' said Edward. 'So she's probably even more trouble than her male counterparts. The widow asked me about Haskins.'

'Haskins?' Cardwell dabbed his nose with his handkerchief. 'Forget about Haskins. She's got no chance of getting to the truth, even with a lady news reporter in tow.'

'But it's troublesome.'

'Yes, but I have every confidence you can deal with it, Edward.'

'Me?' It seemed Cardwell didn't want to share the responsibility.

'Yes. You saw off the chap from Scotland Yard without too much trouble.'

'I'm sure he'll be back.'

'So you'll need to prepare something, Edward,' said Cardwell, steepling his fingers.

'Why didn't he speak to you?'

Cardwell gave a dry smile. 'Perhaps I've been a little more careful than you, Edward.'

He felt a bitter taste in his mouth. He'd always trusted Robert Cardwell. Had he made a mistake?

'So you're telling me your name isn't mentioned once in all those papers that fool Ratcliffe had in his possession?'

'I really couldn't say.'

'You're being evasive, Robert.'

'No, I'm not. I don't know if my name is in those papers. Only Ratcliffe and the police know that. Perhaps the Yard will call on me next time? I have something prepared if they do.'

Edward got to his feet. 'Well, I hope they do. Because I shouldn't be answerable to this alone.'

'Absolutely not. That wouldn't be fair, would it?' Cardwell gave another smile.

Edward left the office wondering if he'd been betrayed.

SIXTY-FIVE

Emma called on Penny after her conversation with Mr Theobald.

'He succeeded in sending me away without me learning anything further,' she told her. 'I feel sure he's hiding something.'

'So you had no success in finding the mysterious Thomas Haskins?'

'No. And no one seems able to tell me where he's gone.'

'Which is surprising when you consider he worked for a company which was also established by Mr Cardwell and Mr Theobald,' said Penny.

'So the two firms are linked as we suspected? How did you find that out?'

'I visited Somerset House earlier today,' said Penny. 'They hold public records there and that includes company records. I asked to look at the record for Fenners and Company and discovered it was established by Mr Cardwell and Mr Theobald earlier this year.'

'Mr Theobald withheld that from me,' said Emma. 'I wonder why?'

'Because Fenners and Company must have something to do with the moneylending,' said Penny. 'James's nephew, Richard, has found more evidence.'

Emma's heart skipped. 'Has he?'

'Yes, he's spoke to five more people on the list of debtors at the weekend. In two cases, he spoke to their families because the men were in prison. They were both convicted of stealing. In two other cases, they refused to speak to him about their debts. And in the final case, a man told Richard that Thomas Haskins had advised him on how to repay the money.'

'Why would Mr Haskins have done that?'

'Richard got the impression Haskins was a debt collector masquerading as a friendly lawyer offering free legal advice. He claimed to wish to help but he was also intent on ensuring every penny was repaid.'

'With interest, presumably.'

'Yes. With a lot of interest. After visiting Somerset House, I went to the reading room today and looked up the convictions in the newspapers. The reports said both men were represented by Thomas Haskins.'

'So Haskins could have been involved with most of the debtors on that list,' said Emma, shaking her head. 'And I can only guess that when Mr Templeman was on top of the Imperial Warehouses, Thomas Haskins heard about it and went there to talk him down.'

'Yes, I think so,' said Penny. 'He didn't want Mr Templeman to jump, did he? Because then the debt would have been harder to recover.'

'So did anyone tell Richard who the moneylender was?' asked Emma.

'Unfortunately, no. They refused to say and Richard suspects it's because they're scared. Haskins has clearly been working for someone and we need to find out who it is.'

'Cardwell and Theobald are connected with this, I'm sure

of it' said Emma. 'But they're not going to answer our questions, are they?'

'No,' said Penny. 'We're going to have to look for evidence.'

'Where?'

'In their offices.'

'How?'

'We go in there.'

'Break in?'

'Sort of.'

Emma laughed. 'No, we can't do that. It's impossible.'

'Is it?' said Penny, giving her a sly wink.

Emma thought about the layout of the offices and the people she'd seen there. She recalled the maid who'd been dusting the portraits in the boardroom. 'Perhaps there's a way we can sneak in.'

SIXTY-SIX

'Everyone ready?'

Samuel Carter drained his tankard and wiped his mouth with his rough coat sleeve. The bar of The Crown public house on Mile End Road was busy this evening. The members of the vigilance committee had just had their meeting upstairs and now, after a swift drink, they were ready to begin the evening patrols.

Mr Mackenzie, the head of the committee, read out the list of names and beats.

'Carter!'

'Here.' He raised a hand.

'You can take our new member with you on the Brady Street beat.' Mackenzie turned to the new member. 'Remind me of your name again?'

'Mr Flynn.'

Samuel didn't like the look of Mr Flynn. He didn't like his oiled hair, obsequious grin and moustache which curled at the ends. Flynn was slight too; he was unlikely to put up a decent fight. Gone were the days when the vigilance committee could choose from a number of well-built volunteers. And now they were down to only two on each beat.

Samuel picked up his stick and checked his coat pocket for his whistle.

'All set?' he asked Flynn.

Flynn grinned. 'Absolutely.'

'See you back here at four,' said Mackenzie as the patrols left by the door.

Outside on Mile End Road, they turned left and headed west to where the thoroughfare became Whitechapel Road. Their rubber galoshes were noiseless on the pavement.

A small crowd thronged outside the assembly hall across the road and the public houses were well lit and noisy.

'So what do you do for a living?' Flynn asked Samuel.

'I'm a cabman.'

'That must keep you busy.'

'It does indeed.'

'And you must know these streets very well.'

'That's right. It's my job to.'

'I have a picture framing shop on Crispin Street,' said Flynn. 'Just behind Spitalfields Market.'

'I know it.'

'Yes, I suppose you would. It was my father's shop. He died ten years ago and now I run it with my mother.'

'Do you do good business there?'

'Oh yes. Very good.'

They reached the crossroads. 'We need to cross over,' said Samuel, leading the way across the street. They passed the Blind Beggar public house and Samuel longed to go inside for a pint of mild ale.

They turned right and walked along Brady Street, passing the Albion Brewery on their right. Its strong malty odour seemed stronger than usual in the still night air.

Samuel stopped once they reached a streetlamp level with

the junction on the opposite side of the street. 'Now this is where we wait,' he said.

'Why?'

'We wait for the constable walking this beat. That road opposite is Buck's Row and, in a moment, we'll see the constable walking towards us. His beat takes fifteen minutes. Have you got a watch on you?'

'Oh yes.' Flynn pulled aside his overcoat and pulled a watch from his waistcoat. It glimmered shiny gold in the light of the gas lamp.

'That's a nice watch,' said Samuel.

'It was my father's. And it's as accurate as the day he first bought it.'

'Good. Well, once the copper's passed us, we wait seven and a half minutes and then we begin our walk around the beat.'

'Why seven and a half?'

'Because if the copper on his beat passes the same spot every fifteen minutes and we follow seven and a half minutes behind him, that spot is then passed every seven and a half minutes. Does that make sense?'

'Ah yes! Ingenious! And seven and a half minutes doesn't give Jack enough time to do his business, does it?'

'Hopefully not. And if you see anything untoward, blow your whistle and everyone within earshot will come running.'

'Buck's Row,' said Flynn. 'That's where they found Polly Nichols, isn't it? And to think the constable on his beat never saw anything. The killer must have waited for him to pass. No one in any of the houses heard a thing! And when they found her, she was still warm.'

'Here comes the constable now,' said Samuel, keen to interrupt Flynn.

A lantern on the street revealed the constable in his long,

belted overcoat and domed helmet. He joined them a minute later.

'Evening PC Harris,' said Samuel. 'Everything quiet this evening?'

'Yes. Let's hope it stays that way.' He checked his watch, then headed off towards Whitechapel Road.

'What's the time?' Samuel asked Flynn.

'Half past midnight.'

'In seven and a half minutes, we follow Harris.'

'How long have you been doing this?' asked Flynn.

'We started our patrols on the tenth of September, after the murder of Annie Chapman. There aren't many of us left from those days. It can get exhausting after a while. Especially if you've got to get up early for work. As a cabman, I can choose my hours.'

'Do you go out every night?'

'I go out as many nights as I can. Some nights I have to work if I'm short of money.'

'Didn't the patrols stop for a while?'

'Yeah, after six weeks we were all getting tired. We were running short of men and money. We kept going until the third week of October, then we had to call it off.'

'I think everyone hoped Jack the Ripper had stopped his tricks,' said Flynn. 'There wasn't a murder in October, was there?'

'No. But then Mary Kelly happened on the ninth of November. So that's why we're all out again now. Lord knows when he's going to stop. I think we'll get him, though. He can't keep getting away with it.'

Eventually it was time to begin their beat, and they walked back down Brady Street to Whitechapel Road. At the bottom of the road, they turned right and passed more public houses, the Working Lads Institute and the railway station. Lights glimmered from the London Hospital on the opposite side of the road.

'It's not just Jack the Ripper though, is it?' said Flynn. 'That gentleman was attacked in Green Dragon Yard. And then there was a woman on Fleur de Lis Street.'

'Very tragic,' said Samuel. 'I don't know what the world's coming to. The gentleman hailed my cab.'

Flynn stopped and gasped. 'You're the cabman who picked him up?'

Samuel nodded. 'Keep walking. We've got to keep pace.'

'Oh yes, of course. Seven and a half minutes. What happened that night?'

'I was coming up this road from the City when he waved me down. I had no idea he was injured, he just looked slightly the worse for drink. He got in and asked to be taken to a lodging house on Canrobert Street in Bethnal Green. We need to turn right here.'

They turned into Baker's Row. The street was much narrower than Whitechapel Road and poorly lit.

'And when you got to the lodging house, you realised he was dead. Is that right?'

'That's right. There was no answer when I opened the hatch. So I climbed down to see if he was all right and there he was. All slumped over.' Samuel shook his head. 'There was a lot of blood.'

'Was there?' Flynn's voice sounded interested rather than appalled.

'Very sad.'

'Yes, very sad indeed.'

They reached the next streetlamp at the same time as a woman in a headscarf and shawl. She carried a bag.

'It's not safe for you to walk around here on your own,' Samuel said to her. 'If you're going to be out after dark, then you must have someone with you.'

'That's easier said than done,' she said sharply. 'I had to go out on an errand. I'm on my way home now. I'll be all right.'

She walked off into the darkness.

'It's not hard to see how these poor creatures fall prey to Jack, is it?' said Flynn. 'A woman like that can't put up any defence at all. It's astonishing how many of them still go out on their own after everything that's happened. I've forbidden my mother from going out after dark. Not that she likes to, anyway. I don't see why any sensible woman would.'

'It gets dark early at this time of year,' said Samuel. 'It's not easy for everyone to stay indoors from half past four.'

'Then women should be accompanied, just as you told that lady. If they all did that, then Jack would run out of prey, wouldn't he?'

Samuel grimaced. He didn't like Flynn's turn of phrase.

'Jack likes writing letters, doesn't he?' continued Flynn. 'Have you read any of them in the newspapers?'

'They're hoaxes.'

'That's what people say. But how can they be so sure? With all the fuss that's being made about him, it makes sense to me Jack would have his say. He sent a kidney to the vigilance committee, didn't he?' Flynn sniggered and Samuel chose not to respond. The actions of the Whitechapel murderer sickened him. That's why he did what he could on the patrols.

They turned right into Thomas Street, then into Queen Anne Street.

'Do you like horses?' Flynn asked.

Samuel sighed, irritated by the man's conversation. 'I've had a few interesting characters pulling my cab, if that's what you mean.'

'I mean the races.'

'I go to them occasionally.'

'I like to offer odds on them. Just for a bit of fun. I've got a very nice tape machine which gets all the updates from

Newmarket to Newbury, Chepstow to Cheltenham. I do it on the quiet, you know. For obvious reasons. Don't go telling everyone about it, otherwise it ruins our fun.'

Although Samuel didn't like Flynn, the thought of winning some money on the horses was appealing.

'I might drop by the next time I find myself near the market,' he said.

'Oh do! Buy a copy of the *Sporting Life* first and see what you fancy.'

A loud peel of a whistle sounded out from a street nearby. Samuel's heart skipped and he tightened his grip on his stick. 'That doesn't sound good. It might be nothing more than a drunken fight, but we should go and find out.'

SIXTY-SEVEN

Emma spent much of the following day at Penny's home as they prepared for their clandestine visit to Cardwell and Theobald's offices.

By half past four they were ready.

'This is only going to work if Mr Theobald finishes work at six,' said Emma. 'If he decides to stay in his office for longer then our plans are scuppered.'

'True,' said Penny. 'There's certainly a risk he doesn't leave work on time. But if we can't get what we need this evening, then we can attempt it again.'

'Really?' Emma didn't like the thought of trying a second time. She didn't think her nerves would stand it.

They arrived at the Bedford Row offices at a quarter to six and paused for a moment in the street. Lights glimmered from the windows and Emma imagined everyone inside busily working. She felt her stomach turn.

'I'm nervous,' she said.

'Me too,' said Penny. 'But you need to pretend you're not.

The trick is to walk about inside the building as if we have every right to be there. If we can appear confident and assertive, then people are less likely to challenge us.'

'That makes sense.' Emma took in a breath, relaxed her shoulders and tried to stand a little taller.

They both wore brown wigs and maid uniforms: black cotton dresses with starched white aprons and white cotton bonnets. Penny had hired the uniforms and also found a pair of spectacles with plain, round lenses for Emma to wear. Having visited the offices twice before, Emma knew there was a risk she could be recognised. She hoped the spectacles gave her some disguise.

'Are you ready?' asked Penny.

'Yes. I'm ready.'

They climbed the steps and Penny pushed open the door. In the marble entrance hall, the clerk peered at them from behind his polished desk.

'Evening, we're here from the agency,' said Penny before he could speak. She marched towards the staircase and Emma followed as if she walked the route every day. To her relief, the clerk said nothing.

They climbed the stairs to the third floor. As part of their preparations, Emma had sketched a plan of the offices so Penny knew exactly where to go.

They passed through the door which opened onto the corridor. With barely a glance around her, Penny turned right and headed towards the boardroom. Emma followed, amused by the bustling gait Penny had assumed for her role as a maid. Emma tried to imitate it as best she could.

In the corridor, they passed the junior clerk with oiled hair who Emma had spoken to on her last visit. She held her breath, trying to remember Penny's words to act confident. He examined some papers as he walked and gave them no acknowledgement. Emma breathed a sigh of relief.

They reached the boardroom. The door was closed.

Emma kept watch as Penny pressed her ear to the door and listened. 'I don't think there's anyone in there,' she said. She turned the handle, and they stepped into the room.

'Right then,' said Penny. 'This looks like it needs a good dusting.' She pulled a rag out of her apron and began rubbing the table with it.

Emma closed the door, trying not to laugh. 'We did it!' she whispered.

Penny grinned. 'It's easier than you think, isn't it? Someone is bound to grow suspicious of us before long, but we mustn't let that worry us for now. We can wait here for ten minutes until Theobald leaves his office at six o'clock. Then we can go in there and have a look around.' She glanced at the row of important-looking gentlemen on the wall. 'It feels like we're being watched, doesn't it?'

Emma nodded. 'None of them look like they'd be much fun at a party.'

Their laughter was cut short by the sound of footsteps out in the corridor. Penny returned to polishing the table while Emma pulled out her duster and wiped it around one of the ornate picture frames.

The door opened and a man with a bald head and wiry eyebrows peered in.

Emma and Penny stopped and smiled.

'Oh,' he said. 'They finished, did they?'

'Yes, they did, sir,' said Penny.

'I thought they were going on until six.'

'They finished a little earlier than planned, sir.'

'I can see that. Very well. Good evening.'

He closed the door again, and Emma and Penny exchanged a grin.

'I'm almost enjoying this,' whispered Emma.

They pretended to dust for a little while longer and then the gold clock on the mantelpiece struck six.

'Right,' said Penny. 'Hopefully Theobald will be leaving now. We need to get into his office before it's locked for the evening.'

They opened the boardroom door and walked back along the corridor. Penny paused a few times to rub her cleaning rag over the wainscoting, and Emma did the same. Gentlemen strode past them in their hats and coats, clearly keen to be heading home for the day.

They reached the door to the offices and Penny marched through it. Emma followed and felt relieved to see no one sitting at the desks between the wood-panelled partitions. The door of Mr Theobald's office at the back of the room was closed.

Emma and Penny dusted the desks as they gradually made their way towards the door.

Then it opened and Mr Theobald stepped out.

Emma startled, crouched down and busied herself with cleaning the legs of a nearby desk. Although she was wearing spectacles, she couldn't risk the possibility that Mr Theobald might recognise her. She turned away from him, fixing her gaze on the woodgrain in the leg of the desk.

He strode past them, but then his footsteps stopped. Emma's heart pounded heavily in her chest. If Mr Theobald recognised her, the plan would be ruined.

'What's going on here?' he asked.

'The agency sent us, sir,' said Penny.

'Why?'

'We were told extra cleaning was needed.'

'By who?'

'I don't know, sir. I only know what the agency told us.'

'Did Mrs Norris agree to it?'

'Yes, I think she must have done, sir.'

'Good.' A pause followed and Emma remained in her

crouched position, polishing the desk leg as thoroughly as possible. 'Extra cleaning, eh?' continued Mr Theobald. 'I think everything looks clean enough. Anyway, good evening to you.'

'And to you, sir,' said Penny.

Emma felt herself relax as he left the room. She got up on her feet, feeling a little light-headed.

'Are you ready?' Penny whispered.

Emma nodded, and they made their way towards Mr Theobald's office. Penny opened the door, and they stepped inside.

The room was spacious and smelled of wood smoke and leather. A fire was dying down in the hearth. Penny switched on a brass lamp which stood on a large, mahogany desk. The desk was tidy, as if Mr Theobald had made an effort to put all his papers away. Bookcases lined the walls, filled with volumes bound in leather with gold embossing. Two comfortable leather chairs sat on an ornate rug by the marble fireplace.

'Let's try the drawers in the desk,' whispered Penny. She pulled out the drawers on one side while Emma pulled out the drawers on the other. She found inkpots, notebooks, blotting paper and a tin of throat lozenges.

'Nothing here,' Penny said.

'Nor here,' Emma remarked looking around the room. 'How about the bookcases?'

The lower section of each bookcase had a cupboard. They crouched and began searching through. Papers were neatly stacked, rolled and tied into bundles with string. The more Emma looked, the less certain she was of what she was searching for. The documents had company names on them and complicated legal language. She reasoned it was easy to hide criminal activity in a dull, long-winded legal document. Few people would have the patience to read and decipher it.

Penny seemed equally underwhelmed by the papers she

was finding. 'There's nothing here, is there?' she said. 'Nothing which makes much sense to me, anyway.'

'We need a few days to search through this office,' said Emma. 'Not a few minutes.' Her heart was beating wildly in her chest. What if they got caught? 'If you wanted to hide something here, where would you put it?'

'The cupboards are too obvious, aren't they?' said Penny. She closed the doors and stood up. Then she pulled a volume out from a bookcase. 'Nothing hidden in here,' she said, leafing through the pages.

Emma ran her eyes over the books on the shelves. Some were older and more worn than others. But a row of black leather volumes seemed different. Each one was identical and appeared shiny and new. She pulled one out. The edges of its pages were gilded with gold. As she tried to open the book, she realised the pages were glued together.

Her heart quickened. 'There's something strange about this,' she whispered to Penny. The volume was large and heavy. She rested it on the floor and Penny joined her as she lifted the cover.

'Good grief!' whispered Penny.

The book contained a rectangular recess where the pages had been cut away. And within the recess sat a small leather folder tied shut with a lace. Emma's fingers fumbled as she untied the lace. She knew if someone walked into the room at this moment, she and Penny would be in trouble. They couldn't pretend to be cleaning with the large book open at their feet.

Once she'd untied the lace, Emma opened the leather folder. Pages of notes had been placed inside it. They contained lines of handwritten numbers.

'More coded messages!' she whispered.

'Take them,' said Penny. 'Put them in your apron pockets. I'll see if there are any more.'

She reached for the next volume as Emma pushed the

papers into the bottom of her apron pocket. Then she replaced the leather folder, closed the book and put it back on the shelf.

'There are more!' said Penny, opening the next volume. She untied the lace of the leather folder. 'Some letters,' she whispered. 'Not written in code. These look like demands for money.'

'Demands? From who?'

'Mr Utterson.'

'Utterson?'

'Yes. And a letter here mentions Barnaby Ratcliffe.'

Emma crouched down next to her to see it.

Your wealthy and reputable clients would be disappointed to learn of your association with the criminal Mr Barnaby Ratcliffe. I will be happy to remain silent on the matter for the sum of fifty pounds.

I request the banknotes be placed in a folded newspaper and left on the bench closest to the fountain in Red Lion Square this Thursday at four pm.

Mr Utterson

'Someone was blackmailing them,' said Penny. 'Someone who knew they were doing work for Barnaby Ratcliffe.

Emma felt nauseous. 'I think I can guess who,' she said. 'Mr Utterson is a character in the *Strange Case of Dr Jekyll and Mr Hyde*. It was one of William's favourite books.'

Penny's jaw dropped. 'You think William wrote this?'

Emma nodded. 'He's disguised his handwriting a little, but I think it could be his.'

'We'll have a closer look once we get out of here,' said Penny, pushing the letter into the pocket of her apron. 'Let's get as much as we can.'

Emma got to her feet and pulled out the next book.

'We can't stay here much longer,' she said hurriedly. 'Someone might find us.'

'I know,' said Penny. 'Just a few more.'

They worked methodically, taking the volumes from the shelves and removing the papers from each identical leather folder.

After five volumes, Emma decided she'd taken enough. 'There's not much room left in my pockets,' she said. 'We should leave.'

'Do another one,' said Penny quickly.

'I think we have enough. We can't take all of them.'

'Just one more!'

Emma felt a prickle of anxiety as she took out the next volume. She wanted to leave while they had a chance. If someone walked into the office and found them there, they would be in serious trouble.

Especially if it was Mr Theobald.

Emma worked as quickly as she could. But her hands fumbled as she hurried to put the book back and it slipped from her grasp. It fell onto the floorboards with a deafening thud.

Emma froze, startled by the noise.

'Oh no,' said Penny. 'Someone will have heard that.'

'I'm so sorry!' whispered Emma, picking up the book.

Penny pushed her book back onto the shelf. 'We must leave,' she said. Emma felt sure she was angry with her. Trembling with nerves, she put the book back and picked up her cleaning rag.

'Let's go,' said Penny, heading for the door. Emma switched off the lamp on the desk and followed her.

Penny opened the door, but stopped as soon as she did so. A stern woman in a black dress and apron was striding towards them. 'Who are you?' she demanded.

'We were sent by the agency,' said Penny.

'Who at the agency?'

'Mrs Carwardine.'

'Who? I've never heard of her.'

'She told us extra cleaning was needed. We've done all we can now, so we'll be off.' Penny stepped past her, and Emma did the same.

'Which agency do you work for?' asked the woman.

Penny continued walking and mumbled something indistinct over her shoulder.

'I didn't hear what you said!' called out the woman.

Penny walked through the door and suddenly took off down the staircase. Emma did the same, jumping down the steps two at a time.

'Come back here!' said the woman. Emma heard her footsteps behind them. Her legs found an extra burst of energy and she caught up with Penny. Her head grew dizzy as they fled together down the staircase.

In the entrance hall, their feet echoed on the tiled floor as they raced for the door. Emma had no idea how close their pursuer was, all she could do was concentrate on getting outside.

Penny pulled open the door, and Emma followed. Together, they leapt down the stone steps outside and reached the street.

'Let's go left,' gasped Penny.

Emma took in a lungful of cold evening air. They made the sharp turn and ran as fast as they could towards the lights of Holborn.

SIXTY-EIGHT

Emma and Penny arranged the papers they'd taken from Mr Theobald's office on Mr and Mrs Solomon's dining table that evening.

'It looks like Mr Utterson wrote five notes asking for money,' said Penny. 'I wonder if they paid him?'

'I can imagine they would have done,' said Emma. 'They would have wanted to keep their association with Barnaby Ratcliffe quiet. If William was the blackmailer, then he might have put the money into his bank account.'

'You really think William could be behind this?'

'I don't see why not. He was ruthless enough to marry me solely for my inheritance. Blackmailing a law firm seems fairly tame in comparison.'

Penny sighed. 'Sadly, I agree. Shall we visit the bank tomorrow?'

'Yes. I have some lessons to teach but I'll be finished by two.'

'Where's the bank?'

'Wyndham and Co on Lombard Street.'

'Shall I see you there at half past two?'

Emma nodded. 'And in the meantime, I'll have a look at these notes written in code.'

'Really? I was planning to take them to Mr Hobhouse.'

'There might be no need. If these have also been written using the Declaration of Independence as the key text, then I think I can decipher them.'

'It's a lot of work.'

'It's fine.' Emma smiled. 'I shall enjoy it.'

SIXTY-NINE

'Agatha would like to learn a song,' said her mother. 'Her cousin can play lots of songs.'

'I will teach Agatha a song as soon as she knows the notes,' said Emma firmly.

'She knows the notes! Don't you, Agatha?' her mother said confidently, giving her daughter a sharp look.

The young girl nodded nervously.

'She knows some of them and she's doing very well,' said Emma. 'She just needs to know all of them so hopefully we can achieve that in the next lesson.'

Agatha was a slow learner, but Emma didn't want to say that to the girl and her mother.

'And when can she play with both hands? Her cousin can play with both hands.'

'When we've learned the notes on the bass clef.'

The mother turned to her daughter. 'Does Mabel know all the notes on the bass clef?'

Agatha shook her head.

'There you go, you see, Mrs Langley. Her cousin Mabel

doesn't know all the notes on the bass clef and yet she's playing with both hands.'

Emma smiled. 'That's impressive indeed. If you would excuse me, I have to be in the City by half past two and really need to leave now if that's all right.'

'Very well. We shall discuss this some more at the next lesson.'

'I look forward to it,' Emma lied, mustering a smile before she put on her hat and coat and dashed out of the door.

She arrived at Wyndham and Co on Lombard Street out of breath and coughing. She was just recovering herself when a four-wheeled hackney carriage came to a stop. The driver hopped down and tied the reins around a bollard. The carriage door opened and an enormous green perambulator edged out.

'Got it!' said the driver, holding the end of the perambulator as it was slowly lowered out of the carriage. Holding the other end was Penny. She smiled when she saw Emma.

'Hello! We won't be a moment. I forgot Mrs Tuttle had the day off today to visit her mother, so I've had to bring the children with me. I'm sure they won't be any trouble in the bank.'

'Oh, I'm sorry you've had to bring your children, Penny. We can do this at another time if you prefer?'

'No need! It will be fine.'

Emma held the perambulator on the pavement while Penny helped Thomas out of the carriage. Baby Florence was tucked up in warm blankets. She stared unblinkingly at Emma.

'Are we in London?' Thomas asked, glancing wide-eyed at the tall buildings around them.

'Yes, we're always in London, Thomas,' said Penny as she paid the driver. 'This is the City of London. There are lots of banks and other important buildings here. Now you're going to be good while we speak to the man in the bank, aren't you?'

Thomas nodded.

He was instructed to hold on to the perambulator while Penny and Emma lifted it up the steps to the bank's entrance. Then Emma held the doors open as Penny wheeled the perambulator into the banking hall with the high vaulted ceiling.

One of the wheels emitted a loud, regular squeak as they crossed the tiled floor to the clerks. 'Oh dear,' said Penny as faces turned to look at them. 'I should have oiled it after that walk in the rain last week.'

'Is this the bank?' asked Thomas.

'Yes, this is the bank.'

Emma spoke to one of the clerks and she was shown to Mr Blythe's office again.

Mr Blythe frowned as Penny tried to edge the perambulator through the doorway. It was barely wide enough.

'Must that come in here?' he said. 'Can't it be left outside?'

'My baby daughter's in it,' said Penny. 'And she's just drifting off to sleep. I'd rather not leave her outside, I'm worried someone might take her.'

'I can't imagine that happening.'

'But you can't be certain.'

'No, I suppose you can't. Do take a seat.' He smiled at Thomas. 'Hello, young man.'

Thomas turned away and hid behind the perambulator.

'How can I help?' asked Mr Blythe, adjusting his steel-rimmed spectacles.

'I would like to look at my husband's bank accounts,' said Emma.

'Mrs Langley, isn't it?'

'Yes.'

'You've looked at them before, isn't that right?'

'Yes.'

'And your solicitor has been in here looking through them, too.'

'Yes.'

'May I ask why you wish to look at them again? As I recall, there's no money left in them.'

'No. But I would like to look at the details of what's gone in and out over the past few months.'

'And your friend here?'

'This is Mrs Blakely. She's assisting me. She's a former news reporter and her husband is an inspector at Scotland Yard.'

'She's assisting you?'

'Yes. I'm concerned there may be some anomalies in the accounts, so she's going to look at them with me.'

'Surely your solicitor can help with anomalies?'

'I would like to do this myself.'

'Oh. I see. I have to say that this is a rather unusual arrangement. And I need to remind you, Mrs Langley, that probate has not yet been granted. It makes matters rather complicated.'

'Are you aware of the circumstances of William Langley's death?' asked Penny.

'Yes I am. It was most unfortunate.'

'Most unfortunate? Is that an appropriate way to describe his brutal murder? A violent murder which was carried out by a culprit yet to be apprehended.' Penny leaned forward, lowering her voice. 'I must say that Mrs Langley has coped with her husband's sudden and tragic death with a dignity and poise which I have never previously observed in a person, Mr Blythe. She has spoken to you today with a brave and respectful politeness which I'm doubting is even warranted. And yet you make comments about an unusual arrangement and matters being complicated.' She paused to stare at Mr Blythe but he gave no response. 'What is so complicated about a grieving widow asking to see the transactions in her late husband's bank accounts?' she asked. 'What more can you possibly ask of her? Do you expect a widow in mourning to kneel at your feet and beg?'

Mr Blythe adjusted his spectacles again and appeared lost for words. 'I shall fetch the accounts,' he said quietly.

Emma was stunned.

'Thank you, Penny... I don't know how you find the words like that.'

'Practice,' said Penny. 'I've met a lot of obstinate people in my time.'

Thomas appeared from behind the perambulator as soon as he left the room. 'Where's the man gone?' he asked.

'He's gone to fetch the accounts.'

'What's the counts?'

'Some important papers. Would you like to play with your train?'

Thomas nodded and Penny pulled the wooden toy out of her carpet bag. Thomas happily took it from her and began pushing it on the desk, making choo choo sounds.

Mr Blythe returned to the room with two folders under his arm.

'Oh hello young man,' he said to Thomas enthusiastically. 'That's a rather fine engine, isn't it?'

Thomas ran back behind the perambulator.

Mr Blythe placed the folders on the desk and opened them. 'This one is the current account,' he said. 'You can see the balance is five shillings. And here is the savings account. There's no balance at all. The remaining sum of forty-seven pounds was withdrawn on the fifth of November.'

'When did William leave the law firm?' Penny asked Emma.

'At the end of July. The twenty-seventh.'

'Let's look that up.' Penny leafed through the pages of the current account. 'Here we are! William received fifty pounds on the twenty-seventh of July.'

'That fits with one of the notes we found,' said Emma. 'It mentioned fifty pounds.'

'That's right,' said Penny. 'What was his salary, if you don't mind me asking?'

'Seventy pounds a year,' said Emma.

'If he earned seventy pounds a year, then his monthly salary would have been about five pounds and thirteen shillings. Let's look at June... yes, there's an amount there which could have been his salary. And the same in May too... and April. It looks like that was his salary. And then, after July, it stops. Which is what you'd expect because he left the firm then. Then he received fifty pounds and then... oh look. Twenty pounds at the end of August. And twenty pounds again at the end of September... This appears to be a regular payment.'

'There it is in October,' said Emma.

'You're right. And November... nothing.'

Florence let out a couple of cries which were followed by a large wail.

Mr Blythe startled. 'Good grief.'

Penny got up and rocked the handle of the perambulator to soothe Florence. The springs creaked. 'So the question is,' she said over Florence's cries, 'where was that payment of twenty pounds coming from?'

'The law firm?' shouted Emma.

'It has to be!'

Florence grew louder. Mr Blythe ran a fretful hand over his thin grey hair.

Penny lifted Florence out of the perambulator and cuddled her to her shoulder. 'And what about the savings account?' she asked over the wails.

Emma looked through the pages. 'I recognise the deposits from the sale of the house and the furniture,' she shouted. 'But the rest of the transactions are withdrawals. He took everything.'

Mr Blythe got to his feet. 'Ladies?'

They both stared at him and he scratched the back of his neck.

'Perhaps you can both come back another time?' he called out over the crying baby. 'Maybe without the—'

'It's all right,' Penny cut in brusquely. 'We've seen enough.'

'Have you?' He smiled with relief. 'Good.'

SEVENTY

Outside the bank on Lombard Street, Florence continued to cry.

'I'm sorry, Emma,' said Penny. 'But I need to get home. Florence won't settle.'

'It's fine,' said Emma.

'I think it's fairly clear William was blackmailing Cardwell and Theobald, isn't it?'

Emma nodded.

'And you know what that means,' said Penny. 'It means he became a nuisance to them.'

'They have a motive for his murder,' said Emma. 'I need to tell Bradshaw this.'

'Yes, we have some evidence now.' Penny winced as Florence wailed loudly in her ear. 'I shall tell James about this and suggest he speaks to Mr Blythe here at the bank.'

Emma hailed a hackney carriage then helped Penny get the children and the perambulator inside it.

· · ·

'Goodness me,' said Mrs Solomon as she peered over Emma's shoulder that evening. 'That looks like a lot of gibberish. What is it?'

'Code,' said Emma.

'And what does it say?'

'I don't know yet. We retrieved these from William's former employer, Cardwell and Theobald.'

'Retrieved?'

Emma didn't want to confess she'd taken them. 'Borrowed. I asked for them and they said I could look at them.' Mrs Solomon gave her a knowing smile.

'And you understand what this code says?'

'Hopefully. All I need to do is use the Declaration of Independence to decode it.' Emma showed her a copy which she had written out at the library and numbered its words. As she explained how the code worked, she noticed Mrs Solomon's face glaze over. She stopped herself and said, 'Actually, there's probably not much use in me explaining the detail.'

'No, there probably isn't. As long as you know what you're doing with it, Mrs Langley, then that's all that matters. Perhaps I could make you a cup of tea?'

'Thank you.'

The work was laborious, but Emma concentrated as well as she could. After a while, she realised she could work quite swiftly. It wasn't too difficult to hold long sequences in her head and she could even memorise a few numbers and the letter they corresponded to.

Laurence the shaggy cat jumped up onto the dining table and observed her for a while. Then he lay down on some of the papers and dozed off.

The note Emma had begun with appeared to be a message with updates on debtors' repayments. As its content seemed mundane, she moved on to another but it was very similar. Emma went through more of the messages, hoping to find some new information. She had to pull some messages out from beneath Laurence, but he didn't appear bothered. Eventually, she stopped and surveyed her work. All the messages had revealed was a discussion about the debts and repayments.

She sat back in her chair and sifted through the coded notes. She felt disappointed that they failed to reveal anything new. She hadn't completed decoding any of them to the end yet because it hadn't seemed worth her while. But as she sipped at her cold and forgotten cup of tea, she noticed a pattern.

Some messages had the same five number pattern at the end. Immediately, she worked to decipher it. She had only translated the first few letters when she suspected what the word was. She continued, just to be certain. Then she wrote it down in large letters and sat back in her chair, exhausted.

The word was a name. Flynn.

SEVENTY-ONE

Emma called on Detective Inspector Bradshaw at Commercial Street police station the following morning.

As she walked, she took in the surrounding sights. The road was busy with carts, carriages and omnibuses. A police officer with white gloves controlled the traffic at the junction with Liverpool Street. A horse pulled a shiny van with *Great Eastern Railway* printed on it in gold lettering.

She passed a gentleman's outfitters, a photographer's studio and a shoe shop. The Metropole restaurant advertised breakfasts, dinner and teas with a ladies' dining room on the first floor. A newsagent had strings of postcards in the window, racks of newspapers and news boards which shouted the day's headlines. A vacant building was covered in bill posters advertising seaside excursions with the Great Eastern Railway to Yarmouth and Clacton-on-Sea.

At the police station, Emma sat with Bradshaw in the room with the grey wainscoting. Smoke rose from the pipe beneath his red moustache as he listened.

'My husband was blackmailing his former employer, the law firm Cardwell and Theobald,' she said. 'Here are the notes he sent to them.'

The inspector examined them. 'Mr Utterson?'

'A character from his favourite book, the *Strange Case of Dr Jekyll and Mr Hyde*.'

'But you have no proof your husband actually wrote these?'

'The amounts he requested correspond with the amounts deposited with his bank Wyndham and Co on Lombard Street. I feel sure they paid him the money these notes ask for.'

'I see.'

'I've also found a list of people who borrowed money.' She passed a copy of the list to him. 'It was originally written in code and hidden in the frame of a painting which my husband had owned. The painting had been framed by Mr Flynn in Crispin Street.'

'This list was hidden in a picture frame?'

'Yes. Some of the debtors have been traced, we know many of them were involved with a lawyer called Thomas Haskins. He worked for a law firm called Fenners and Company. The firm is actually owned by Cardwell and Theobald.'

She sat back in her chair to allow the inspector a moment to understand the information. He took out his pipe and scratched his temple with it.

'I found more notes in Cardwell and Theobald's offices which discussed the debtors and the money they owed. The notes were signed by someone called Flynn.'

'The picture framer?'

'It has to be. I think Flynn is the moneylender and Cardwell and Theobald were assisting him.'

'And what does this have to do with your husband's murder?'

'He was blackmailing Cardwell and Theobald. They wanted to put a stop to it.'

'And the list in his picture frame?'

'I can't be certain he knew about it. But if he did, then maybe he was working with Flynn.'

His brow furrowed. 'I see.'

'And then there's Lady Lou to consider,' continued Emma. 'Last week, Mrs Blakely and I saw her visit Flynn's shop—'

'Mrs Blakely?'

'She used to be a news reporter for the *Morning Express*. She's married to Inspector Blakely at Scotland Yard and she's helping me.'

He shook his head. 'I recall her from the distant past.' Emma sensed his opinion of Penny was unflattering.

'Mrs Blakely and I believe we overheard Flynn and Lady Lou arguing.'

'About what?'

'We don't know. But we do know Lady Lou is associating with Flynn. And I don't think she can be trusted as a witness. She's supposedly the last person who saw my husband before he met his attacker, but we only have her word for that.'

'True.'

'And she carries a knife with her to protect herself. She said it came in useful when she came face to face with Jack the Ripper.'

The inspector smiled. 'If I had a penny for every person who's told me they've met Jack the Ripper, I'd be a rich man by now. Did she make a report to the police about it?'

'I don't know. But she was frightened enough by the incident to leave Whitechapel.'

'Where is she now?'

'In the West End. We spoke to her in the Adelphi arches.'

'You spoke to her there? With who?'

'With Mrs Blakely. We don't think Lady Lou can be trusted.'

'No, she probably can't. She's that sort of character, I'm afraid.'

'Can you question her again to be sure about what she told you?'

He exhaled a cloud of pipe smoke. 'She may not be a trustworthy character, but I found her reliable enough when she made her statement about meeting your husband in Green Dragon Yard.'

'But she's been inconsistent about the time she saw him. She told the inquest it was half past twelve, but told me it was half past eleven. And she had a knife with her and she could have attacked him for the case he was carrying.'

'His case?'

'Yes. He had a case of personal papers which he left with Miss Drummond for a while. Then he collected it from her on the day of his death, and Lady Lou said he had it with him when she saw him. Have you ever found his case?'

'No.'

'Perhaps Lady Lou has hidden it somewhere.'

'If she took it. That doesn't sound like Lady Lou.' He sat back in his chair. 'You do realise that I, and the other officers at this station, are extremely well acquainted with Lady Lou? She's been arrested more times for soliciting and drunkenness than I've had hot dinners. She's many things, but she's not a murderer.'

'And what about Mr Flynn? Can you speak to him?'

He scratched behind his ear. 'You believe he's a moneylender?'

'Yes. I have coded messages he sent to Cardwell and Theobald to prove it.'

'Where did you find the messages?'

Emma paused, realising she had to be careful about admitting to wrongdoing. 'I found them in their offices.'

'You took them?' His eyes widened.

'I took a few. But only because I've been desperate to find out what happened to my husband, Inspector. At least now I have some evidence of wrongdoing.'

'Evidence? It seems to me you've collected an enormous jumble of information and concocted a far-fetched story out of it all.'

'This isn't far-fetched—'

'Spending time with a news reporter is not helping you at all, Mrs Langley.' He gave a snort.

'I disagree. She's helping me enormously.'

'If I were you, Mrs Langley, I'd be careful about who I was spending time with. Although I don't know Mrs Blakely myself, during her days as a news reporter for the *Morning Express* she had quite a reputation.'

'For what?'

'For telling police officers how to do their jobs.'

'She solved cases.'

'Yes, she did. That's because she enlisted the help of Detective Inspector Blakely at Scotland Yard. You don't think she solved all those cases on her own, do you? She had a police officer doing most of the work. And these days she's clearly struggling to accept her career is over now she's married. Quite disgraceful behaviour and I feel sorry for Inspector Blakely. I expect he's tried to put his foot down but she walks all over him, poor fellow.'

Emma felt a snap of anger. 'That's not the case at all! And I don't appreciate you talking about my friend in that way!'

'I can clearly see you're under her influence, Mrs Langley. What a shame. She's encouraged you to meddle in things you don't understand,' he said bitterly.

Emma tried to breathe out her anger. This conversation was proceeding much as she had expected it to. She wished she hadn't come.

'Perhaps you choose not to listen to me, Inspector. But I

warn you now, Mr Flynn is up to no good. The police need to speak to him.'

He blew out a sigh with a puff of pipe smoke. 'The police here have enough to be getting on with, Mrs Langley. Ever heard of Jack the Ripper?'

She felt the anger return. She gathered up her papers and got to her feet, her chest burning with rage. 'You're doing absolutely nothing to investigate the murders of my husband and Miss Drummond! I'd like to take that damn pipe of yours and...'

'And what, Mrs Langley?'

She marched out of the room before she said something she would regret.

SEVENTY-TWO

Outside, Emma leaned against the wall of the police station to recover herself. She had never felt so frustrated and powerless before.

A passer-by stopped. 'Mrs Langley? This is a surprise.'

'Miss Fairchild?' Emma felt immediately irritated by her pretty, smiling face.

'How are you?' asked Miss Fairchild.

'As well as can be.'

'You looked a little bit upset. I can imagine it must be awfully difficult for you at the moment.' Her blue eyes were wide and sympathetic. 'Would you like to come to our stall for a cup of tea?'

'Thank you for the offer, Miss Fairchild, but I'd like to get home.'

'Of course. I completely understand. Have you just had to speak to the police again about your husband's murder?'

'Yes, I have.'

'And do they know who did it?'

'Not yet.'

'How dreadful for you! There's nothing worse than not knowing, is there?'

'No.'

'Do you have family to support you?'

'No. But I have some good friends.'

'Well that's something, isn't it?'

Emma was keen to get away. She couldn't help feeling Mary Fairchild was being nosey.

'Where do you live?'

It was an odd question. 'Clerkenwell.' She turned to leave.

'Oh, very nice. And not too far from here.'

'Not far, no. I must be on my way. It was nice seeing you again, Miss Fairchild.'

'And you too, Mrs Langley. Do take care of yourself, won't you?'

Emma headed off in the direction of Liverpool Street station.

The first time she'd met Miss Fairchild had been in the same place she'd spoken to her just now. Had it been a coincidence? Or had Mary been watching and waiting for her?

'Look out! Lady! Move!'

Emma heard a clatter of hooves behind her. She turned to see a horse and carriage had mounted the pavement and was heading directly towards her.

Emma froze. She wanted to move, but her feet remained stuck to the ground.

A blow from her left sent her tumbling into the road. Someone was on top of her. They were heavy and the ground was wet and mucky. She felt the ground shudder as the horse and carriage thundered past.

The person on top of her groaned then moved. 'Blimey,' he said, getting up. He was holding some newspapers. As Emma turned to look at him she realised he was the newspaper seller she had passed moments earlier.

'Are you all right, madam?'

'I think so. I couldn't move. You saved me!'

He laughed and held out his hand to help her up. 'I'm glad you didn't break any bones. He was heading straight for you! For a moment then I thought you were a goner.'

SEVENTY-THREE

Edward Theobald had been right about the Scotland Yard inspector. A little over a week after his last visit, he was back again.

In his last conversation with Detective Inspector Blakely, Edward had felt the need to defend the firm. But now he had doubts about Cardwell's loyalty, he didn't feel compelled to do so. It wasn't fair that he was the one the police insisted on speaking to. Cardwell had clearly protected himself, so Edward decided to do the same. He was going to be as honest with the police officers as he possibly could.

'I visited William Langley's bank first thing this morning,' said Blakely. 'And I looked at his bank accounts.' He opened the file which he had brought with him again. Edward desperately wanted to see what was in it. 'Can you confirm what Mr Langley's salary was when he worked here, Mr Theobald?'

'About seventy pounds, I believe.' He folded his arms and jutted his chin, preparing himself for a slew of questions.

'And was any money paid to him after he left your employment on the twenty-seventh of July?'

'I believe an amount was agreed on his parting.'

'Do you know how much?' asked Blakely.

'No.'

'Would fifty pounds sound about right?'

'It sounds like an awful lot of money to me. But it wouldn't have been my decision, it was likely to be Cardwell's.'

'So the fifty pounds which Mr Langley received on the twenty-seventh of July is likely to have been paid to him by this firm?'

'Yes, I believe so.'

Blakely sat back in his chair and fixed his gaze on him. 'Can you remind me of the circumstances in which Mr Langley left this firm, Mr Theobald?'

'I can do better than that, Inspector.'

'You can?'

'I can tell you exactly why he left. But before I do, I need to come to an arrangement with you.' He unfolded his arms and rested his hands on the desk.

'What sort of arrangement?' asked Blakely.

'I'll tell you everything I know about William Langley. And I really do mean everything. And in return, I request that my work with Barnaby Ratcliffe be overlooked. Not the firm's work with him. You can carry on looking into that all you want. Cardwell was probably involved in a good deal of it. But I'm talking about my own personal involvement.'

Blakely leafed through the papers in his file, rubbed his chin then gave a sigh. 'All right then, Mr Theobald, tell me everything you know about William Langley.'

'And you won't prosecute me over Ratcliffe? As I've said, you can prosecute anyone else in this firm over him. I'd just like immunity for myself.'

A pause followed as Blakely gave this some thought. 'Your information about Langley had better be good,' he said.

'Oh it is. It's very good indeed. In fact, there's quite a lot I can tell you. Make yourself comfortable, Inspector, you'll enjoy this.'

SEVENTY-FOUR

'William Langley came to work for us in early 1887,' Edward Theobald told Detective Inspector Blakely. 'Initially, I was quite impressed with him. He presented himself well, he seemed knowledgeable, and I knew our clients would like him. He had a certain charm about him, as it were. Initially, all went well.

'He'd been with us for about six months when I received a complaint from a client that he hadn't done some work thoroughly enough. I had a conversation with Langley about it. He was extremely apologetic and assured me it wouldn't happen again. But I'm afraid to say that a few months later, we had another complaint. Then there were unexplained absences from work and I found out he would sometimes ask the clerks to complete work which he was supposed to be doing.

'Before long, it was quite apparent he was arrogant and insubordinate. He had little respect for his senior colleagues and considered himself better than everyone else. I hadn't taken up his reference when he first joined us because I'd been very impressed with him. But when I looked into the reference, I realised he'd falsified it. I dismissed him. But then there was a problem.'

'What was the problem?'

'Langley had discovered the firm was carrying out some work for Barnaby Ratcliffe. He'd heard from somewhere that Ratcliffe was carrying out fraudulent activities. So Langley sent us some notes demanding money.'

'You paid him?'

'Yes, Mr Cardwell decided we should do so.'

'So Mr Cardwell knew about this?'

'Oh yes.'

'And was Langley paid any more money after that payment at the end of July?'

'Unfortunately, yes.'

'And how did you give him the money?'

'Well, we had to keep it under wraps because we didn't want anyone to find out about the arrangement. So we had a clerk meet a friend of his in a park or gardens somewhere and it was handed over that way.'

'Do you know who the friend was?'

'I couldn't say. This was all arranged without my close involvement.'

'Would the clerk remember?'

'Possibly.'

'Excellent. We can speak to him about the identity of the friend,' said Blakely. 'Langley was expensive for your law firm. Presumably he was going to continue demanding money indefinitely?'

'I suppose so. But we made the mistake of working with Ratcliffe and we had to pay our way out of it. That's the way we viewed it.'

'Were there any discussions within the law firm about bringing the arrangement with Langley to an end?'

'Murder him, you mean? No. The money wasn't a lot to us. We had to spend it to cover up our mistake.'

'What did you do on the night of Saturday, the tenth of November?'

Edward laughed. 'Ah, here we go. You wish to establish an alibi for me. That's quite straightforward. I went to see the Royal Italian Opera Company's performance of Verdi's *Ernani* at the opera house in Covent Garden. It was very good, I can recommend it. I went with my wife and my friend, Mr George Piggott, with his dear wife, Catherine. My wife will still have the ticket stubs if you ask her. We dined beforehand at the Grosvenor restaurant just off Piccadilly. They will have a record of our booking.'

'What time did the performance end?'

'About ten o'clock and then we enjoyed a few drinks with the Piggotts at their home in Fitzrovia afterwards. You can call on them to verify it, Inspector. They're on Rathbone Place, number eighty-seven. We were there until at least one o'clock. We rather overstayed our welcome, I'm afraid. They had to practically kick us out!' He chuckled.

'And what about Gideon Flynn?'

Edward startled. He thought his explanation was over. 'Who?'

'Mr Flynn, a picture framer on Crispin Street, Spitalfields. Ever heard of him?'

Blakely had clearly found some evidence, so Edward reasoned there was no use in lying.

'Yes, I know Mr Flynn.'

'In what capacity?'

'He came to us asking for advice.'

'For what?'

'He'd got himself into a slight mess. He'd made the mistake of lending money to the inhabitants of Spitalfields and Whitechapel and he was struggling to recover the debts.'

'People weren't paying up?'

'No. And that's what happens when you lend money to poor people. They have no means to repay it. He made a very silly mistake.'

'So what advice did you offer?'

'Presumably if I tell you, my own personal involvement will be overlooked in return for what I told you about Langley?'

'That depends on what you're going to tell me.'

'Oh come along now, Blakely. We had a deal!'

Blakely pulled at his ear. 'Very well.'

'Thank you. Well we offered some advice to Flynn but he wasn't happy with it for whatever reason. So we reached an agreement whereby we bought the debt from him.'

'You took on the debt?'

'Yes.' The inspector raised an eyebrow and Edward could tell he'd interested him now. 'We took on the debt because we could add our own favourable rates of interest and ensure the debts were recovered effectively.'

'Effectively?'

'Yes.' Edward chose his words carefully; he didn't want Blakely thinking any threats were made. 'We asked a respectable lawyer to provide free advice to each debtor to make sure he could repay what he owed in a timely manner.'

'Is the respectable lawyer Thomas Haskins?'

'Yes.' Edward raised a cautious finger. 'Now you're not supposed to know any of this, Blakely. We set up a separate firm to conduct this work. But I'm telling you all about it now so that everything is clear. I realise what we've been doing is not entirely legal but at least I'm being honest with you. Once this is all explained, you can rest assured we're hiding nothing else.'

'I appreciate it, Mr Theobald.'

Edward smiled. Talking about these long-held secrets was helping him feel a little better.

'So that's the situation, Blakely,' he said. 'We paid Flynn a decent sum of money for the list and he helped us with some of the administration. That involved keeping records and keeping Haskins informed. We managed to recover quite a lot of the debts.'

'At what cost?'

'At no cost to us. We've been making good money on it.'

'I mean the cost to the debtors. Some stole to repay you and at least one man jumped to his death.'

Edward grimaced. 'Sadly the type of people Flynn lent to are the sort who have many problems in their lives. Many are addicted to vices such as drink and gambling. They're the sort of people who lead short, tragic lives.'

'So you accept no responsibility for their fate?'

'They borrowed money from an unauthorised lender and had no means to pay it back. What else could they expect?'

'Well, it's been a long and interesting day,' said James when he returned home that evening. The children were already in bed and James's dinner had been kept warm on the sideboard for him.

'What happened?' Penny joined him at the dining table as he ate.

'Mr Theobald gave us a full explanation of William Langley's departure from the law firm. And it turns out your theory was correct, Penny. He was blackmailing them.' Penny listened as her husband told her about the details between mouthfuls of turkey pie.

'So they could have murdered William to stop him blackmailing them,' she said, once James had finished.

'Possibly. But Mr Theobald said twenty pounds is a negligible amount for a firm of their size. And besides, he has an alibi for the night of Langley's death.'

'And Cardwell?'

'I spoke to him afterwards. He has a strong alibi too.'

Penny sighed.

'I have to say I thought Theobald spoke fairly honestly this time,' said James. 'This business with Ratcliffe appears to have created some bad blood between him and Cardwell. Both men seemed keen to blame the other for poor judgement and mistakes.'

'So will they be prosecuted for working with Ratcliffe?'

'There's quite a bit of work to do yet. We need to build the case against them and there's a lot of paperwork to go through. Cardwell certainly appears to have been the cleverer of the two. Unfortunately for Theobald, quite a lot of Ratcliffe's paperwork has his name on it.'

SEVENTY-FIVE

'Good morning, Mrs Langley,' said Mr O'Brien from Cardwell and Theobald the following day. 'How are you on this fine morning?'

Emma could see the morning wasn't fine at all. A brisk icy wind whipped at the solicitor's thin brown hair and low grey clouds rolled over Northampton Square. The hansom cab which had brought Mr O'Brien here hadn't yet departed.

Now was Emma's chance.

'I do apologise, Mr O'Brien. I should have notified you before you made your journey here this morning. I no longer require your services, thank you.'

He scowled. His pointed nose was red from the cold. 'I don't understand, Mrs Langley.'

'I no longer require your services. I have an uncle who's a solicitor, and he's offered to do the work instead.' Her heart thudded in her chest. Would he shout at her? She wouldn't know what to do if that happened.

'Your uncle? Which firm does he work for? I might know it.'

The cab began to move away. Mr O'Brien spun round and held out a black-gloved hand to halt it.

'I'd rather not say,' said Emma.

He turned back to her. 'You'd rather not say?'

'That's right. I don't have to, do I?'

'No. You don't. But you do realise you're making a big mistake, Mrs Langley? Your husband died intestate and I've been working extremely hard on your application for probate.'

'Thank you for your help. I appreciate it.'

'And may I remind you that Cardwell and Theobald provided my services to you entirely free of charge?'

'Yes. Thank you. You've been very helpful, Mr O'Brien.'

She gripped the handle on the door, keen to close it.

'So that's it?' he said.

'Yes.'

'I see.' He put on his hat. 'Well, I've warned you that you're making a mistake, Mrs Langley. No doubt Mr Cardwell or Mr Theobald will call on you shortly to sort this matter out.'

He turned on his heel and marched back towards the cab. The driver raised a hand in acknowledgement and she realised it was Samuel Carter. She waved in response, then closed the door.

She returned to the sitting room, her body aching from the tumble she'd taken the day before. The horse must have bolted out of fear. That's what she assumed. But the newspaper seller's words repeated in her mind: 'He was heading straight for you!'

SEVENTY-SIX

'What time is your next piano lesson, Mrs Langley?' asked Mrs Solomon. Emma was in the hallway, packing some piano instruction books into her bag.

'Eleven o'clock,' she said. 'In Marylebone.'

Mrs Solomon glanced at the grandfather clock. 'I've got a few minutes to speak to you, then. I won't keep you though, I don't want to make you late. Ronald and I have been talking.'

'Oh?' Perhaps they'd decided it was time for her to move out. Emma could understand why. They had been generous to her for long enough.

'We'd like to offer a reward,' said Mrs Solomon. 'A reward for finding Mr Langley's murderer. It would only be twenty-five pounds, but that might encourage someone, mightn't it? It's better than nothing.'

'That's very kind of you,' said Emma. 'I don't know how to properly thank you both!'

'Oh, don't worry about that. I know you're grateful. We think it's awful the police haven't done much yet and we just want to do our bit to help. And sometimes a reward works, doesn't it?'

'Yes, it does.' Emma smiled. 'Thank you again.'

As Emma travelled by the underground railway to Baker Street, she considered Mrs Solomon's offer. A reward was only useful if people knew about it. How could she advertise it? She could paste up bill posters around the East End, but that would take a lot of work. Perhaps a few posters in public houses and assembly rooms would be better.

And perhaps an advertisement in a newspaper. Maybe Penny could negotiate something with the *Morning Express* newspaper.

So, after spending half an hour on 'Twinkle Twinkle Little Star' with her new pupil in Marylebone, Emma made the short train journey to Penny's home in St John's Wood.

'How kind of your landlady to offer a reward,' said Penny. 'I'm sure the editor, Edgar Fish, will put something in the *Morning Express* for us. We can go there now.'

'Or another day, you're probably busy.'

'I'll check with Mrs Tuttle, and if she's fine minding the children then we can go down to Fleet Street. There's no time like the present.'

On the underground train, Penny told Emma that James had spoken to Edward Theobald the previous day.

'He admitted everything,' she said. 'He told James that William had blackmailed the firm and that Mr Flynn was a moneylender. James says he was forced to own up to it all because of the evidence we found. We were right all along!'

'Good.' Emma breathed out a sigh. 'Do you think James will explain it all to Detective Inspector Bradshaw? He refused to listen to me.'

'Yes, he's visiting him today.'

'That's excellent news! And did Mr Theobald mention Thomas Haskins?'

'Yes. He worked for them collecting the debts. They set up Fenners and Company so he wouldn't be associated with them.'

'And then housed the company in the same building,' said Emma. 'They're not as clever as they say they are.'

'James says Mr Cardwell and Mr Theobald both have alibis for the time of William's death,' said Penny. 'And apparently the amounts of money they were paying him were relatively small for the firm.'

'So James doesn't think they could have murdered William?'

'No.'

'I suppose it's good to have fewer suspects to consider. I can only hope Bradshaw looks into Flynn and Lady Lou now.'

'Hopefully he will.'

Emma told Penny that she had sent the solicitor, Mr O'Brien, away that morning.

'And how did he take it?'

'He was quite grumpy about it. He told me I was making a mistake and that Mr Cardwell or Mr Theobald would probably call on me.'

'Well they've got no right to! You can choose whichever solicitor you like. It sounds like he didn't take the news well.'

'And you think he was watching me and reporting back to the firm?'

'I think it's possible. It could explain his grumpiness because Cardwell and Theobald probably won't be happy you turned him away.' Penny reached out and patted her arm. 'But please don't worry, Emma. Now that we've managed to get the truth out of Mr Theobald they should leave you alone.'

Raised voices could be heard beyond the newsroom door when Emma and Penny arrived at the *Morning Express* offices.

'Sounds like a normal day in the newsroom,' said Penny with a grin.

She pushed open the door, and they entered a scruffy room with piles of paper on every surface and a grimy window looking out over Fleet Street. The air smelled of stale tobacco smoke.

The editor, Edgar Fish, stood with his hands on his hips in the centre of the room. A corpulent, curly-haired gentleman sat with his feet on his desk and his hands cupped behind his head.

'I didn't fall asleep!' protested the curly-haired man. He removed his feet from his desk and got up from his seat when he noticed Emma and Penny.

'You must have been asleep, Potter,' said Edgar. 'Otherwise, how did you miss half of Mr Parnell's speech about the second reading of the Irish Land Purchase Bill?'

'It was probably too boring to follow.'

'And you nodded off.'

'I didn't nod off!'

Edgar shook his head and turned to Emma and Penny. 'Good morning, ladies. As you can see, Mrs Blakely, little has changed here.'

'How lovely it is to see you again, Mrs Blakely.' The curly-haired reporter gave a little bow.

'Hello Frederick,' said Penny. 'It's lovely to see you again.' She turned to Emma. 'This is Frederick Potter, a colleague I worked with for many years.' She turned back to Frederick. 'I'm helping Mrs Langley investigate the murder of her husband, William Langley, and his friend Lavinia Drummond.'

'And how's it going?' asked Edgar.

'Not very well, so far. The police are too busy to do much and because I'm not a reporter anymore, it's not as easy to go about asking questions. In fact, I've come here to ask a favour.'

Edgar grimaced. 'I can't employ a woman who's married and a mother, Mrs Blakely. We discussed this. But the offer of you writing the occasional article for us on an ad hoc basis still stands.'

Penny laughed. 'I'm not asking for my job back, Edgar! Mrs Langley's friend has offered a reward of twenty-five pounds to find William Langley's murderer and we need to publicise it.'

'So you'd like it mentioned in the newspaper?'

'Yes please.'

'How about we do something even better than that? How about the *Morning Express* newspaper adds another twenty-five pounds and we make it fifty?'

'Thank you!' said Emma.

'That's wonderful, Edgar,' said Penny. 'You're getting generous in your old age.'

'Where are you going to find twenty-five pounds from, Fish?' asked Frederick.

'Mr Conway the proprietor will agree to it.'

'And if he doesn't?'

'I'll find it, don't worry. It's not a problem. The *Morning Express* is a newspaper which likes to help. We can print some posters too. As long as we can put the name of the *Morning Express* somewhere on them.'

'Will that be all right?' Penny asked Emma.

Emma nodded. 'Of course.'

'Good,' said Edgar. 'I'll get onto the compositors and printers now. And I meant to say to you on your last visit, Mrs Blakely, that you must pass on my congratulations to your husband. He did a good job of arresting that Barnaby Ratcliffe.'

'There was a team of them working on it.'

'All the same, I've heard he did a lot of investigative work so they could find him. And it seems Ratcliffe has had help from a lot of people over the years. Many of them with professional reputations who should know better. There's a bookkeeper's firm involved and also that law firm in Holborn... Cardwell and Theobald. That's the one.'

'How do you know about them?' Penny asked.

'I've got an ace new reporter,' said Edgar. 'He spends his time sniffing around London. He's like a bloodhound. You haven't met him yet because he's rarely here. He's always out and about.'

'Sniffing,' added Frederick.

'That's right.'

'What's his name?' asked Penny.

'Harry Wright. He can smell a story before it even becomes a story.'

'What an interesting skill.'

'And his name is Wright as in write,' said Frederick. 'When you think about it, he writes for a living. Harry Wright writes.'

'And sniffs as well by the sound of things.'

'That's right, Mrs Blakely,' said Edgar. 'He's heard about these professional firms helping Ratcliffe but don't worry, we're not publishing anything yet because we don't want to jeopardise your husband's investigation.'

'Good.'

'And Cardwell and Theobald is an interesting connection,' said Frederick. 'There was all that lawyer in the river business fifteen years ago.'

'Lawyer in the river?' said Penny. 'I've not heard about that.'

It sounded alarming to Emma.

'A lawyer who worked for the firm was found in the river,' said Frederick.

'How did he end up there?'

'That's the mystery.'

'And this was fifteen years ago?'

'Yes, 1873 I think.'

Edgar glanced at the clock on the wall. 'Oh dear, look at the time,' he said. 'And that clock's slow. You need to finish your report on the second reading of the Irish Land Purchase Bill, Potter.'

'I know.'

'We'll leave you to it,' said Penny. 'But I'm interested to know, Frederick. What's it like working for Edgar?'

'Awful.' He shook his head in mock dismay. 'Every day I hold out hope Mr Sherman will march through the door again.'

Penny laughed.

SEVENTY-SEVEN

Emma and Penny visited the reading room at the British Museum after they left the *Morning Express* offices. They were keen to learn more about the lawyer in the river.

In the newspaper room, Penny pulled out the first volume for 1873, and Emma helped her carry it to a desk. 'I shall check January to March,' said Penny. 'Would you like to check April to June?'

'Of course.'

They pulled out the second volume, placed it on a desk, and began leafing through.

Emma was almost dizzy from searching through the pages when a headline caught her eye: *Lawyer Found Drowned in the Thames.*

'Here!' she said to Penny.

Penny joined her and they read the report of an inquest.

An inquest was held Thursday last at the Rose and Crown, Collingwood Street, Blackfriars Road, by the Coroner for East Surrey on the body of Mr Joseph Moore, 32, of Gordon Place, Bloomsbury. The deceased was found in the river near Westmin-

ster Bridge. He held a responsible job as a solicitor for a law firm, Cardwell and Theobald in Holborn.

From the evidence heard, Mr Moore was last seen on the third of October at six pm at his place of work. His wife, Mrs Harriet Moore, grew concerned about his absence that evening and considered it out of character. She reported his disappearance to Hunter Street police station at half past eleven that same evening. Mrs Moore stated she did not know why her husband would have gone to the river that evening and that he had shown no sign of any desponding condition before his death.

The report went on to say the inquest had been adjourned until December to allow for further investigation by the police.

'So it was considered suspicious!' said Penny.

They read the December reports on Mr Moore's inquest which stated the jury had returned a verdict of 'found dead in the river'.

'How disappointing,' said Penny. 'They never managed to establish how he ended up there.'

SEVENTY-EIGHT

'Gentlemen.' Gideon Flynn fixed a wide grin on his face. 'How can I help?'

The red-haired man removed his pipe from his mouth and showed him his warrant card. 'I'm Detective Inspector Bradshaw from Commercial Street police station.'

'Ah yes. Just up the road.' He turned to the other man. 'And you, sir?' He recognised him as the man who had been waiting by the lamp post for the two ladies who had visited earlier in the week.

'Detective Inspector Blakely of Scotland Yard,' he said, also showing him his warrant card.

'And how can I help?'

'We'd like to speak to you about William Langley,' said Bradshaw. 'Did you know him?'

'A little. Why don't we have a chat over tea?'

He turned and led them up the narrow staircase. He could only guess the two ladies had asked the police to visit him. But why? They had no evidence that he'd done anything wrong.

His mother lingered in the doorway at the top of the stairs.

'Fetch us some tea, please,' he said. Then he added in a quiet hiss, 'It's the police!'

She pulled a worried expression and hurried off.

The detective inspectors made themselves comfortable in the sitting room. 'I've received a couple of reports about you, Flynn,' said Bradshaw. 'And I've asked Inspector Blakely to join me because we've agreed the Yard can assist with this case.'

'What case?' Gideon grinned and crossed his legs.

'William Langley,' said Bradshaw. 'You do know what happened to him, don't you?'

'Yes, of course. The chap was murdered in Green Dragon Yard almost three weeks ago now. Terrible.'

'Did you know him?'

'Yes. A little. In fact, his widow visited me last week. Poor lady. She had a friend with her. A delightful pair of gentlewomen.'

'So how well did you know Mr Langley?'

'Not very well. I knew him as Billy, though. I think everyone around here knew him as that.'

'Did you lend him money?' asked Blakely.

The question surprised him. 'Excuse me?'

'Did you lend William Langley money?'

'I er...' Gideon pulled at his ear and felt his neck grow hot. What did the detectives know about him? They had clearly been told he had once been a moneylender. If he lied too much then they could trip him up. 'Yes,' he said. 'I lent him some money.'

'How well did you know him?'

'Quite well, I suppose. I shall be honest with you, gentlemen.'

'Good,' said Blakely. 'We like honesty.'

'I like money,' said Flynn. 'I like to invest it and make more of it and I used to lend it too. Investments have always interested me, you see. I study them all the time in the financial press. It was always my hope to work in finance, but my father insisted on me taking over the family business instead.'

'You have some disgruntled customers, don't you, Flynn?' said Bradshaw.

Gideon's mother brought in the tea tray and he felt pleased by the interruption. After she had placed it on the little table, he busied himself with pouring out the tea.

'Mr Flynn?'

'Yes?'

'You haven't answered my question.'

'What was it again? Oh, disgruntled customers. Well, you always get those.'

'I had a report from Mr Gallagher.'

'Oh, him. How much milk do you like, Inspector?'

'Just a normal amount. Mr Gallagher is well known around here, isn't he? Owns a boxing club and a shop on Commercial Street. He's not the sort of man you want to annoy.'

'No. Absolutely not.' He handed the teacup to Bradshaw, trying to keep his trembling hand as steady as possible.

'Mr Gallagher tells me you took his money.'

'Now that's the trouble with investing. You explain to people that returns can vary and they pretend they've understood every word. It goes well for a month or two and they're pleased with the results. Then there's invariably a month or two when it doesn't go quite as well, and then they accuse you of swindling them! I'm sorry Mr Gallagher has wasted your time, Inspector.' He turned to Blakely. 'How much milk would you like, sir?'

'The same will do me, thank you.'

'What do you invest in, Flynn?' asked Bradshaw.

'Now that would be telling. I can't reveal my secrets.'

'Gallagher told me it was horses.'

'That's a part of it, yes.'

'He also told me you run an illegal bookmaker's on these premises.'

Gideon kept his eye on the thin trickle of white milk he was pouring into the teacup. 'Did he? Well, that's quite an accusation.'

'Is he right?'

'The description "bookmaker's" is overstating it a bit.' He grinned as he handed the cup of tea to Blakely. 'Biscuits?'

'No, thank you.'

'Gallagher told me he spoke to you and you refused to refund him,' said Bradshaw.

'That's because investments don't work like that.' Gideon poured out his own cup of tea.

'How many customers have made similar complaints?'

'None.'

'Gallagher seems to think he's not the only one.'

'Does he? Well, I suppose he would say that.' Gideon sat back in his chair and crossed his legs again.

'Was Langley a disgruntled customer?' asked Blakely.

'I lent him money.'

'Did he give you money for your investments too?'

'Yes.' He scratched his nose. 'This is a little confusing. He first approached me with some money to invest. So I did that and then, like Gallagher, he was unhappy with his returns. So then I agreed to lend him some because he'd run out completely. Billy was hopeless with his money. He loved to gamble. That's what I heard, anyway. In the end, we came to an arrangement that he would do some work for me.'

'Doing what?'

'Visiting people who owed me money. Or who wanted to give me money. He helped me with my financial business.'

'For which you have no banking licence.'

'That's right. But I told you I'd be honest with you, didn't I? I'm admitting to some wrongdoing.' Gideon hoped if he could be pleasant enough about it then his punishment wouldn't be too severe.

'If Langley worked for you then you clearly knew him quite well,' said Bradshaw. 'Did you have any disagreements?'

Gideon felt his heart thud. 'None.'

'None? When did you last see him?'

'On the day he died. In the Ten Bells.'

'Did you speak to him?'

'Briefly.' Gideon tried to keep his voice even. What were they getting at?

'What were you doing on the night of the tenth of November?' asked Blakely.

'I was here. My mother will tell you that.'

'All night?'

'Yes.'

'And what were you doing?'

'Reading. Writing. That sort of thing. If you think I went out onto the streets of Whitechapel and murdered Billy Langley, then you're completely mistaken, Inspector. I'm doing what I can to help this area become a better place. I've even joined the vigilance committee patrols. I went out four nights ago. We thought there was trouble at one point, but it was just a fight outside the railway station. We broke it up and everyone went home safe and sound. That's the sort of thing I do, gentlemen. I don't murder people!'

Bradshaw put down his cup and got to his feet. 'I'd like to have a look around.'

Gideon's heart sank. The tape machine was in the back room. 'Why?'

'Have you got anything to hide?'

'No.' He felt his throat tighten.

SEVENTY-NINE

James was late home that evening. He tucked into cold chicken pie and Penny listened intently as he told her about his interview with Gideon Flynn.

'So Detective Inspector Bradshaw allowed you to accompany him?' she asked.

'Yes. We've agreed to work together on Langley's case and Gideon Flynn has been arrested.'

Penny grinned. 'I can't wait to tell Emma!'

'There's a lot of work to do yet,' said James. He finished off his pie and rested his cutlery on the plate. 'And there's something else I need to tell you about Flynn.'

'What's that?'

'It seems he has an unhealthy interest in the Whitechapel murders. During our search of his property, we found drawers filled with newspaper cuttings about the atrocities. We also found several well-sharpened knives.'

Penny gave a shudder. 'Well, newspaper cuttings are one thing, I admit to having a collection of those too. But knives?' She recalled him gleefully telling her and Emma how he liked to cut the canvases from their frames. 'Does he use them for picture framing?'

'They weren't in his workshop,' said James. 'They were in a drawer in his sitting room.'

'Where Emma and I sat when we visited him last week.' She shuddered. 'What a horrible thought!'

'He's a strange character.' James untucked his napkin from his collar and rested it next to his plate.

'Have you ever heard about the lawyer in the river?' Penny asked him.

'No. A lawyer in the river?' He raised an eyebrow.

'It happened in 1873.'

'That's before I joined the police.'

'And I had just begun working as a reporter but, for some reason, I don't recall it. Emma and I went to the reading room today to look up the details.' Penny stacked their empty plates and told James what she and Emma had discovered.

'How intriguing,' he replied. 'I wonder what the explanation could have been?'

'Someone pushed him into the river.'

'Oh, Penny. You always assume there's skulduggery behind these incidents. Perhaps he jumped in intentionally? Or fell accidentally?'

'It would be interesting to look at the police files from the case.' She held his gaze, her eyes narrowing.

'Yes, it would. But it's not something I'm going to be looking into. We have enough work to do!'

'But don't you think it's quite the coincidence that Mr Moore worked for Cardwell and Theobald?' she asked.

'You think one or both of them pushed him into the river?'

'They could have done.'

'I'm not going to revisit a fifteen-year-old case,' said James. 'Not for the time being, anyway.'

'That's a shame,' said Penny, getting up from her seat. 'I suppose you're too busy.'

'Yes I am.' James got to his feet and cleared his throat. 'Was Francis Edwards in the reading room?'

'No.'

'I suppose I should be relieved about that.'

'Oh James, that rivalry was years ago.' She felt her face flush.

'He was extremely fond of you, wasn't he?'

'We don't need to remind ourselves about all that.' She picked up the plates and carried them into the kitchen. James followed.

'I wonder where Francis is now?' said James. 'He went off to Egypt, didn't he? That was his plan, anyway. But that was three years ago, and I thought he would have returned to the reading room by now. He enjoyed his work there.'

Penny felt uncomfortable discussing Mr Edwards. James had been envious of him once. 'I don't know where he is,' she replied. Although she'd never reciprocated Francis Edwards' feelings for her, she had always been fond of him. She missed him. 'I thought he would write,' she said.

'He did, didn't he? Once or twice.'

'No. I've heard nothing from him since we said goodbye at Euston railway station.'

'Oh. You seem rather sad about that.'

'No, not sad. But I would like to find out what he's doing these days. So much has happened since then.'

EIGHTY

'You can't put that there,' said a guard at Liverpool Street railway station. 'No bill posters are allowed.'

He pulled the reward poster off its tack and handed it back to Emma.

'But I want people to know about the reward that's being offered to find my husband's murderer,' she said.

'All the same, you can't put it there.'

'Is there anywhere in the station I can put it?'

'You need to speak to someone in the accounts office at the Great Eastern Railway. All advertisements need to be paid for and approved by them.'

'But this isn't an advertisement. It's a request for help.'

'Whether it's a request for help or a picture of a bar of Sunlight soap, my answer is the same, madam. You can't put it there, and I politely request you move along now, please. My job is to ensure the trains depart punctually and safely and you're causing a distraction which could endanger the convenience and safety of our passengers here at Liverpool Street station.'

'Come along,' said Penny, taking Emma's arm. 'We'll have to try somewhere else.'

They left the station and entered Bishopsgate. 'Well, it was worth a try,' said Emma. 'The guard could have turned a blind eye, couldn't he?'

'Yes, he could. But never mind. Many of the passengers passing through the station may not know this area well. But there's one place I can think of which seems obvious to me.'

'The Ten Bells?'

Penny smiled. 'You read my mind.'

They walked along Brushfield Street, heading for the tall spire of Christ Church Spitalfields at the end.

'James told me yesterday evening that Flynn has been arrested for running an illegal bookmaker's,' said Penny.

Emma felt a grin on her face. 'What good news! A bookmaker's? I thought he was a moneylender.'

'He was. It will take the police a few days to find out exactly what he was up to. He told James that William worked for him.'

'Really? So that explains the coded message in the picture frame. I'm growing increasingly convinced that Flynn could be the murderer. Maybe William learned too much about his business and Flynn wanted him silenced?'

'It's a possibility. And with Flynn in custody now, I hope Bradshaw asks him those questions. James also told me Flynn is extremely interested in Jack the Ripper. He's got a collection of newspaper cuttings about the murders and also a collection of sharp knives.'

'He talked to us about using a sharp knife, didn't he?' Emma shivered at the memory, recalling the slashing action he had made and his awful, insidious grin. He had done it deliberately to scare them.

She thought for a moment. 'Do you think Flynn could be responsible for the Whitechapel murders?'

'Jack the Ripper?' Penny's voice dropped to a whisper.

'After what James found in his office... I think they'd be fools not to consider it.'

A man and a woman fell out through the swing doors of the Ten Bells public house as Emma and Penny arrived. The couple giggled and staggered off arm-in-arm down Fournier Street.

Emma wasn't looking forward to going inside – she knew her and Penny's presence would draw attention.

Penny pushed open the doors, and Emma followed.

The warm air smelled of hops, tobacco and unwashed bodies. A soggy layer of sawdust covered the floor.

'Oh, hello!' said a cheerful, gravelly voice. 'Who've we got here then?'

'Gentlewomen!' said another. 'They're here to help the deserving poor.'

'Not you, Jack. You're the undeserving poor. The gentlewomen won't be helping you.'

'More's the pity.'

Emma dared not look at the men who were talking, but instead followed Penny to the counter. She recognised large-framed Albert Bexley, the landlord who had spoken at William's inquest, serving beer.

'Excuse me,' Penny said to him. 'Do you mind putting up one of our reward posters in here? Fifty pounds is being offered to find the murderer of William Langley and Lavinia Drummond.'

The landlord held out a large hand for the poster, then examined it.

'Yeah,' he said. 'How many have you got?'

'Fifty.'

'Give me three,' he said. 'I'll put one at this end of the bar, one at that end of the bar and one in the window.'

'Thank you very much,' said Penny, handing him two more posters. 'It's very kind of you.'

'It's the least I can do. They both used to come in here and it's a shame the police have done nothing about it yet. There's bound to be some folks in here who saw something or know something. Fifty pounds will serve as a little reminder, I'm sure.'

'Give me a hundred pounds and I'll go to the coppers right now,' said a yellow-faced man with a stained shirt and greasy neckerchief.

'You know something, do you, Fred?' asked the landlord wearily.

'I do if there's a hundred pounds going.'

'It's not a hundred pounds, it's fifty. And either you know something or you don't.'

'If they offered a hundred pounds, I would make something up,' said Fred.

'But it doesn't work like that,' said the landlord. 'They can check your story out. Anyone can go to the coppers and tell a load of lies. But it ain't worth it because they know when you're lying. Especially you, Fred, you're the worst liar I've ever known.'

Fred gave a hoarse laugh. 'Oh, I ain't that bad. Don't listen to a word he says, ladies.'

The landlord glanced at Emma and narrowed his eyes. 'You're the widow, aren't you?' he said. 'I saw you at the inquest.'

'Yes.'

'Hopefully, this reward you're offering will come to something. I saw Tommy Fletcher in here earlier. He played cards with your husband that night, didn't he?' The landlord raised himself onto his toes and looked over the heads of the drinkers in the bar. 'Yeah, there he is,' he said. 'In his usual corner.' He put his hands around his mouth to magnify his voice. 'Tommy! Over here!'

Moments later, the labourer appeared. 'What?' he said.

'The widow.' The landlord pointed at Emma. She gave a

nervous smile. By now, most of the drinkers in the bar were looking at her.

She noticed a flash of alarm in Tommy's expression.

He didn't want to talk to her.

'Oh, right,' he said. He stepped closer. 'Sorry about your husband.'

'Thank you. My friend, Mrs Blakely, and I are letting people know about a reward being offered to find his killer.'

'Oh, right,' he said again, hitching up his trousers. 'Well, I've said all that I know about it.'

'Which is what?' asked Penny.

'Weren't you at the inquest?' he asked her.

'No.'

'Oh, right. Well, we saw Billy in here that day.'

'The tenth of November?'

'Yeah.'

'What time?'

'Blimey, it's like being interviewed by the police again.' He wiped his nose with his hand. 'It was the evening. About eight, maybe. I was over there playing cards.' He pointed to the far end of the bar. 'There were three of us and we thought it would be better with four. I saw Billy standing about on his own, so I asked him if he wanted to join us and it turned out that he did. He'd had a bit to drink. We all had. And then we thought we could play with a bit of money, you see. Well, we didn't want to do that in here because Albert doesn't allow it and that's fair enough. So we went to mine.'

'Where do you live?' asked Penny.

'Finch Street. It's over that way.' He pointed to the far end of the bar again. 'It's about a five-minute walk from here. It's not far. So we went back there, and we played for a bit of money. It didn't go too well for Billy because he lost a bit and he wasn't too happy about that.'

'What did he say?'

'He accused us of cheating, which we weren't, obviously. I don't cheat at cards, I like to play fair. All of us did. But he wasn't having that, and he got a bit angry. I thought I'd make a joke just to cheer everyone up, but that made it worse.'

'What joke did you make?' asked Penny.

'Well, it ain't funny when I say it now, but I thought it was funny at the time because we'd all had something to drink. Everyone laughed but, well... Billy didn't laugh. I told him he looked like Jack the Ripper.' He wiped his nose again and had the grace to look slightly embarrassed. 'Not funny, is it? But you say these things when you've had a few drinks. So after that, he left.'

'What time was that?'

'Oh, I don't know. Midnight I suppose.'

'And how close do you live to Green Dragon Yard?'

'Oh, quite close. It's about fifty, sixty yards. Doesn't take long to walk there.'

'Lady Lou has given two times when she saw him there,' said Penny. 'Half past eleven and half past twelve.'

'Well, it must be the half past twelve one because he left us about midnight.'

'And it took him half an hour to walk fifty or sixty yards?'

'Well, he was lost, wasn't he? He must have been wandering about somewhere. Either that, or I've got my times wrong, and he left about a quarter past midnight or twenty past. It's hard to remember it all exactly because we'd been drinking.'

'Did he have a case with him when he played cards with you?' Emma asked.

'Oh yeah, he did have a case. We asked him what was in it and he said it was nothing important. Then when I joked he was Jack the Ripper, we said he kept his knives in it. Like I said, it's not funny now.'

EIGHTY-ONE

'It seems Tommy Fletcher feels guilty about how he treated your husband,' said Penny as they left the Ten Bells.

'I can see why,' said Emma. 'But I don't blame him for making jokes at William's expense that evening. It seems William got annoyed with them all after he lost at cards. If you're going to play cards, then you have to expect you might lose at it.' She glanced around the street and recalled the strange encounter she'd had with Mary Fairchild when she was last here. 'There's an odd lady I think you ought to meet,' she said to Penny. 'I'd like to hear your opinion of her. She's approached me a couple of times when I've visited this part of the city and I'm sure I noticed her watching me once when we were looking for Lady Lou.'

They walked up Commercial Street, turned right at the top and headed for Mary Fairchild's tea and soup stall outside the Sunday school.

'There she is,' said Emma as they approached. She could see Miss Fairchild and her companion, Doris, standing at their stall with the large steel urns. 'She'll come across as very pleasant. A bit too pleasant.'

'Suspiciously pleasant?' said Penny.

'Yes.'

'Mrs Langley!' Mary Fairchild's face broke out into a wide smile. 'How are you?'

'Very well, thank you. This is my friend Mrs Penny Blakely.'

'How lovely to meet you, Mrs Blakely! Would you like some tea?'

'Oh, no thank you,' said Penny. 'Please save it for the people who need it the most.'

'It's no trouble at all.' Miss Fairchild set about filling two cups from the urn. 'It can't sit in here for too long because it loses its flavour after a while. We can put the kettle on in the Sunday school whenever we need to. Here.' Two steaming cups of tea were thrust into Emma's and Penny's hands.

'I'll go and put the kettle on again,' said Doris. She disappeared into the red-brick building behind them. Emma sipped her tea, which tasted surprisingly good.

'I heard Gideon Flynn the picture framer has been arrested,' said Miss Fairchild. 'What a surprise that was! They say he was running a bookmaker's from his shop and was lending money. Shameful. he'll probably lose his shop now and I don't know what that will mean for his poor mother. It's been the family business for over fifty years.' She shook her head in dismay. 'Very sad. Oh look, here comes Mrs Bridewell.'

A woman shuffled towards them with several children in tow. They were all poorly dressed and ranged in ages from two to fifteen.

'Hello Mrs Bridewell!' chimed Miss Fairchild's voice. 'I haven't seen you yet today, I was beginning to worry about you. How are you?'

'I've been better.' Mrs Bridewell coughed.

'I'm sorry to hear it. Are you unwell?'

'A little. But I'm not at death's door just yet. Can I have some soup, please?'

'Of course. How's your mother, Mrs Bridewell?'

'She's not doing too good.'

'Oh no, I'm sorry to hear it.'

The children grew bored as the women talked. Three girls began playing with a skipping rope while a couple of boys kicked at some rubbish in the gutter, perhaps hoping to find something useful or valuable.

The youngest child toddled off towards Commercial Street with no one but Emma and Penny noticing. Emma strode after her, gently took her arm and guided her back to the stall.

'Come and have your soup!' Mrs Bridewell shouted at her children. She then returned to her mother's list of ailments as Miss Fairchild patiently listened.

Emma drained her tea and was about to suggest to Penny that they went on their way when she spotted the young girl toddling off down the side of the Sunday school. Once again, no one in her family appeared to have noticed.

'I'll fetch her,' said Penny.

'It's all right. I'll go. You've still got some tea left.'

Emma followed the child down the narrow, dingy passage-way. It was cluttered with broken pallets and barrows which the young girl managed to successfully clamber over.

'Come back!' Emma called out to her. 'Your mother will be worried!'

The little girl laughed and continued on her way, pushing past more rubbish in the passageway. Emma caught her shin on a leather case and looked down to move it out of the way with her foot.

Three initials caught her eye: WJL. Emma stopped. The case was wet and grimy. Her heart skipped a beat. It couldn't be. But it was unmistakably William's case, the handle worn as she remembered. It was the case he'd been carrying on the night he'd died. She picked it up and grimy drops fell onto her foot.

Then she remembered the little girl. There was no sign of her now. While Emma had been distracted, she had disappeared around the corner at the far end of the passageway. 'Where are you?' she called out.

A little smiling face peered around the corner.

'Can you catch me?' said Emma, smiling back.

The little girl laughed and toddled towards her. Relieved, Emma made her way back to the street, checking over her shoulder that the child was following.

'Oh, there she is,' said Mrs Bridewell, grabbing her daughter's arm. 'This one's always disappearing somewhere. Come and have your soup.'

Emma saw Penny staring at the case. 'Is that...'

'Yes,' said Emma, still bewildered that she'd found it. 'It's William's.'

She turned to Miss Fairchild who stood stony-faced and silent.

EIGHTY-TWO

Emma carried the case into the Sunday school and set it down on a trestle table just beyond the door. Penny joined her.

William had kept the case locked with a padlock, but there was no sign of it now. Her fingers fumbled as she undid the leather straps. She pulled it open and gave a relieved laugh as she saw William's belongings. His brush, comb and shaving mirror were there. And lots of papers too. They were damp and crumpled, but still readable.

'I wonder if everything's here?' she said.

'You'll have to go through it all carefully,' said Penny.

Emma nodded. 'True. The padlock has been removed so I suppose someone could have opened it.' She lifted a pile of papers which looked like financial statements. They felt heavy, as if something was caught in between them. She separated them out and something fell back into the case with a thud.

Light flashed on a shiny blade. But it was only partly shiny. The rest of the blade was covered with rusty stains of blood.

Emma cried out and stepped away from the case, her gaze fixed on the bloodstained weapon. Penny gasped and swiftly closed the case again.

Nausea swam in Emma's stomach and she staggered towards the wall to support herself. Miss Fairchild dashed in through the door. 'Is everything all right?' she asked.

Emma turned on her. 'What was the case doing here?'

'I don't know.'

'But you must know! It was hidden by the side of this building. How could you not have noticed it? You set up your stall here every day.' Then a thought occurred to her. 'Did you hide it here?'

'No,' said Miss Fairchild. 'Absolutely not. I realise this is upsetting for you, but I can assure you I had nothing to do with it.' She stepped forward to rest a reassuring hand on Emma's arm.

But Emma didn't trust her. 'Get off me!' she railed. 'Stay away!'

Miss Fairchild stepped back, her eyes and mouth wide with shock.

'You did this!' said Emma, pointing at the case. 'You thought you could get away with it!'

'No!' protested Miss Fairchild. Tears sprung into her eyes. 'No, Mrs Langley, you're mistaken!'

EIGHTY-THREE

'Miss Fairchild says she had no idea the case was there,' said Detective Inspector Bradshaw. Emma and Penny stood with him in the reception area of Commercial Street police station.

'She's lying,' said Emma, rubbing her temples. Her head was pounding. 'She didn't look surprised when I first found it. She only denied knowing about it once I discovered the knife.'

'I have just spent twenty minutes speaking to her,' said the inspector. 'And she's very shocked indeed. Although I realise this find is extremely upsetting for you, Mrs Langley, it's excellent news that we've found the murder weapon.'

'We?' said Penny. 'You're including yourself, Inspector? Mrs Langley found it.'

'Actually, it was Mrs Bridewell's youngest child,' said Emma. 'If I hadn't followed her down that passageway, then I wouldn't have come across it. But I swear Miss Fairchild knows something. It's why she's been acting strangely!'

'What's she been doing?' asked the inspector.

'Approaching me and watching me.'

He frowned. 'Can you explain a little more?'

'She introduced herself to me when I was leaving this

station. Then she happened to be in the same place a second time, as if she was waiting for me. And then I saw her watching me once.'

'Where?'

'On Commercial Street.'

'Is it possible you're mistaken, Mrs Langley? Miss Fairchild is a friendly and prominent member of the community here. She doesn't even live here and yet she did everything she could to support the matchgirls in their strike. She comes here each day to provide hot tea and soup to the poor. And she's been doing so for years. I know that because her stall is less than a hundred yards from this very station.'

Emma sighed. The inspector clearly believed Miss Fairchild could do no wrong. 'How do you explain how my husband's case ended up in that passageway?'

'It's quite simple, Mrs Langley. The murderer left it there. And the murderer is not Miss Fairchild.' He turned to Penny. 'Perhaps you can ensure your friend gets home safely? She's had quite a shock, and she needs to recover.'

Emma gritted her teeth at his condescending tone, but chose not to argue. 'What about my husband's papers?' she said. 'When can I have them?'

'We'll have a look through them first. I'd like to find out if there are any more clues in that case.'

Penny took Emma's arm. 'Come on,' she said. 'Let's go and find a cab.'

EIGHTY-FOUR

The following Monday, Emma had four piano lessons to teach. Her final one that day was in Finsbury Park.

'You play very nicely,' she said to her pupil, Georgina. 'But you need to slow down a little bit.'

'I like to play fast,' said Georgina. They sat at an upright piano in a large dingy room with heavy oak furniture.

'But when you play too fast, your fingers slip on the notes and sometimes you play them out of sequence or out of time.'

'I don't like playing slowly.'

'But some songs sound better when you play them slowly. It's nicer for the listener too. They can hear the phrases clearly and the change in tone and emotion.'

Georgina shrugged. 'I don't understand what that means.'

When Emma returned to Northampton Square, she found a telegram waiting for her in the hallway. It was from Edgar Fish at the *Morning Express*:

Lady Lou wants to meet you in the Ten Bells.

Emma wondered why the telegram had come from Edgar Fish. Then she realised Lady Lou must have seen or heard about the reward poster which had the *Morning Express* newspaper's name printed on it. Lady Lou must have gone into the newspaper offices which were quite near the Adelphi, and told them she had some information. It seemed the fifty-pound reward was encouraging her to be a little more truthful about her encounter with William that night.

The telegram had been sent at ten o'clock, it was now a quarter to three. Lady Lou hadn't specified a meeting time. Was she planning to spend all day in the Ten Bells waiting for Emma? Or had she left now?

Emma hurried back out into Northampton Square and looked for a cab to hail.

Ten minutes later, she arrived at the public house. Had Lady Lou seen the murderer that night but been too afraid to tell? Was she going to admit to murder herself? The admission was probably unlikely, but Emma hoped Lady Lou had something useful to tell her and wasn't wasting her time.

The landlord noticed her enter the public house. 'Lady Lou's been looking for you,' he said. 'Seems she wants her fifty pounds.'

'Do you know where she is?'

'She left about half an hour ago. I don't know where she's gone.'

Emma's heart sank. She glanced around at the drinkers, hoping the landlord was mistaken. A toothless man grinned at her and raised his tankard in a toast.

'Is there another public house she could have gone to?' she called over to the landlord. He was busy now serving drinks.

'Don't know,' he said.

'Who's that then?' said a wide, red-faced man with a grey beard.

'Lady Lou.'

'She was in here.'

'I know,' said the landlord. 'But she's gone now.'

'Probably gone for a walk,' said the bearded man.

'Where does she like to go for a walk?' Emma asked.

'Oh, I don't know. Here, there and everywhere. But it ain't exactly walking country round here!' He laughed and took a gulp from his tankard.

Emma balled her fists in frustration.

'All right then. Thank you,' she said to no one in particular, and left.

Outside on Commercial Street, she looked left, then right, wondering which way Lady Lou could have gone. It was likely she'd returned to the Adelphi. But perhaps she was keen to meet Emma in the Ten Bells and hadn't strayed far.

She turned right and walked north to the next junction where she turned right into Hanbury Street. It would get dark in an hour, so she decided to use the time to find her. If she was unsuccessful, then she could go to the Adelphi the following day.

She continued along Hanbury Street, passing tired, shabby houses and down-at-heel shops. A rickety ladder was propped up outside a business offering general repairs and she moved out of the way to let a grime-covered chimney sweep push his hand-cart past. She walked south along Great Garden Street turning into Chicksand Street, then Osborne Place. She reached the junction with Brick Lane and turned north again. She felt like she was wandering aimlessly now.

'I'm looking for Lady Lou,' she asked a woman who was about to step into a public house on Brick Lane. 'Have you seen her?'

'No, sorry about that.'

Emma had better luck with a woman further up the street. 'Lady Lou? Yeah, I saw her about half an hour ago.'

'Where?'

'Near the brewery.' She pointed up the road. Emma thanked her, quickening her step. It was getting darker now.

An icy wind whipped down Brick Lane as Emma headed for the Truman Brewery with its tall red chimney reaching up into the low grey cloud. The smell of malt grew stronger, and she passed alongside the tall brick brewery walls which flanked both sides of the street. A heavy cart lumbered towards her, laden down with barrels.

She reached a crossroads. Which way would Lady Lou have gone from here? There was a public house on the opposite corner and the brewery occupied the buildings to the left and right of her. Ahead was a row of shops and workshops and beyond it a railway bridge passed over the road. Emma decided to head as far as the bridge and then look in the public house.

As she walked, Emma felt sure she could hear someone singing – just as she had heard beneath the arches of the Adelphi. An old music hall song.

Was it Lady Lou?

She continued on, past a laundry and a general store.

The street ended, and the road continued over a railway line. Ahead of her was the railway bridge she had seen from the crossroads. A bridge crossing another bridge. And close by, in the fast-dimming light, she saw Lady Lou with her tall hat and her shawl over her shoulders.

She was sitting on the wall of the bridge, her back facing the road and her legs dangling over the railway lines.

EIGHTY-FIVE

The lady continued to sing, unaware of Emma's presence.

'Lady Lou?' she said cautiously. She didn't want to startle her, given that she was sitting in a precarious position.

The lady turned. 'Mrs Langley? Oh, you're here at last. I've been wanting to talk to you all day.'

Her speech was slurred by drink. Emma felt worried for her perched on the wall of the bridge above the railway line. 'Why don't you get down from there?' she said. 'It's not safe.'

'Oh, I like it up here. I like to watch the trains. I can see the trains down here and I can also see them up there.' She pointed to the higher bridge. As if on cue, an engine pulling coal trucks passed over the upper bridge, puffing steam and smoke into the darkening sky.

'That one's going into the goods yard,' said Lady Lou once they could hear themselves again. 'And the ones down here go into Liverpool Street.' She pointed in the direction of her feet. 'I love the trains. My father worked on the trains. That's what my mother told me, I don't really remember him.'

Emma walked up to the wall and rested against it. 'What did you want to speak to me about?'

'Oh yeah, I heard about the reward. Fifty pounds. Polly told me they'd put up notices about it. I can't read, you see. But she told me it was the *Morning Express*. I didn't even know what that was until she told me it was a newspaper. She said I should go there. Well, I've never been to a newspaper before! She went with me to Fleet Street and we found the offices and I went inside and spoke to them in there. They said I could speak to you or some other lady. I forget who. Well, I remembered you because you're the widow. So I asked them to send you a message. I didn't know how to go about any of that. And I thought of the Ten Bells because everyone knows it, don't they? So I waited there, and you didn't turn up.'

'I got there at three o'clock,' said Emma. 'And they told me you'd just left.'

'Oh watch out, here comes a train!'

Emma heard it approaching behind them, and they paused as it passed beneath the bridge. It let out a whistle and a cloud of steam engulfed them.

Lady Lou let out a loud laugh. 'Oh, I love it when they do that! Sometimes I think the engine drivers know I'm here and they sound the whistle on purpose!' She laughed again as the steam cleared and she steadied herself with her hand as she wobbled a little on the wall.

Emma felt her throat tighten. 'Are you sure you won't get down from there?'

'Don't you worry, I'll be fine. You should come up here too!'

'No, I won't, thank you.'

She looked down at the drop and it was about twenty feet beneath Lady Lou's thin legs and buttoned boots. Her head span for a moment and she quickly looked up again.

'What did you want to tell me?' she asked gently.

'Oh yeah. Your Billy. He was a handsome chap he was. I always liked the look of him. But he was keen on Lavinia. I hope you don't mind me saying that because you were his wife.'

'He knew her before we met.'

'Oh yeah. Well, he was keen on her, but he wouldn't marry her. Sometimes I thought he might marry that soup lady.'

'Soup lady?'

'Yeah. The one who does the soup. Do-gooder lady.'

'Mary Fairchild?' Emma felt her blood run cold.

'Yeah, she's the one. She has that stall outside the Sunday school. Just along that way.' She pointed ahead and to her left.

'Are you sure about that?' Emma asked.

'Yeah. He sometimes helped. I think she probably told him to. I saw him there a few times when I went to get my soup.'

Mary had given no sign that she had known William.

'How long ago was this?' she asked.

'I don't know. Last year. Maybe this year. Can't remember. But she was keen on him and I reckon she was hoping he would propose marriage, but he didn't.' She turned to Emma and smiled. 'He chose you instead, didn't he?'

'He married me for my money,' said Emma flatly. 'He didn't love me.'

'Oh. Well, that's not nice then. I didn't realise he did that. I don't think so well of him now.'

'What happened that night?' asked Emma, growing impatient.

'Well, Tommy spoke to me about it.'

'Tommy Fletcher?'

'Yeah. And it wasn't his fault. He didn't know what was going to happen.'

'What do you mean?'

'I told him I'd do it, but only if there was money in it. So I got five shillings, but I should've got more after what happened.'

'I don't understand, what did Tommy Fletcher tell you to do?'

Another train passed beneath them.

Emma's jaw clenched. 'Please Lady Lou, just tell me who attacked William!'

But Lady Lou didn't hear her, she was too busy watching the carriages pass beneath the bridge.

'Who killed my husband?' Emma asked once the noise subsided.

'It wasn't me, if that's what you're thinking. And I swear on that.'

'If you want the fifty pounds reward, then you need to tell the police who attacked him.'

'Yeah, I'd rather talk to you. And there's something I want to say, Mrs Langley. I betrayed your husband that night and I've been feeling bad about it ever since.' Her voice cracked. 'He trusted me and he shouldn't have. And because of me, he died! I never knew it would happen that way. I only did it for five shillings. And what did I do with that? Spent it on drink. Like I always do.' She wiped her eyes and Emma saw her sunken cheeks were wet with tears. 'I don't deserve to be here still. He's dead, and he was such a handsome chap.' She reached into a pocket. 'Where's my handkerchief?'

'Have mine,' said Emma.

'I've got one somewhere.' Lady Lou wobbled as she turned to check another pocket.

Emma felt a sickening twinge in her stomach. 'Please come down from the wall and you can use mine.'

'I've got it.' Lady Lou turned back. 'Oh!' She wobbled again and put out a hand to steady herself. 'I nearly went then.'

'Careful,' said Emma, her heart racing as Lady Lou swayed unsteadily. The woman's eyes were unfocused, her movements growing more erratic as she fumbled for her handkerchief.

'I've got it somewhere,' Lady Lou muttered, patting her pockets with clumsy fingers. Her elaborate hat tilted precariously as she twisted to search another pocket.

Emma took a step forward, every muscle tensed. 'Please, just take mine—'

But Lady Lou had shifted too close to the edge of the wall. For a horrible moment she teetered there, arms windmilling, before the weight of her legs pulled her down. Emma glimpsed her face, mouth stretched in a silent scream, eyes wide with sudden terrifying awareness. Her thin bony hand made a desperate attempt to grip the top of the wall, but it merely made a sharp slapping noise against the bricks as she fell.

'No!' Emma cried out.

Lady Lou plunged onto the tracks beneath, her skirts and shawl billowing as she went.

'Help!' shouted Emma, desperately looking around. Her heart pounded in her throat.

A passing cart pulled up. 'What's happened?' asked the driver.

'Someone's fallen onto the tracks. We need to help her!'

He cursed, jumped down from his box and ran over to the wall.

Emma felt an icy dread rise within her as she heard the approaching sound of a train.

'Oh no.' Her voice was weak and her mouth was dry.

The engine sounded its whistle as it passed beneath the bridge.

EIGHTY-SIX

Emma had to relive the horrific incident again as she related it to Detective Inspector Bradshaw at Commercial Street station.

He took pity on her and gave her a blanket to put around her shoulders and a warm cup of cocoa.

Emma couldn't stop shivering. And she couldn't get the image of Lady Lou falling out of her mind. The look of horror on her face. Her hand slapping on the wall. Her clothing billowing as she fell.

And then the train.

'If the train hadn't come, we could have saved her,' she whispered, barely able to get her words out.

'They're very regular in and out of Liverpool Street, it would have been too dangerous to venture onto the tracks,' said the inspector. 'You did all you could. She'd had a lot to drink, and she'd chosen to sit on that wall. You asked her to get down, and she refused. It's a tragic accident.'

'Tommy Fletcher,' said Emma. 'You need to speak to him. Lady Lou said he told her to do something, and she received five shillings for it.'

The inspector wrinkled his nose. 'You are aware Lady Lou was a prostitute?'

'It was nothing to do with that. It was something to do with William. She said she'd betrayed him. She felt sad about it. She cried. And she said Tommy didn't know what was going to happen. It's as if...'

'What?'

'It's as if they didn't expect William to die.'

'I don't quite follow.'

'I'm not surprised. Lady Lou was quite muddled in her words. But Tommy told me William was angry he lost his money at cards.'

'Yes, I recall that from the inquest.'

'So there was an argument. And perhaps it didn't end once William left Tommy's house in Finch Street. Perhaps it continued. Perhaps they wanted to hurt him, but they didn't want him to die.'

'Very well. I'll speak to Tommy Fletcher about this. While you're here, I'll give you your husband's belongings and his case.'

He left the room and returned a short while later. 'I'm afraid it suffered a bit from being out in the cold and wet.'

'Thank you. Did you find any clues in it?'

'Apart from the murder weapon, I'm afraid not, Mrs Langley.'

'And you're quite sure Miss Fairchild had nothing to do with this?'

'Quite sure.'

'Lady Lou suggested Miss Fairchild and my husband had a love affair.'

'Is that so?' He stroked his chin. 'I shall bear that in mind. However, for the time being, I feel quite certain Miss Fairchild had nothing to do with your husband's murder.'

'And Flynn? What about him?'

'He's an interesting character.' His expression softened and he tilted his head. 'I'd like to apologise to you, Mrs Langley, for not listening to you before. I may have been a little rude to you and I regret that. I have a lot of suspicions about that man and will tell you my thoughts once I've finished questioning him.'

EIGHTY-SEVEN

'Awful,' said Mrs Solomon the following morning. 'Simply awful.'

Emma sat in the parlour with a warm shawl over her shoulders. She had slept little. Would the awful images ever leave her mind? Or were they destined to stay with her forever?

'Have you got to teach any lessons today?' asked Mrs Solomon.

'Yes. Beatrice at two o'clock.'

'Tell me the address and I'll send a telegram. You're in no fit state to teach anyone.'

'But they're expecting me today.'

'And you're in shock. There's no use in even attempting to teach a lesson. You won't be at your best and that's not fair on Beatrice.'

Laurence the cat rubbed against Emma's shins. She leaned forward to stroke his warm, shaggy fur, and he purred.

'I think you should take to your bed,' said Mrs Solomon. 'That's always the best cure. I'll bring you up some soup.'

Soup.

The word sent a jolt through Emma's thoughts as she

recalled Mary Fairchild. Lady Lou's words echoed in her mind – Mary had wanted William to propose. The same Mary who'd played at being so concerned, so friendly. Who'd just happened to be waiting outside the police station that day. Who'd watched from street corners when she thought Emma wouldn't notice.

The pieces clicked into place with sickening clarity.

'Mrs Langley?' Mrs Solomon's voice seemed to come from far away.

Emma blinked, pulling herself back to the present. 'I'm sorry. What did you say?'

'The soup – would you like some?'

'No.' The word came out sharper than she intended. 'No soup. Thank you.'

'But it's the best thing when you're not well.'

'I'm well. I'm just a little shocked.'

'You need to rest.'

'Very well.' Emma gave Laurence another stroke, then got to her feet.

She would rest now just to keep Mrs Solomon happy.

And then she wanted to speak to Mary Fairchild.

EIGHTY-EIGHT

Penny had barely slept all night. Florence had cried for most of it and now she was sleepy. But her face was flushed red and her skin was hot.

Penny felt sick with worry. Nothing she did made Florence any better. In fact, her condition was worsening. The baby lay in her cot while Penny applied a cold flannel and prayed the fever would abate.

But the cold compress had no effect. Penny wanted to pick Florence up and cuddle her, but she needed her daughter to cool down. Cuddling her would only make her warmer.

'She doesn't want any milk,' she said to James before he left for work.

'Maybe she's tired after she kept us awake all night.' James's face was lined and pale.

'I'm worried about her. I think she has a fever.' Her throat felt tight and there were tears at the back of her eyes. This was the first time Florence had been unwell. Was she overreacting?

'See what Mrs Tuttle thinks when she gets here. And you'll let me know how she gets on, won't you? Just send a telegram to the Yard.'

'I will.' Penny hoped the housekeeper would be able to reassure her.

Mrs Tuttle arrived ten minutes later. 'Oh dear,' she said. 'Florence isn't her usual self, is she? In fact, she looks quite unwell. I'll fetch a doctor.'

'What's wrong with Flonce?' asked Thomas. He couldn't quite say her name properly yet. Penny picked him up and cuddled him.

'I don't know,' she said. 'But the doctor is going to make her better again.'

She silently prayed she was right.

EIGHTY-NINE

Emma spent some time looking through the damp belongings in William's case. She guessed the items which had been in contact with the bloodstained knife had been removed.

She found receipts for bank deposits and withdrawals and they appeared to confirm the information she'd already learned about the state of William's finances.

She put his brush and comb, shaving mirror and favourite cufflinks with the rest of his belongings in his trunk.

It was disappointing that there was nothing in William's case which could give her any more clues about his murder.

But there seemed to be something missing still. His diary.

When Mrs Solomon went out to the shops that afternoon, Emma put on her coat, hat and gloves and left the house.

She chose to walk, hoping the cold air would clear her head. But thoughts of Lady Lou kept returning.

What had it been like for her when she'd realised she was falling? And had she been knocked unconscious by the fall or had she heard the train approaching?

Emma screwed her eyes shut and grimaced, trying desperately to clear the thoughts from her mind. It was awful. Too awful.

When she opened her eyes, she noticed a woman looking at her with concern. Emma gave her an embarrassed smile and continued walking. She had to turn her thoughts to Mary Fairchild.

It took forty minutes to reach Quaker Street. The final part of her walk took her along a bridge over the railway lines into Liverpool Street station. The sound of a train caused a swill of nausea in her stomach. She hurried on, hopeful to find Mary Fairchild at her soup stall.

As she approached, she could see a woman standing behind the large urns on the stall.

It wasn't Mary, it was Doris.

'Good afternoon, Mrs Langley!' Her cheery greeting felt out of place. Emma couldn't even return her smile.

'I'm looking for Miss Fairchild,' she said. 'Is she here?'

'Oh yes. She's just inside boiling the kettle.' She gestured at the red-brick Sunday school behind her.

Emma marched in through the door. What had Lady Lou called Mary Fairchild? A do-gooder. The sort of person who did good things to hide the bad things.

'Oh hello, Mrs Langley!' Miss Fairchild stood by the iron range. A large black kettle sat on top of it. 'You've come to join me by this nice, warm spot?'

She smiled and Emma could see why William had found her attractive with her fair hair, blue eyes and heart-shaped face.

Mary's smile faded as she realised Emma wasn't sharing her enthusiasm.

'Why didn't you tell me you knew my husband?' she said.

'Did I not?'

'When I first met you, you told me you'd heard about his murder, but you didn't mention you knew him.'

'It must have slipped my mind.' Mary's face stiffened, and she didn't look quite so pretty anymore. 'Most people around here knew him, so I suppose I assumed you knew I did, too.'

'You deliberately withheld it from me. Why?'

'It wasn't deliberate. You were upset about his death and I was more concerned about you than I was about myself.'

'That's a lie. You weren't concerned about me at all. Instead, you were intrigued about the wife of the man you wanted to marry.'

'Marry?' She spat out the word and her face flushed red.

'It's true, isn't it?' Emma took a step towards her.

'Who told you this?'

'It doesn't matter. But instead of telling me the truth, you pretended to be my friend.'

Mary stepped back, her eyes wide. 'I couldn't tell you the truth!'

'Why not?'

'You're a grieving widow, how could I admit such a thing to you and make you feel even worse?'

Emma clenched her teeth; she had never wanted Mary Fairchild's sympathy. 'I don't believe you were being that thoughtful, Miss Fairchild. I think you didn't tell me because you have something to hide.'

Mary shook her head. 'I have nothing to hide.'

Emma felt sure she was lying. 'Even though I found William's case by the side of this building? Only the murderer could have put that case there. William had it with him when he was attacked.' She fixed Mary's gaze. 'You've done a good job of persuading the police you had nothing to do with it. But you can't fool me! You had a love affair with William and wanted to marry him.'

Mary's lower lip wobbled and Emma could tell from her expression that this was true.

'You must have got very upset when he refused,' continued Emma. 'And when did you find out he was married? Was that when you lost your temper with him altogether? Is that what happened in Green Dragon Yard?'

'No!' Mary flung her hands over her face. 'No! It's not true!'

'Then you took his case from him and hid the knife in it. You dumped the case in the narrow passageway and hoped no one would ever go down there and find it. What a foolish place to hide it. Why not throw it into a canal?'

'That's what I would have done!' said Mary, her face stricken. 'Do you think if I was the murderer I would have been stupid enough to leave the case in a place where someone could find it? In a place I work from every day?'

Emma felt her anger seep away. Mary was right. 'So why did you lie?' she asked.

'Please just let me explain,' she said, her hands fidgeting with her apron. 'I first met Billy last year. I'd seen him with Lavinia Drummond, then I heard she'd left him for someone else. He passed by the stall one day and we began talking and I said he could help us if he liked, and he did. We got on well.'

'You had a love affair with him?'

'Yes. And only because I thought we would marry.'

'You were in love with him?'

'Yes. Briefly. But there were two sides to him, weren't there? When I learned he liked to drink and gamble, I was disappointed. But I thought I could change his ways.'

Emma couldn't resist a laugh.

Mary pursed her lips. 'I don't see why you think that's so funny.'

'William only looked out for himself,' said Emma bitterly. 'No one was ever going to change him.'

'We know that now, perhaps. But you must have felt the same when you married him, Mrs Langley?'

'I didn't want to change him.'

'No. Because you didn't fully realise who he was, did you?'

Emma felt her eyes begin to smart. It was true.

'We were both naïve,' said Mary. 'We were both charmed by him. We all were.'

'All?'

'Yes. All the ladies who fell for him. He enjoyed it, didn't he? He enjoyed playing games with us. I believe the only woman he ever loved was Lavinia Drummond. I think it was the greatest sadness of his life that he couldn't marry her.'

'He could have done if he'd really wanted to.'

'No, he couldn't. He wanted to maintain his respectability. He needed it to balance out his vices. If he'd married her, then he would have had no respectability left. But if he kept it, he could continue working as a lawyer and charm gentlewomen like you and I, Mrs Langley. Unfortunately for him, I didn't have any money. But you did.'

Mary's words were uncomfortably close to the truth. 'How long did your love affair last for?'

'Until I found out about you.'

'Which was when?'

'Last month. I saw you in Northampton Square together. I happened to be passing through and I saw you walking arm-in-arm.'

Emma recalled those walks. William had helped her around Northampton Square to build her strength again after her illness.

'I confronted him after that,' said Mary. 'And he told me the truth.'

'And what was the truth?'

'That he wasn't in love with you, but he needed the money.'

Although Emma had grown accustomed to this unpleasant

fact, hearing it now from Mary Fairchild seemed particularly hurtful. Her eyes grew damp and she willed the tears away.

The kettle's whistle pierced the silence. Mary lifted it carefully, the cloth wrapped around its handle, steam billowing as she set it on the iron trivet. Her movements were precise, controlled – at odds with the tremor in her voice.

'Tell me what happened when you confronted him,' Emma pressed, her throat tight. 'Were you angry?'

Mary's hands stilled on the kettle. 'Angry? I was furious. Betrayed.' She gave a bitter laugh. 'Though I should have known better. I knew exactly what kind of man he was.' Her voice dropped. 'And that's why his death... it's my fault.'

NINETY

'You're responsible for my husband's murder?' gasped Emma. 'How?'

'I introduced him to Gideon Flynn,' said Mary Fairchild. 'Gideon is my brother.'

Emma felt her jaw drop.

'Obviously I don't want a lot of people to know that and it's why I changed my surname. I grew up in the rooms above that shop on Crispin Street. Our father was a bully. Unfortunately, Gideon bore the brunt of it, because he was the boy. Father made Gideon take over the shop from him.

'Mother has always worked in the shop. She worked there for Father, and she does the same for Gideon now. She's always carried on doing the same thing, year in, year out. Always loyal.

'I got away as soon as I could. I went to live with my aunt in Poplar when I was fourteen. The aunt who knows Annie Besant who helped the matchgirls. She's an elderly lady now, but she inspired me to get involved with helping the matchgirls' cause. They lost out on their wages, but we did what we could to support them. I suppose that's why I've always wanted to help those in need.'

Emma felt a pang of guilt for thinking that Mary Fairchild had been a do-gooder, almost too pleasant for her own good.

'I suppose I'm trying to explain why Gideon is like he is, and why I am like I am. I'm not proud of him at all. I feel ashamed of what he's become. He's a strange, lonely, twisted man.

'I mistakenly told Billy about my brother. I complained about him to Billy one day and then he called on him. I should have kept them completely apart. From that day onwards, Gideon had him in his grasp. He offered to invest money for Billy for large returns but that didn't come to anything. To appease him, he then lent him money so Billy was in debt to him. Gideon put him to work collecting his debts for him. What a horrible, unpleasant job. All those poor people who found themselves on hard times. Then Billy told me Gideon had passed on the debt to someone else. So it became someone else's problem and Billy continued to spend time in his company. Gideon was running his bookmaker service from the shop and Billy helped. He also spent every penny he had on Gideon's various investments that he created. Their fortunes went up and down. Sometimes they would make a lot of money, and I suppose that's what encouraged them to carry on, but before long they lost it all again.'

'A few minutes ago, you told me you were responsible for his murder,' said Emma. 'What do you mean by that?'

'It pains me to say it, but I'm certain Gideon murdered Billy. They must have fallen out over the money once and for all, and it was Gideon who attacked him that night. He took his case from him, broke the padlock, put the knife in the case, and then he left the case at the side of this building. A place where I never went but close enough to where I do my work so that it would look like I'd put it there.'

'Your own brother framed you for William's murder?'

'Yes.' She gave a shaky sigh. 'That's what I believe.'

Emma rested a hand on her arm, hoping she could persuade her to do the right thing. 'You know what you have to do, don't you, Miss Fairchild? You need to tell everything you've told me to the police.'

'But Gideon is already in custody, isn't he?'

'Exactly. They already have him. And if you truly believe that he murdered my husband, then he can be tried for murder, can't he?'

Mary rubbed her brow. 'I know it's the right thing to do,' she said, 'but I've been in such a quandary over this for weeks. I want to tell the police what I believe, but I don't know if I'm definitely right. And despite everything, Gideon is still my brother. I know my mother will die of a broken heart if Gideon is found guilty of murder.'

NINETY-ONE

Emma walked to Liverpool Street station, paying little attention to her surroundings. Her conversation with Mary Fairchild repeated in her mind and she felt unsure what to think. Had Mary told her the truth? Or did she lie as much as her brother?

Despite Mary's heartfelt explanation, Emma believed she would have been upset and angry when she'd discovered William had been married. Angry enough to murder him?

She reached the station ticket office and rubbed at her neck which ached with tension. How far could she trust her own judgement? Her mind felt so muddled that she couldn't be certain of anything anymore.

It was time to ask Penny what she made of it all.

Emma travelled by the underground railway to St John's Wood. It was raining when she emerged from the railway station and she'd forgotten to bring her umbrella. She hurried on to Penny's home in Henstridge Place.

Mrs Tuttle answered the door. She looked as tired and weary as Emma felt.

'I'm afraid Mrs Blakely isn't here,' she said. 'It's poor baby Florence. They've had to take her to the hospital.'

'Oh, goodness!' Emma's heart dropped like a stone.

'She has a fever. A bad one.'

'I'm so sorry for disturbing you at a time like this.'

'Please don't worry. You weren't to know. I'm here minding Thomas. Hopefully, his little sister will come home soon.'

'I hope so too.'

Emma walked slowly back to the station, her hat and coat growing wetter in the rain. Her argument with Miss Fairchild seemed petty now when compared to the delicate life of a young child.

Emma's footsteps echoed in the empty hallway. A cream envelope lay on the hall table, innocent-looking except for the unfamiliar hand that had written her name. Her fingers trembled slightly as she broke the seal. The message inside was brief, the writing neat and precise:

I know you pushed Lady Lou. Leave London now before they come for you.

She read it twice, her breath catching. The threat was clear – someone wanted her gone. Or silenced.

NINETY-TWO

Nothing happened for two days.

Emma didn't leave London. But she didn't leave the house, either. She cancelled her lessons for the week.

Fortunately, no new notes were posted through the door. Surely no one believed she'd pushed Lady Lou? She had explained everything to Detective Inspector Bradshaw and he'd been sympathetic. If he suspected her, then he would have questioned her again by now.

And who was going to come for her? Hopefully the threat was meaningless.

But there was also the risk it wasn't. She thought again about the incident with the horse and carriage which had almost knocked her over on Commercial Street. An accident? Or had someone driven directly at her?

And she'd never managed to establish the identity of the man who had watched her and Lavinia Drummond at Liverpool Street station.

Emma wanted to discuss the note with Penny before she informed the police. Penny had told her about threatening messages she'd received while working as a news reporter. Perhaps Penny could help her work out who'd sent the note.

But there had been no word from Penny since Emma had learned about Florence's illness. Emma wanted to call at the house and find out how the baby was doing. But she felt wary of bothering the family at a difficult time.

Penny would be in touch again when she felt ready. If she ever did feel ready again.

By Friday, the walls of her room felt like a prison. Emma paced, her mind racing between fragments of conversations, half-formed theories, dead ends. She couldn't bear another hour of wondering, waiting.

She needed to see it all fresh. Start over. Retrace every step.

NINETY-THREE

It was another foggy day in Whitechapel. Emma stood where Green Dragon Yard met Whitechapel Road. The exact spot William had stood on the night of his death and hailed the hansom cab.

So Emma did the same.

She asked the driver to take her to the Whitstable Guest House on Canrobert Street in Bethnal Green. As the horse moved off, she lifted the hatch and asked the cabman for the time.

'It's just after eleven, madam.'

They passed through the cold, foggy streets of Whitechapel, heading north. After passing beneath the railway lines, they reached Bethnal Green where the streets were equally dismal.

When the cab reached Whitstable Guest House, Emma asked the cabman for time again. 'Almost quarter past eleven, madam. That will be a shilling for the fare.'

'I'm not getting out here. Can you take me to Liverpool Street station now, please?' Emma asked, an idea forming.

At the station, she stood where it had begun – where William had left her that misty morning. Methodically, she began reconstructing his movements, seeing the pieces with new clarity. The pattern was there... She could hear Penny's voice in her head... *Keep pulling at the threads.*

Another envelope was waiting for Emma on the hallway table when she returned that evening. This time, it was a telegram. And it bore good news:

> Florence recovered. We are home. Please call on us tomorrow.

Emma smiled. The timing was perfect.

NINETY-FOUR

Emma bought a copy of the *Morning Express* on her way to the station the following morning. An article caught her eye as she read it on the train:

A picture framer, Gideon Flynn, was charged yesterday at Worship Street police court with using his premises on Crispin Street, Spitalfields, for betting purposes. Two detectives found a tape machine in a room above the shop and a large amount of cash books and papers were seized. The case was adjourned.

There was no mention of the knives found in Flynn's drawer. Although storing them there wasn't illegal, surely the sinister find had raised the police's suspicions?

It was heart-warming to see Penny and her family when Emma arrived at their home. Young Thomas sang to himself as he played with his spinning top and Tiger the cat strolled through the sitting room, her tail held high.

'I can't believe how well Florence has recovered!' said Penny. 'It's as though she was never unwell.'

'Let's not forget how frightening it was in the hospital,' said James as he cuddled the happy baby on his lap. He looked pale with dark circles beneath his eyes.

'But she's better again, James,' said Penny, tickling Florence's cheek. 'And I don't want to set foot in any hospital again for a very long time. But that's enough about that.'

'I've just been reading about Gideon Flynn,' said Emma. 'He's been charged with betting offences.'

'That's right,' said James. 'It's all we can get him for at the moment, but our work continues.' Florence grabbed his finger and he winced as she bit on it.

'Do you think Flynn could be Jack the Ripper?' Emma asked him.

'He's one of H Division's suspects. But they have quite a few suspects. They'll have to work hard now on accounting for his whereabouts at the time of each attack.'

Penny sighed. 'They have a lot of work to do. But having met Flynn, it wouldn't surprise me if he's the man behind the murders. At least he's in custody now and can't harm anyone else.' She turned to Emma. 'How have you been? I read about Lady Lou's death in the newspaper.'

'Yes, so tragic.' Emma chose not to elaborate. It seemed inappropriate to discuss something so horrific within earshot of young children. Thomas was sitting on the rug carefully building a tower of blocks while Tiger the cat watched him.

'Shall we talk in the dining room?' whispered Penny, somehow reading Emma's mind.

Penny made some tea, then they sat in the dining room together while Emma told her about Lady Lou and Mary Fairchild.

'I was quite convinced Mary was William's murderer,' said Emma. 'But although she must have been angry to discover he hadn't told her about his marriage to me, would she really have murdered him in revenge? Although I don't like her, she seems fairly measured and rational in her thoughts.'

Emma then showed Penny the threatening note.

'How horrible,' she said, pulling a grimace. 'But it's a good sign.'

Emma gave a puzzled laugh. 'Good? Why?'

'It means you're worrying someone. They think you're going to find out they're the person behind this. These threats often come to nothing, they just want to frighten you.'

'Well it's worked.'

Penny stroked her chin as she thought. 'So if it wasn't Mary,' she said, 'then who could it have been? Mr Theobald has confessed his part in it all, and so has Mr Flynn. Lady Lou didn't do it, although it's possible she was tricked into helping someone. Was it Tommy Fletcher?'

'No,' said Emma. 'The answer is simpler than that. In fact, I'm surprised we didn't consider it before.'

'Then who?'

'It was the cabman,' said Emma confidently. 'Samuel Carter.'

NINETY-FIVE

'Explain it to James,' said Penny as they entered the sitting room.

'Explain what to James?' he replied from the rug where he was sitting with Florence and helping Thomas build a wall with his wooden blocks.

Emma and Penny sat down.

'I'm certain Samuel Carter the cabman murdered my husband,' said Emma.

'The cabman who picked him up on Whitechapel Road?' James looked surprised.

'Yes. It explains why William didn't ask to be taken to the hospital when he hailed the cab. He wasn't injured at that point.'

'Of course!' said James. 'We said he probably hadn't realised how badly he had been injured, but we were mistaken.'

'If he'd been injured then he would have asked for help,' said Emma. 'He would have asked for a doctor, or he might have asked to be taken to the hospital. He might even have attempted to walk to the hospital, it wasn't far away.'

'I agree,' said Penny.

'Then there's the lodging house,' said Emma. 'Carter said William asked to be taken to the lodging house on Canrobert Street. I spoke to the lady who runs it. She told me Carter hammered on her door at half past one that night, asking for help. William was already dead by then. She said the cabman was very shaken up. He could have been acting, though, couldn't he?

'I couldn't understand why William had arranged to stay at that lodging house,' continued Emma. 'The landlady told me he'd never stayed there before, nor had he booked a room for that night. He carried a case around with him that evening. Surely if he planned to stay in a lodging house, he would have booked a room in advance and left the case there so he didn't have to walk about with it?'

'So this suggests the cabman decided to drive William to the lodging house to make it look like William had planned the destination and happened to die on the way there,' said Penny.

'Yes,' said Emma. 'I'm quite sure William had never heard of that lodging house before and had never planned to stay there.'

'He must have planned to stay somewhere, though,' said James.

'I think he planned to go back to Lavinia Drummond,' said Emma. 'She told me he'd turned up on the Saturday afternoon expecting to stay with her for a few days. She turned him away because he was drunk. He was probably planning to go back to her house in the hope she had changed her mind.'

'So William could have got into the hansom cab and asked to be taken to Miss Drummond's house,' said James. 'Remind me where she lived.'

'Fleur de Lis Street,' said Emma. 'Just under a mile from Green Dragon Yard.'

'But instead, Carter drove William to Canrobert Street in Bethnal Green.'

'Yes,' said Emma. 'I estimate that distance is just over a mile. I tested the route in a hansom cab yesterday. The journey time was almost fifteen minutes. We were held up in traffic a few times and I think the journey would be much quicker in the early hours of the morning.'

'Yes, it would,' said James.

'The landlady of the lodging house said Carter brought William to her at half past one,' said Penny.

'Yes,' said Emma. 'And this is where Carter has made his mistake. He says he picked up William from the junction with Green Dragon Yard at a quarter to one. That timing fits with what Lady Lou said if we believe the last time she saw William was in Green Dragon Yard at half past twelve. And that also fits with Tommy Fletcher's claim that William left his home between midnight and quarter past.'

'Carter says he picked up William at a quarter to one,' said Penny. 'The landlady says Carter arrived in Canrobert Street at half past one. Carter took forty-five minutes to make a journey which is just over a mile and normally takes ten or fifteen minutes by cab.'

'Forty-five minutes unaccounted for,' said James. 'Carter did make a mistake. He should have said quarter past one to cover his tracks.'

'But then it wouldn't have tied in with what Lady Lou and Tommy Fletcher said,' said Emma. 'It would have meant William took forty-five minutes to walk through Green Dragon Yard.'

'Carter was probably hoping no one would question the times too much,' said Penny.

'So during those forty-five minutes,' said James. 'Carter drove William somewhere, stopped the cab and...' He glanced at the children. 'You know what.'

'Somewhere quiet,' said Penny. 'There may even be witnesses who saw his cab making its detour that night.'

'Good point,' said James. 'You've thought this through excellently, Mrs Langley. But there's one big question remaining. Samuel Carter may have murdered your husband. But why? What was his motive?'

'I can't think of one,' said Emma. 'So I think he was paid to do it.'

'By who?'

'Cardwell and Theobald.'

NINETY-SIX

'This can only be a theory, Mrs Langley,' said James. 'You can't be sure of it.'

'No. But I suspect Samuel Carter has been working for Cardwell and Theobald as a cabman. When I first visited the firm to speak to Mr Theobald about William, I saw Samuel Carter on his cab by their office on Bedford Row. He mistakenly thought I was going to hail him and told me he was already booked.'

'So he was there to pick up someone from the law firm?' said James.

'I think so. And I saw Samuel Carter again recently,' said Emma. 'Just over a week ago, I turned away the solicitor from Cardwell and Theobald, Mr O'Brien. I spoke to him on the doorstep of the house I'm staying in on Northampton Square. I could see the hansom cab he had arrived in behind him. And guess who was driving that cab?'

'Samuel Carter,' said Penny. 'They must employ him as a regular cab driver.'

'And possibly to do a few other things, too. But if Cardwell and Theobald planned this attack on Mr Langley, several things had to fall into place. They needed him to be on Whitechapel Road that night so Carter could pick him up in his cab.'

'Which is where Lady Lou and Tommy Fletcher come in,' said Emma. 'I think they were paid to take William to Fletcher's house that night, then guide him down to Whitechapel Road. Fletcher was inconsistent in his account of what happened that evening. At the inquest, he said William had approached him and his friends and asked to play cards with them. But when Penny and I spoke to him a week ago in the Ten Bells, he said they'd asked William to join them.'

'True,' said Penny. 'I remember that.'

'So Fletcher took William to his house, then arranged for him to leave about midnight and fall into the hands of Lady Lou,' said William.

'Lady Lou had been asked to do something,' said Emma. 'Although she wasn't entirely clear about what it was. She was quite drunk when I spoke to her and she clearly felt bad about her actions. She suggested she and Tommy had been asked to do something and she said she had been paid five shillings. From what she told me, I don't think either of them expected William to be murdered. They both seemed genuinely upset about his death.'

'So they were paid to lead him into a trap,' said James. 'But they had no idea the outcome would be so serious. How did Cardwell and Theobald know William would be in Whitechapel that day? His supposed plan was to travel to Suffolk.'

'Maybe they had someone watching him?' said Penny.

'I suppose so. There could have been a few people running around passing on messages, couldn't there? If this is what happened, it's quite a masterful plan. And to think Theobald told me they weren't bothered about twenty pounds a month! I think it's time we paid them a visit. What day is it? Saturday. Some workplaces close at lunchtime on a Saturday, but if we're quick, we might catch them there. Hopefully Carter will be there too.'

'We can pass by Mrs Tuttle's house and ask her to mind the children for an hour,' said Penny. 'We can pay her double.'

'Good,' said James. 'I'll go to St John's Wood police station now and ask them to send a wire to Detective Inspector Bradshaw. He can meet us there and also send some men out to look for Carter.'

NINETY-SEVEN

A large black windowless carriage and two horses was waiting for them on Bedford Row.

'Don't tell me Bradshaw's parked the Black Maria right in front of their offices!' fumed James. 'If that's not going to tip them off, I don't know what will!'

He jumped out of the hackney carriage and ordered the Black Maria to move out of sight.

Emma glanced nervously at Cardwell and Theobald's offices as she and Penny waited on the pavement. All seemed quiet, perhaps they hadn't noticed the police carriage. Was anyone even in the office?

'I hope I'm not mistaken,' she said to Penny. Her heart thudded heavily.

'I don't think you are. And James doesn't, either.' Penny gave her a reassuring smile. 'I think you've done an astonishing job of piecing together all the information and conversations from the past few weeks.'

. . .

Mr Theobald was surprisingly welcoming, his heavy jowls wobbling as he greeted them. 'You've caught us just in time, Inspector,' he said to James. 'We don't work too late on a Saturday. And how are you, Mrs Langley? It's lovely to see you again.'

His insincerity made Emma's toes curl. She politely gave him a thin smile.

'I'd like to put some things to you, Mr Theobald,' said James. 'And while we're talking, my colleague, Detective Inspector Bradshaw, and his men would like to search your offices, please.'

'Of course! Let's talk in the boardroom.'

Emma thought he seemed too genial. As if he had a trick up his sleeve.

He led them to the room with the long, well-polished table and portraits of gentlemen hung on the wall.

'Will Mr Cardwell be joining us?' said James.

'You'd like him to? Oh, of course.'

Mr Cardwell was a bird-like man with a long, sharp nose and a flat, balding head. He was less enthusiastic than Mr Theobald and made a point of examining his watch as soon as he sat down.

Emma's mouth was dry. She felt anxious about a confrontation, but she couldn't bear the suspense of waiting for it. 'May I ask a quick question first?' she asked.

'Of course, Mrs Langley,' said Mr Theobald.

She opened her bag and took out the anonymous threatening note. 'Do you recognise this?' she asked, pushing it across the table to him.

She watched as Mr Theobald read it, then passed it to Mr Cardwell. They both shook their heads.

'Who's Lady Lou?' asked Mr Theobald.

'I think you sent me that note because I turned away Mr O'Brien,' said Emma. 'He was unhappy when I asked him to leave, and I think that's because you sent him to keep an eye on me.'

'We were merely looking out for the widow of a former employee, Mr Langley.'

'A former employee who blackmailed you.'

'Yes. We've been over this.' Mr Theobald sighed and turned to James. 'Are we going to discuss anything new, Inspector? Or merely cover old ground?'

Emma felt her shoulders slump. Mr Theobald had evaded her accusation.

'You didn't send Mrs Langley the threatening note?' asked James.

'Absolutely not. We've got far better things to be getting on with.'

'And I don't have a lot of time,' said Mr Cardwell, tapping his fingers on the table.

'I'll get on with it,' said James. 'But before I begin, I should explain this detective work is not mine. Mrs Langley is the lady who worked this out.'

'With a lot of help from Mrs Blakely,' said Emma.

'Not that much help,' said Penny. They exchanged a glance and Penny smiled.

James got to his feet and explained the actions he believed Samuel Carter had made on the night of William's death. Both Cardwell and Theobald listened impassively. If they felt any emotion, they didn't show it.

'Does Samuel Carter work for you?' James asked them.

'Occasionally,' said Cardwell. 'He works for a lot of people. He's a cab driver.'

'Do either of you know where we can find him?'

Both men shook their heads.

'You don't know where he lives?'

Theobald turned to Cardwell. 'I suppose we have a record of it somewhere, don't we?'

Cardwell scratched his nose. 'Somewhere I suppose.'

'It's important we speak to him as soon as possible,' said James. 'We believe you paid him to kill William Langley. And it shall come as no surprise to the pair of you that I'm going to arrest you both today for murder.'

Cardwell chuckled. 'All because of a fantastical story cooked up by a hysterical woman?'

Emma felt a burn of anger in her chest.

'We'll see about that,' said James. He strode over to the door, and opened it. 'Bradshaw!' he hollered down the corridor.

'There's no need to shout,' said Theobald. 'Awfully uncouth.'

Moments later, Bradshaw appeared, calm and officious.

'Have you found anything?' James asked him.

'We've found some interesting volumes on the shelves of Mr Theobald's office,' said Bradshaw. 'Their pages have been removed to accommodate secret papers.'

'That's because we deal with highly confidential matters in this law firm,' said Mr Cardwell.

'I'm sure you do,' said Bradshaw. 'Is that why you had William Langley's diary hidden away there?'

Emma and Penny exchanged a glance. They hadn't had time to check all the volumes, so they had missed the diary.

'His diary was in his case,' said Emma. 'The case he had with him on the night he was murdered.'

'Interesting,' said Bradshaw. 'Perhaps you gentlemen can accompany me to the station and explain how you came by it?'

NINETY-EIGHT

'You'll need more than Langley's diary for evidence, and you know it,' spat Mr Cardwell.

'Perhaps this isn't the first time you've murdered an employee,' said James. 'What happened to Joseph Moore, the lawyer in the river?'

'That was fifteen years ago,' said Cardwell.

'So you remember him then?'

'It was an accident,' said Theobald with a roll of his eyes. 'And the coroner ruled it as such.'

'I'm sure the case can be revisited if new evidence presents itself,' said James as he paced the room. 'And I'm looking forward to speaking to Mr Carter too. I'm quite sure he'll assist us.'

'If you can find him,' said Cardwell.

'If? So you're not going to tell us where he is?' James placed his hands on the table and leaned over him. 'That's your feeble attempt to scupper our plan, is it?'

'At least tell us what happened to Lavinia Drummond,' said Emma. 'She didn't deserve what happened to her.'

'Miss Drummond?' said Mr Cardwell. 'I don't recall her. Do you, Edward?'

Mr Theobald shook his head.

'She knew something,' said Penny sharply. 'That's why you had her killed. Did you ask Carter to murder her, too?'

A long pause followed. Cardwell examined his nails. 'Let's put it this way,' he said. 'When Langley blackmailed this firm, there had to be a method of getting the funds to him with no one else making the connection. Carter delivered the money to an associate of Langley's.'

'And the associate was Miss Drummond?' said Penny. 'The money was left in a newspaper on a bench near the fountain in Red Lion Square, is that right?'

'You'd have to ask Carter.' Cardwell steepled his fingers. 'If you ever find him.'

'I'll interpret that as yes,' said Penny. 'You murdered Miss Drummond because she knew Mr Langley was blackmailing you. You couldn't bear the thought of her mentioning it to anyone. Especially after you murdered Mr Langley. To you, her life was cheap.'

Emma felt her fists ball with anger as she regarded the nonchalant expressions on the two men.

'Right then,' said James. 'Bradshaw, you can help me make these arrests and we'll get them into the Black Maria outside.'

Emma and Penny left the room. They waited outside on the pavement and watched as Cardwell and Theobald were marched, handcuffed, to the police carriage.

'Well done, Emma,' said Penny. 'You must be exhausted.'

'I am. And I'm angry too. Somehow, watching them being taken away doesn't take away the anger, too.'

'Perhaps you'll feel better once they're convicted,' said Penny. 'And I'm sure you'll feel a lot better when they arrest Samuel Carter. He can't have gone far.'

James walked over to them. 'I need to go with Bradshaw and

his men to accompany the prisoners to the station. Then we'll get looking for Carter. Will you take a cab home?'

'Yes,' said Penny. 'We'll share a cab.' She took Emma's arm. 'I can get back to St John's Wood via Northampton Square.'

'Are you sure?' said Emma. 'It's a bit of a detour.'

'Of course.' Penny turned back to her husband. 'Good luck, James. And well done!'

He waved goodbye, and Emma and Penny walked up Bedford Row. 'There's a cab now,' said Penny, hailing it.

NINETY-NINE

'Cardwell and Theobald have no remorse, do they?' said Emma as the cab took her and Penny north along Bedford Row.

'I'm afraid not. But that's probably because they're still thinking they can somehow get out of this. They'll probably try to blame Carter for it all. Let's not forget they're both lawyers, they think they're going to be quite good at arguing their case.'

The horse came to a sudden halt. Then the cab rocked a little.

'Oh!' said Penny, gripping Emma's arm. 'What's happening?'

Emma lifted the hatch. 'Is everything all right?' she asked.

'Yes,' said the cabman. 'Someone tried to rob me just then, but I shook him off.'

'Oh no!' said Penny. 'How worrying. You wouldn't expect that in Bedford Row.'

The horse took off at a trot.

'Fancy trying such a thing when the police are close by,' said Penny. 'I suppose the robber tried his luck while they were distracted.'

The cab slowed as it reached Theobald's Road, then crossed over it and into Great James Street.

'Shouldn't we have turned right on Theobald's Road?' said Penny.

'Yes,' said Emma. 'But we can also turn right at the end of this street.'

'I wonder what your husband's diary had in it which Cardwell and Theobald were so interested in.'

'Something which they presumably wanted to keep hidden. I suspect Carter must have taken the case to them once he'd murdered William. Then they must have gone through William's belongings, looking for anything which could implicate them in his murder. Correspondence about the blackmail, that sort of thing.'

'Yes, I think you could be right. The diary must have had something in it of that nature. Then, once they were finished with the case, Carter must have put it in the alleyway next to the Sunday school so Mary Fairchild would be suspected.'

'Yes. He'd probably hoped someone would have discovered it sooner. And I keep thinking about the runaway horse on Commercial Street.'

'Which horse?'

'I forgot to mention it to you. A newspaper seller had to knock me out of the path of a bolting horse about nine days ago. I assumed the horse had bolted but I wonder if it was deliberate.'

'Carter?'

'He could have driven his carriage at me, couldn't he? I didn't get a chance to look at the driver's face. It happened so quickly. But the more I think about it, the more I'm convinced Carter tried to harm me.'

'Tried to kill you by the sound of things,' said Penny. 'Thank goodness the newspaper seller was so quick thinking. Where are we now?'

'Taking a roundabout route to Northampton Square, I think. But the driver seems to be in a bit of a hurry.' The horse trotted briskly past terraces of neat townhouses.

At the top of the road, they turned right into Guilford Street, then left into Gray's Inn Road. The cabman urged the horse to move faster.

'I don't think this is right,' said Penny. 'We're not heading in the direction of Northampton Square, are we?'

'No we're not,' said Emma. She lifted the hatch. 'Stop here please, driver!'

But there was no response.

'Can you stop the cab please?'

'He can't hear,' said Penny. 'Or he's ignoring us.' She pushed at the pair of doors which closed over their legs. They could only be opened by a lever which the cab driver operated.

Emma and Penny stopped talking, both alert to their surroundings.

The cab weaved its way through the traffic, narrowly dodging a horse tram.

A cold sickening sensation grew in Emma's stomach. 'I don't like this,' she said.

'Me neither,' said Penny. 'Something odd is happening.'

Emma felt even worse. She had hoped Penny would have some positive words to reassure her, but if she was worried then the situation was clearly dangerous.

The cab man urged the horse into a canter. Emma and Penny lurched from side to side with the movement.

'Stop!' they called out.

Drivers on other vehicles called out curse words as the cab sped past them.

'No!' said Penny. 'He's taking us somewhere, isn't he?'

Emma felt a cold sweat break out. She pushed at the doors again, hoping they would somehow budge.

'Slow down!' she called out. 'Wherever you're taking us, slow down!'

Gray's Inn Road came to an end, they lurched to the left and Emma caught sight of King's Cross railway station on their right.

'Help!' called out Penny. She waved frantically at people on the pavement. Someone waved back, assuming she was in high spirits. Other people ignored her.

'Why won't someone help us?'

They made a sharp turn to the right and Emma gripped the side of the carriage, worried it would tip over. They passed along the road between King's Cross and St Pancras stations.

'The goods yard and the gasworks,' said Penny.

They exchanged a fearful glance. He was taking them to a place where there would be few people about.

'There are two of us,' said Emma. 'And only one of him. We can overpower him.'

'And if he has a knife?'

Emma didn't know what to say.

They took another turn to the right, and the horse cantered along the road between the tall cylinders of King's Cross gasworks.

Then the cabman pulled the horse to a sudden halt. Sweat had broken out across the horse's haunches, and Emma felt desperately sorry for the poor animal.

The doors in front of them opened and they jumped out as quickly as they could.

The cab had stopped on a bridge over the Regent's Canal. The water was deep and filthy. Around them were the gasworks, goods sheds and railway sidings. Emma glanced behind them. The yard behind was a dead end.

Samuel Carter jumped down from his seat. Emma had never realised until now how unpleasant his appearance was with his rough skin and pale eyes. He wore a long black coat and something sharp and shiny glinted in his hand.

He walked towards them. 'Did you enjoy the ride, ladies?'

'Get away from us,' said Penny.

'No one will hear you scream around here,' he said. 'Although if you want to get away, you could always jump into the canal and swim for it.' He laughed. 'The cold will incapacitate you within minutes. Which do you prefer? Drowning or my knife?'

'Neither,' said Penny. 'We're not ready to die.'

'No? That is a shame. Because the pair of you have become a terrible nuisance in recent weeks.'

'Did you drive your carriage at me?' asked Emma.

He laughed again. 'Oh yes, that was a good one. It's a desperate shame I didn't succeed.'

'And the note?'

'There was truth in it though, wasn't there? You pushed Lady Lou to her death. She sent your husband to his death so you did it in revenge.'

'I did not! And Lady Lou had no idea what she'd got caught up in!'

'Because she was stupid. Give people a few shillings in a place like Whitechapel and they'll do anything for you. That said, she did her job admirably. She sent him down to the place where I was waiting for him. It was all remarkably easy.' His expression hardened. 'Until you two came along. Now, all I've got to do is decide who's first. The trick is to do away with the stronger one before the weaker one. Now which one of you is it?' He stared at Emma. 'You're younger. But does that make you stronger? It doesn't always follow.'

'You're a cruel, heartless man,' she said. 'You murdered my husband and Lavinia. And you've mistreated this poor horse.'

'Oh, he'll be all right. He's a tough one.'

'How much did they pay you to murder?' asked Emma. 'Do you really have so little regard for human life?'

He stepped closer to her. 'I suppose I'll have to do you first because you're the noisy one. Some of you women never know when to stop talking, do you?'

'No!' Penny screamed as he grabbed Emma's arm. She tried to pull away, but he was too strong. The blade glinted in his hand. If only she could duck it...

Carter crashed to the ground. His grip on her arm suddenly went.

Emma stepped away, panting. There were two men on Carter's back and he was squashed, face down, into the ground.

James and Detective Inspector Bradshaw.

'Are you both all right?' said James.

'Yes,' said Penny.

'We followed in another cab but worried we were going to lose you.'

'But you didn't,' said Emma. 'Thank you.'

'And well done,' said Penny. 'You found Samuel Carter.'

ONE HUNDRED

The hackney carriage which James and Detective Inspector Bradshaw had taken was stopped behind the hansom cab. Two constables had accompanied them. One was attending to the distressed horse while another helped James put handcuffs on Samuel Carter's wrists.

'Are you all right, ladies?' asked Bradshaw.

'I think so,' said Emma. 'We're not physically harmed.'

'No,' said Penny. 'Just rather shaken up. I'm just relieved there wasn't an accident on our way here. I really hope the poor horse is going to be all right.'

'I think he will be,' he said. The constable had untethered the horse from the cab and was walking him up and down the road to keep him calm. 'He doesn't look lame at all, but we'll make sure he's checked over by a veterinarian. The poor animal has had a fright just as you have.'

'I don't even understand where Samuel Carter came from,' said Penny.

'I suppose he must have been in the building when we were there,' said Emma. 'And Mr Theobald or Mr Cardwell must have got word to him that we were leaving.'

'Yes, I suppose that could be the case,' said Penny. 'They could have asked a member of staff to inform him to watch us leave.'

'We were too distracted with putting Cardwell and Theobald in the Black Maria,' said Bradshaw. 'The last thing we expected was the hijack of the cab you were in. The first we knew about it was when the poor driver came running down the road to tell us that a man had jumped onto the side of his cab and threatened him with a knife. He told him to get down from his seat, otherwise he would attack him and his horse. The driver reluctantly complied, but he told us that two women were in the cab, and that's when we knew the pair of you were in danger.'

'He jumped onto the side of the cab?' said Penny. 'Emma and I were too busy chatting to notice that!'

Bradshaw rolled his eyes and smiled. 'That's ladies for you. Luckily we hailed a hackney carriage but four-wheelers aren't as fast as hansoms.'

'But you did your best, and you got here on time,' said Penny. 'Thank you.'

'Get to your feet!' James shouted at Carter. The cabman stood up. Emma shuddered as she saw the knife lying in a puddle on the ground.

James and the constable guided Carter to the hackney carriage.

'You ladies really do need to get home now,' said Bradshaw. 'I'll hail a cab for you on Euston Road.'

'No, it's quite all right thank you,' said Penny. 'I think we'll walk to King's Cross station and take the train.'

ONE HUNDRED AND ONE

'Oh, I love babies,' said Mrs Solomon, bouncing Florence in her lap. 'We're still waiting for our grandchildren to arrive, aren't we Ronald?'

There was no answer from her husband.

'Ronald?' she shouted.

'What?'

'I said we're still waiting for our grandchildren to arrive, aren't we?'

'Oh yes. Yes we are.'

Emma and Penny exchanged a smile.

Mrs Solomon had insisted on inviting Penny, James and their children around for afternoon tea to celebrate the arrest of Cardwell, Theobald and Carter.

Laurence the cat rested on the hearthrug and Thomas rested his toy train on his shaggy fur. He was very amused when the cat didn't flinch.

'More sandwiches, Mrs Blakely?' said Mrs Solomon. 'Do help yourself. I'm not handing them round because I'm too busy with your darling daughter.' Mrs Solomon carried on cooing at Florence who gurgled back with joy.

'Thank you, but I'm completely full,' said Penny.

'Nonsense! You've hardly eaten anything. I like my guests to get their fill when they're here.'

'All right then.' Penny politely helped herself to another cucumber sandwich from the neatly stacked arrangement.

'So Mr Blakely,' said Mr Solomon. 'What's it like working at Scotland Yard?'

'I enjoy it very much,' said James, loud enough for Mr Solomon to hear. 'But I'm quite sure the ladies don't want to be bored hearing about it all.'

'Well from what I can work out, the police haven't done very much recently, anyway,' said Mrs Solomon. 'The person who solved William Langley's murder was his own wife!'

'With a lot of help from Mrs Blakely,' added Emma.

'Only a little bit,' said Penny, winking at Emma.

'No, it's true,' said James. 'It's fair to say both ladies solved this case. I've been saying for a long time we need to allow women to be detectives in Scotland Yard.'

'I agree with that,' said Mrs Solomon.

'I don't,' grumbled her husband. 'It's not suitable for ladies.'

'Very well,' said Mrs Solomon. 'But try telling that to Mrs Langley. I think she's got a skill for detective work. The next time Mr Blakely needs a murder solving, he'll be calling on her for help. Just you wait and see.'

'I think a walk would be nice,' said Emma. The room suddenly felt warm and stuffy.

'A walk?' said Mrs Solomon. 'Where?'

'Just around and about.'

'Yes you look like you need some air,' she said. 'A walk will put a bit of colour in your cheeks. I'll stay here and mind the babies.'

ONE HUNDRED AND TWO

Emma and Penny walked around Northampton Square together while James remained with Mr and Mrs Solomon and the children.

It was mid-afternoon and the sky was grey. A drizzly fog was settling over the square and covering the crowns of the bare trees.

'Everything is going to feel strangely quiet now,' said Emma as they strolled past the railings which encircled the gardens in the square. 'I suppose I shall have to spend some time getting accustomed to widowhood.'

'I think you could train to be a news reporter,' said Penny turning to her.

'Oh no! I'm hopeless at writing.'

'But you're good at investigating.'

'I'm not sure about that. I did what I could because I wanted to find out what happened to William. I was driven by curiosity and a desperate need to know the truth about the man I married.'

'And you discovered it,' said Penny, 'and got his murderer arrested.'

'I couldn't have done it without you, Penny.'

'And I couldn't have done it without you either, Emma. We worked on this together. And I think you need to realise how much of it was your work. You were strongly motivated to do it, but you did it, and you did it well. You do realise that you could set yourself up as a lady detective?'

'No. I shall remain a piano teacher,' said Emma. 'I would be too embarrassed advertising my services. And I'd be worried about letting people down.'

'I can understand that,' said Penny. 'I just don't want you to underestimate yourself. But if music is your calling, then that's what you need to do.'

'And you?' asked Emma. 'What will you do now?'

'Edgar told me that I'm welcome to write articles for the *Morning Express* if I would like to do so. I would like to write a series of articles about the challenges of motherhood. There have been times when I would've liked to have read helpful articles myself! And don't forget we have some more investigating to do. We need to find out more about the lawyer in the river. And also those mysterious entries in William's diary.'

'Yes, those entries are puzzling,' said Emma.

Having looked through the diary, they'd found references to his blackmail of Cardwell and Theobald. The law firm had clearly taken the diary to keep his actions hidden. But other entries were marked only by a mysterious symbol and Emma was puzzled about what they could mean.

'When you feel ready to look into it, we can work on it together,' said Penny.

Emma smiled. 'I'd like that.'

A LETTER FROM THE AUTHOR

Thank you for reading this Emma Langley mystery. I hope you enjoyed it!

Would you like to know when I release new books? Here are some ways to stay updated:

Click here to be the first to know about my latest releases with Storm:

www.stormpublishing.co/emily-organ

Join my mailing list and receive a free short mystery: *The Belgrave Square Murder:*

emilyorgan.com/the-belgrave-square-murder

And if you have a moment, I would be very grateful if you would leave a quick review of my books online. Honest reviews of my books help other readers discover them too!

emilyorgan.com

f facebook.com/emilyorganwriter

g goodreads.com/emily_organ

BB bookbub.com/authors/emily-organ

HISTORICAL NOTE

Whitechapel and Spitalfields, just east of the City of London, have a long history shaped by immigration and industrial growth. By the late 1880s, the area had fallen into disrepair, marked by poverty and overcrowding. The East End endured significant bomb damage during World War II, and sizeable areas have been redeveloped. Some of the older buildings which remain have been restored and a few streets offer a flavour of what the area would have looked like in the nineteenth century.

The Whitechapel Murders of 1888 cast a shadow over a part of London which was already struggling with poverty and poor living conditions. Mary Ann Nichols (known to her friends as Polly), Annie Chapman, Elizabeth Stride, Catherine Eddowes and Mary Jane Kelly were believed to have been murdered by the same man.

In this story, Emma Langley comes across the funeral procession of Mary Kelly. Her funeral was held on 19th November and crowds thronged the streets to watch as the cortege passed through the East End from St Leonard's Church in Shoreditch to Mary's resting place at St Patrick's Catholic Cemetery in Leytonstone.

The name 'Jack the Ripper' emerged from a letter sent to a news agency in September 1888, beginning with the infamous words, 'Dear Boss'. This letter is widely believed to have been a hoax and hundreds of similar letters were sent to newspapers and the police. One letter stood out – the so-called "From Hell" letter sent to George Lusk, the chairman of the Whitechapel Vigilance Committee. Enclosed with the letter was half a human kidney, leading to ongoing debates about whether it was sent by the murderer.

During this time, Whitechapel was on high alert. Tensions ran so high that a man mistaken for the murderer was beaten by a mob and had to be rescued by the police. Crowds often gathered outside police stations whenever a suspect was arrested. People were desperate for answers.

The local community began to lose faith in the police's ability to catch the killer. This led to the formation of vigilance committees and the Whitechapel Vigilance Committee was founded in September, funded by donations from local businesses. Volunteers armed with whistles and truncheons patrolled the streets at night, timed to fill the intervals between constables' scheduled beat times. By the end of October, the strain of the nightly duties led the committees to abandon their patrols, but they reformed after Mary Jane Kelly's murder on 9th November. The work continued into January 1889 before finally disbanding.

The murderer dubbed Jack the Ripper was never caught and debate continues today about his identity.

The Ten Bells pub stands close to Christ Church Spitalfields and its name is believed to be inspired by the bells of the church. It's rumoured that two of Jack the Ripper's victims, Annie Chapman and Mary Kelly, were regular patrons. The pub has become a destination for people interested in exploring sites connected to the Whitechapel murders, especially as many other historical sites are now gone.

The police station on Commercial Street where Detective Inspector Bradshaw is based still stands and has been converted into flats.

The Whitechapel Working Lads Institute, where the inquest into William Langley's death was held, was founded to support homeless young men. The inquests into the deaths of Mary Nichols and Annie Chapman were held here. Whitechapel didn't have a coroner's court at that time, so coroner's inquests were held in public buildings (quite often pubs). The building still stands on Whitechapel Road next to the tube station and has now been converted into flats above a shop. The charitable work of the original Working Lads Institute still continues as the Whitechapel Mission which helps homeless and marginalised people in the area.

The matchgirls' strike took place in the summer of 1888 after an article by the social reformer Annie Besant exposed the appalling working conditions at the Bryant & May match factory in Bow, east London. Many of the workers faced long hours, harsh fines for minor infractions, and health risks, including 'phossy jaw' – a debilitating condition caused by exposure to white phosphorus, which led to necrosis of the jaw.

One of the workers was dismissed following the article's publication, prompting approximately 1,400 women and girls to go on strike. Negotiations led to the agreement of better terms, and the success of their efforts led to the formation of the Union of Women Matchmakers, which became the largest union of women and girls in the country. This victory not only improved conditions at Bryant & May but also inspired a growing trend of collective organisation among industrial workers.

The Adelphi, located between the Strand and the Embankment in London's West End, was an ambitious eighteenth-century architectural feat. The grand houses were lavishly designed with a terrace supported by a row of large arches.

Beneath these arches lay a network of vaulted spaces. The subterranean lair was mentioned in Charles Dickens's novel, *David Copperfield*. In the 1860s, a new river embankment was constructed, and the arches were filled in. The subterranean area became a refuge for beggars and criminals. It was rumoured the ghost of a murdered woman, 'Poor Jenny', haunted the tunnels. In the 1930s, the houses were demolished to make way for a modern building. Part of the tunnels can still be accessed via Lower Robert Street. And it's still spooky.

Liverpool Street railway station opened in 1874 as the terminus of the Great Eastern Railway. The railway served the counties northeast of London as far as Norfolk. During excavation work for the Elizabeth Line in 2013, a mass burial ground was uncovered a few feet below the station. This was the New Churchyard burial ground where 25,000 people were buried between 1570 and 1739 – many of them plague victims. The Bethlem Hospital (nicknamed Bedlam) also used the burial ground, having been located on the site in the seventeenth and eighteenth centuries. 3,300 of the internments were excavated to make way for the new ticket hall. They were reburied at Willow Cemetery on Canvey Island, Essex, in 2015.

Bedford Row in Holborn, where the offices of Cardwell and Theobald are located, is a tree-lined street lined with large houses built in the early eighteenth century. It has a long association with the legal profession with many law firms located here. Much of the street remains unspoiled and well-preserved.

Northampton Square, where Emma Langley lives, was originally surrounded by townhouses, and the area had an association with clockmaking and jewellers. Today, much of the square is dominated by the buildings of City University. Some of the original townhouses remain.

Lombard Street, where Emma Langley visits the bank Wyndham and Co, has been synonymous with banking since medieval times. The street is home to the thirteenth-century church of St Edmund, King and Martyr. Until the late twentieth century, most of the UK's major banks had their headquarters here, before moving to modern office spaces.

William Langley is buried at Abney Park Cemetery, Stoke Newington. The cemetery was one of the 'Magnificent Seven' Victorian cemeteries built in the nineteenth century. The cemetery fell into disrepair during the late twentieth century and nature has reclaimed it, turning the space into a haven for wildlife. It's a peaceful place to visit. The cemetery's chapel, which sat derelict for thirty years following a fire, has recently been restored and reopened.

The iconic circular reading room at the British Museum, where Penny Blakely likes to work and research, was in use from 1857 until 1997. During that time, it was also used as a filming location and has been referenced in many works of fiction. When the British Library moved to a new location in 1997, the reading room was restored and subsequently used for exhibition space. The room was closed to the public for a decade, but reopened again in 2024 for weekly guided tours.

Printed in Great Britain
by Amazon

59708861R00233